Joe's Legacy

Joe's Legacy

J.M. Williams

PARTRIDGE

Print information available on the last page.

To order additional copies of this book, contact
Toll Free 800 101 2657 (Singapore)
Toll Free 1 800 81 7340 (Malaysia)
orders.singapore@partridgepublishing.com

www.partridgepublishing.com/singapore

For my dearest Rebecca
With thanks and gratitude for your
enthusiasm and encouragement.

I thought I'd shut the cruel world out by choice.
It is now not so, the world has shunned me.
I had nothing to give, I had no voice.
I was an itch on a cur, a mere flea.
I lost the purpose of my confined world.
My mind and my heart were darkened by cold.
There was no light in the place where I dwelled.
I'd have taken my life were I so bold.
I opened the door for one brief moment.
Light poured in and destroyed isolation.
Lost in this land yet I felt no torment.
Truth came quickly, gone was desolation.
A vision stood where no vision should be.
It turned my way and chose unworthy me.

CHAPTER ONE

"Mum knew Jimi Hendrix"

The three young women were looking in a clothes shop window on Oxford Street and the backdrop was a poster of the rock legend.

It was Karen who had offered this information and she was on a shopping mission with her older sister Mary, their friend Pauline and their mother, who was currently looking for headache pills in Boots the chemist.

Pauline was sceptical until Lou Leeson appeared at their shoulders and said "Oh poor Jimmy"

"Did you really know him Mrs Leeson?"

"Not well but I used to see him in or around the shops in Clarendon Cross. He used to stay in Lansdowne Crescent sometimes, with his girlfriend I think."

"Did you ever speak to him?"

"Oh yes. He'd always stop and pass the time of day. He was a really nice boy, no airs."

"Did you know he was famous?"

"The butcher told me but I'd never heard of him. Anyway I wasn't sure I believed him because he said that he played his guitar upside down."

"That's true Mrs Leeson; it was something to do with his being left handed."

Lou looked puzzled then started laughing uncontrollably.

"Mum what's so funny" asked Karen.

When she finally calmed down she was able to tell them. "My sister Elsie's left handed and I had a picture of her standing on her head doing her ironing."

Now they were all laughing. Mary composed herself and told her mum that it was the guitar that was upside down, not Jimi Hendricks.

This just made them laugh all the more.

They headed for Selfridges, to buy new outfits for a local wedding. Heads turned as they walked along the street. It wasn't just that they were in fits of laughter it was because Karen was a very striking young lady. She was eighteen, tall, blond, blue eyed and liked to show a lot of flesh.

Mary was a little shorter and dark like her mother. She had a very pretty face, very rarely wore make-up and dressed modestly. She was training to be a nurse and would soon be qualified. She was two years older than her sister and, as different as they were, they got on extremely well. She was Julie Andrews to Karen's Bridget Bardot.

Once inside Selfridges Karen and Pauline tried on lots of really expensive clothes, knowing full well they couldn't afford them. Mary found what she was looking for and was admiring herself in the mirror.

"Mary can't you be a little more adventurous. Mum, tell her. She's got a great figure but she hides it in clothes like that."

"It looks lovely. Just because she doesn't walk around with her tits hanging out, doesn't mean she doesn't look good."

Lou was modest herself but couldn't help being proud of Karen. The admiring looks she always received from the entire male population touched her. She had another reason to be proud of her youngest. Karen was to start university in September and both Lou and her husband Maurice were over the moon about it. That didn't happen often in their neighbourhood.

Mary had left school at eighteen to pursue her dream of being a nurse and now Karen, who wasn't quite so intellectually bright, was going to university to study communications. She wanted to get a job in P.R. as it sounded so glamorous. You got to go to lots of functions and meet famous people or that's how she saw it.

When the shopping was concluded to everyone's satisfaction they set off westward to Marble Arch. Lou suggested that, as it was such a lovely day, they take a stroll through the park to Lancaster gate and catch the bus from there. Their bags weren't heavy so the girls humoured Lou and headed for the park.

"Ben Johnson said if you don't like London you don't like nothing"

"Mum it was Dr Johnson and he said......"

"Miss know-it-all, Mary, it was Ben Johnson who told me"

"What, who's he?"

"The man in the paper shop"

Lou did love London and she would often go for long walks on her own and sometimes the girls would tag along. Maurice was "a lazy bugger" and she could never get him away from the television.

They lived in Notting Dale which has a rich history as Lou was fond of telling her children and later her grandchildren. She loved telling them stories of old. Her favourite was about the gypsies.

Notting Dale is defined by the hill. You would go up the lane (Portobello Road) and down the bush (Shepherds Bush). Even their street had a top and bottom even though it was relatively flat in the Dale.

The area was once called the piggeries and potteries. In the nineteenth century there had been a gypsy encampment there. There was a short lived race course frequented by the gentry. It was closed down as it was rumoured that gentlemen were catching syphilis from the gypsy girls or as Lou would relate it "something nasty".

The gypsies were resettled into permanent accommodation built in the area as trust property, some of which still exist. One Octavia Hill set up the trust, which is named after her and that is where the Leeson family resided. There's still a potters kiln on Walmer Road, opposite the recreation ground but the only evidence of the race course lies in the name of a small narrow road at the end of Pottery Lane called Hippodrome Place.

Lou told her progeny that a lot of the older residents in the area, when she was growing up, were from gypsy stock and she would proudly proclaim "That includes me." She certainly looked like one and superstition abounded in the Leeson household, that being a gypsy legacy.

The park was full of sun worshippers, stripped down to their bare essentials, as always every time there was the promise of a tan. There were the energetic joggers, cyclists, dog walkers and young people playing ball games.

They stopped for an ice cream at the kiosk at the Lancaster gate entrance and continued walking. They had walked further than they intended and exited the park at Queensway. It wasn't now worth catching a bus so they wandered down towards Notting Hill Gate. They stopped at a pub on the way and had a much deserved drink and a rest.

The day of the wedding arrived and Karen was taking her new boyfriend. Mary was to be a singleton as usual.

Mary had dated a few boys but was always disenchanted by their reactions when they saw Karen. That night at the reception she danced a few times and generally had fun. She liked the people around her. She knew most of them; it was a real local party. Those events were getting fewer as the denizens had started moving out of central London and the rich and wannabes had started what seemed like a headlong rush to move in.

One young man, whom she hadn't met before started to take an interest in her. He was good looking and well dressed. They danced, drank and chatted for about an hour when the inevitable happened. He asked her if she would introduce him to Karen. She picked up her drink and left him not to return.

She loved her sister dearly and she was her only real friend. She wasn't jealous in fact she was proud of her. She was waiting for a man who would be interested in her for who she was. She was to have a long wait.

Mary walked home with her mother. Karen had disappeared an hour before with a young man she had met at the party. The deserted boyfriend was left searching for her. Karen was an attention seeker and she never had to look far for it. She changed boyfriends as often as most people change their clothes as Lou would say.

CHAPTER TWO

Karen started university the following September and took to it like a duck to water. She studied hard and tried desperately to avoid the attention she was constantly offered. At the end of the first year she succumbed to the charms of one Nials. He was blond like her, tall, good looking and obviously rich. He drove a sports car and dressed in a way she thought opulent people did. She was smitten.

She stuck to her studies but half way through her third year she fell pregnant. She decided not to tell Nials; she would quickly and secretly have an abortion.

Nials had his own flat near the university and Karen spent most of her free time there. They were sitting in the kitchen when she looked up at him and a thought struck her. Why should she go through this alone? It was his responsibility too. At least he could support her through the abortion and if he wouldn't then he wasn't someone she wanted to be with. She told him.

His reaction came as a total surprise. Nials was delighted and insisted they get married as soon as possible. He was besotted with her. They married and Karen finished her degree with three months to spare.

His family were extremely good about the whole thing and for a wedding present they bought their only child a small house in Seven Oaks, close to them.

Everything worked out perfectly for Karen. She got her degree, she got a handsome, rich husband and after the birth of the baby a job in Nials' family's business as the PR Director. Nepotism maybe but it didn't bother her one bit. She excelled at her job and all were happy.

Mary continued her nursing career and approached it with a passion. She had a few boyfriends along the way but always lost interest. She concluded that she just wasn't interested in men or sex. She liked men well enough but she didn't enjoy the groping and grunting that occurred when they disrobed.

By the age of twenty five she had abandoned the search for a half way decent partner.

She had just had her thirtieth birthday and had attained the position of ward sister at Charing Cross hospital. A new patient had been admitted to her ward and she was instructed to give him her personal attention. He occupied one of the private rooms so she assumed he must be a person of some importance but nobody explained what made him important.

The man had been in a bad car accident just outside Bonn in Germany. The driver of the car, in which he'd been a passenger, had died. He had been in hospital in Germany for six weeks and at his own request had been transferred to London when he was well enough to be transported.

Both his legs were in plaster and his right wrist. His internal injuries had healed and it was just a matter of time before his bones did likewise.

Mary was present during the admission and she studied his details. His name was Joe Martinez, aged forty three. He had no spouse or relatives domiciled in UK. His address was an apartment on Portobello Road, a block of flats she knew well. Here was a dichotomy, why was a council flat dweller being given first class treatment?

When he was comfortably installed she watched as the doctor checked him over. Everything was satisfactory. The journey hadn't caused any complications. When the doctor left Mary introduced herself. She tidied his bed and offered him water which he drank readily.

He looked up at her and grinned. "Are you my angel of mercy" he said in perfect English which surprised her. She had expected a Spanish accent and wondered why.

"Whilst I'm on duty, I'm responsible for your care and comfort. Are you English?"

"My name is Spanish, as were my parents but I was born here. My name is Joe."

"Ok Joe, we'll get to know more about you later after they've run all the tests and x-rayed your broken bones. Are you comfortable?"

"Yes thanks. What do I call you?"

"Sister will do"

"You have a name?"

"Yes I do but it is sister to you OK?"

He gave her a huge smile and half laughed. Mary almost blushed. Joe was obviously not his normal self yet. He looked sallow and drawn, yet he was still extremely handsome. When he smiled he had shown a perfect set of pearly white teeth. She had felt her heart flutter hence the near blush.

Over the next three weeks, they had many conversations. Joe was a great flirt and he always made Mary laugh. He had visitors every day who consisted of two work colleagues and a group of friends who between them made sure Joe got a visit every day. They would always come in the evenings and bring decent food so Joe didn't have to eat the hospital slop. He had a few female visitors who seemed not to be romantically attached.

When Joe was due a shower he made it very clear how disappointed he was that sister didn't help him. To his chagrin, it was a male nurse who performed the duty.

Mary had taken Joe's temperature and when she removed the thermometer he asked "Sister, how many boyfriends do you have?"

She looked up as though counting. "That would be about none. How many girlfriends do you have?"

"At last we have something in common, same number."

Joe thought she must be lying. He thought she was warm, amusing and very pretty. Mary couldn't believe that this handsome, funny, exotic looking man didn't have a partner somewhere. His colour had returned, his hair shone black and curly, with a few silver flecks and she lost her heart every time he spoke to her.

After two weeks he was able to get around on crutches and a week later he had the plaster removed from both legs. He remained for another week having physiotherapy to strengthen his leg muscles but his wrist and hand remained in plaster. He was relieved to find his fingers were working as without the proper use of his hands he'd be unable to do his job.

Mary was doing her rounds and after the general ward she went to check on Joe. She entered the room whilst looking at his charts which she had in her hand. She closed the door behind her with her foot without looking up. When she did, she saw Joe standing by his bed stark naked. She'd seen many naked bodies in her years of nursing but to her they were just that, bodies in need of help. Joe didn't rush to cover himself. He was looking in his cupboard for clean underwear and continued to do so as Mary fumbled with her charts. He found what he was looking for and started to dress. He had put on his underpants before Mary spoke. She had kept her composure and now helped him button his shirt.

"What are you grinning at?"

"I think you blushed. You must see naked people all the time and it's not the first time you've seen my private parts either."

"I didn't blush and I wasn't paying that much attention" she lied. He had looked so wonderful and she had almost fled the room.

"Now you're dressed, we have to talk about you going home."

"Must I? Can't I live here with you forever?"

"Stop that. Now do you have anyone at home to help you? You're going to have to keep that plaster on your wrist for a few more weeks. That might make it a bit awkward for you."

"No one, I used to have my dad but he died last year so I'm all alone. I can manage though. I still have my left hand and I can do wonders with that" he said the grin having returned.

"You're still a bit unsteady on your feet and you must be careful not to overdo it."

"When am I leaving?"

"Tomorrow, you OK with that?"

"I'll be fine, thank you"

"I'm off duty now for a week so I won't be here tomorrow when you're discharged. I'll stop by later and say goodbye."

A couple of hours later she returned to Joe's room and he presented her with a huge bouquet of flowers. He thanked her for all she'd done for him and kissed her on the cheek.

"Would you have dinner with me one night?"

"Joe, that's probably not a good idea. I'm going now so look after yourself," she left with her heart pounding.

Joe was discharged at two pm the next day. He caught a taxi home and carried his belongings in his left hand up the one flight of stairs to his floor. He opened the door and the musty smell hit him immediately. He dropped his bags and went around opening all the windows.

It was a three bedroom flat with just one bathroom, standard for the period in which it was built. He had removed everything from the fridge before he had left as he was to be away for three weeks on his last assignment. He put the kettle on and made himself a cup of black coffee. He sat at the kitchen table wishing he had some milk when the doorbell rang.

He limped to the front door and on opening it he saw a female he didn't immediately recognise.

"Mary, what a nice surprise, you look ….. different."

"No uniform, aren't you going to let me in" She had made an effort to look nice and even wore some discreet make up.

He stepped aside and beckoned her in. She was carrying a plastic supermarket bag which she deposited onto the kitchen table.

"Do you like your coffee black?"

"Not really, I just haven't got any milk."

"Well you have now."

She emptied the contents of the bag onto the table. She had bought milk, bread, butter, ham and cheese.

"It occurred to me that you might not have any food so I thought it my nursely duty to buy some basics."

"Thank you. I'll make some more coffee, would you like some?" She accepted the offer.

He had never seen her in civvies. Her hair was loose where it was usually pulled off her face. She was wearing a little make-up around her eyes and her dress summery but modest.

They made sandwiches and sat at the table and ate and drank their coffee having put the rest of the purchases in the fridge.

Mary noticed that the place smelt musty and there was a fair amount of dust everywhere.

"When we're done I'll help you clean up."

"You don't have to do that but thanks for offering."

She did anyway. First she put clean linen on his bed and then set about dusting. Whilst she went about her work Joe vacuumed the carpets watching her as he did so. This was not how he envisioned their first date to be but was very pleased she was there.

When they had finished they had more coffee. Sitting at the table, he took a hard look at her.

"Hiding behind your uniform you still look beautiful you know. Today you look the same only fresher and a lot younger."

"Stop flirting."

"I'm not, well maybe but it's true."

Mary was struggling to keep her self-control. She knew she should leave but didn't want to.

"You up for a short walk Joe?"

"Sure, where're we going?"

"It's six thirty so you must be ready for dinner. We'll grab a bite to eat at the café around the corner and then shopping for some proper food supplies."

"Yes nurse." His normal patter seemed to have deserted him. This never happened. Every girl he had ever met had expected him to take care of them and this didn't feel right. He felt he wasn't in control and this was his home.

They did as planned and returned with the groceries. Mary left Joe to put everything away as she didn't know where he stored provisions. She looked at her watch and told him she had to go. That was a lie, she was just feeling nervous. Joe had stopped flirting and she felt she'd made a horrible mistake.

Joe saw her to the door.

"Mary that's the nicest thing any woman has ever done for me. I'm lost for words, me Joe Martinez lost for words. Will I see you tomorrow? Please?"

She didn't know what to make of the situation but said she would drop by the next day. He asked what time.

"Why, are you planning to go out?"

"No, I just don't think I'd like the uncertainty of not knowing."

"I'll be here at twelve to get your lunch O.K.? You can manage your own breakfast I think."

She was about to leave when he lent forward and kissed her cheek.

That night Joe lay in bed and thought of Mary. Then his thoughts turned to his father who had died the year before.

CHAPTER THREE

Joe's grandparents had emigrated to England from Spain just before world war one. They settled in the East End and granddad had worked in the building trade. He was skilled at what he did and, with the help of some Spanish friends he was soon able to start his own business. Joe's dad had been born in nineteen twenty and was a full British citizen. When he was eighteen he joined the police force where he stayed until retirement in nineteen eighty. He married a British girl who was also of Spanish parentage. This resulted in Spanish being the only language spoken at home. Joe wasn't sure what his first language was, until he started work where he spent most of his waking hours.

Joe was born in nineteen forty five just as the war ended and when he was four years old the family moved into a council flat on Portobello Road. He was bright, playful and loved sports.

He had a loving upbringing and being the youngest of three, he was a little spoilt. He excelled at school and went on to university to study electronics. Joe had great respect for his parents and, unlike many sixties teenagers, he stayed close to his family.

Joe's dad was always playing flamenco music and he was a proponent of the dance. Joe was taught at an early age and took to it with a passion and developed a great talent for it. Like most things he committed to, he excelled and flamenco was no different. Joe was to continue dancing for the rest of his life, even taking part in shows to the Spanish community and anyone else who cared to watch. He also taught the dance when he found time.

Through his mid to late teens Joe would go out with his friends at the weekends to pick up girls. Friday night was the Goldhawk where the resident band was the Detours who morphed into the Who. The main bands were the big ones of the day, the likes of The Kinks and The Animals. They were too young to drink but that was OK. Occasionally they would go to the Bedsit on Holland Park Avenue which stayed open until the early hours of the morning. There was always someone outside selling purple hearts, black bombers and

French blues. Joe would take a handful which did little for him but keep him awake. Inside everyone was high and they would get into long discussions about nonsense with nobody really listening to each other. The band was always blues and whenever he went there it just sounded like a monotonous thumping of drums and guitar. The singers invariably were inaudible over the noise of the musicians and the constant hubbub of the so called in-crowd.

That was short lived for Joe as he found he still couldn't sleep when he got home and he felt like he'd been sucking blotting paper all night when he woke in the very late morning.

He always managed to pick up a girl and went for the rich ones as they would always invite you in. It was almost impossible for a girl to say no to him. He was good looking, sensuous and had the right moves on the dance floor. Besides which this was the sixties and it wasn't cool to be a virgin. He got plenty of sex and played the field like a professional.

There was one time when he was sitting on a girl's bed naked watching her remove her clothes. When she had stripped down to her Eve impression she produced a joint. He'd never tried before and was up for it. They passed the spiff to and from each other until it was done. Joe felt great, relaxed and almost floating. They lay back on the bed and started talking. Joe was feeling exceeding mellow and hadn't noticed that the girl had fallen asleep. What the fuck, he thought to himself and closed his eyes and drifted away. He slept the sleep of the innocent and didn't wake up until seven the next morning and it was a school day. He was in deep trouble.

After that incident he only smoked before going out and then only in the company of his friends, now happy friends.

His passion, other than flamenco and getting laid, was football. He and his dad went to watch QPR at every opportunity. He lived through the golden age of Rodney Marsh. March 4th 1967 was the highlight of his football supporting life. QPR were playing at Wembley for the first time. It was the league cup final, third division QPR versus first division West Bromwich Albion, who were also the previous season's winners. West Brom started with a bang and led two nil at half time. You knew how bad it was when the Rangers fans started being philosophical about how well they had done to get so far. Everything changed in the second half. Rodney must have found his magic in the changing room. First a goal by Roger Morgan, then one by the man himself and in the dying minutes Rangers rose from the dead with a winner by the aptly named Mark Lazarus. There were about ten thousand real QPR supporters, amongst the almost hundred thousand spectators, on the day and they nearly all cried. In later years there came Stan Bowles and then, the gentleman of football himself,

Les Ferdinand. Joe felt lucky to be a QPR supporter; surely this must be the best football team in the world, just unlucky.

At twenty one, he graduated University with a BSC in electrical engineering. He applied for a number of jobs and one in particular caught his attention during the interview. It was a company that provided electronic security solutions for homes and offices. They also installed safes and surveillance equipment. They made their own alarm systems and were considered amongst the best in the country. The job on offer included installation and development of refined and tailor made systems. Joe was offered the job and he accepted.

When he started work, he planned on moving out of his parents' home. His brother had left four years earlier for a teaching job in Montevideo. His sister had become a nun many years before and was currently in Manila leaving Joe the only offspring left at home. He had discussed it with his father who seemed a little disappointed. Joe loved his parents dearly and rather than hurt them he told them he'd changed his mind. The following year his mother died which meant that his father would be alone if Joe moved out. There was no way he would do that, not after all his parents had done for him. He loved his dad and really didn't have a problem staying. They settled down to a comfortable routine but Joe was neither allowed to pay for any household expenses or make a financial contribution. He knew there was no arguing so he calculated how much that would really cost him and started investing that sum every month.

His social life changed as he got older. He had lots of friends and there was always something to do. The clubs gave way to eating out and parties. Joe was never short of a female companion.

He really liked his job and he was very good at it, often developing new systems as technology changed. His boss treated him well and Joe was soon earning a very good salary for his age. The company was going from strength to strength on their deserved reputation, which was to a large extent due to Joe's contribution. As technology became more sophisticated so did Joe's enthusiasm. He loved tinkering in the company's workshop trying and testing new ideas. They became known in the market as innovators and work orders piled up.

Seven years into his job, Joe attracted the interest of a client. He was replacing an old alarm system with a state-of-the-art system of his own design. Whilst he was working on some wiring the client approached him and asked how long the job would take. Joe told him that he'd be finished by the end of the week, which seemed to satisfy.

"I hope you don't mind me saying this but whoever recommended your old system must have been really dumb, I don't think it would have kept the least experience burglar out and that safe is as good as useless."

The client was obviously taken aback. "That was the work of our own security department and we have some of the finest people in the country. The only reason you're here is the alarm broke and they were too busy to work on it themselves. You came recommended. What do you mean about the safe and how did you know there was one there?"

"Sorry sir but you have a picture on the wall over there and it kindda looks out of place, so I took a peek. The safe looks like one of those you buy in a toy shop."

"It serves its purpose and I'm assured it's secure."

"OK but if you give me a few minutes I'll show you what I mean."

The client looked dubious but agreed. Within two minutes the safe popped open. The clients jaw dropped.

"How did you do that, what happened?"

"You obviously took some bad advice. There's a lot of crap out there and you have to be careful."

Joe was asked to sit down and they had a lengthy conversation about security systems. Joe explained a lot of things about new technology and how you had to stay beyond the capabilities of would be thieves. He also said that apart from being his job it was his hobby and passion.

It turned out that the client was with the foreign office and part of his job was to ensure security for embassies and diplomats homes. His officer in charge was, as he now thought, fortunately due to retire in a few months and they were looking for a replacement. Joe didn't know this at the time.

Wednesday of the following week his boss called him into his office and told him he was wanted at the Foreign Office.

"Fuck, what for?"

"They said it was something to do with a safe you opened, not been up to anything silly have you?"

"No I just showed the guy that he had a piece of crap."

"Well it turns out that the guy works for the foreign office and you've been summoned there. Go face the music Joe. It's tomorrow at ten. Hope they don't lock you up" he laughed.

He gave Joe the name of the person he was to see and the address.

The next day Joe kept the appointment, heart in mouth. It wasn't what he expected. He was ushered into a meeting room and who should appear but the safe owner with a cheerful grin on his face.

"I hear that you thought you were in trouble young man, far from it."

They were joined by two other men who, without explanation, grilled Joe about security systems. Joe was able to answer all their questions and offer more, which seemed to impress.

When the interview was over Joe asked the safe man, who he now knew as Major Lever, the purpose of the interview. The reply was terse. They would be in touch. He was baffled.

Late the following week Joe was summoned by his boss.

"They've been on the phone again, that lot from the foreign office. They asked for your CV so I faxed it to them. I told them that it wouldn't tell them much about what you did because it ends with you graduating university. They asked me how good I thought you were and being the government and all I couldn't lie."

"What did you say?"

"I told them you were the best I've seen. Then they asked me loads of questions about you, personal like." He had a satisfied look on his face."

"Why are you looking so happy?"

"I think we're going to get a nice big fat government contract out of this."

"If we do and, as you said, I'm the best you've seen, does that mean I'm going to get a big fat raise to go with the big fat contract?."

How wrong could they be? One month later Joe was working for Major Lever. His old company was in fact awarded a contract for UK work which of course was overseen by Joe. All were happy. Joe had been a problem for the F.O. as the job he was given was of a grade that meant, even at the bottom of the range, his salary doubled. They had never had such a young person in the job before and they had no way of adjusting salaries to fit the situation and Joe was only twenty eight and so started his career as a civil servant.

CHAPTER FOUR

Joe's job was to ensure all Embassies and related offices and accommodation in Europe and North Africa were secure. It had become generally known that Joe was the best in his field. He'd worked very hard in his first year on the job to learn everything he could about what was available where, as he was having to source in different markets. Where he couldn't get the quality he wanted he hired a team from his old firm and did it himself. He upgraded his skill sets by learning as much as was available around new technology in his field. Here he had some help as one of his staff turned out to be a computer whizz who was into everything new. Between them they just about covered everything they needed to.

He travelled on average once every two months. He would do site checks himself along with an assistant whom he was training. He'd oversee new installations and upgrades and if there was a quick fix needed he'd do it himself, just to keep his hand in.

Joe loved the job and the travelling. He was very popular amongst the embassy staff, especially with the females. He was never one for long term relationships so the life style suited him admirably. He soon had a girl in every port of call, on tap whenever he was around. When travelling he lived on expenses so he was spending even less than before so his savings and investments grew substantially.

Life was great and he had been doing his job impressively for five years and his boss was more than happy with his performance and often told him so.

One fine sunny afternoon the boss's secretary came looking for him and told him Major Lever wanted him. He went immediately to his office and knocked on the door. No open door policy in this establishment. Major Lever opened the door and offered Joe a seat at the small conference table where two men were already ensconced. Joe didn't know either of them and before the conversation proper started one of them reminded Joe that he was bound by the official secrets act and whatever was said at that table was for no other ears. Joe thought this odd and wondered if there was a problem.

"We're with the Secret Intelligence Service. You probably know us as MI6."
Joe's ears popped. "Have I done something wrong?"

"Absolutely not, it's what you've done right that interests us. First off we want to know about your current situation. There were extensive background checks done when you first joined the Foreign Office. Tell us about your private life now."

Joe looked concerned. "If you're MI6 you probably already know."

"Tell us anyway."

"Not much to tell really. I live with my dad, who's British of Spanish decent, as am I. Mum died some years ago. We speak only Spanish at home. I don't have much of a social life these days as the job takes up a big part of my life. I like women and get what I need in that area. Nothing ever serious, I'm not into long term relationships. When I joined the Foreign office I started renting a lock-up in Shepherds Bush where I experiment with new security things, that's because there are no real facilities here for the engineering side. It's also my hobby. That's it really. Oh and I'm an ardent QPR supporter."

What do you experiment with Joe?"

"Surveillance equipment mostly and listening devices, technology changes so rapidly, you have to keep up to date and be ahead of the curve where possible. That's important for what I do. Most of the equipment you can buy today isn't that reliable so I modify or make my own."

They spoke for about two hours on Joe's area of expertise, question after question. At the end of the interview Joe was dismissed without explanation.

Two days later he was summoned to MI6 headquarters. He was shown to a room where the two men he'd met previously were sitting together with a woman and another man. Introductions were made by name not function.

After a brief chit-chat they came to the point. They wanted Joe's assistance for some vital work connected with national security. This wasn't a full time job. Joe would retain his current position and be called on as and when required. They explained what they wanted him to do and Joe agreed as long as he had the right to decline if he thought the task beyond his capabilities. The response was, if he could convince his contact of that then, yes.

"Joe, you live on Portobello Road. Are you considering moving at all?"

"No I like it there. It's the only home I can remember and dad's happy there."

"Good. The money you will be paid for each assignment, whilst not frequent, will be significant. You being a single man living with a parent, means you have few outgoings as shown by your bank balance." Here Joe smiled, the bastards knew everything.

You're saving and investments are impressive for a man of your age. We just don't want you drawing attention to yourself by splashing out or going upmarket on the home front."

"Is there anything you don't know about me? Look I'm not moving and I'm certainly not one to draw attention to myself."

The female spoke for the first time." There's a girl in Zurich, one in Bonn another in Cairo etcetera. Whilst we don't want to spoil your relaxations we do insist on discretion. Oh and I understand that your flamenco is divine."

Joe shook his head in disbelief.

"Would you like me to tape record all my dates, heavy breathing and all? You have nothing to worry about. I never talk to anyone about my work except those in the office and then not everything. Even my dad doesn't know what I do."

"We know that. Your father is a policeman so it wasn't difficult to find that out."

Joe laughed.

"Well I think we have an agreement then. Joe come with me I'll show you around and introduce you to some people you might find useful."

They walked around the office areas and descriptions of areas of responsibility were touched on. They entered a large enclosed space which looked like a workshop cum laboratory.

"This I think will be of special interest to you. Nigel, let me introduce you to Joe our new addition. He has clearance so you can answer any questions he asks. Joe has his own workshop which he'll be relocating here so find him a decent space. I'll leave him with you and when you're done bring him to my office he has a few papers to sign."

Joe was amazed at the cheek of the guy. Without asking he'd effectively told Joe to close his workshop but when he looked around, he thought maybe that wasn't such a bad thing. He was given a tour and whilst it wasn't Q's lab it was extremely impressive. He was allowed to talk to the technicians and was fascinated to learn what they were doing.

Nigel stopped at a work station and said it might be of particular interest to Joe, now knowing what he did. They were working on a new miniature camera which could be secreted almost anywhere without detection. The problem was it was still too big. Joe offered a few suggestions and impressed his audience immensely.

He explained to Nigel that because of the amount of time he spent on his day job he had to do his research at night or weekends.

"Don't worry about that. We're open twenty four hours a day and seven days a week. I can't get these guys to go home. The place is yours whenever you want."

When they had finished the tour Joe was deposited back to his point of origin.

"I assume you found that interesting, you've been gone three hours, now for the formalities. He was given some documents to read and sign which he did without having any questions. He was told how much and how he would be paid for each assignment. Joe was surprised. It wasn't a huge sum but generous and it was to be paid into a bank in Switzerland so effectively tax free. Joe asked himself if that was legal and concluded if HMSS did it, then it must be.

He didn't feel comfortable about the job requirements. He was to be given another identity and they would supply him with the necessary documents. All his assignments would start and finish in Zurich, hence the bank account or vice versa. He was to get himself a deposit box in that bank to store his documents. He was beginning to feel like a very nervous James Bond.

He was told that he should move whatever he needed from his workshop to the lab at the weekend and he had immediate access. This really pleased him. The prospect of using the most up to date equipment and technology was better than Christmas.

CHAPTER FIVE

Funnily enough Joe's MI6 contact was named James but not Bond but the uninspiring Jones, he was Welsh.

Joe was sent to Zurich under the pretence of reviewing the security system, which he had only upgraded six months before. He opened a bank account with a banker's cheque for ten thousand Swiss francs, which was given to him in a sealed envelope by one of the consulate staff. He also requested, as instructed, a safety deposit box for which they supplied him with his own key.

After two days hanging around the consulate he was taken to a private room where he was given a small package. He was left on his own to discover the contents. Inside was a Spanish passport using Joe's real name, a driver's licence and a credit card. Joe was now a different person with the same name; at least he wouldn't forget who he was. A note instructed him to place these in his safety deposit box at the bank. He did this within the hour, checked out of his hotel and caught the first available flight back to London.

Life returned to normal for a while.

His first assignment came two months later when James called him to MI6. He was told briefly what the purpose of the assignment was and the role he was to play. He was given a plan of a large house and the details of an alarm system. It was very straightforward. He knew the system well and could disable it with ease which pleased James.

He went via Zurich to Rome. He'd collected his false documents from the bank and left his real ones there. He booked the flight to Rome and the hotel with the credit card without a problem. Going through immigration at Zurich airport and then Rome, he felt extremely nervous and hoped no one noticed he was sweating but again there was no problem.

He was contacted by an agent at his hotel. They were to do the job the next night. They had a window of opportunity from eight in the evening until midnight. The agent needed about an hour so with a safety cushion that left Joe two hours to disable the alarm and then reset it. That wasn't a problem.

That night Joe didn't sleep well. He kept wondering what he had let himself in for. He felt like slipping out of the hotel and going home.

The allotted time arrived. They drove from the hotel to one of the wealthy Roman suburbs. The agent parked the car and they walked along an unlit street to their destination. The house was in darkness. Joe's heart was beating so fast he thought he might faint. The agent seemed utterly calm.

Joe calmed himself by breathing deeply and set about his task. When they entered the house the agent went from room to room secreting listening devices. Joe wanted desperately to leave and after about fifty minutes they did. He reset the alarm and walked back to the car.

Then it hit him. He felt strangely elated and started laughing. The agent turned to look at him and said "Scared shitless were you. First job is always like that. Now you probably feel real pleased that you did it without being caught. The adrenalin kicked in late. It gets better but let me tell you now it's always scary and if you ever think it's not, be careful, that's when you make mistakes."

"You seemed so calm."

"Compared to you I was but I still got the adrenalin rush, its fear and in a strange way excitement. By the way you did a really good job, nice working with you"

Every couple of months Joe would be called on to do similar assignments. Sometimes he was also required to open safes. One time he was presented with a plan which he said was beyond his capabilities and they just said OK, no problem. He had really started to enjoy this part of his life. The fear, although not completely gone, had turned to excitement. After each job he seemed to be on a high for days.

He continued with his normal job but MI6 always took priority.

He never seemed to spend any money. His work was taking up a lot of time and his social life in England only revolved around football and the occasional tryst. His bank balance and investments were in six figures.

In the early eighties the local council offered their flats to the tenants for purchase at a very good price. Joe paid cash for theirs.

His dad had been retired for three years and in nineteen eighty seven, very unexpectedly, he died of a massive heart attack. Joe was desolate for a while. Every time he came home he expected to see his dad and it brought a lump to his throat. He considered moving but decided this was still home.

The following year he was talking to a neighbour who said he wanted to move out and was looking to sell. Joe made him an offer which was accepted. His dad had been a frugal man and had left all his money to Joe, which was more than enough to buy the neighbour's flat.

He rented it out to wealthy students who wanted to live in a happening place or so they said. Joe's income and assets continued to grow but not his outgoings.

In late spring of the same year Joe was given an assignment in Germany. It seemed straightforward enough. On the way to their destination they were hit by a large truck. Joe had been looking out of the passenger window at the time and knew nothing of the incident. He woke up in hospital two days later being lucky to have survived. The agent had died instantly.

When he was well enough he received a visit from James who was most concerned with Joe's wellbeing. He had asked Joe what he remembered which, was nothing. James said that a car had passed shortly after the accident and had called the emergency services. Had it been longer Joe would have bled to death. The driver of the truck had disappeared and the truck, they discovered later, had been stolen. It was all a little odd. He asked if anyone had known where Joe was going to be at that time and Joe told him as always he didn't know where their destination was to be.

He heard no more of it but it did leave him with a few doubts.

When he was well enough he was transported to England at his own request. He had to travel on his Spanish passport, his real one being in the bank in Zurich.

CHAPTER SIX

After Mary had left Joe settled himself in front of the TV and watched the news. He rarely watched but he felt tired and unable to do much. He went to bed early and thought of her as he drifted off to sleep.

Mary was restless and couldn't get comfortable in her own bed. Her mum had gone to stay with Karen for two weeks and she was supposed to join them for a few days but right now she was alone with her thoughts. It was early September and unseasonably warm. It wasn't the heat that was keeping her awake.

The next morning she arrived at Joe's full of courage. She was early, it was only eleven o'clock. He answered the door and was obviously pleased to see her. They sat, as before, in the kitchen and chatted about his stay in hospital. Mary inquired as to who the visitors had been. Joe explained that some were old friends who he still went to watch football with and some were work colleagues. Some were relatives who had come over from Spain just to see him and the others that she may have thought looked foreign, were friends from the Spanish community.

"You're obviously a QPR supporter from the snatches of conversation that I heard. Your workmates were very different. I couldn't understand most of what they were talking about. What do you do?"

He knew how much he could tell her but wondered how much he should. He opted for saying he worked with security devices at the Foreign Office. She seemed satisfied with that.

Mary made lunch and then washed the dishes. It was two o'clock and she suggested going out for a short walk to give Joe's legs a little exercise. Then her courage failed her when Joe said "Would you like to see me naked again?"

"Stop that Joe I hardly know you."

He smiled that amazing smile and she felt very nervous.

"Come on, you've seen me naked before."

"That was different, it was in the hospital. I think I should go."

He looked straight in her eyes still smiling. Her heart was pounding and her ears were ringing. She felt like a stupid schoolgirl.

"I tried having a shower but I can't without getting this thing wet, so I thought you might like to help me."

Mary's innards were dissolving and she cursed herself for feeling like a timid virgin. She stood up obviously distressed and said she had to go.

Joe found this totally disarming. He got up and walked along the passageway with her, to the front door. Joe put his good hand on her arm and she turned to face him.

"May I at least kiss you goodbye?"

She hesitated but nodded nervously. He embraced her and kissed her a long, soft and sensuous kiss. He pulled his head back still holding her in his arms. He had a puzzled look on his face whereas Mary now appeared relaxed. This time Mary initiated the kiss. They parted their embrace and Joe just stood there silent. She turned and opened the front door but didn't move to leave. She closed the door and turned back to face him.

"It wouldn't do if I didn't help a patient in need, would it?" All her courage had returned.

"Let me help you out of these clothes."

They didn't move out of the passage and there she undressed him down to his shorts. She led him to the kitchen and found a plastic shopping bag which she tied around his plastered wrist. Then she took him to the bathroom and ran the shower. She removed his shorts and helped him step into the bath.

Joe had said nothing since the kiss. He was normally so at ease with any situation around women and although he wasn't at all anxious he was wondering what the outcome would be. It was almost as if he didn't want to break the spell. He felt himself getting an erection so thought of pain to distract him. It was time to say something.

"Won't your clothes get wet washing me?" he said doing his best not to smile.

"No" she said and removed her clothes and stepped into the shower with him.

"I think I need a cup of coffee. Would you like one?"

"Yes please Joe."

He got off the bed and walked naked into the kitchen.

She stayed on the bed and stretched. She told herself that she had never had sex before, not real sex. That was so wonderful. No grunting or groaning, no pawing, just pure sensual pleasure and a few laughs in trying to ensure Joe didn't damage his wrist. She felt amazingly happy.

She got off the bed and slipped on Joe's tee-shirt. Joe was standing by the kitchen counter waiting for the coffee to ready itself. He looked so natural standing there naked. He had no inhibitions and a beautiful body. He was just under six feet, his chest was hairy but his back smooth and erect. She put her arms around his waist and advised him to beware of the hot coffee.

They took the coffee back to the bedroom.

"I bet you've had many conquests in this bed."

"No I haven't you're the first"

She looked doubtful.

"I've never brought girls back here, dad wouldn't have liked it."

He told her of his father's death and how much he missed the old bugger.

"After university I was going to find my own place but mum died and dad would have been all alone. He was so upset and I don't think he ever got over it. He was a good dad."

"Do you miss him?"

"Yes, very much, both of them, we only spoke Spanish at home and I miss that too. I've been going to Spain every summer for as long as I can remember and still do. It's good to talk about them to our relatives, shared memories and all that."

"Will you stay here?"

"Yes, it's my home and I own it, so no point in moving."

They talked for a while until Joe getting amorous again said, "You didn't have an orgasm."

"I don't think I can, I've never had one."

"Not even a do-it-yourself one?"

"Especially not that."

"There are ways you know, we'll have to remedy that," and he did.

It was five thirty and Joe had fallen asleep. Mary got up and had a shower, dressed and prepared dinner.

Joe appeared about half an hour later, naked still.

"Go and put some clothes on or I'll not be able to concentrate on dinner."

Mary again helped him shower and dress. Joe found a bottle of wine, Spanish of course and they sat down to dinner. It all seemed so natural and right to both.

He complimented the cooking and it really was good. This woman had many talents it seemed.

"When I kissed you the first time it was like I'd never been kissed properly before. It was perfect."

"I bet that's a standard line."

"No really, I've heard of chemistry but until now never really understood. It was magic. I thought you felt it too."

She laughed. "It was enough to get me naked into the shower with you. Is that magic enough?"

"Will you stay tonight?"

"I have some things to do at home and I'll need clean clothes for the morning, so no."

He tried unsuccessfully to hide his disappointment.

"Would it be alright if I stayed tomorrow night?"

His face lit up. "Stay as long as you like. Do you know you have the most beautiful body I've ever seen? That includes at the pictures."

"So you go and watch sex movies do you?"

He shook his head and grinned.

"You're a real smoothy Joe Martinez and I shouldn't trust you an inch. It is nice to hear though, even if it's not true."

"It's true, honestly and the prettiest face in the world."

"You're not bad yourself."

Mary went home at nine and returned early the next morning with enough clothes for three days. She really didn't need to bother. Who needs clothes when Joe's around?

Mary moved in three weeks later.

Joe had never had a long term girlfriend, two months being about the longest. The women overseas, well that was different. He wasn't sure what was happening to him, maybe he was just getting old and mellow, but he liked it.

She never asked him for anything and didn't try to impress him. She was soft, smooth and beautiful to his eyes. He supposed he was in love for the first time in his life at the age of forty three.

There was one test Joe had to pass, Karen. She was coming to London that week to go shopping with Mary and she wanted to meet the mystery man. They arranged to have dinner at Julie's on Portland road and booked a table for seven o'clock.

When Joe arrived they were sitting drinking wine. He kissed Mary and offered his hand to Karen. "No kiss for me then"

"Oh sure, sorry," he stood up and pecked her on the cheek.

Joe looked excited about something. The doctor had discharged him and he demonstrated that his hand was now in perfect working order. He could go back to work the following week.

He kissed Mary again only this time full on the lips. Through the evening he was polite to Karen and conversed with her as he would with most people.

Towards the end of the evening Karen commented on how well they went together and how nice it was nice to watch.

Mary couldn't help but look and feel triumphant.

CHAPTER SEVEN

It was New Year's Day and they slept late. They had been out with some of Joe's friends the night before, celebrating. Mary woke first and got up and made coffee, which she took into the bedroom. She kissed Joe on the forehead and he stirred, opened his eyes and smiled.

"I'm on the night shift tonight, so I'm going to sleep all day."

"Then I'm cooking dinner, Joe's special paella."

"Sounds great."

They settled into a routine and Joe was back at work. His hand was in perfect working order but he hadn't been given any assignments. His assistant had been standing in for him and had done an adequate job, which pleased him.

His first overseas job was in April, two weeks in Paris installing a state of the art system in the embassy. He'd asked Mary if she could get time off to join him but the hospital was short staffed so that wasn't possible. It occurred to him that he had last travelled on his fake passport so arranged to go a day earlier than normal and flew to Zurich to exchange documents.

Paris was beautiful in the spring and he'd missed her. He had behaved himself non-the-less. When he returned, Mary was at home waiting for him. He asked if she had missed him.

"I immersed myself in my job and did a few extra shifts, so no, not then. It was when I came home that first night it was horrible so I went to stay at mum's. She was pleased to have me there but it was then that I missed you. Did you miss me?"

"With every breath I took."

"You're so lovely, I almost believe you."

They went to the bedroom at six and after about an hour of making out, Joe lay on his back looking at the ceiling and said he wanted to talk. Mary put her head on his belly and listened.

Joe told her most of his life story. He explained that he couldn't tell her everything he did at the Foreign Office as they weren't allowed, even to those closest to them. He told her about all the women he'd been with and how little they had meant to him, they were just fun. At that point he yelled "Ouch, what was that?"

"You had a large grey hair growing out of your belly, so I removed it for you."

"You were punishing me and I deserve it."

He finished his story and asked if she still loved him.

"I'll have to think about that. Ummm, yes of course I still love you, always."

"I do have one dark secret that I haven't mentioned, though."

Mary wasn't sure if she really wanted to hear dark secrets but said, OK, what."

"I dance."

She laughed. She had a vision of Joe gliding around a ballroom in tails.

"I dance flamenco. I've not been since the accident but I usually practice or teach on Saturday mornings and the dance group are desperate to have me back. I'll go this coming Saturday. They're putting on a show soon and as I'm the star performer, I need to start rehearsing."

"Can, I come to watch if I'm not on duty?"

"Sure, I'd really like that."

Joe got off the bed and made Mary do the same. He knelt before her and couldn't resist kissing her pubic hair. He looked up and said,

"Mary Leeson, will you marry me?"

Mary was truly shocked, she hadn't seen this coming.

"Joe we've only known one another for a few months. Don't you think it's a bit soon?"

Joe stood up and looked serious for once. He held her in his arms and pointed out that, with his hospital stay, it had been almost a year.

"I feel that I've known you all my life and I want to marry you."

Oh, Joe knew how to sweet talk but this was different, serious. She wanted to say yes but nothing would come out of her mouth.

He let her go and went to the bathroom looking dejected. He came back a few minutes later with a toothbrush in his mouth and apologised through bubbling toothpaste for assuming too much. Mary laughed as she couldn't make out all he said but got the gist. Joe returned to the bathroom and Mary heard the shower running. She got dressed and left without saying goodbye.

Joe hadn't heard her go and was extremely miserable when he realised she had. How could he have got it so wrong? She meant everything to him but obviously that feeling wasn't reciprocated.

He sat at the kitchen table with a book on micro technology but couldn't concentrate. He grabbed his wallet and went to the pub where, unlike him, he got drunk. He stayed until closing time and then walked unsteadily home.

He woke the next morning with someone hitting him on the head with a hammer. He sat on the side of the bed, head in hands.

"Well, that's no way to solve your problems."

Mary was standing over him with a glass of water in one hand and Panadol in the other. He took them gratefully and fell back onto the bed and pulled the covers over his head. He wasn't sure if he was embarrassed, hurt or just plain stupid.

Mary pulled the covers back and exposed his aching head.

"Aren't you going to ask me where I went?"

"I know where you went, out."

"If you're going to act like a spoilt brat I'll leave."

He rolled over onto his back and slid his legs over the side of the bed, just managing to stand up unaided.

"You must have been really drunk; you've still got your socks on"

He looked down and saw two black things at the end of his legs.

"Is this what you do every time you don't get your own way, get drunk?"

"Mary, I haven't been drunk since university and I've never been that hurt before. I'm not blaming you, I just thought ...."

"What did you think Joe?"

"I thought that you loved me and wanted to be with me forever."

"Who said I didn't?"

"Sorry I'm not understanding, I'll have a shower, it might make my brain get itself together."

When he was dried and dressed Mary fed him breakfast. When he had finished she told him to put his coat on and to bring his wallet. She led him along Portobello Road to the antique shops. They entered one that specialised in Jewellery. Joe looked around whilst Mary spoke to the shop owner.

"OK Joe, pay the man. It's one thousand seven hundred pounds."

Joe handed over his American Express card and the shopkeeper made a call. Joe signed the record of charge and they left. He hadn't seen what she had bought and he hadn't said a word since they had left home. His head was spinning and he felt decidedly wobbly. Mary held his arm and took him home.

"What did I just buy?"

"I'll tell you later but first you are going back to bed and I'm coming with you and no sex, just sleep."

Mary hadn't slept much the night before, she was too confused. Now they both slept.

He woke up at three and turned to face Mary and saw she was watching him.

"Feel a little better, misery?"

"I'm sorry, really sorry. It won't change anything, will it?"

"Sure Joe it'll change everything"

"Oh fuck."

"Not yet."

He almost smiled.

"Get up and put your clothes on."

He obeyed and she did likewise. She handed him a small box. He looked puzzled.

"Now down on your knee Joe Martinez and do it again."

He opened the box and then it registered. He gladly obliged. This time she accepted. He hugged her, kissed her and did a little flamenco and hugged her and kissed her again.

"You're such a kid Joe but I still love you."

"Wasn't I supposed to choose your ring?"

"What if you bought me one I didn't like? I'd be stuck with it for the rest of my life."

"You are so practical. What happened, where did you go last night?"

She had walked home and passed St Francis of Assisi on the way. The lights had been on, which was unusual for the time of night, so she went in, seeking guidance. There was a sign saying there was a vigil for the victims of the Hillsborough disaster. She sat at the back of the church and wondered what she should pray for. Then it occurred to her that she had everything she wanted, and as the families of the dead football fans knew, life was too fragile and too short to not spend as much time as possible with your loved ones. She prayed with the congregation and sat in silence for half an hour. She then went home and told her parents that she was getting married.

They sat and chatted for a while. Her dad was a little concerned that Joe was a bit old for her but relented when he was reminded that there was an even bigger age gap between him and Lou. Mary went to her room and collected the remainder of her belongings and threw them into a holdall. She arrived back at Joe's at eleven thirty.

"You were here all night?"

"Yes I made the bed up in your dad's room and slept there. There was no way I was getting into bed with you. You were talking and shouting in your sleep and then snoring and you stank of beer."

Joe was feeling a little nervous. "What did I say?"

"Lots and lots."

"Like what?"

"I don't know it was all in Spanish."

He felt himself relax. Mary asked about the chest that was in his dad's room. She said it looked totally out of place and should be in one of the antique shops down the road. Joe explained that it was a family heirloom and had been in his family for generations so it had sentimental value.

"Come on let's go."

"Where?"

"To your parent's house, I have to ask your dad for permission to marry his daughter."

Mary hugged him and guided him to the bedroom.

"We'll have a little celebration first."

The wedding was in July and they went to Spain for their honeymoon. Apart from the year before, Joe had spent every summer that he could remember in Spain. They visited his relatives and were feted at every house they entered. Joe spoke Spanish most of the time but managed to ensure that Mary didn't feel excluded. She even learnt a few phrases with the help of his female cousins.

On returning to London they settled into a comfortable routine. Both had their work interests which kept them apart on occasions, Mary having to do shift work and Joe still travelled every couple of months.

CHAPTER EIGHT

One year into the marriage Mary's dad died. Joe told Mary that she should invite Lou to come and live with them. Mary loved Joe for many reasons and his generosity of spirit was just one of them.

She extended the offer to her Lou who thanked them but said that she was going to live with Karen. Mary was very disappointed as Karen hadn't mentioned it to her. She called her.

"Mum says she's going to live with you. When's this going to happen?"

"You sound upset, what's wrong?"

"You could have told me." Now Mary sounded really peeved.

"Oh I see, I didn't ask mum recently. I told her a long time ago that any time she and dad wanted, they could live in the granny flat above our garage, its news to me that's she's coming."

Mary felt ashamed of herself for thinking badly of her sister and apologised.

She went round to see her mum to talk about it. She said she was surprised that she wanted to go and live in Kent. Lou loved the convenience of London, having the shops nearby and the freedom to walk anywhere. Didn't Lou always love London?

Lou explained that she didn't think it was the same anymore. All the real people had moved out. They had tarted up the houses and now it's all posh knobs in the area. They keep themselves to themselves and it just wasn't the same friendly place it used to be.

Mary said she understood and made it clear that if she ever changed her mind she could always go and live with her and Joe.

Lou moved a few months later. Mary really missed her, which meant Joe's trips abroad became hard for her.

Joe returned from Cairo where he had been for three weeks. He looked darker than ever. Mary was so glad to see him as she had felt lonely. She knew it was her own fault for not making friends but she was starting to resent Joe's excursions.

Joe unpacked and had a shower whilst Mary made their dinner. After dinner Mary said she wanted to talk but Joe had other ideas. Later that evening when they were sitting in the front room, Mary asked if Joe wanted children. She had never mentioned it before, so he was a little taken aback. He said he wouldn't mind, whilst thinking to himself how much he would love a son.

She pointed out that they used no protection and reminded him how often the opportunity for her to get pregnant occurred.

"Do you think there's something wrong with me? Do you think I should go for a test? I could easily do that being at the hospital all day but if you're not interested in having kids then there's no point, is there."

He looked at her lovingly choosing his words carefully.

"Mary my love if that's what you want to do, then do it. If you want me to be tested I'll do that. If it's just for me because you think I'm getting old and would like children before its too late, don't worry. I have everything I want sitting right in front of me. Anything else would be a bonus."

"Joe, you're so good and I love you dearly. I'll give it some more thought. There's something that I keep wanting to ask you, what is it exactly that you do? Can you explain what did you do this time in Cairo?"

"That's easy; I spent three weeks sitting by the pool in a luxury hotel. Can't you tell by the tan?"

"Joe, be serious, I'm your wife and I should know."

He dreaded these questions because there was only so much he could tell her. This would be OK but another time he'd have to tell her that it was classified information or he'd have to lie, the latter being something he didn't want to do.

He explained step by step how he'd been upgrading at the ambassador's residence and had done a thorough check on the embassy. He went into minute detail to the point where she almost wished she hadn't asked.

"That's it in a nutshell, get it?"

"That was a bloody big nut but I think so."

He asked her if she could get three weeks off in September as his cousin's villa in Malaga would be free and they could stay there. She said she could and he called his cousin right away, anything to deflect.

The arrangements were made and Joe hugged Mary and said, "It'll me just you and me. We can try twice a day to make a baby."

"Only twice" she teased, "You're getting old Joe Martinez."

"You're very cheeky, tell you what let's try now."

"We tried, as you put it, half an hour ago. I think you might want to refill your tank first."

September came and they had a wonderful holiday, just the two of them. October arrived and Mary missed her period so she did a pregnancy test, which was positive. Joe was away so she'd have a nice surprise for him when he got back.

He was delighted with the news. They were both really happy. Come February Mary miscarried. Joe was very good about it. He hid his disappointment well but Mary couldn't. She cried at odd moments for two weeks.

Life returned to normal. The year progressed pretty much like the previous one. Christmas came and went and winter dissolved into a pleasant spring.

On a late April Sunday, Mary woke and sat on the edge of the bed. Joe was asleep. She felt very nauseous. She ran to the bathroom and was sick. What had she eaten? She went back to the bedroom feeling terrible. She had missed her last period and wasn't keeping track of when it should be due, she had shut it out of her thoughts. She ran to the bathroom again and was sick again. This time Joe had woken and was just about to get up when Mary came back into the bedroom.

"You all right love?"

Mary started crying.

"Hey, what's wrong?"

When she settled down she sat on the bed with her back to Joe.

She sniffled. "I think I'm pregnant. No, I know I'm pregnant."

Joe knew not to show too much excitement. He had to tread carefully after the last disappointment.

"That's great but let's not get too excited this time. If it happens, it happens."

"Yes your right, let's not."

He got out of bed and sat next to her with his arm around her. She started to cry again and he comforted her as best he could.

By September they were confident that this time it would all be OK. They skipped their holiday to Spain and stayed home together. Joe wanted to decorate his dad's old room for the new baby but Mary said no.

"We are not going to buy anything for this baby until he's born, neither of us."

Had Joe heard right? "Did you say he or was that just a figure of speech?"

"Do you remember the last scan? Well the radiologist told me afterwards. I couldn't bring myself to tell you. I'm sorry. It's definitely a boy. I've known for three months."

Joe was elated but kept it down. "Oh well now I know." He wanted to jump up and down but held his excitement until it just burst out. He yelled at the top of his voice and started his flamenco dancing around the front room.

"I take it you're pleased from your little outburst."

"Sorry but oh god we're having a boy."

It pleased Mary immensely that Joe was so excited.

"But no decorating or buying anything promise?"

"Yes, but….."

"No buts OK."

"Can I at least put his name down to play for Rangers?"

She agreed to that knowing full well it wasn't something you could do.

Joe had one more assignment before the end of the year. It was for mid-October and it was for MI6. He had wanted to decline but the job was straight forward and he needed some excitement in his life. He hoped Mary wouldn't ask him about it and she didn't. Maybe he should give up that part of his job. He'd seriously consider it after the baby was born.

He had saved his vacation time so he could take all of December and part of January to be with Mary. He would be present at the birth and be around for a month after to give Mary support.

CHAPTER NINE

The baby was born on the seventh of December 1992.

That had agreed that his name would be registered as Juan but they would call him Jonathan which satisfied them both. Joe didn't have to be at the Foreign Office until the second week of January so he did all he could to help with the baby. Jonathan was a placid infant and cried only when he was hungry, which meant always in the middle of the night.

As Mary was no longer working she had no income. Their domestic finances had been a loose affair, Joe paid the bills and Mary used her cash when necessary. Joe changed his banks accounts and investment accounts to joint accounts and, without telling Mary, had the ownership of the second flat put into a trust fund for Jonathan. The rent would accumulate so that there would be sufficient to pay for his education when the time came.

When Mary opened the first bank statement addressed to them both she was amazed at how much money Joe had. She asked him if he'd robbed a bank. Joe explained how little he had needed to live and how his investments had been giving a regular return. She now knew how much he earned and as well as how much he was worth. He also had the flat in which they lived put into joint names. Mary never had to ask him for money which suited them both. Their income exceeded their outgoings and continued that way as Mary, although not mean, was frugal.

Joe went back to work and Mary coped well enough with the baby. Joe's first assignment of the year was a short maintenance trip to Brussels and he was gone for a week. When he returned Mary seemed distraught. She hadn't imagined that it could be so hard being alone with a baby. She had no friends or family close by so she had felt very isolated.

Joe was at home the next weekend and her mood seemed to brighten but come Monday when he went back to work her mood darkened again. Joe had no travelling abroad for the next two months so he was around for support in the evenings and weekends.

He didn't go to football at weekends and spent all his spare time with his beautiful son, Juan. He was growing fast and Joe had stopped being nervous holding him thinking he might break.

They didn't have sex during this time and although Joe assumed it was a hormonal thing he still felt neglected. Mary knew it wasn't just hormones. When she thought about it logically she realised that she was resentful. Joe got to go to work and have a life whilst she felt imprisoned by her responsibility. She knew she should be happy that Joe was so good with Jonathan but even started to resent that. Joe got all the good bits and she now had no life away from the baby.

Joe loved Mary and was concerned by her attitude but assumed that would pass. He spent every free moment at home and as the baby grew he felt more love for the child that he could ever have imagined. They had agreed that Joe would speak Spanish to Jonathan and now this was starting to annoy Mary.

In late May Joe had an assignment in Germany, his first there since the accident. It was a big job and he would be gone for a month which didn't please Mary at all. He felt terrible. This was his job and had been when they met and now it just seemed like a problem.

"Mary, this is supposed to be the happiest time of our lives. We have one another and we have a beautiful, healthy baby boy."

"He is beautiful but he has an absentee father," she said sourly.

"That's my job and has been as long as you've known me. What do you want me to do?"

"I don't know. All I do know is I'm alone most of the time and I'm not happy."

He was lost for words. He didn't know how to respond.

"I'm going to stay with Karen whilst you're away. At least I'll have some real support there."

Joe nodded and went into the front room and switched on the television.

He was leaving the next day and they hardly spoke until he was about to leave, suitcase in hand.

"Whilst you're gone I have some serious thinking to do."

"About what?" he said in a very hurt voice.

"About us, this life."

He looked at the woman in front of him and didn't recognise her. His face flushed with anger and he turned and left.

Mary sat down and cried

Joe's assignment was to be at the embassy in Bonn and the consulates in both Hamburg and Düsseldorf. MI6 also had two jobs for him to do. He had always felt extremely nervous when about to embark on what could only be called criminal activity but this time he felt a rush of excitement. It was as if he didn't care. With the exception of the joy the baby gave him, his life had been so dull and miserable the last few months that the thought of danger pleased him.

He'd been assigned to a different intelligence officer, one Gideon Charles. Gideon himself worked under a newly promoted boss Charlotte Tully. James Jones had taken early retirement and she was his replacement. He wondered if he'd been demoted as it was made very clear to him that he would report to Gideon and have no dealings with Ms Tully. Joe thought this a little odd at the time but being in his frame of mind, let it go.

They had two jobs, both in the old East Berlin. Joe had reviewed the building plans and it all seemed straightforward and they turned out to be that way. He was amazed how antique everything in this part of the world was.

He was never told why they were doing what they did, just what was expected of him. They didn't tell him from where the plans had been acquired or how they knew the site would be unoccupied. In both cases Joe had to gain access to a property, disable the alarm and open a relatively uncomplicated safe. Gideon photographed the contents and that was it. Joe reset the alarm and they left without a trace. Usually they would plant listening devices but not this time. Joe knew better than to ask and in fact he didn't want to know.

Whilst in Bonn Joe had dinner with a woman he'd known for about ten years. It was very pleasant and when they had finished eating they sat talking for a while finishing their bottle of wine. He was tempted to ask her back to his hotel room, knowing she would be willing. He so needed some affection but also knew he was vulnerable and not in a position to make a good value judgement. They said goodnight and parted company.

When his work was done he returned home, hoping against hope that all would be well once more.

There was nobody home. He supposed Mary was still at Karen's as there was no sign of life in the flat. He unpacked and lay on the bed for a while wondering what to do. He made coffee and called Karen. Mary was brought to the phone and she sounded cold and distant. She told him they would be home the following week.

"Mary I don't understand. What have I done that's so wrong? I want to see my son."

"Joe we'll be home Friday next week." She hung up.

Karen had heard part of the conversation and resolved to say something. She told Mary that they were going out for dinner that night and Lou would look after the baby, girls' night out.

At dinner they chatted and Karen took her opportunity when she saw it.

"You've not really been happy since mum came to live with me have you? It's strange you were always so dependent on her. I mean how many thirty year olds still live with their mums. You're very lucky you know. Most women would give their eye teeth to have a husband like yours and you've been treating him like shit. He's so good to you and all you do is complain especially when he has to travel. That's his job for Christ sakes." She felt herself getting angry so she took a breath and a glass of wine.

"Joe's handsome, generous and bloody sexy. He's great with Jonathan and he's given up just about everything for you. He doesn't even go to his beloved Rangers anymore. What have you done for him? You desperately wanted a baby and when you miscarried he was there for you, no thought on your part that he might have been disappointed. Then you have the baby and blame Joe because you have no life outside of him. You don't deserve him."

Mary hadn't seen that coming. She was quiet for a while and then agreed. "I'm acting like a spoilt brat I know but I get so lonely"

"You'll be lonelier when he walks out the door and who would blame him. He's your husband and you should be looking after him not always the other way around. Grow up."

Joe spent all his spare time, including the week-end at the MI6 lab. He was refining a surveillance camera and the challenge absorbed his thoughts. At least he wasn't miserable when he was doing one of the things he liked most.

Friday arrived as did Mary and the baby as promised. Joe was amazed to see that there was a noticeable difference in the size of Jonathan, how he had grown in just five weeks. Joe took him and held him close and was sure the beautiful child knew who he was.

Mary said it was his bed time and took him into his room and fed him. Joe was sitting in the front room when she had finished. She sat in an armchair and asked if he'd had a good trip.

"Yes thanks, I did. How was it at Karen's? How's Lou?"

"Good and good thanks, it gave me time to think. What have you been doing since you came home?"

It was all a little stilted and Joe knew then that whatever it was that made him love Mary had gone, forever.

"I spent most of the time at work. There was nothing to do here."

"Joe something isn't working and I just can't understand what. It's not that I don't love you, it's just everything is different."

"I know, I don't even think I know you anymore."

"What shall we do?"

He hadn't told her about the trust fund and just to change the subject he thought this might be a good opportunity, so he told her he'd been to see a solicitor that specialised in financial matters. She looked shocked. "You want a divorce?"

He almost broke into a smile and looking at her through a reality lens he said, "No I've asked him to set up a trust fund for Jonathan. I'm changing the ownership of the other flat into Jonathan's name and the rent will go into his trust account. That will pay for his education and give him a start in life. Everything else I've settled on you as you know so you're financially secure. If you want me to leave none of that will change."

Mary stood up and went to the bathroom. She was gone for half an hour. When she returned she asked him one more question.

"Would you like to see me naked?"

They both laughed and history repeated itself, well almost.

They lay spent on the bed. Mary was the first to speak. "I'm really sorry Joe. I thought I had all this burden and you just see it as joy. You think of all our futures and I haven't been able to see past the next nappy. I'm a selfish cow."

Joe was saved having to reply as Jonathan started crying. He leapt off the bed and went to get him. He placed him on the bed and lay down on his elbows over his son. He started talking to him in Spanish and making weird noises that made the baby smile. He picked him up and placed him on Mary's bare breast and he suckled hungrily.

"Apart from talk to him, I don't really know what to do. I've never been around babies and maybe it's my age but I feel like I should do more. I can't feed him, you do. He doesn't need me he needs you. The best I can do is, change his nappies." None of this was really true. If he had to he would bring the child up single handed. The old Joe had suddenly emerged and without thinking he was giving her a line.

"When he's a bit older it will be different Joe. You can take him down the Rangers. I want to say sorry again. I do have a problem with the separations and I know it's your job. You like your job and it was there when I met you and I don't want that to change. When I was at Karen's she made me go to a support group for new mothers and it was OK. They gave me an address for one round here so I'll try that."

"When I'm here love, I'm here in mind and body but if you want me to change my job I will." He lied.

There was no way he was going to quit his job, especially now that his fear had turned to thrill. This really pleased her but she said he mustn't quit.

Joe decided there and then that if it was lies that pleased her then lies she would get.

"No Joe, I remember when you were in hospital, one of the men you work with told me that you were the best he'd ever seen at the job you do. I'm proud of that even if I still don't understand exactly what it is that you do. Perhaps you'll be able to tell me properly one day.

"Perhaps." An evil thought occurred, maybe he could get MI6 to eliminate her as a security risk. He bit his bottom lip hard to stop himself laughing.

The baby finished feeding and Joe returned him to his previous position and continued their conversation in Spanish ignoring Mary. Joe felt happy all of a sudden. All he had to do was tell Mary what she wanted to hear even if that meant lying. He felt that somehow she had betrayed him and no longer deserved his loyalty. Viva the old Joe. His strategy worked. He gave her a load of old flannel and it kept her happy. He had no conscience about what he was doing. What he had was a beautiful son and sex on tap from a still very attractive woman.

The next couple of months, life went well. Mary was a very observant person and she knew that something had changed in Joe and knew she was the one responsible for making it happen. The light in Joe's eyes had turned from love to lust in the bedroom. He acted the same was still very good to her and he obviously adored his son but she knew.

They planned their summer holiday. They were going to Spain in September. Joe's relatives wanted to see the baby so they would go to Madrid for a week and then down to Malaga. Joe had one more assignment before then, a security job in Switzerland.

Mary had access to their bank accounts and somehow that gave her a sense of security. She could see if Joe was spending any unusual amounts of money, which he didn't. She didn't know about his bank account in Switzerland which he used if he needed any extra for any extras. She was the joint owner of the flat and Jonathan's financial future was secure. She had made some acquaintances through the baby clinic and she occasionally went to a baby group so she wasn't feeling so isolated. Joe had changed and this she had to live with. He didn't love her or least not how he used to but she felt she was better off than most.

CHAPTER TEN

The assignment was for two weeks at the embassy in Berne, a routine job. He just needed to tweak the existing system which wouldn't take long. The ambassador's secretary was an old friend and she looked better than she had ever in Joe's eyes. He was finding that generally woman looked better and knew it was his rediscovered mental freedom that was responsible.

He asked her out for dinner. Anna accepted readily. They skipped dinner and went instead to Joe's hotel room. Anna had always been very physical in the past and it seemed that her appetite had doubled. It was five years since they last played bodies together and they made up for lost time. They took a break and ordered room service. Anna had some very inventive ways of eating without utensils. They drank champagne and enjoyed one another until two in the morning. This was the first time he'd been unfaithful but that didn't stop him sleeping the sleep of the innocent.

Whilst working the next day, Joe's thoughts turned to the previous night's pleasures. Anna was terrific. In the cold light of day, he felt no pang of conscience and he understood why. Mary had betrayed his love, she had shunned him and that changed everything. If being married allowed her to treat him that way, what might the next drama be. The old Joe had been resurrected and was not going back into his coffin any time soon. He felt strangely happy.

That evening they gave a repeat performance. Anna was as keen as Joe and they continued in this vein every night Joe was in town.

On the Wednesday, Joe got a call from Zurich, it was Gideon. He was to meet him at the consulate in Zurich the following Monday.

Joe packed an overnight bag and caught the early train on Monday morning. He arrived at the consulate at ten thirty. He was shown to a small room where Gideon was sitting at a desk drinking coffee. He beckoned Joe to sit and poured him a cup.

There was an urgent assignment and Joe was the only person available. The target was just outside Turin and the window of opportunity was from two am until seven am the following day. That left plenty of time to do the job with some to spare. Joe was given the plans of the house in question and the safe type. He studied them for a while and agreed it would be straightforward. Gideon was pleased with the assessment.

"There's something different this time Joe."

Joe inquired as to what.

"I've been called back to London and there are no other field agents available, so it's down to you."

Joe was shocked and was about to protest when he stopped to consider. Why not, it might be just the buzz he needed right now.

"OK I'll do it."

Gideon looked relieved and pleased at the same time. Joe had been booked on an evening flight to Turin. He collected his second passport from the bank in Bahnhoff Strasse and also his driving licence and credit card and stored his genuine documents.

When he arrived at Turin airport he rented a car to be dropped in Zurich the next day. He showed his credit card but was told the rental had been pre-paid; he thought this strange but just shrugged. His stomach was churning but he knew he should eat. He stopped at a nondescript restaurant and ate what he could and drank three double espressos. If he thought he was buzzing before he knew he was now. He set off for his destination at ten o'clock. It took him an hour to find the house which was large and set in its own grounds with nothing near it for a quarter of a mile in either direction. He was early so he drove passed, noting there were lights on. There was a small copse about two hundred yards further on where he pulled off the road and out of sight to any passing vehicles not that there were any.

He took his tool bag out of the boot and wandered along the road back towards the house.

When it was in sight he looked for a viewing point from which he could see the house but not be seen. He chose a large tree with a wide trunk about ten feet off the road. It was still only eleven thirty so he had a long wait. He shone his torch on the house plan and knew it was accurate as always. He double checked his equipment. The task was to enter the house, empty the safe and remove anything that looked vaguely valuable. It was to look like a straightforward robbery. As usual he wasn't told the purpose.

At one forty five the house lights went out and two cars left the house driveway and turned right onto the road. Joe waited until two o'clock looking for any signs of life. He walked nervously up to the house and then around the periphery. No life was noted. He disabled the alarm system with ease and opened the front door with his tools.

He found the safe which was almost an antique and opened it in a matter of minutes. He put the contents into his bag. There was a number of documents and a wad of US dollar bills. These had been concealing a gun and a box of bullets. Joe hesitated but remembered his instructions so he took these as well. He collected a few trinkets from a jewellery box in one of the bedrooms and stashed them into the bag with the rest of the booty.

His heart was pumping hard. The adrenalin rush he was experiencing made everything more focussed. It was still only three thirty. Something told him that it was just too easy.

This was supposed to look like a robbery so he didn't reset the alarm, would a burglar do that? He walked quickly back to his car and set off north towards the Swiss border. He crossed a bridge over a small river and stopped on the far side. He checked to make sure there were no vehicles approaching. He took the gun and bullets out of the bag, walked back to the bridge and dumped them in the river. About a mile further down the road he parked in a lay by. He repacked his tool bag, placing the acquired items under the removable hard base false bottom. He then stored it under the spare tyre in the boot and set off for the border.

His passport, driving license and credit card were in his own name but this was a different Joe. The fictitious Joe was a Spanish national who lived and worked in Madrid for a security company. If anyone had checked they would have found that both the person and company existed. They would have also found that Joe was paid a salary every month. If they had checked further they would have discovered that Spanish Joe's bank account was emptied every so often with the balance being transferred to an account in Zurich. Joe would appear one hundred percent genuine to most scrutiny.

Even with this knowledge Joe's heart was in his mouth when he reached the border. The sleepy Italian officers hardly noticed him drive through. The obviously alert Swiss ones ignored him. He gave an enormous sigh of relief. About half an hour before Zurich he stopped and retrieved the tool bag. He took his ill-gotten gains out and examined them. There were a number of documents, some in Italian and some in English. There were numerous bearer bonds but Joe didn't understand what they were. They all had US dollar values on them of fifty thousand. He counted them, there were twenty. If each was actually worth that much then that was a million dollars he had in his hand. He counted the cash and without rechecking it amounted to about forty thousand dollars. The trinkets were real or not, he didn't know. What was the aim of the operation? Was it the documents, the bonds or some obscure thing he was missing?

It was best not to think about it. The job was done and that was that.

He returned the car at Zurich airport and caught a taxi to his bank. He swapped over his documents and then it suddenly hit him. Who would know if there was cash in the safe, nobody? He sat and counted the dollar bills which amounted to fifty two thousand. He put five thousand in his pocket, forty five thousand in his deposit box and two thousand in the large envelop he had for the documents. He fingered the jewellery and thought, fuck it. He took an attractive looking bracelet and put it in his pocket together with his newly found dollars and put the rest in the envelope, which was addressed to Gideon.

He went to the consulate and they took possession of the envelope which would go into the diplomatic bag, no questions asked.

On the train back to Berne he was staring out of the window when he suddenly started to laugh out loud. He felt like he'd never felt before. Joe was bad, wasn't that fantastic. The other reserved Swiss passengers ignored him. The train arrived at seven so he still had time to meet Anna.

That night they went to the most expensive restaurant the hotel concierge could find a reservation for at such short notice. Over dinner Joe surprised Anna with a gift, the stolen bracelet. This was becoming more enjoyable by the minute. The meal and wine was extremely expensive but Joe didn't bat an eyelid when presented with the bill. He took out his credit card and then as if an afterthought, he asked the waiter if they took US dollars and was answered in the affirmative. He fished out his wad and paid the required amount leaving a generous tip. That night they didn't sleep.

The next day he asked one of the embassy staff if they knew what bearer bonds were. It was explained that they were forms of value which could be redeemed by anyone holding them. Not being very secure instruments they were not much used in the present day.

Joe swore to himself. Fuck, he'd just handed over a million dollars to Gideon Charles and maybe all they wanted were the documents or did they?

He still had the plan in his possession, which he should have destroyed but for some reason hadn't. He wrote on the back of it exactly where he'd been, what he'd taken (except the dollars and diamonds he'd filched) and who had given the instructions. He had a strong feeling that something wasn't right. Was this just a robbery and nothing to do with MI6? He stopped himself thinking along those lines as in truth all his MI6 assignments were nothing more than criminal.

He had two more nights in Berne so he and Anna made the most of it. When he checked out of the hotel he paid for his numerous extras with US dollars.

He returned to Zurich for a short maintenance job before leaving for London. Whilst there he went to the bank and placed the plans with his notes and the balance of his dollars, less five hundred dollars pocket money, in his deposit box.

He was still on a high so he called a woman he knew but she was unavailable. He had dinner and went to his hotel. He was restless so he went out for a walk. He wandered around and after a while was lured into a brothel where he happily indulged himself. He was living on the edge and it was great.

CHAPTER ELEVEN

When he arrived home Mary was waiting. This time she seemed happy to see him.

"You look tired Joe."

"I'm fucked truly fucked." He had to hurry to the bathroom so that she wouldn't see him laugh. He composed himself and the home loving Joe kicked in and he settled easily back into home routine.

He spent as much time as possible with Jonathan chattering away in Spanish getting no response other than a smile or a gurgle. He and Mary took him for long walks in his push chair and he seemed to be taking in his surroundings.

It was during this period of domestic bliss that he was called to MI6 to help with a new piece of equipment they were developing. On his way to lunch with Rupert, his technician friend, he bumped into Charlotte Tully. He asked if she had a minute but she looked at him as though he was a piece of shit and told him she didn't converse with contractors. If he wanted anything he had to go through Gideon Charles. He shrugged it off and told himself that he had at least tried to share his discomfort with the last job. He made a note of the encounter when he next opened his safe deposit box.

September came and Jonathan was crawling and almost walking but no words only indecipherable noises. They enjoyed Spain and Joe's relatives were over the moon with Jonathan. They all said he was the most beautiful baby they had ever seen, classical Spanish and Joe and Mary readily agreed.

The whole of the next year things remained on an even keel. Joe was the perfect husband when at home and a wild animal when overseas. He wondered if it was mid-life crisis kicking in but decided not. He was just having a great time, life was fun again.

It was October and Jonathan was coming up for two. Mary had been concerned that he wasn't talking and had taken him to see a paediatrician. He asked Mary many questions and tested Jonathan's motor skills and declared him normal. He explained that sometimes bilingual children were late talkers.

This she thought stupid as how could he be bilingual when he wasn't even monolingual?

The doctor explained that Jonathan responded non-verbally when spoken to in English and explained how. He then asked if he did the same when spoken to in Spanish. Mary confirmed that he did but still didn't say anything at least nothing understandable. He reassured her that her child was perfectly normal and she left feeling a little happier.

Joe was away for most of November and when he returned home he found his wife in the kitchen spoon feeding their son, his son, his beautiful precious son. He kissed them both and picked up Jonathan who was squeaking with delight at seeing his father. Joe babbled away in Spanish and played with him and made him smile and giggle. Suddenly Joe stood still, to his amazement Jonathan had repeated something that he'd said. He said the few words again and Jonathan obliged by doing the same. Joe hugged and squeezed him and turned to Mary with a huge smile.

"When did this start?"

Mary knew enough Spanish to know what had just happened. "Just then, the boy speaks Spanish first and no English. I'm left out in the cold." She said not really caring just relieved that her son could talk.

Jonathan's speech came in leaps and bounds and soon he was saying English words to Mary, which pleased her immensely.

Joe continued with his Jekyll and Hyde existence and enjoyed both roles. He loved being at home and Jonathan gave him more pleasure than he could ever had imagined. His relationship with Mary was good even though not what it used to be. They both knew that they had broken something.

Joe was enjoying his work more than ever, especially the MI6 assignments. He rarely had to work with Gideon, who assigned him to various agents, which somehow pleased him more. It wasn't that he didn't like him it was just somehow he wasn't sure if he trusted him. Since the Turin job, he had kept a copy of each plan and had written what had been required and what had transpired. He felt it was a sort of safety net should he discover that he was, as he suspected, sometimes being used to do things that weren't kosher. It also occurred to him that if the job was not MI6 generated then Charlotte Tully must be involved as she was the only one who had access to the information required, which enabled them to do the job. That would explain her refusal to talk to him as she needed to keep her distance. He had no recourse to anyone senior to her so he decided not to rock the boat. He had tried to talk to his boss at the foreign office but was quickly shut down. It was made very clear that MI6 business was not his.

CHAPTER TWELVE

Jonathan started school when he was five. He was already able to read and write in both English and Spanish so Joe decided they should send him to a private school where he would get more individual attention with a smaller class size. One was found just behind Notting hill Gate and although expensive it gave Joe and Mary a certain peace of mind.

Mary found a part-time nursing job at a local clinic. She was able to take Jonathan to school and pick him up which she did unless Joe was around, then he gladly did it.

Mary felt happier than she had for many years. They had a comfortable routine, no money worries and Jonathan was already excelling at school. On Saturday mornings Joe would take his beloved son to judo classes and then onto his own flamenco classes. Jonathan wanted to be just like his dad and so he started to learn flamenco too. Now he was old enough they went with Joe's old football buddies to watch QPR's home games. Jonathan loved it. The noise the excitement was infectious. He heard all kinds of swear words that were never used at home and he thought this very grown up. He tried a few his self only to be told he must never do that anywhere else.

Life was good but like most mother's Mary still worried. Jonathan had no trouble settling into school but he didn't have any interest in the other children. He'd happily partake in any organised games but refused invitations to other children's homes for friendship or parties. He had been to one party and hadn't enjoyed it so avoided social occasions.

Mary expressed her concerns to his teacher who said that he was very focussed and didn't interact much his classmates but was great to have in her form.

Mary only worried more, strange things started going round her head. Maybe Jonathan had some type of autism, Aspergers maybe so she took him to see a child psychologist.

The doctor spent an hour with Jonathan putting him through numerous tests whilst Mary sat anxiously in the waiting room. When the doctor appeared he had a broad grin across his face and invited Mary into his surgery leaving Jonathan outside in the care of the receptionist.

"Mrs Martinez does Jonathan interact much with you and your husband?"

"Yes especially with his father. We do things together and Joe takes him here there and everywhere he goes, apart from work."

"What do they do?"

"Joe plays football with him, takes him to watch QPR, judo, flamenco and they're always reading books together usually in Spanish. He really likes all those things and he adores his dad."

"Does his father talk to him as a child?"

"I don't know about the Spanish bit but no he speaks to him as if he were an adult, why?"

"Your son is extremely bright and there are two reasons that he doesn't particularly want to interact with his peer group. One is that he is mentally far more mature and the other is he's just not that interested in other people. It appears you supply all the stimulation that he needs. He says he loves to read which he finds rewarding and he likes to learn new things. School doesn't stretch him enough so he makes his own challenges. Some children, and of course adults, don't have the conventional need to constantly have people around them and Jonathan is one such. He's just highly introverted and there's absolutely nothing wrong with that unless he's pressured to act otherwise. The only advice I can give you is to carry on doing what you've been doing. Keep him stimulated by stretching him academically. He's a very smart boy and the reason I was grinning when I came out was I asked him why he didn't like children's parties and he asked me if I did. As I said he's a very smart boy. When I asked why he didn't have any friends he just shrugged and asked why he should, as his mum doesn't."

Mary wasn't sure she wanted a smart boy. She wanted a normal boy.

"Should we send him to a special school?"

"Absolutely not, Jonathan is a very happy child and you're fortunate to have him. I find him delightful. If his school suggests that they put him up a year I would resist that. He's probably way above his peer group but putting him with older children would disadvantage him physically. You have nothing to worry about but a lot to be proud of."

Mary thanked the doctor and on the way home she began to feel more comfortable. Her son was a beautiful, happy bright child, albeit a little different, so why was she worrying? She thought about what Jonathan had said about her having no friends. She had her sister and her mother and some acquaintances, so it was her fault he was like he was. She sighed.

Jonathan was now eight and learning French at school and was finding it frustrating much to Mary's pleasure. At last there was something he wasn't good at. He told his father that as he couldn't hear it outside of school he was finding it difficult to get the right pronunciation and to increase his vocabulary. Joe took him to W.H.Smith's and they bought CDs and VCDs and Jonathan set to work perfecting his French, which of course he managed very quickly. It wasn't that he was competitive he just had a need to learn that which he needed to learn for school.

Joe was so proud of his son. He could dance flamenco, his judo was coming on well and he'd grown to love QPR as much as his father.

Joe was fifty five soon to be fifty six and was considering retirement. He still felt young and the thought of inactivity didn't enthral him. He didn't feel the ravages of time and his vanity wouldn't allow him to want to get old. He decided to give it a few more years. His sexploits were still rewarding and he still entered the bedroom with relish, anyone's bedroom. The thrill of his MI6 assignments, were as fresh as ever and he loved the high they gave him.

He still kept meticulous records of everything he did. He knew why but wasn't sure what he could ever use them for.

That summer he was in Zurich doing security work and Gideon turned up at the consulate. He had a job, an easy one. He couldn't do it so Joe was to go solo again as there was no other agent available. This was the fifth time this had happened so Joe wasn't fazed. He checked out the layout from the security plans and decided it was a piece of cake so he acquiesced.

The target was a detached house in the suburbs of Zurich and it would be empty the next day for two whole days. Joe decided he'd do it on the first available day. Gideon told him not to be surprised by what he would find. He was to take everything from the safe and make it look like a straight forward burglary.

Joe did the job the next day as planned. He emptied the safe and was surprised by the contents; maybe it was the documents that were important. He took a look around the house and knew something was not right. He had the strongest feeling yet that he was being used, in fact he was certain. This was a normal family home evidenced by the items scattered around and the family photographs. The people in the frames were European and artefacts around suggested they were Christian. He left as soon as he had finished and returned to his hotel. It was dark but not late. He emptied his loot onto his bed. There were two velvet bags. He opened them and his worst fears were confirmed, diamonds. Maybe there was still a reason so he scrutinised the documents which were bills of sale from a diamond merchant. The rest of the documents were mainly import and export licenses and looking at the company name and description it became apparent that the owner was a jeweller. The diamonds were therefore probably the raw materials for making jewellery for retail sale.

He felt extremely angry. It was the family photographs that had touched him. He thought of returning everything but that would be stupid he might get caught; the damage was done. He placed a call to Gideon.

"What the fuck have you made me do? This was no MI6 job; it was an ordinary family house. Have you had me stealing for you all these years? I'll fucking tear your balls off, you bastard."

Gideon remained calm. "Joe your role isn't to question. You do as you're told. I can't and won't tell you why you do what you do so just keep quiet." He hung up.

Joe made his notes and instead of taking his haul to the consulate for the diplomatic bag, he went to his bank. He put everything in his deposit box. He needed time to think so he just went about his work.

He returned home the following Wednesday to a warm greeting from his family. They were sitting down to dinner when Mary related a strange incident.

"I dropped Jonathan at school on Monday and was walking to work when a van pulled up alongside me. Before I knew what had happened I was inside the van with a bag over my head. About five minutes later the van stopped and I was pushed out. I took the bag off my head but the sudden brightness meant I couldn't see properly, not the men or the van and by the time my focus returned, they were gone. I was on Ladbroke Grove so I walked to the police station and told them what had happened. I think they thought I was making it up.

"They sat me down and gave me a cup of tea and I made a formal statement. They eventually believed me, I think. I couldn't tell them anything about the van or whoever it was that dragged me into it. It was all so weird Joe."

Joe sat listening trying to stay calm. He knew exactly what had happened. It was a warning.

He finished his dinner with difficulty and went into the bedroom and took out the phone he only used for Gideon. He pressed the dial button and connected.

"You piece of shit you leave my family alone."

"Now, now Joe, don't get angry, it doesn't help. Just remember you're not dealing with ordinary folk here. There's been nothing for me in the diplomatic bag so I suppose you have something for me."

Joe took a deep breath and lied. "Yes I do. What do you want me to do with your lovely diamonds, drop them down the drain?"

"Joe that would be exceedingly silly of you, meet me tonight and this will all be over. Say nine o'clock at Shepherd's Bush market, under the bridge.

Joe agreed. He hadn't thought what he would do but he just wanted to kill Gideon or at least teach him a lesson. Joe could be a little naïve at times.

Joe was there at nine sharp and Gideon was waiting. Joe couldn't help himself, without either of them saying a word, He attacked Gideon savagely. Gideon wasn't alone. Two bulky figures appeared out of the shadows and Joe was outnumbered. He fought furiously but to no avail. He fell to the floor and was kicked a multitude of times before he slipped into unconsciousness.

Midnight came and Joe hadn't come home. Mary was worried. Joe rarely went out and when he did he was never this late. She waited up. One o'clock came and went and at two she called the police. She thought that they'd think her stupid but they were very kind and said someone would be round soon if she was still going to up. She said she would and hung up. She knew then that something was terribly wrong. It was as if the police were expecting her to call but why?

There was a gentle knock at the door. Mary opened it and admitted two policemen.

"Are you Mrs Martinez?"

"Yes"

"And your husband is Jose Martinez?"

"Yes, I told you that on the phone. Has something happened to Joe?" she said with panic in her voice.

"Please sit down Mrs Martinez. Is this your husband's driving licence?"

"Has something happened to Joe? Has he been in an accident?"

The policeman looked at her with compassion and asked her the question again.

"Yes that's Joe's driving licence."

"I'm afraid then we have bad news. Your husband was attacked about nine o'clock. It looks like a mugging. His wallet was empty and his pockets. The only thing not taken was this. That's how we were able to identify him."

"Is he OK? Where is he, poor Joe."

"I'm afraid he died on the way to hospital."

Mary shook her head. Words wouldn't come out of her mouth. Her head was swimming and she wanted to scream. She couldn't cry. She was totally immobilised. Then Jonathan appeared at the door. She mustered all the power left in her and stood up and lead him back to bed. "Go back to sleep. It's alright."

Jonathan got out of bed again and listened at the kitchen door. He could hear his mother crying. He heard words that said his father was dead. He opened the door and walked over to Mary and put his arms around her neck and they both sobbed uncontrollably.

One of the policemen said under his breath, "I hate this fucking job."

CHAPTER THIRTEEN

Mary learnt at the inquest that a young courting couple had found Joe and called the police immediately. They had seen three men walking away in the opposite direction from which they had come. The verdict was death by person or persons unknown.

The funeral was held ten days after Joe's death. Lou was unwell and couldn't help out so Karen stayed with Mary and Jonathan through that period. She'd made all the funeral arrangements and booked a local hall for the mourners to be given food and drink. She hadn't wanted to order alcohol but Mary had insisted, saying Joe would have wanted people to be entertained properly. Karen was appalled that entertainment could even be considered in these circumstances but Mary still insisted.

Ten of Joe's relatives from Spain would be attending along with Joe's football friends, some work colleagues and a few neighbours. That coupled with Mary's family meant there would be about fifty people.

The service was held at the local catholic, church and the crematorium at Mortlake.

Mary arrived at the church with Jonathan and Karen in a car following the hearse. When they entered the church, it was full. Mary was oblivious to the fact; she held on tightly to Jonathan and looked ahead. She didn't want to make eye contact with anyone as it was likely to make her cry.

Just before the service ended, Karen's children, Martin and Philipa, who were in their early twenties, stationed themselves at the exit. Karen had prepared an invitation to the crematorium with a route map. On the reverse side was an invitation to the after gathering, also with a map. She had printed a hundred to be on the safe side but not expecting such a crowd. As people were generally in pairs or groups, there were enough to go around, just.

The trip to the crematorium took about forty five minutes. There was to be a short service and Joe's coffin would be placed on a conveyor belt. Mary was asked if she wanted to see the coffin leave or if she would prefer for it to remain until they had all left. She opted for the prior as she thought it would give them some sort of finality to the whole painful thing.

To Karen's surprise there were at least a hundred people present half of them standing as the chapel was small. When the service was over the coffin started to move. There was absolute silence. Jonathan suddenly stood up and cried at the top of his voice, "No please, please don't take him away." He was sobbing. The child felt so much pain. Mary held him close. Even the toughest in that chapel found it hard to hold back a tear. The Spanish contingent had no problem showing their emotions. Men and women cried openly and many Brits followed suit.

On the way to the hall, Jonathan calmed down.

He told his mother that he didn't want to go to the party.

"Jonathan it's not a party. It's a send-off for your dad."

"I saw my dad go, can I please go home?"

Karen suggested that it might be a good idea. Martin would take him and stay with him.

"Please mum, let me stay at home with Martin." She couldn't refuse.

When they reached the hall everything had been prepared. Tables to accommodate sixty people had been set out and there was a long buffet and a well, stocked bar.

Mary and Karen were the first to arrive and having checked everything, were satisfied that all their requests had been fulfilled. It was three thirty and the invitation had stated four o'clock.

People started drifting in just before four. The first to arrive were Joe's football friends, who had brought their partners with them. Then there were a large number of Joe's relatives from Spain. Including Mary's family there were already nearly forty people. Then the rush started. Neighbours, Joe's work colleagues and people that Mary had never seen before suddenly filled the hall. There were over a hundred people. Karen sprang into action and arranged with the staff to provide more food. The bar was well stocked so that wasn't a problem.

People introduced themselves to Mary and offered their condolences. There were a lot more people associated with Joe's work than was expected. At one point three very attractive, immaculately dressed women approached and all kissed Mary on the cheek continental style. None were English. Mary asked where they were from and how they knew her husband. The last part of the question she thought she already knew. They were embassy staff from different parts of Europe and two of them said they had known Joe for many years. The third one was much younger so hadn't known him so long. Mary studied the very attractive ladies standing before her and asked them why they had travelled such distances.

"What did Joe mean to you?"

One of the ladies offered, "We've been asking each other the same question. We've never met before today but we all came here for the same reason. I've known Joe for twenty years the others a little less but we're all of one mind when it comes to Joe. When he was around the whole place would light up. He was friendly, funny and not one bit impressed by our pomposity. You know embassy staff do tend to put on airs but Joe saw through everyone. He was very popular and he even used to get invited to the Ambassador's functions if he was around. Everybody loved Joe. That's why we're here."

She wasn't lying, all three women really loved Joe but put in general terms it sounded like something else. They hadn't discussed their romantic love for Joe with each other but they all knew, unfortunately so did Mary now.

There were two titled people there who were very nice and sympathetic to the widow. Mary was in a muddle. All these people she had never met before or even knew existed coupled with her grief was making her head spin. The hall was very noisy with people talking and laughing and generally celebrating Joe's life. Mary felt very sad and at the same time very proud.

Towards the end of the evening a man approached and introduced himself as Gideon Charles a work associate of Joe's. He said he had worked closely with Joe on a number of occasions and said what a privilege that had been. He spoke in general terms about their relationship and asked Mary if it would be appropriate to ask her something work related. Mary consented.

"When we cleared out Joe's work station we expected to find a key but it wasn't there. If you come across one you don't recognise at home can you give me a call, please?" He handed her a calling card that bore just his name and telephone number. She shuddered, the man gave her the creeps but she assented. She wondered how Joe could have worked with someone like that. Everyone else she had met that day had been really nice but this man was creepy.

CHAPTER FOURTEEN

The hall emptied just after ten o'clock and Mary walked home with Karen, neither saying much. When they arrived Martin was watching television and Philipa, who had left the gathering earlier, was in the kitchen making tea. Jonathan was asleep in his room and had been since eight o'clock. He had been exhausted by the events of the day and Martin reassured Mary that he had been fine once they arrived home.

Philipa offered them tea but Karen said she needed something stronger so they opened a bottle of wine. Karen told Martin to turn off the television and go into the kitchen with his sister. She wanted to talk to Mary alone.

"How many of those people did you know?"

"About half, Joe was obviously more popular than I thought."

"The glamorous women, who were they?"

Mary related the conversation she'd had with them and Karen looked sceptical. She didn't want to say anything upsetting but she knew her sister so she came straight out with it.

"Your Joe was a very sexy man. I suppose you knew that better than most."

Mary bit her lip and started to gently cry. Karen put her arm around her. When the tears subsided she looked at Karen and asked her what she had meant.

"Your husband was not only very good looking, he was also extremely sensuous. He used to send a shiver down my spine and I'm a happily married woman. Don't tell me you didn't have great sex. That man managed to get my straight laced sister into bed in no time and you soon went back for more" she laughed.

Mary managed a rueful smile.

"It all changed after Jonathan was born."

"That's usually the way. Kids take up so much of your time and I seem to remember you weren't being very nice to Joe after the birth."

"It wasn't the baby. Joe gave up so much for me as you could see today and I gave up very little. He had loads of friends and I had chosen to have none. When Jonathan arrived it was great until Joe had to go on a trip. I felt isolated and blamed him. I continued staying with you even after he came home. I think that did it as it was never really the same afterwards. Before we got married he told me all about his women and I accepted that, as he was being honest and making a new start with me. Those three women were probably amongst his old flames but I think after the way I treated him he rekindled the flames. I drove him into other women's beds. It's true, if you have something precious then you should treasure it not treat it like a piece of shit."

Karen sighed, "Men, its all water under the bridge now he's gone. Just remember the good times. He was good to you. In fact most women would give their eye teeth to have a husband like him."

"I know and I let him down. He loved Jonathan so much. He spent all his spare time with him. I don't know how this is going to affect the poor boy. He really loved his dad."

"He's a remarkable child and he'll work it out. He just needs time. He'll be fine, you'll see."

Karen stayed for another week. Jonathan stayed off school for two weeks. He didn't want to leave the flat and he spent most of the time alone in his room. The Friday after Karen had left he walked into the kitchen and announced that he would be going to school the following Monday and life then seemed to return to a sort of normality.

CHAPTER FIFTEEN

Jonathan was fine at school if only a little more withdrawn than usual. There had been an incident in the playground and he told Mary exactly what had occurred. She couldn't help but smile to herself and wondered if she should make an issue of it but decided to let it go. Events took over, she was asked to go and see the Head Mistress the following day.

The story was that Jonathan had thrown a boy to the ground during one of the breaks. The Head Mistress was sympathetic as she had discovered that Jonathan was being teased at the time because he was a loner. No damage had been done except to the boy's pride.

Mary gave the Head Mistress a surprising smile and asked if she could confirm that the school had a zero tolerance policy when it came to bullying. It was confirmed. Mary smiled again knowing the woman sitting in front of her was not telling the full story.

"Do you know what actually happened?"

"I told you."

"You told me just part of the story. Jonathan told me what had happened and he doesn't lie. When I was asked to come and see you I called a few parents and asked if their children would be prepared to back up Jonathan's version and they said they would be only too glad to if it meant a stop to the bullying that goes on in the playground."

The poor woman turn a whiter shade of pale and denied knowing anything further.

"Then I shall tell you. The boy in question is two years older than my son and his name is Sherman, his father just happens to be the chairman of the school board, and he and two of his classmates have been bullying the younger children for the best part of this year. When they picked on Jonathan he defended himself. Now this I can prove so will the boys in question now be expelled given the schools bullying policy?"

The Head was lost for words.

"Let me tell you what will happen, now. You will apologise to me, Jonathan, the other children and their parents for not being aware of the situation. You will tell the bullies' parents and they and their children will also apologise. If this is done then it will go no further."

The poor woman looked as if she would disappear under her desk. She thanked Mary for her information and assured her that all her requests would be met and they were. Jonathan was looked upon with a new respect and the bullying ended.

Mary did have to ask Jonathan one question, "Are you allowed to use Judo like that?"

"It's a martial art of self-defence. I defended myself."

Mary was pleased that her son could look after himself even if he was quiet and somewhat withdrawn. She felt a great sense of pride in her quiet unassuming angel.

The next two years went well academically and Jonathan slowly came out of his shell. He played sports and took part in various school activities but still resisted out-of-school invitations. Mary had many conversations with him about this and one time he relented and accepted an invitation to a classmate's home to 'hang-out'. The boy wanted only to play computer games and watch television both of which Jonathan found boring. He'd tried for his mother's sake but only the once.

When he was eleven he went to a catholic boys' school just off Holland Park Avenue. The atmosphere at the school was to Jonathan's liking. He was encouraged to learn and no one objected when he opted to stay in a classroom at lunch time to study. He'd been at the school for two months and had settled down to a workable routine. His maths lesson had taken them up to lunch so he remained behind and worked at some equations that were giving him a little trouble. He had his head buried in his book and hadn't noticed he wasn't alone. It was only when he heard a noise did he turn to see a smallish boy sitting with his head on his desk, crying.

Jonathan went over to him and asked "What's the matter, aren't you having lunch today? Your name is Nigel right?"

The boy looked up and nodded but continued crying.

"Come on Nigel what's wrong?"

Nigel sniffled and said through his tears, "I can't go into the playground there are three third years that keep hurting me and taking stuff. They said that if I didn't bring them something good today they will beat me up. I said I'd report them but they said if I did that they would find out where I live and come and get me."

"Well that seems very unlikely but do you know who these boys are?"

"The big one is called Sherman but I don't know what the others are called."

"Is one ginger and the other one tall and skinny?"

"Yes do you know them?"

"Well I think so they used to go to my primary school. Let's go and sort this out."

"I can't go out there they'll beat me up and you as well."

"Trust me Nigel that won't happen."

Jonathan gave the boy instructions on what to do and he reluctantly obeyed. He walked into the playground with Jonathan a few paces behind and stopped when he saw his tormentors approach. He wanted to run but as Jonathan passed him he said some words of encouragement.

The third year boys surrounded Nigel and Sherman gave him a prod and a big smirk. Jonathan had walked up behind them and tapped Sherman on the shoulder. "Hi Pug I didn't know you were acquainted with my friend Nigel."

The three boys all turned and looked at the greeter.

"Hi Jonathan, people don't call me that here and we were just talking here."

"That's nice of you. Seeing as you've reformed maybe there's something you can do for me?"

The three bullies had put a little distance between themselves and the two younger boys, trying their hardest not to look nervous.

"What do you want Jonathan."

"Well Pug, my friend Nigel here has been having a bit of a problem with three guys and I said I'd help him sort it out. The problem is we can't find them so I wonder if you'd do me a big favour and watch his back for me."

Pug nodded, "Sure Jonathan, no problem."

"Great then I'll leave you four to continue your friendly conversation. I'll see you in class after the break Nigel and you can tell me about your new friends. By the way Pug my mum asked me if I'd bumped into you. I say hello for you shall I?"

Pug waited until Jonathan was out of earshot and then apologised to Nigel and wandered off with his two henchmen across the playground. Nigel was completely nonplussed but felt so much better. After the next lesson he stopped Jonathan in the corridor and thanked him and asked how he'd done that. "I don't know if it was my imagination but they seemed afraid of you."

Jonathan laughed, "Who'd be afraid of me? We're just old friends."

"You talk like a grown up."

"Thanks, I suppose that's a compliment. Now for class, see you."

Jonathan's love of learning had been fed by the new challenges he was facing and he studied very hard. Studying was magic to him. He loved to learn new things and he'd go beyond anything they were learning in class. He excelled at examinations but never flaunted his skills in front of the rest of the class for fear of seeming like he was showing off but he couldn't hide it when it came to examination results. He played rugby, joined different school societies and generally fit in well with the other boys although he still didn't socialise outside of school.

Mary had thought he would grow out of his introversion and she asked him if he was happy not having friends. He told her he didn't need any, he was far too busy with his studies. He'd decided he was going to be a barrister and wanted to study at The London School of Economics. He knew what he needed by way of subjects and grades and what other activities were looked for in potential students and therein lay his focus. To gain admittance, he had to achieve A's and A+'s at A-level so he needed good grades in his GCSE's to be able to choose the subjects of his choice. This was the most important thing in his life at that point and he didn't want any distractions and therefore no social life. He assured Mary that he was very happy and loved school and his own time. Mary remembered what the child psychologist had said some years before, he was just different.

Jonathan's world changed completely when he entered the sixth form.

The school year started mid-week and now he was to face a new challenge, girls were admitted to the sixth form and he was a young testosterone filled man.

The subjects he selected were very much determined by his ambitions, which were Maths, Economics and French with philosophy as an extra subject at AS level. It was strange to have girls in the classroom but he wasn't distracted by that at least not for two whole days. On the Friday afternoon it was the first philosophy class. He sat at the front, as he chose to do in all lessons, and a girl came and sat next to him. He smiled and nodded. She stared at him with a look he couldn't define.

"No introduction then."

"Sorry I didn't mean to be rude, I'm…"

"I know who you are. You're Jonathan Martinez, the smartest, best looking guy in the school."

Jonathan returned her stare feeling challenged.

"I don't think either of those things is true but if they were only the first one would be in anyway important."

She smiled at him and he felt his heartbeat quicken. She was tall and beautiful in a way he seemed to recognise. She had long black wavy hair and her large brown eyes were vaguely oriental. She looked like she was from another age but he couldn't think why.

"Modest as well, I'm Gabriella Lee and I think we're going to more than good friends."

Before he could think of a reply she asked where he lived.

"That's great I live just off Camden Hill Road so you can walk me home. Not today though, I don't spend my weekends in London so I'll be picked up straight from school this afternoon."

Jonathan was lost for words. She said all this in such a fashion as if he had no choice. He'd never met anyone so direct before. He shrugged and looked towards the front of the classroom.

The lesson started and they both listened intently hardly glancing at each other throughout. It was Greek philosophers today and they were given a book and instructed to read the first five chapters before the next lesson and they would discuss what they learned the following Tuesday.

It was the last lesson of the day and when they left the classroom they walked to their lockers and retrieved what they needed for their weekend homework. Gabriella walked with Jonathan to the school gate and held his arm in the process. He didn't object and he didn't feel uncomfortable. He didn't know what he felt. This tall willowy beautiful girl had some other quality he still couldn't define it was almost as if they had met before. As she left him she gave him a piece of paper with her address and told him to be there at eight o'clock on Monday morning. He assented with a big smile; she had said it in flawless Spanish.

"How comes you speak Spanish and how did you know I do?"

"I saw you on Wednesday and I asked some of the guys about you. I did some research you see so I already knew that you live on Portobello Road so it's just a short detour to my house, so will you?"

"Sure, eight o'clock then."

Just then a large blue Mercedes pulled up in front of them.

"See you Monday at eight" She kissed him full on the lips and stepped into the waiting car.

He stood and watched the car move away, dumbstruck. A group of his peers gathered around him having watched what had happened and pumped him for information. He didn't know what to tell them so he tried to act nonchalantly. The general consensus was that Gabriella was hot and very different from the rest of the girls and Jonathan was clearly a very lucky bastard.

He walked home slowly, oblivious to the world around him. He contemplated what had happened and felt strange. He'd never really kissed a girl before, in fact he still hadn't she had kissed him. He felt light and somehow elated.

When he got home Mary took one look at him and asked what had happened. She was very good at reading people's emotions and if she knew them well, their intentions. He shrugged and said nothing but couldn't help a huge smile light up his face. A million thoughts went through Mary's head because her first thought just couldn't be right.

Jonathan found it easy to shut out potential distractions when he was studying and he managed to do so then except every idle moment he got his thoughts went to that strange, beautiful girl.

CHAPTER SIXTEEN

Monday morning arrived and he did as instructed. On the way he tried to find a logical reason for what had happened and more to the point, why he was doing as she had asked. The house was easy enough to find. It was an imposing four stories high house and looked very opulent. It was only seven forty five when he rang the doorbell. A middle-aged man appeared almost immediately.

"You must be Jonathan. Come in please. Gabriella is in the kitchen, I'll show you the way."

"Are you Mr Lee?"

"No, I work here. My name is Todd."

Gabriella was reading a book and drinking coffee. She looked up and smiled.

"You're a little early. Would you like some coffee?"

Jonathan accepted and was just about to sit down when she stood up and embraced him and again kissed him on the lips. It was like they were long time lovers. He wasn't sure what to do so he followed his instincts and returned the kiss. This time it was long and what he thought must be passionate.

They sat down to drink their coffee and before he could think of anything to say she jumped in, speaking Spanish.

"You want to know why I speak Spanish. Well my mother is from Madrid and my father is British. He was born in Hong Kong and his mother was English and his father Chinese. Hence the name Lee and it also accounts for my vaguely oriental eye shape. Anymore questions?"

"I haven't asked any for there to be anymore. You're not a witch are you because I have one of those at home? What's happening here?"

"My beautiful Jonathan, we're falling in love."

He didn't know what to say. It was all so alien to him. There in front of him was the most beautiful girl he'd ever seen and she wanted something from him which she called love. It was all so unreal.

She laughed at him and said they should go to school and talk on the way. She instructed him to speak to her only in Spanish when they were alone but not in company because that wouldn't be polite. He desperately wanted to kiss her again but she was insistent that they leave.

She held his arm as they walked. They discussed the courses they had elected to take. Philosophy was the only one they had in common and Gabriella was taking that as an A-level, together with Psychology and Spanish.

"Why are you not taking Spanish, you're sure to get an A+?"

"That's why I'm not taking it, my dad used to tell me that I should always stretch myself and learn new things or I'd end up as a one dimensional middle class bore."

"I know your dad died when you were young but how young if he spoke to you like that."

"Eight, he always spoke to me like I was an adult. I don't think he knew any other way but it was great."

"So how's your French? Nowhere near as good as your Spanish I suppose."

"I'm fluent and I read as much as I can of French literature. I downloaded Satre at the weekend, thought it would kill two birds and all that."

"You're the smartest person in school so people tell me. We'll see this evening."

"What's happening this evening?"

"You're walking me home and you're going to stay for dinner at my place and we're going to study together, in silence. Somewhere in there we're going to make love. I want to know if this all consuming passion I feel for you is real."

"I think you're a little crazy."

"I'm a lot crazy. Crazy for you and no one else is going to have you. I'm usually a very level headed young lady from Roedean but you do something to me and I'm not going to miss what might be the love of my life because of some convention. Look at us; we even look a bit alike. We're a match made in heaven, if there was a heaven that is."

"You really are nuts."

She feigned a pout. "Don't you like me?"

"I don't know I'll have to find out." He said this whilst shaking his head in disbelief. He couldn't help smiling a broad smile.

She squeezed his arm. "That's not a no then so there's hope for me and please don't smile at me in public or I'll cry with frustration." She kissed his cheek.

"I'll meet you at lunch break and we'll ignore the world, then we can walk home together after school."

"I'm taking some first years for Spanish conversation so I won't be finished tonight until four thirty."

"That's OK I'll help you."

"I think you'll need permission from the Spanish teachers to be able to do that."

"Well that's not a problem, I've Spanish this morning. Consider it done."

They lunched together with eyes watching from every direction, to which they were oblivious. Gabriella was true to her word and had been given permission to assist Jonathan that evening. Jonathan was very serious about the class. The pupils learned a lot but thought him to be a little too stiff. This lesson was very different.

Gabriella was alive and sparkling. She made them laugh and generally made the whole process more enjoyable. Jonathan wasn't sure that this was a good thing but she assured him that they learnt more when they were having fun. He wasn't totally convinced as he didn't learn that way. He loved learning so that was a joy in itself. He considered what he'd experienced and concluded she might be right given the audience.

The previous year's first years had a number of pupils that never really engaged and he wasn't sure he was getting through to them all. Today everyone was eager to take part. Horses for courses, her way seemed to work with this group.

On the way to Gabriella's, he called his mother and told her he was going to a friend's house to study and would eat dinner there. Mary was amazed. Jonathan didn't have those sorts of friends. She was happy for him but curious. The same thought kept coming back, it's a girl.

They arrived at the Camden Hill house and Gabriella took him straight up to her room. His own bedroom could fit into this space at least four times. They put down their books and she held him close. They kissed and embraced but he stiffened.

"My parents don't live here so relax."

After a few minutes they were lying on her bed.

"Are you a virgin?" she asked.

He felt embarrassed but owned up to being so.

"So am I, isn't it wonderful?"

He hesitated and then bashfully said, "I've never even really kissed a girl before."

She laughed and said "I only once kissed a boy and that was when I was about 10. There was no opportunity in an all-girls school and I'm glad. Now stop talking and let's discover what it's all about."

He kissed her and held her in his arms and to his amazement he felt a surge of love. This time the kiss was far more pleasurable, less rushed and there was more enjoyment of the nearness.

After about an hour they lay on their backs looking at the ceiling.

"I love you Jonathan. I hardly know you but yet I do if you know what I mean. I knew the first time I saw you."

Jonathan was silent for a while. "I don't know what it means to love someone, romantically, the only people that I've ever loved are my family and that's very different. I mean to love someone in this way, well it feels like something wonderful that I can't explain."

"Don't analyse it, you're too intellectual. I know you love me and I just knew you would. Just accept it."

"I feel like I've never felt before so maybe it is love."

"We'll tell the philosophy class tomorrow and ask their opinion."

He laughed and rolled over on top of her. "You would too. OK I love you Gabriella Lee" and he did.

"Get off me, we need to study."

Gabriella changed into a dress she took out of her wardrobe. It was subtly floral and slightly loose fitting. When she moved it took the shape of her body. She looked more mature and extremely vivacious.

He held her tightly.

"Let go, we have dinner waiting and studying to do."

"I don't want to let go, ever."

"Tough, come on my beautiful love we must depart my boudoir and go eat and work."

They picked up their books and she led him down the stairs to the dining room.

They studied at the table, each doing different subjects, saving their joint philosophy until last. After about half an hour Jonathan looked up and saw she was looking at him with a smile on her face.

"What's funny?"

"Nothing's funny, it's just that I can see why you've never had a girlfriend. When you opened your book it seemed like it had devoured you. I ceased to exist."

Jonathan looked hurt but she continued smiling. She picked up the book he was reading and kissed it.

"What was that for?"

"I would kiss every book you've ever read just to thank them."

He was truly puzzled. "I don't understand."

"Your books kept you safe. They knew I was coming so they saved you for me, thank you books."

"You truly are nuts."

"Yes I am but it's still true."

He nodded in a bemused way and leant over and kissed her.

"None of that or your books will get jealous."

They resumed their studying and about twenty minutes later a woman entered the room carrying a tray.

"You must be Jonathan, I'm Frances. Gabriella has told me all about you. I thought she was exaggerating but you are really a beautiful specimen of youth. There's a similarity between you, you could be related, a mirror image thing is it?"

"Frances stop embarrassing him. He's a sensitive soul and he's all mine, so I have to protect him from evil people like you."

Frances put the tray down and set the dinner plates at the other end of the table.

"Now eat young things. You my lad make sure she eats all of her dinner. She eats like a sparrow and it's not good for her."

"You'd have me obese if you had your way, now be gone woman."

Frances laughed and departed.

Jonathan inquired as to whom Todd and Frances were. Gabriella explained that they were employed by her father as house cum child minders. They were married and moved around as instructed by her father. They had been around as long as she could remember. They looked after everything including her and she added that she loved them dearly.

Jonathan asked where her parents were and was told that they lived in different places depending on where her father's business took them. They had a house in Southwold which her mother preferred when they were in England as she didn't like London and they had the house they were in now. They also had a house just outside Rome and two in Spain. Her mother always preferred to be in Madrid so that's where she spent most of her time. She had been unwell for a number of years with a wasting disease and wasn't expected to live for more than a year or so.

"Oh I'm sorry, that must be very hard on you."

"The only hard thing is I have to spend most weekends with her, my father insists although he's hardly ever around. My parents don't really like me; I think they had me just because they thought they should. There were certainly no more after me."

"Does he own all these properties?"

"All, except this one. I own this house and only because it's useful for tax purposes so he tells me."

"What is his business?"

"Do you know I'm not sure, he says he's a trader but that could mean anything?"

"He must be very rich to own all those properties and fancy cars."

"He's exceeding rich unfortunately."

"Why unfortunately?"

"He doesn't handle it well. He thinks it gives him the right to treat people like shit, he's an absolute pig."

"What about Todd and Frances, is he not nice to them?"

"He barely ever sees them but no they seem to be the exception. Todd always stands up to him and father dear like all cowards generally backs off. Only Todd can do that and I've always wondered why but I suppose some things just are. Let's eat."

Whilst they ate Gabriella asked about Jonathan's upbringing and was touched by his obvious love for his parents especially his father. There really wasn't a lot to tell but she listened intently and sighed with envy at the seeming simplicity of his story.

They finished their dinner, or Jonathan did. As Frances had predicted, Gabriella ate just a few mouthfuls.

They returned to their books and eventually got around to their philosophy reading. They quickly read their chapters and discussed what it all meant. Jonathan was surprised at how insightful and bright Gabriella was although he didn't say so.

"There's nothing in there about love, so my beautiful lover I shall have to bring it up tomorrow."

They finished their studying at ten and Jonathan reluctantly went home.

CHAPTER SEVENTEEN

It was ten twenty when he walked through the front door. Mary was in the front room watching the news. She heard him come in and got up to find him. He was sitting at the kitchen table engrossed in his laptop.

"Didn't you finish your homework at your friends then? You've been gone long enough."

He looked up at her and he seemed to have a sort of glow about him. Peaceful came to mind and perhaps even happy. Mary saw it for what it was without asking.

"We finished OK and we did some preparation for later in the week."

She had planned not to ask but couldn't help herself. "And who is this friend, anyone I've met."

"No mum she's not."

"She? You don't have girls at your school. Oh of course they do in the sixth form. You've been back at school less than a week and you have a friend who's a girl? That was quick."

"Yes I suppose so."

"What's her name?'

"Gabriella."

"Is she English?'

"Half Spanish like me and a few other things thrown in."

"Oh and will you be doing your homework with her again?"

He laughed, "Nosey, yes I will."

"What are you looking at?" She leant over and read what it was.

"The philosophy of love, I hope that's not about any feelings you have?"

"It's our philosophy class. It's all a bit inconclusive. Did you love dad?"

"Of course I did."

"How long did it take him to know he loved you?'

She thought for a bit then decided to be honest. "Wow, now I think of it, not long really maybe a couple of days."

"Only, does it always happen like that?"

"I don't know. I've only ever loved one man and I think I knew that before I really knew him."

"What is it, love I mean?"

"Well you know how I love my theatre and I love South Pacific. There's a line in a song that says fools can explain it wise men never try. I don't think you can define it, it's different for everyone. It just happens. I really hope this is for your philosophy class."

He tapped the side of his nose and turned his laptop around. Jonathan had always found it hard to lie so didn't. He'd learnt from his mother if you didn't want to tell then don't answer.

She recognised immediately what he'd done and wasn't sure whether to be alarmed or thrilled. He never had a friend he'd spent time with outside of school and he'd certainly not taken any interest in girls. This just wasn't like him. She knew something had happened and felt uneasy.

The next morning he called at Camden hill and Gabriella answered the door. "I'm not inviting you in or I'd be sorely tempted to play truant amongst other things."

He pulled a face and she said, "Don't do that, I'd never want to disappoint you and if you want to play truant I'll do it gladly with you."

"I don't think you could disappoint me but then I hardly know you."

"You're a horrible liar, you know me like you've known me all your life and I'm all yours."

He felt so happy and warm inside and and a million other things he'd never felt in his short life. "Where does your boldness come from? You're really outrageous."

"Only with you, I can't help myself. I lay awake last night trying to understand and I even read about love from the philosophical point of view but it really didn't describe what I felt."

He didn't tell her that he'd done the same and also felt the same as that would sound too trite. They walked arm in arm along the avenue oblivious to everything and everyone around them.

At registration Gabriella was the centre of attention. All the girls in her group surrounded her and asked about Jonathan. They all thought him handsome, dreamy, hot and many other adjectives that seemed to go on endlessly. She smiled enigmatically and said in a sexy voice "We're just good friends."

"Tell us, tell us" they demanded

"Nothing to tell, love is private." The last bit had slipped out unexpectedly.

"Love, you're in love" they said in chorus and all feigned faintness.

"I didn't say that so now bug off and leave me to my beautiful thoughts" she laughed.

They took their seats reluctantly.

Jonathan's classmates watched him like he was an alien. He seemed different and had a look on his face somewhere between a smile and a look of pleasure, definitely not the Jonathan of old.

One of his almost friends said that they had seen him walking home last night with one of the new hot chicks and coming back with her this morning.

"Did you sleep with her?"

Oh how he wished. He could answer because of the way the question was put. "No stupid, she lives on the way home."

"Oh and I suppose she was holding your arm for support."

Jonathan suddenly felt very proud but just shrugged.

They skipped lunch and went for a walk in the park and stole a kiss or two, hidden by trees. Love was better than food any day.

Philosophy was again the last class of the day. The teacher went through some points which Jonathan found interesting as he had read the meanings a different way. He wasn't sure the interest was universal but generally the class was engaged.

There were fifteen in the class small enough to let everyone have a say so they were all asked individually what they had focussed on in their reading homework and why. There were some very good insights offered and it seemed he was wrong; there was an air of enthusiasm from all.

When it came to Gabriella's turn she said she had read about love. There were a few guffaws to be heard but she didn't let it distract her. She had found it a bit confusing because there seemed too many philosophical aspects to it. The teacher asked if she was trying to understand the different types of love or romantic love specifically. He was no fool but it engendered more suppressed noises.

"Romantic love but even then there seems to be differences of opinion."

The teacher threw it open to the class and there was a heated debate.

"That proves the case in point. Over two thousand years later we still can't agree as couldn't Plato and his pupils. Jonathan you haven't said anything. Do you have any thoughts?"

"I asked my mum last night and she told me a line from a song which said fools can explain it wise men never try."

"Or wise women so it seems."

"There was one thing that struck a chord, whether or not it's right, it sounded right."

"Go on.'

"Socrates said love is two bodies one soul. I think I can understand that. When you meet that special person it's like you found the part of yourself that you didn't realise was missing."

At that point Gabriella started to cry. The teacher asked if she was alright, was she ill or something.

"No I'm fine it's just that was so beautiful."

Most of the class started laughing and some of the other girls were crying. Jonathan just looked puzzled.

"Jonathan you're obviously not completely satisfied with that, what are thinking."

"Aristotle says you have to be egotistic, in a good way, because you first have to love yourself. That's the bit I don't get. Isn't love supposed to be totally unselfish?"

"Ok class, we're nearly done for the day. Your homework is to research self-love and we'll discuss your thoughts on Friday."

On the way home Gabriella held Jonathan's arm tightly.

"Everyone says you're really clever but you're more than that. You have deep feelings and you need to understand them."

"I don't know about that but I do have a need to generally understand everything that comes my way."

"When you said the bit about finding the piece of yourself that you didn't know was missing did you mean me?"

"That's the way you make me feel."

She stopped and hugged him.

The evening repeated itself except it somehow felt even better.

By Friday Jonathan knew with absolute certainty that he was in love.

There was much discussion about self in philosophy until the teacher said "Emma you wish to say something?"

A pretty blond girl at the rear of the room said in a soft voice," I read lots of references and the one that rings true to me is right here on our doorstep. We're all catholic and we know the teachings of Jesus and he gave this great importance. The only commandment he gave us was to love our neighbour as ourselves. That tells us that we need to love ourselves doesn't it?"

The teacher looked at Jonathan and asked for his opinion. He sat still for a while and then turned to look at where the voice had come from. "Thank you Emma, that was great and now it's self-evident. I understand, thank you very much."

Emma turned bright red as he clapped as did the rest of the class.

Jonathan walked to the school gate with Gabriella. Todd was picking her up and she was booked on a flight from Heathrow to Madrid.

"What will you do this weekend" she asked.

"The same as I've done for as long as I can remember.'

"What's that?"

"I'll go to Judo class tomorrow morning and flamenco class after that. On Sunday I may go to mass with mum but only if she asks. I'll watch some football on TV and study. Then it'll be Monday and I'll have you back."

"Jonathan you're full of surprises. Flamenco eh, why and are you good?"

The answer had to wait as Todd drew up in the Mercedes. He wanted to kiss and hug her so badly but being at the school gate he thought better of it. They kissed briefly and gently and she got into the car.

He knew why she had to go and he didn't want her to feel guilty about doing her duty, he understood that. He knew he already missed her and wondered if she felt the same but knew the answer to that one too.

As he watched the car move away he felt a tap on his shoulder. It was Mr Roberts his house master. He asked Jonathan if he could spare a few minutes and they went back into school to an empty classroom.

Mr Roberts said that it had come to his attention that Jonathan had taken up with one of this year's intake of girls and he was concerned that it might be a distraction. The school tried to discourage such things.

Jonathan had seen it coming and was more than ready with a response.

"I'm sorry sir I'm not sure I understand. I suppose you're referring to Gabriella Lee my friend. In fact the only friend I've ever had in my whole life. Are you saying that I'm not allowed to have a friend or is it a sexist thing?"

Mr Roberts was surprised by this response and all of a sudden he felt like he was skating on thin ice and he got a bit tongue tied.

"It's neither of those things. I'm just concerned that it might be a distraction. You're the brightest pupil I've ever seen in this school and I don't want to see you waste that at this stage. Girls can bring a lot of disruption to one's life."

Jonathan gave him a disarming smile. "So it is a sexist thing, shame on you sir. I can assure you that whatever my relationship is with Gabriella it will not disrupt my studies. We study together and I don't know if you're aware but she's extremely bright and we help one another, she's great. I've never been more, happy in my whole life by having a real friend so thank you for your concern but I think it's misplaced."

"Jonathan, there are friendships and friendships but romantic attachments are different and I'm not being sexist about this. I would like you to think seriously about getting involved when you're both so young and vulnerable."

"Sir we've both more mature in many ways than our peer groups and both know exactly what we're doing. I think you are being sexist because you have a long term romance in our year and I doubt you've ever had that conversation with those pupils."

Now the teacher looked puzzled. "Who do you mean?"

Jonathan shook his head. "I'm sorry sir but the whole school knows, well at least the pupils do. You say I'm a bright pupil, what pupils come after me?"

He thought and said "Well, that's Johnston and Murray but their close friends and that's good for them."

"Sir I don't wish to be argumentative but I've known those boys since I was five, we went to the same primary school. They've been inseparable all the time I've known them and it's a great love story and I think it works fine."

Mr Roberts suddenly blushed and asked what he was inferring.

"I'm not inferring anything but any one with eyes can see they love one another and what they get up to is no business of mine but for sure they'll still be together many years from now. They're great guys but as I said earlier you've not had this discussion with either of them have you."

The teacher did know, so did the whole faculty but it was never discussed, just swept under the carpet.

"Jonathan I should have known better than to try and dissuade you but as I said be careful."

Jonathan smiled again and said he would and thanked him for his concern.

Mr Roberts was left pondering his own miserable love life or lack of it.

CHAPTER EIGHTEEN

On the way to school on Monday Gabriella announced that she was going home with Jonathan that evening. She very much wanted to meet his mother. He called and Mary said she'd like that and she'd get dinner for them.

"We can't do what we do in my house with my mother around, it's so small."

"Does that matter? I thought you loved me and love means making sacrifices sometimes." She was trying hard to look serious. He looked disappointed.

"I haven't seen you all weekend and now I have to keep my distance. That's harsh."

She couldn't help herself and she laughed.

"What's so funny, don't you want me?"

"I thought you were clever but it seems I was wrong."

He asked why and she obliged with "Well you will walk me home after, won't you?" The penny dropped and he was happy again.

On the way home from school they stopped at Gabriella's so she could change and couldn't resist an abbreviated love making session. They arrived at Portobello Road at five thirty. Introductions were made and Gabriella kissed Mary on her cheeks. Mary eyed her up and down and when Jonathan went to change Gabriella said" Well will I do?"

"Oh sorry I didn't mean to be rude so please don't take offence."

"None taken and it's only right that you should check me out after all I am your son's lover."

Mary was shocked, not by the information but the way it was delivered. "What did you say?"

"We're in love."

"That's not something I want to hear, you're just children?"

"We're not children, in fact we're old enough to get married with parental permission."

Mary shook her head.

"Mrs Martinez, I really wanted to meet you and I really want you to like me but I don't want that to be based on a lie. I want you to like me for who I am."

Mary sat down. "I don't know quite what to say."

"Please say what you like and I don't mind of its not nice as long as it's truthful."

"I supposed it would happen one day, although I had my doubts, and I suppose I should be thankful for your honesty. It's just, this is Jonathan."

"He was surprised too. He told me that he'd never as much as had a real friend before except his dad. Now he loves me and I love him."

"My dear it's too much too soon to know that and you're so young."

"Jonathan told me what you said about you and his dad falling in love. This is no different. You didn't expect it to happen and neither did we but it did and it's real."

At that point Jonathan returned. "Are you two getting along alright?"

"I'm not sure I like this young lady but I'll tolerate her for your sake."

Gabriella stood up and hugged her. "Thank you so much.'

Mary shook her head and went over to the cooker to put the dinner on. Her head was spinning. Was she angry and if so why? She almost put sugar in the vegetables such was her distraction. She thought about it as she went about her business.

The loving couple studied at the table and when dinner was ready they cleared their books and Mary served. They sat in silence for a while which was broken by Jonathan's question as to what had happened.

"I told your mother about us. All of it and I think she's angry with me."

"Mum, are you angry with me too?"

Mary looked at them both and saw two beautiful angels. Gabriella actually resembled him not just in looks but in her gestures, facial expressions and his inability to lie. They could have been brother and sister apart from her eyes, her beautiful eyes.

"I'm not angry with either of you. I suppose I'd rather be an ostrich. There are some things that parents might not like to hear, which in itself is stupid. It's just a double shock. Jonathan you've never had a real friend and now you say you're in love with someone you hardly know. It's all a bit much to take in."

"That's OK mum, if Gabriella hadn't told you I would have sooner or later. Anyway I don't understand why it's a shock, you already knew."

"How did she know, nobody knows but us?"

"My wonderful mother and I mean she is wonderful, has a knack of seeing things, so I doubt she didn't notice a change in me and put two and two together."

"Did you know Mrs Martinez?" asked a puzzled looking Gabriella.

"Sort of, he's not looked this happy since before his father died so something had happened. It wasn't hard to work out. He had found a friend, a female friend, and he has a glow about him. I saw that same thing in his father so I suppose I knew. I just didn't want to for some stupid reason."

"So if I hadn't told you, you would have liked me better."

Mary thought about that for a while.

"No I wouldn't have. In fact it wouldn't have mattered if I liked you or not. Now I have to make a choice. I'm glad you were honest so let's leave it at that for now."

Gabriella was just about to say something when Jonathan interjected. "When she says enough she means it."

"Oh, sorry, I was just going to ask something different, so I'll just stay quiet."

"No I'm sorry, I know you're not insensitive that was stupid of me, ask her whatever it was."

"What were you going to ask young lady?"

"I wondered if you tell me about Jonathan when he was growing up.

Mary smiled as it was her favourite subject. This girl is smart as well as honest.

They spent almost an hour at the table eating and Mary telling her boy's story.

"Thank you Mrs Martinez, that was great both the food and the story."

Gabriella stood up and started clearing the plates.

"Hey you sit down and finish your homework, I'll do that."

"No I have to help you wash up. My grandmother told me it was rude not to do that. Anyway I have to put my hands in the same water as you at the same time and we'll be friends."

"Oh you're not a gypsy are you?'

"No I don't think so, why?"

"Mum's part gypsy and has loads of superstitions."

"Are you really? How exciting, so you understand?"

Mary nodded, superstition was stupid but it did give one a feeling that everything would be alright if you complied. They put their hands in the water at the same time and Gabriella leant over and kissed Mary on the cheek. Mary liked that.

When the dishes were done and the homework finished it was time to go. The young couple took their leave and went to Camden Hill. He left at around ten thirty but so wanted not to so he jogged all the way home to put distance between them so he was not impelled to turn back.

When he got home Mary was in bed. He was tired so he also went to bed and lay there thinking for a while. His thoughts went back to the philosophy class when Emma had reminded them of Christ's one and only commandment. He had always been happy within himself and now he was happy making someone else happy. He thought about how he interacted with others and although he wasn't going to become gregarious he decided he would open himself up to other people more readily. He fell asleep and dreamt of war. Dreams are so strange.

When he got up the next morning Mary was still in her room. He knew she wasn't asleep, she never slept late but he had a good idea why she hadn't come out to get his breakfast.

After school they went and sat in Holland Park for a while. Gabriella asked if Mary had said anything about her and Jonathan said he hadn't seen her. He supposed she was avoiding him.

"Does that tell you anything?"

"Yes it means she hasn't made up her mind yet."

"Then you must go home now and give her the chance to tell you."

'I'm not going to ask her anything, she'll only say something when she's ready."

"I didn't say ask her. Go home and just be there, at least that way she has the opportunity. I'll see you at my place at eight, OK?"

He thought about it and decided she was right.

Mary was reading The Evening Standard in the kitchen. She looked up and asked him why he was home.

"I do live here."

"You could have fooled me."

He ignored her comment and sat down opposite her and did his homework.

"Are you here for dinner?'

He nodded.

"Where's your friend?"

"At home."

"Had a row?"

"No."

She busied herself with making dinner. Then she suddenly stopped what she was doing.

"Then why are you home, have I caused a problem?"

"I don't know, have you?"

"Stop talking in riddles, what's happened?'

"Nothing."

"She's a bit strange that girl. She reminds me of someone out of the sixties. The way she dresses, the way she talks openly about things. She's very beautiful and after the initial shock, I appreciated her honesty. If it wasn't for you I'd like her a lot."

Jonathan looked up from his book. "Do you still want to know why I'm home?"

"Yes I suppose so."

"Gabriella told me to come home and give you the chance to tell me what you thought of her and us."

"The witch, I think she's evil."

"So do I mum, now I have two evil women in my life."

"I just worry about you."

"I know but you worry when I don't do things and then you worry when I do. If I don't allow myself this now that I really feel something I might as well be a priest."

"Heaven forbid."

"Even if I get hurt I'd have learnt something. I can't ignore the world forever."

"You two are too smart. OK I bloody well like her so she can come here anytime she wants, that please you?"

Jonathan stood and hugged her, a rare occurrence and she whispered, "My little boy's a man."

He ate his dinner as fast as he could, saying he was starving and then ran all the way to Camden Hill.

CHAPTER NINETEEN

"You're looking very smug, what happened?"

"She hates you and I told her I wouldn't see you anymore."

"Lies, lies, what really happened?"

He told her and added, "She said you are a witch and I suppose that's why you'll get along. She likes you for you, how great is that? Thank you for being you."

"I love you so much Jonathan."

They went up to her room and closed the door firmly.

"I went to the library at the weekend and read all about grown up love stuff." Jonathan admitted

"Why didn't you just look it up on the internet?"

"My mum may have seen me and she'd start asking questions."

"Was the book pornographic?"

"No it had a few diagrams, that's all."

"I suppose I should do the same."

"No I'll tell you, that'll be much more exciting."

"I'd like that."

"I know, I love you."

Time was too short and he soon had to go home.

The next day there was a Philosophy class and the teacher told them that he'd really enjoyed what they had done so far and appreciated that they were fully engaged in the topics. The problem was they had veered from the syllabus and if they were to get good grades they needed to follow that. He didn't want to curb their enthusiasm so he said he would be willing to run an after school session, when they could discuss topics of their choice and not be restricted, that is if anyone was interested.

The class was unanimous with a resounded yes please. Socrates Fifteen, as they called themselves, was born to meet every Tuesday following their scheduled lesson.

Philosophy crept into their everyday thoughts and Gabriella especially used it to work out why they couldn't be together all the time that, coupled with practicality.

They were studying after dinner and Jonathan looked up knowing he was being watched. "What's up?"

"Nothing and everything."

"Is that a new philosophy?"

"I hate being away from you. I want us to be together all the time. I know that's not possible and I know that's mostly my fault."

"It's not your fault. You have a duty to your parents and if you didn't take that seriously then you wouldn't be you and we wouldn't be here."

"You always make situations seem right for me but I want to spend my nights with you. I want to wake up in the morning and feel you next to me. I want so much, too much."

"Can we do that sometime, spend the night together?"

"How, when and would your mother allow that?"

"Yes when we're eighteen and old enough to vote and die for our country. Let's enjoy what we have and when the times right we'll be able to do that without upsetting anyone."

She sighed,"I don't get holidays or even weekends for myself, I have to go where they are."

"I don't think you really explained that one. Why do you have to be home every weekend yet they let you stay here alone?"

"They travel a lot that was their excuse for putting me in Roedean and they wanted me to stay there but it was stifling me. This is already a compromise and as far as my father is concerned a big one. I'm like you an only child and dear father insists that I spend as much time with them as possible without disrupting my studies. What he really means is they didn't want me at home full time but their willing to suffer me when it suits them. Very often he's not around anyway. He thinks his deep pockets represent fatherhood."

"Is your dad very strict?"

"Not really, he doesn't care enough for that but if he tells you to do something, you do it."

"He sounds tough."

"He is and I know it's wrong to feel it but I really don't like him. He's an oaf and a bully. Everyone is scared of him except me and Todd, especially my mother. I stand up to him then he threatens to stop paying for all my living expenses. I can't win. I'd gladly cut off all ties with him if mother would leave him. Of course there's no chance of that she likes the fine things in life and he supplies them by the bucket load. I'd like to think that she loves me but she doesn't. Like me with them, it's just duty."

"Would she leave him?"

"No chance, especially now that she's not well. Every time she seems better it just comes back again only worse. They say she hasn't got much longer to live. Then it will be just me and my monster of a father."

Jonathan's heart went out to her. His own father had been so great. Every memory of him was comforting. He still did the things his dad had wanted him to do like Judo and Flamenco lessons on Saturday mornings but he didn't go to the Rangers anymore, somehow that just wouldn't be the same without watching him get totally out of control with excitement and exasperation.

He asked her if her parents would be staying in Madrid long term or moving on. She laughed and said that two months was long term for them but as her mother was getting worse then she didn't know. She was going to have to fly to Madrid every weekend for the foreseeable future.

"Would he really make you do that, isn't it really expensive?"

"Yes and yes but money is no object with him. Look at this house I'm the only one who lives here. Todd and Frances are only here because I am. The thought of spending Christmas and the whole of next summer in Madrid is hell."

A huge smile came over Jonathan's face.

"Why are you looking so happy when I feel so miserable at the prospect?"

"Guess where I spend my summers?"

"If you tell me Madrid then we're skipping homework and going back upstairs."

He stood up, took her hand and led her up the stairs and they still managed to finish their homework.

At ten thirty he stood up to leave but sat down again.

"I've known you just a couple of weeks and we talk as if this is forever. Do we need to do a reality check; is it real or just hormones? I did some research trying to see what philosophers said about young love and there was nothing. After I wished I hadn't because it seems they were all lacking in that department. The Greeks preferred young boys. I even tried the modern ones only to discover that Satre had an open relationship and Russell, who had said, divorce would destroy the fabric of society, married three times. He changed his view to suit his own circumstance it seemed. There was nothing there to help. I'm not saying I don't love you, I know I do but we have no point of reference."

She gave him an indulgent smile. "You have to intellectualise everything and I love you for that because it means you do things with your eyes open. That tells me that this is real. Anyway you were looking in the wrong place. Only poets have really been able to express it. Shakespeare did a pretty good job of it. If they hadn't experienced it then they couldn't have written about it so passionately. They say love at our age is the most intense but I don't think that means it's not real. Let's worry about tomorrow when it comes. Jonathan just love me please and if you ever don't you're free to go. Love is freedom not a prison."

"O speak again, bright angel for thou art as glorious to this night being o'er my head as is a winged messenger of heaven."

She kissed him," That's better, I far prefer Romeo to Socrates for company. Just love me for as long as it lasts."

On Friday Jonathan went straight home from school having watched the Mercedes glide away. Gabriella had been to his home the night before and had spent the entire evening helping and talking to Mary. They had really started to enjoy each other's company. Mary had said she looked so much like him that she felt she'd found a long lost daughter. Both the teenagers said at the same time that they were glad that wasn't the case. Mary ignored the remark, the sex thing being shut tightly somewhere at the back of her mind.

Gabriella had told the truth which only needed to be said once, so all was well.

Mary asked him why he was home so early and where was Gabriella. He reminded her of the situation and she said she thought only Saturday and Sunday.

"Unfortunately not but even that would be too long. She doesn't have a choice so I have to be supportive and not make it worse for her. So I'll just fill my time as I've done every weekend since dad died."

"Doesn't the fact that you miss her distract you?"

"No, you know me when I'm learning I'm totally focussed. I do have a strange feeling in the pit of my stomach when she's not around but I have to learn to live with that. My problem is when I come up for air then I miss her so much. It's worse for her at least I'm somewhere I want to be with someone I want to be with."

"Who's that?" she said with alarm.

"You stupid."

Jonathan had never been affectionate towards her, that was saved for his father so it was a genuine surprise to hear him say those words. She felt feelings of pride and affection coursing through her.

CHAPTER TWENTY

A routine was established. They ate and studied at each other's homes on alternate nights. It was a sweet natural way of being but Fridays always disappointed. Jonathan made it as easy as he could for her focussing on their Monday reunion and not the coming painful separation. She knew what he was doing and loved him more for it.

They both studied hard and enjoyed their chosen subjects. They loved the Tuesday after school philosophy debates as did the rest of the group. They spoke of many things and researched many philosophers. It was very interactive with many opposing views, which kept it lively and engaging.

At one session they discussed good and evil. The problem they encountered was a definition of evil. There were many interpretations and many sources of opinion and it lead them through a maze of thought. Someone had read a book on the subject by Terry Eagleton who spoke about Theodicy which they really couldn't grasp. The conclusion was that the subject was too difficult to define therefore they would debate what it meant to themselves in daily life. After all they were all now philosophers and had a right to an opinion.

Murray pointed out that they were all now at least sixteen which is a milestone. They could all now have sex with one another legally so does that mean they should experiment and do what the law allows or not. When one reaches the age of eighteen you are given the vote and you are expected to exercise that right so is it the same. He sat back with a huge grin on his face.

It was put to the vote and they all agreed that they should and there was much laughter.

The teacher said as they were running out of time they would continue that discussion the following week and advised them to wait until then before deciding to rush out and lose their virginities. He asked for suggestions for the next debate. Emma suggested they revisit love. They had never really concluded the last debate and it had been held in class time so which wasn't as conducive to honest debate. The sex at sixteen would also fit into that so all agreed.

The following Tuesday Emma was invited to introduce the subject and share her views.

"I listened to the points made the last time we discussed love and I came away knowing there were various types of love. We're all teenagers and I think what interests us most is romantic love."

There were a few groans from the boys and noises of assent from the girls.

"We're all probably going to experience that in some way but not many of us have yet. I liked what Jonathan said last time but how enduring can it be. Is romantic love, just a brief adrenalin rush and to Murray's point should we all experiment now we're legally able. I see Jonathan and Gabriella and it's obvious to the whole school that they are in love. They're so close that they're exclusive they lose all awareness of other people when they're together. All the girls are envious and the boys too but they won't admit it. I'm sure our parents were like that but not any longer.

"My parents exist together; have shared responsibilities but not many common interests. Maybe that's nature's way of making the final separation easier or it might just be ennui. We're all too young to have experienced that and with a few exceptions, to experience romantic love. The only enduring love we read about ends in tragedy. How can we know what true love is or doesn't it really exist? That's my point for debate."

There was a buzz in the room and someone asked if romantic love can be separated from sex. Emma suggested they ask Gabriella and Jonathan.

Being at the front of the room Gabriella had to stand and turn to address the question which obviously hadn't made her feel uncomfortable.

"It seems odd to me that you notice what we have. I say that only in the sense that we've not observed too well what goes on with others. We have more than romantic love. We share a love of learning and a number of other things and we do things together not because of the romance thing but because we do them well together. My own parents show no sign of love for one another but did they ever I suppose so.

"Will I always feel this way? I don't want to know. If I saw a mundane future I wouldn't be in love. So maybe love is just about the now. Love for me is in the future of one person. I don't want to imagine a future whereby I didn't feel that way. How do I know my love is real? It's not something I can explain. It consumes my whole being and makes me a little crazy I think. It wasn't planned. I saw it and I wanted it. Maybe it's just nature calling after all we are of child bearing age. At this point in my life I just see it as hope and fulfilment."

The room was quiet. Jonathan offered a question.

"We're young. In philosophy it appears there isn't a case for true romantic love but it happens but doesn't appear to endure. Does it serve a purpose other than to encourage procreation? There are two people in this room who have been in love in some way or other for the last eleven years and still are maybe one of them could help?"

Everyone knew to whom he was referring and to everyone's surprise Johnston stood up.

"My parents are divorced and it wasn't a pretty site seeing their marriage disintegrate. Murray's parents always seem so happy together so at the weekend we asked them. Murray's dad said there's romantic love and true, unselfish love for a person. The first can only endure with the second. Even then we should expect the romance to wane once it's served its purpose of bringing people together. If the second one is strong it more than compensates for the fireworks. Then love is enduring and sex becomes a bonus not the focus of the relationship.

"We're young and if our parents seem content rather than madly in love that might be exactly what they want and the best that we can hope for. I'd gladly settle for that if it's with the right person. That's love."

The debate continued and as usual the teacher was surprised by the level of maturity and honesty.

That evening, Gabriella clung tightly to Jonathan.

"I don't think I liked today's debate. It frightened me."

"I could see that and I understand why. Whatever happens to us, our feelings, opinions and thoughts, we must remember to talk about it. Everything I've read says breakdowns in communications are a big part of breakdowns.

"I really liked what Johnston said and I'd gladly settle one day for a life shared without the fireworks as long as it's with you."

"Has that started to happen already, has the rot set in so early?" She laughed and pinched him. He rolled on top of her and gently kissed her.

CHAPTER TWENTY ONE

As winter drew in they became closer. Jonathan found himself asking himself what Gabriella would do when faced with a problem. He began to wonder if he'd lost his ability to be an individual. When he mentioned it to her she said she felt the same. Was losing your individuality a bad thing? They concluded maybe that's what was meant by one soul.

Just before the Christmas break Emma approached Gabriella and told her that the Socrates fifteen were planning a dinner to celebrate both Christmas and their fellowship. She said that she knew Jonathan never took part in social functions but maybe if Gabriella asked he might. They all wanted them to be there.

"He just over there, why don't you ask him, the worst he can do is say no?"

So she did and to her amazement he said he would like that very much. Jonathan attended his first non-family function since his one and only children's party when he was five years of age. He even enjoyed it.

The weekends had been dull for both of them but when the Christmas break arrived the thought of three weeks apart was almost unbearable. They had stopped emailing and texting each other because there was no end to it and it really didn't make things better if you couldn't be physically together. There was just no comfort in it. It just accentuated the longing. As Gabriella put it, "Parting is not such sweet sorrow, it's fucking awful."

Jonathan tried his best to enjoy Christmas for his mother's sake. She knew how much he missed Gabriella and only mentioned it once just to acknowledge the fact. She told him that she missed her too which she did. That girl had got under her skin and had become in her mind the daughter she would have loved to have but she kept that to herself.

They spent Christmas Eve to Boxing Day at Karen's. He liked his close family, they were always so good him and he had a sense of belonging when they were together.

Lou was in good form and got tiddly over Christmas dinner and announced that she had a boyfriend and was having great sex. Her daughters were horrified but her grandchildren found it hysterical offering her much encouragement. They later discovered that the mystery man lived two doors away and was eighty. Now they all saw the funny side of it.

The first Monday back at school Jonathan arrived early at Camden Hill. Todd let him in and told him that Gabriella wouldn't be back until that evening as something had happened over Christmas which had delayed her departure. He asked him to inform school and suggested he return about seven that evening. He gave him coffee and toast as he was very early for school and they sat and talked about nothing in particular.

Jonathan trudged to school feeling empty. A part of him had been missing and this disappointment made it doubly worse. They were both now seventeen and he thought more mature. The problem was his disappointment belied that maturity. His mother had told him that not letting disappointment get you down was a sign that you had grown up. If that was the case then he was now about six.

After school he decided not to go home first but to go directly to Camden Hill and wait there. He was overjoyed when Gabriella opened the door. She'd managed to get on an earlier flight and was now just as pleased to see him. They embraced as though they would never let go much to the amusement of Todd who was standing in the hallway.

Life had returned but Gabriella had a sad demeanour. Her mother had died over the holiday and she had felt very guilty for not loving her.

"How can you not love your own mother? Is there something wrong with me?"

"You probably did in a way but you always expect more of yourself. You said she didn't love you but I bet she did in her own way."

Gabriella burst into tears. "That bastard of a father couldn't wait to get her into the ground. He was visibly relieved, can you believe that? I'm trying very hard not to hate him. I don't want him to poison me with his mean ways. I don't want to be like him so please help me not to hate him. This is the first time I've cried since she died. Hold me and don't let me go."

When they kissed Jonathan was as tender as he could be and she cried again.

Winter ended and spring blossomed. Gabriella's father had insisted that she still go home at weekends but as soon as he realised that this was an imposition to himself he only insisted on every other weekend.

On those free weekends Jonathan still did his Saturday things and Gabriella spent that time with Mary. They would wander around Portobello market or go shopping in the West End. They would lunch together and increasingly Mary would want to mother her but stopped short in case she gave offence. Whilst out shopping one day someone stopped them and introduced himself as an old school peer of Mary's. They hadn't seen one another for twenty years or more. He looked at Gabriella and said he wasn't surprised that Mary had such a beautiful daughter. Before she could reply Gabriella thanked him for the compliment.

When he departed they both started laughing. Gabriella asked if Mary had minded to which the reply was a huge smile and a hug. She really loved this girl as her own and now she needn't hide it.

Summer arrived and school ended. Mary had booked their tickets to Madrid and she had chosen the same flight as Gabriella and although she was staying only three weeks, Jonathan's return was synchronised with that of his heart's desire. There had been a condition to Jonathan's extended stay; he would have to spend a week with his mother in Marbella.

Gabriella had been booked on first class so she swapped seats with Mary so she could sit next to Jonathan. Mary didn't object, and she loved the attention she got saying afterwards that she would now only fly first class.

When they reached Madrid a car was waiting to pick up Gabriella so they got a ride to their destination. Gabriella told the driver to note where they were and said she'd be back in the morning.

Summer in Madrid was sweltering. The young lovers didn't mind as long as they were together. They walked the wide boulevards, lunched in Plaza Major or went to the museums. The both loved the Prado and spent hours viewing the Goya collection and the crazy Hieronymus Bosch paintings. Whilst looking at Bosch's painting of hell they both had the same thought.

"Do you remember the discussion we had on evil well….."

Jonathan finished her sentence.

"We should have just shown this picture." They laughed and hugged.

There was no opportunity for love making but that didn't bother either of them. They were more than happy that they could share this time together.

Jonathan introduced her to his relatives and they loved her immediately, not least because she was half Spanish and spoke it just like him, Juan.

When the day arrived that they were to leave for Malaga his heart sank. Their bags were packed and Gabriella's driver was waiting to take them to the airport. They said their goodbyes and got into the car and to his surprise Gabriella was sitting in the back seat.

"I've come to take you to the airport."

Mary looked at her and gave a mock scowl.

"Don't be cruel. That's lying by omission and you don't lie young lady."

Jonathan wondered what she meant and he looked from one to the other questioningly.

"I'm coming with you."

"But how, I mean that's fantastic but how?"

Mary had called Mr Lee and told him she was inviting his daughter to spend a week with them in Malaga. Unexpectedly he had agreed without question other than to ask who Mary was.

"Thanks mum you're the best."

Mary fished through her bag and brought out a gift wrapped package.

"Gabriella dear, I bought you a Christmas present but forgot all about it and I found it in my drawer while I was packing. Here, a very belated Merry Christmas."

Gabriella opened it and was lost for words. She kissed Mary and said, "So you approve. Thank you."

"As long as it doesn't end that way."

Jonathan leaned over to look. It was a beautifully bound book, Romeo and Juliet.

They arrived in Malaga in the late afternoon. It was sunny but much fresher than Madrid. The villa belonged to Joe's cousin. Jonathan had stayed there several times before and knew there were only two bedrooms and wondered where he was to sleep.

Mary showed Gabriella her room so he asked the question. "And where am I going to sleep, on the veranda"

"That's up to you but I don't need to know."

They looked at Mary in amazement.

"Don't you dare say thank you. I've no idea where you're sleeping young man. Now unpack quickly, you and I are going to the shops for provisions."

"Am I not coming?"

"No, you're staying here to dust and wash the floors. When you've done that, you can make as many beds as you see fit."

"But that will take ages."

"That's ok we'll be gone for ages."

The ladies left arm in arm. He watched them depart anticipating what was to come.

Jonathan woke during the night and looked at the bedside clock, it was four fifteen. He got out of bed, slipped on his shorts and went in search of Gabriella. He found her on the veranda sitting at the table drinking water.

"What are you doing out here?"

"I was thirsty and a bit hot so I came out for some fresh air. It's such a beautiful night or should I say morning?"

Jonathan sat down and shared her water and appreciation of the cool night air.

They went back to bed and it was a strange but wonderful experience to not have to part at the front door.

Mary had the day planned for them and she received no objections. They had everything they needed and wanted so the rest didn't matter.

The days passed slowly and peacefully. It felt and acted like a tight family unit, something Gabriella hadn't ever experienced. Romeo and Juliet had brought books with them which they read between Mary's impersonations of a tour guide.

When their week was done they returned to Madrid. Neither of the lovers wanted to go but Mary had promised Mr Lee that his daughter would be home that day.

Mary returned to England and Jonathan stayed on. They met every day and sometimes Gabriella stayed for dinner. One morning she arrived looking a little distressed and when asked why, she told Jonathan that her father wanted to meet him. He was invited to dinner that evening. She had a terrible feeling of foreboding.

That evening the car took them to the Lee establishment in a very expensive part of town. The house was not overly large but beautifully decorated and furnished. Mr Lee was nothing like Jonathan had imagined. He had expected a large overbearing oath of a man but instead saw a slim person slightly smaller than himself and slightly, Chinese looking and he spoke English beautifully. He had expected him to be about sixty as Gabriella had told him that the age gap between her parents was the same as his. He'd forgotten to take into account the fact that Gabriella's mother conceived when only twenty one. Mr Lee was about the same age as his mother,

Introductions were made and they went straight into the dining room for dinner. Mr Lee said that he'd been told that Jonathan was the brightest pupil in his school and wanted to know what he was going to do with that asset.

Jonathan told him about his plans to go to LSE and to become a barrister which seemed to please. There was general chit chat and although the young couple felt nervous nothing untoward was said.

"Gabriella tells me that you only speak Spanish when you're not in company of non-speakers such as me. I'm sorry my Spanish really isn't very good but if you want to converse in Cantonese I'll gladly accommodate."

"I'm sorry but I don't really speak Cantonese only a few words and then not very well."

Mr Lee burst out laughing, Jonathan had said that in Cantonese and he was very clear.

"So young man, you're a linguist as well are you?"

"No sir, when I was twelve I watched a few Cantonese movies and it interested me so I started to teach myself with the help of language tapes. I gave up when someone told me that I'd never be able to speak it accent free because I started too late."

"A perfectionist, are we? Well young man you did ok. How is it that you still remember?"

"I have good retention which helps when taking exams. That's one of the reasons I do well at school."

"And the other reasons?"

"I have a passion for learning and I love books. My favourite place is the British Library but I don't get many opportunities to go."

"Surely in this day and age you can get all the information you need on internet?"

"That's true and I do but I love the feel of a book. They talk to me in a more personal way. That probably sounds stupid."

"Not at all Jonathan, not at all, Gabriella I think I like this young man."

"So do I daddy."

The rest of the evening passed amicably and when Gabriella showed him to the door he said he almost liked her father.

She was amazed at how polite her normally horrible dad had been and thought that he'd probably hired an assassin to dispose of her 'friend'.

Jonathan left Madrid on the last Friday of the school holiday and Gabriella the following Sunday.

School started the following week, their last school year. They slipped back into their previous routine, only their studies were more intense. School also felt different as they were now the seniors. They would both be eighteen before Christmas and they felt more mature than last term.

They were having dinner at Gabriella's on the first Thursday back at school. Jonathan stopped eating.

"Not hungry"

"I've been thinking about us since we've been back. I can't escape this feeling that you're always with me, in my head. I have conversations with you and you speak just as you do and I'm sure you say exactly what you would say, if you know what I mean. It's almost like there are two of us in my head, we've become one person."

"Two bodies one soul"

"Clever guy that Socrates, sad that he probably never experienced it himself."

"Maybe he did secretly although there is no evidence that he was ever in love, otherwise how would he know?'

"It's philosophy, it doesn't have to be a personal experience, just a thought. Poor guy he didn't know what he was missing, it's so real for me."

He was hoping she'd say she felt the same and to his joy, she did.

"We'll be eighteen soon and legally be able to do almost anything."

"Jonathan what are you suggesting?"

"I want us to get married. Will you marry me? I'm supposed to get down on my knee and asked and I will if you want."

Gabriella was silent for a while, she stood up and put her arms around his neck and kissed him.

"No Jonathan. I won't marry you, we're far too young. Try again once you've been called to the bar. Then I'll say yes."

He knew there would never be another woman in his life and it made sense to him that they should enjoy one another whilst they were young and full of vim. To please her he said she was maybe right. That didn't stop him wanting to sleep in the same bed as her every night and wake up next to her every morning, feeling her warmth and softness. He wanted everything.

Jonathan's grade was such that he was allowed to continue his philosophy class as it didn't clash with any of his chosen A level subjects and the teaching staff were confident that it wouldn't be a problem for him.

They passed their eighteenth birthdays and had a miserable three week separation at Christmas. Gabriella's father had started being nice to her since her mother died and now he was positively attentive so she didn't like to ask him if she could return earlier. She had been feeling odd over the holiday so her father had taken her to see a specialist. They could find nothing wrong with her but she had a sense of foreboding. Maybe that's all it was, just nerves or separation anxiety.

When she returned to London she didn't feel any better. When she was with Jonathan it was fine but when he wasn't around she wasn't comfortable.

They had a half term holiday in February and she went to America with her father. When she returned she seemed just a little bit different. Jonathan noticed only too well.

"Is something bothering you, are you feeling unwell or something?'

She gave him a heart melting smile and said that she was fine but had been thinking a lot lately. She had decisions to make about where to study and what she should do once she had graduated.

He knew it was more than that but didn't pursue the point, she would tell him when she was ready.

That term they studied very intently and on the weekends Jonathan spent all his spare time with his nose in a book, nothing distracted him.

The Easter holidays arrived and Gabriella went to New York again with her father. She had seemed unwell of late and had grown pale. Jonathan was worried but she said she was just missing the Spanish sunshine. Jonathan was even more certain that it was more than that. He had a bad dream that she died which made him ill at ease the whole time she was away. He spoke to his mother about it and she agreed that she wasn't looking well but suggested they didn't worry too much about it until she returned. Maybe it was exhaustion from all the studying and she might just need a break.

The day school started Jonathan arrived at Camden Hill at seven forty five. Gabriella answered the door and looked her old self much to his relief. They embraced and kissed and he didn't want to let her go. Todd coughed discretely and they broke their hold and went and had coffee and toast in the kitchen. They exchanged stories of their Easter break, he having little to tell and she excitedly talking about New York. It would had been much better had they been together but it was still OK. Jonathan felt a little miffed but said nothing.

"I went to see a doctor whilst we were in New York. Father insisted as he said I looked horrible. He has a nice way with words. I'm suffering from anaemia would you believe. Anyway that's sorted so now I'm fine." That was partly true the rest he would discover later.

They walked to school and through the school gates to their last term in secondary education.

Time seemed to fly and June soon came around and with it their A level exams. Jonathan was confident he had done well but not so Gabriella. She thought she had done enough to pass but wasn't sure her grades would be good enough to get her into the university of her choice.

There was just their graduating prom to attend and then school would be behind them forever.

Mary insisted that Jonathan use some of his trust money to buy a good dinner suit. She marched him to a high class tailor in the West End where he spent close to a thousand pounds much to his dismay and Mary's delight.

When he went for his final fitting Mary said he looked fantastic and even he thought he looked a bit James Bondish.

The night of the prom he ordered a taxi and went to pick up Gabriella. He hadn't seen her all day as she said she would be very busy. The taxi driver drew up outside her house and Jonathan stepped out. He walked proudly up the few stairs and rang the doorbell.

Todd answered the door and ushered him inside. Before he followed Jonathan inside he paid the taxi driver and told him to go. Jonathan assumed that meant they would be going in the Mercedes. Todd led him into the kitchen and asked him to sit down.

"Is Gabriella still getting ready?"

Todd took a deep breath. "She's not here."

"Where is she, will she be long?"

"She left for Madrid this morning. Her father came to collect her."

Jonathan thought he had misheard. "What, she can't have, she would have told me?"

"It was all rather sudden. She asked me to tell you that she would write to explain."

"When will she be back?" Jonathan asked in an unsteady voice.

Todd looked at the floor and didn't answer. Panic started to rise in Jonathan's chest. "When?"

"Jonathan I'm sorry but I don't think she will be coming back. Mr Lee has asked me to close the house up and give the keys to an estate agent."

Jonathan wasn't taking the information in clearly, he was stunned.

"I'm sorry, this was your prom night and you're all dressed up looking like a film star. I'll drive you home or anywhere else you want to go."

Jonathan followed Todd and got into the car and was driven home. He had found it hard to put one foot in front of the other and had to struggle up the stairs to the flat.

Mary wasn't at home. He undressed and hung his clothes in his wardrobe. He lay on his bed not knowing what to think. He tried calling her mobile but it was disconnected. He resolved to go to Madrid the next day. He opened his laptop and used his debit card to book a flight.

He called his dad's cousin in Madrid and told him that he would be arriving the next day, knowing he would be welcomed. He packed a bag long enough for a week. He couldn't sit still and tried lying down but that was no good. His heart was pounding because he knew something was terribly wrong. He could feel her. He could hear her but she was drawing away this couldn't be happening, it mustn't be happening.

He got dressed and went for a walk. Halfway along Portobello Road he got a panic attack. He couldn't breathe so he sat down on the curb and put his head between his legs and gasped. A few people stopped to ask if he need help. He thanked them as best he could but remained where he was until he felt some strength and control return to his body and mind. He walked until he found himself in Paddington. He didn't want to see his mother, so he continued his wandering until such time he thought she'd be asleep. He arrived home at one o'clock. The flat was in darkness so he went straight to bed. He lay there tossing and turning not able to sleep.

He heard his mother moving around at seven o'clock. He checked himself in the mirror. He looked awful. His flight was at one o'clock so he needed to leave about ten. He went to the bathroom and had a shower. He felt marginally better but looked almost normal. He dressed and went into the kitchen.

"Did you have a nice time love?" She had her back to him when she'd asked. She turned and knew immediately that something was wrong.

"Something happened and Gabriella had to go to Madrid. I'm going today."

"So you didn't go to the prom?"

"No"

"What happened?"

"I don't know. She left without telling me. Todd didn't know either."

She knew not to ask too much as he was obviously distressed. "How long will you be gone?"

"I booked for a week, I might stay longer if I can be of use. I've got the whole summer."

"OK, whatever it is tell her my thoughts are with her won't you" she said full of foreboding.

Somehow her words filled him with hope. He felt better, stronger and of course he would find her and everything would be fine.

When he reached Madrid his dad's cousin, Fernando was waiting to take him into town. Jonathan told him what had happened and asked if they could go straight to Gabriella's house and he obliged. Jonathan rang the doorbell and an elderly, very elegant looking woman answered. Jonathan's mind started getting jumbled when he was told that the Lees didn't live there any longer. They had sold the house to her son in January. Asked if she knew where they lived now, she was unable to help other than to say she thought they were still in Madrid. Fernando gave him comfort by saying it wouldn't be difficult to find a wealthy foreign family in Madrid.

When they arrived at their home the whole family offered to help in the search. They checked for Lees in the telephone directory and found a few but that drew a blank. They tried the internet and even visited the police station, nothing. Jonathan was very despondent. He walked the streets of the wealthy neighbourhoods and asked people coming out of houses if they knew the Lees. He thought he saw her once but when he got close the girl didn't resemble her one bit. The days weren't long enough. When it was almost time to go home, he decided to change his ticket to stay longer but Mary called and changed his mind. A letter had been hand delivered and it was from Gabriella to him. He asked what it said but she hadn't and wouldn't open it.

She didn't tell him that she had also received a letter so she had a good idea what it might say. She had cried on and off for two days and only now was she able to call her son without breaking down.

His search seemed hopeless and he wanted to know what Gabriella had written so he returned home on the due date. Mary gave him the letter and he took it into his room to read. He read it over and over again as if in hopes the words would change. Mary resolved not to cry again, he needed her support not her tears. Jonathan was only eighteen and he'd already lost the two people he'd loved most in his short life and both in a way that didn't make sense.

She had gone. He would never see her again, never. He knew she meant every word. He even understood what she had said. When he read the words he heard her voice and knew there was nothing he could do to change the outcome. All of a sudden he got up and ran to the bathroom. He was sick and it seemed that he would never stop being sick. He felt as if his stomach would be expelled through his mouth. He didn't care. He didn't want to exist anymore.

Mary didn't tell him about her letter because it expressly asked her not to and she thought that wise. Jonathan hadn't cried as she had and she wondered why.

CHAPTER TWENTY TWO

Jonathan spent most of the next two days lying on his bed thinking. He tried to apply logic to what had happened. He asked himself if it had been real and if it had then why had she written, what she had written, had philosophy made her unsure of their future. What was he to do now? He eventually tuned into her voice and listened to her words. He understood what she said and knew even if he could see her he wouldn't be able to change her mind. He would love her forever and she would love him. They had that and he wanted to keep her and she was there in his mind.

He'd never loved before other than his father but that was different. What would he do now? He'd opened himself up to love and he got burnt. He would never put himself in a position again where he could be hurt. Although she may never know, he would do what she had encouraged him to do, be a successful barrister.

His A-level results wouldn't be published until the following month but he knew he'd got the grades he needed and would be going to LSE in October. He'd throw himself into his studies which would close his mind to his loss.

He left his room just as Mary was entering hers.

"How are you feeling my love" she said with a lump in her throat.

"I'm Ok, I have to be."

"You have to get some food inside you or you'll get ill as….." she'd cut her sentence short but he didn't notice.

He forced some food down and when he had finished he told her that he was going out to buy a bicycle. She didn't question him.

He came back about three hours later and parked his new mode of transport in the hallway.

"You need a shave. What have you got in those bags?"

"New clothes"

She felt encouraged until she saw them. He'd bought round neck printed t-shirts, torn jeans and drab looking hoodies.

"Are you going to wear those?"

"Yes mum, I'm going to become invisible. I don't want anyone looking at me and I won't be shaving often, Ok?"

"God and your father gave you a beautiful face, it's wrong to hide it."

"Yes and look where that got me. I'm going to get lost in the crowd. I don't want anyone to think I'm anything special because of the way I look."

"But you are special, you're exceptionally special."

"Not anymore mum, not anymore. I'll do my best to be the best I can be intellectually but my physical appearance means nothing."

Mary felt wretched but understood why he felt that way.

CHAPTER TWENTY THREE

Jonathan wasn't one to waste time when it came to learning opportunities. He had nothing to study because he hadn't started his course but that wasn't going to stop him. He rode his bicycle every day to the British library and read various books on law. His initial object was to find out which branch of law interested him most. They all had their attractions except contract law which seemed to focus on divorce as much as anything. At the end of a week's solid research he decided it would be criminal law.

It was now the first week in August and as he was sitting down at dinner with his mother a thought occurred to him.

"Mum, aren't you going on holiday this year?"

"Yes I am but I thought you wouldn't want to go to Spain so I'll go later in the year when it's not so hot."

"Mum, my course doesn't start until October so if you want me to come with you now I will."

"And you'll spend every day looking for that sweet girl. No I'll go on my own later but if you wanted to go somewhere else we could do that."

"No thanks mum, I'm not going anywhere if it's not Spain. At least here I can have access to books that will help me in the future and I'm learning as much as I can."

"Jonathan if that helps then that's good. You've taken to hiding yourself physically and if you want to immerse your thoughts in other things to hide from the truth then do that but the truth will always be there. You have to face up to it and get on with living."

"I know that and I'm doing it the best way I know how. Before she came along I wasn't exactly a social person and that was alright. I will not become a total recluse, although that does sound an attractive proposition. I'll deal with this and I promise I'll be alright."

Mary sighed and thought about how he'd once been and having him revert to that wasn't something that made her comfortable. He wouldn't really talk to her. He hadn't told her what was in the letter and she hadn't asked, although she had a good idea.

"I'm starting back at Judo and flamenco at the weekend. Does that please you?"

She smiled and said it was a start.

The A-level results were published in the middle of August and he achieved an A+ in all four subjects, even philosophy. He checked Gabriella's results and she got an A in psychology and A+ in both Spanish and philosophy. He wondered where she would now go to university. She had been accepted by two universities in London but obviously she wouldn't be doing that. Where would she go?

The night he received his results he lay in bed and many thoughts came into his head. Who am I? What am I? He knew he'd always been a serious introvert but there was a period where he had opened up and that wasn't so bad really. He'd experienced love and even a degree of friendship from his peers. Should he really go back into that impenetrable shell? He realised that he'd done that for the last month and he'd shut Gabriella out of his thoughts at every opportunity. He hadn't allowed her to talk to him in his thoughts and yet today he did and it felt somehow comforting not painful anymore. He wanted her in his head. He still loved her and always would. Whatever reason she had for leaving it would never have been to hurt him. She was a mystery and she'd gone just as quickly as she arrived. He smiled to himself at that thought, the suddenness of it all. He would remain invisible but not totally isolated. He would find some mindless time when she could enter his thoughts but how?

The answer came the very next day. He decided that he would ride his bicycle to LSE to assess the time he would need to get there. He already had a good idea as it wasn't that far from the British Library where he'd been so often that last month. He felt better that day than he had since Gabriella's departure. The thoughts of the previous night had helped clarify a lot.

He needed some more clothes as what he'd bought wasn't enough to satisfy the washing cycle. It was one thing being scruffy but he neither wanted to be dirty or smelly. He set off for Soho to buy some more invisibility cloaks a.k. Harry Potter. He brought some sweat shirts and some really out of date cotton trousers and was pleased with his purchases. He pushed his wheels through Berwick Street and turned down one of the side roads where a notice in a pub window caught his eye. He glanced at it and moved on then something registered and he went back to the Flag.

The sign was a staff wanted sign. He wheeled his bicycle into the bar and asked for Len, the name on the sign.

Len was a kindly man and he sat Jonathan down at a table and asked him a few questions. It was all settled. Jonathan would work Monday to Friday from 6pm until midnight, maybe later on Fridays. Len almost apologised about the pay but to his relief Jonathan had said it was more than enough. He would start the following Monday.

He'd found what he was looking for. He now had some mindless time when he could let Gabriella into his thoughts and he would have to study that much harder with a shorter period in which to do that. He'd have no free time at all and that pleased him.

He settled quickly in his bar job and by the time he started university he'd mastered the pumps and optics. He shaved only on Saturday mornings and only then because the Flamenco instructor had threatened to throw him out of her group, if he insisted on looking like a down and out. Generally his ploy to become invisible worked and apart from at LSE he was ignored.

When he had to speak to people in the pub he did, he would also listen to people's problems and Gabriella was there to give him advice on how to answer. Life was not perfect but getting better. If he needed time off from the pub Len was obliging and he reciprocated should they have a need for extra staff at the weekend.

Mary went to Spain at the end of October and didn't return until mid-December. When she came back she looked exhausted.

"Wow been partying mum? You look done in."

"Something like that, I had a wonderful time. I'm going back in February. Madrid is beautiful when it's not hot. I don't think I ever appreciated it before."

CHAPTER TWENTY FOUR

They arrived at Heathrow and a car was waiting. George Wilson sat in the front seat and his son David in the back. George turned and gave his son a look of bewilderment.

"You haven't said a word, not one fucking word since I picked you up. So are you going to tell me?"

David looked at his dad and thought how much he wanted to tell him. The problem was he knew what the reaction would be. He'd say he would be better off dead.

David was nineteen and was on a gap year. He was due to start at LSE in October. George, not knowing how it was going to pan out had requested a deferment for a year which was granted.

When they got home David went straight to his room and stayed there. He only came out at meal times and he didn't utter a word for a month. Every time he was about to say something he pulled back for fear of the questions that would ensue.

George thought the boy had gone nuts so he asked his doctor to recommend a psychiatrist. David didn't object when told, he just shrugged, so they made an appointment.

David went into the consulting room and George waited outside. When David emerged George was called in. The doctor told him that David had spoken and suggested that George tried talking to him about anything other than the last year.

"Why, did he tell you what this is all about?"

"No and he won't whilst he feels threatened."

"Threatened, who's fucking threatening him? Maybe I should. I should beat it out of him. That'd fucking cure him."

"Mr Wilson, that's part of the problem I think. He wants to know that you'll stop asking questions about the last year and he wants to hear you say that. He said you're a man of your word and if you say it, he'll believe it."

"What, me the problem?"

"Part of it, will you have a conversation with him, in my presence please."

George agreed and David was brought in. George made his promise but qualified it by saying he'd only agree to that if David continued seeing the psychiatrist.

David spoke to his dad for the first time since he'd been home.

"Thanks dad, and yes I'll do that."

George shook his head in disbelief. They made an appointment for the following week and left.

When they got home, Stella, David's stepmother, opened the door.

"Well?" she inquired.

"Fucking miracle, the boy's talking but you mustn't ask him any questions. Can you fucking well believe that?"

David went to his room and lay on his bed. His dad sounded tough and although he was of only average height, he looked tough. Nobody messed with George Wilson. He thought about his own appearance and concluded that he was a streak of piss with a blond mop on top and a public school accent to go with it. He had a big scar down the side of his face which he thought probably made him look like a victim rather than tough. He was six feet four inches and weighed just about twelve stone.

He'd been packed off to boarding school when he was eight, a year after his mother died. George had tried to raise the boy but was hardly ever at home and couldn't cope when he was. His sister Carol was older and pretty much self-sufficient so she was allowed to stay home.

David always suspected it was a ruse to get him out of the house so that his dad could invite his girl-friends home.

David did well at his prep boarding school and sailed through his common-entrance exam. He was offered a place at Harrow much to George's delight.

"One up theirs right. All those toffee nosed gits that think I'm a bit of rough. Now I've shown them." He said to anyone who would listen.

David had only left Harrow a little less than a year before but it seemed a lifetime ago.

An image of himself grew in his head. If he beefed up and spoke like his dad, no one would dare bother him and there would be no repeat.

The next day he went and bought a bench and a set of weights. He bought books on nutrition and how to gain muscle, big muscles. He soon started seeing results which pleased him but he still had the accent.

George owned betting shops and a tacky casino in Bayswater and here Dave saw his opportunity. He asked his dad if he could work in the casino as he had a year before he started university.

"Are you sure? Aren't you sick?"

"No dad, I really think it will be good for me and I'll get to learn your business."

George was surprised and in a strange way pleased.

"And kid, stop taking the piss."

"About what?" knowing full well what he meant.

"You're starting to talk like me."

"I thought I should. You know, going into your business one day. You don't want your lot to think your son is a toffee nosed git do you?"

George looked up to heaven. "I don't know fucking anything anymore. I spend a fortune making you into a gent and now you want to be like me."

"Dad it was money well spent. I've worked hard and I'm pretty clever. It's just a front. Oh by the way can you call me Dave from now on."

"Now you are taking the piss."

CHAPTER TWENTY FIVE

David, now Dave to all except George and Stella, worked hard at the casino. He spent most of his time in the back office learning the operations and financial aspects of the business. He occasionally wandered onto the casino floor just to get a feel of what went on and learn about the clientele.

When he went home he would go to his room and push weights. He increased his calorie intake and he was starting to see results. He had a severe problem sleeping. Most nights when he did manage to drop off he would have horrific dreams which would wake him up sweating and gasping for breath and sometimes shouting and screaming. He found by taking naps during the day it enabled him to work into the early hours of the morning in the casino so his need for longer sleep periods was diminished.

When the year had passed he was ready for university. Dave Wilson was now seventeen stone with muscles like Schwarzenegger. He'd perfected his London accent and when he spoke to himself in the mirror he was pleased with the result. Dave Wilson looked and sounded like a hard case and nobody was going to mess with him.

George was sick of David's nightmares and told him that now he was about to go to university he should consider living out.

His heart sank, he was being sent away again.

"Dad, I didn't apply for halls of residents so where will I live?"

"We've got that flat just off Holland Park Avenue, in Lansdowne Road and the tenant has just moved out, you can live there."

"Isn't that a bit big for me?"

"No, it's fine and it's my personal property not the company's so you can take care of my investment."

George was never mean with money and he knew how to make it. He was just mean with time and family responsibilities.

"Are you sure dad? Well thanks."

George thought that he mustn't sigh with relief and say thank fucking Christ out loud. Instead he said "You go for it son. I'll hire a housekeeper so that you eat properly and the place stays clean. You'll enjoy it, it's just around the corner from the station which is on the central line so straight through to Holborn and LSE."

George was from Notting Dale but had moved to Esher when his first child had been born. Carol was a beautiful baby and grew up to be a stunner. Dave was a mistake and made up for his lack of good looks with a razor sharp brain.

He'd bought the flat in Lansdowne Road as a statement, telling himself that he'd crossed the tracks. It was a short distance from where he was born but a totally different world. It would suit David down to the ground he told himself in justification.

Dave moved in the following week. It was half a four storey house. It had three bedrooms, all with en-suite bathrooms and a small box room situated on the top floor which was above street level but not exactly what you'd call a ground floor or a first floor. The lower part of the flat was just below street level, a semi basement from the front but garden level at the back. The small back garden had a gate that opened onto a large communal garden. There was a large kitchen at the front, a dining room, a large lounge and a small room that he would later use as an office.

It all looked a bit shabby but Dave resolved to make it his home. He arranged for the whole flat to be redecorated before he bought any furniture other than a bed and kitchen table. The first bedroom to be finished he turned into a gym and bit by bit he furnished the whole place simply but tastefully. Tasteful costs money and George willingly paid; a small price for his own freedom from his nutcase son.

Dave continued to see the psychiatrist on a monthly basis. He had managed to tell him the whole miserable story. He actually felt a bit better for doing so but he was still far from whole. The dreams continued to haunt him but their intensity had lessened. The doctor had told him that like many victims he blamed himself so their main focus would be on relieving the guilt. Dave needed to find redemption and much to Dr Marks' disappointment, he turned to the church. This had happened at the time he started university. There was a catholic church nearby at the end of Pottery Lane, St Francis of Assisi. He went intermittently and sometimes he struggled about going, not being in a state of grace, in fact far from it. He decided to go to confession but then decided against it as the priest might recognise him and would know what he'd done. He didn't go.

CHAPTER TWENTY SIX

He was taking economics and if he graduated to be followed by an MBA, four years of study. He had wondered if his problems would have affected his ability to learn. He'd hardly picked up a book in two years. His fears were allayed the first day. He was a fast learner and had excellent retention. He would go early and fill his time between lectures in the library. He was free of all his problems when he was immersed in Adam Smith and the like. When he submitted his first paper his lecturer ask him to see him. He was very nervous about the meeting and his thoughts were of failure.

The truth was quite the opposite. The lecturer commended him on his excellent work and asked if it was ok to make some personal observations. Dave didn't respond which the lecturer took as a yes.

"I looked at your application and I noted your age and educational background. You're twenty but you look a lot older and you dress as if you were going to work in the city. It makes you stand out like a sore thumb. You don't interact with the other students in fact you seem to isolate yourself from everyone. Is there something I could help you with? There are lots of societies that could use your contribution and might help you integrate better.'

Dave looked at the man and stood up.

"I'm here to learn not to fucking integrate." Once the words were out of his mouth he regretted them and duly apologised and left.

If there were no lectures in the afternoon he would go to the British Library and stay there until six. He loved the library, access to millions of books and the tranquillity of the place. Nobody ever tried to strike up conversations in this temple of learning. He felt at home with all that knowledge around him. It soothed his troubled soul.

The housekeeper George had employed was a Mrs Hayes. She had a spare key and would let herself in. She cleaned, did the laundry and cooked something for Dave's dinner which she left in the oven. They met rarely but on the first time of seeing Dave, Mrs Hayes realised he needed large portions of food to feed that large frame, so she cooked enough to feed two people.

Occasionally his dad and Stella would stay the night, when they were out on the town. He knew he shouldn't but he began to find this intrusive.

After a day at university he would go home and work out for an hour. He would then eat his dinner and then nap on the couch, setting his alarm for nine thirty. He'd get up and shower. At ten he would set off for the casino where he stayed until two o'clock. There was a car and driver at his disposal to take him home.

He was thankful that his days were full and as time passed he began to feel less fearful. He still had the weekends to fill. On Saturday he'd get up around seven have a huge breakfast and then spend the morning studying. If he had completed his assignments he would still study. He knew what was coming up so he'd get ahead of himself.

He'd cook himself lunch and then go for a long walk. This left him alone with his thoughts but he knew he needed to confront them. He increasing found that his surroundings interested him and his dark thoughts began to abate. In the evenings he would pump iron until he was exhausted.

Occasionally George would call round and take him to see Chelsea play. He enjoyed his dad's company when all there was to talk about was football. After the match they would go to George's favourite pub which was full of his cronies. He would talk to everyone there except Dave, who didn't mind one bit.

Sundays followed the same pattern except as time progressed he found himself attending mass more frequently but not at St Francis. On one of his walks he had passed Brompton Oratory and noticed they had sung Latin mass and that became his church of choice, he loved the music and the choir, he found it all very soothing. The church was also big enough for him to slip in and out unnoticed.

He had been in a band with friends at Harrow and it was agreed by all that he had an undeniable talent. Music had become important to him again. He listened whilst he studied and sometimes just played current songs and learned the words so he could sing along and air guitar.

After Christmas, which he had found a struggle, he returned to his lectures, with much relief. He was on his way to the canteen when something caught his eye on the notice board. The poster said that a band formed by the students was looking for new members and they would be auditioning at four that afternoon. Dave read it a few times and decided to go along. He'd forgotten his love of music until he heard sung mass which revived his passion.

There were a number of musicians at the back of the room and potential band members, who were few, seated facing them. Dave took a seat. One by one they were called up to perform. One played guitar well, another sang badly and generally the rest were adequate. Dave was the last to arrive and therefore last in line. All but the band had left and they seemed to be about to start packing up. Dave stood up and asked where they were going. He was told that they had finished the auditions and were leaving.

"What the fuck you think I'm here for, to listen to that crap?"

The band members looked one to another and the lead guitarist addressed Dave.

"I'm sorry sir but this is open to students only.'

"I am a fucking student" and looking menacingly at all of them "don't I fit your mould."

The guitarist raised his shoulders and apologised and asked Dave what he could do.

"Play guitar, drums, keyboard and sing the arse off you lot."

"Oh well which one do you want to do?"

"Which one do you need most?"

"We're desperate for a singer, a rock singer."

"Ok what can you play?"

"How about Kryptonite?"

"I'll give it a shot, give me a guitar."

They obliged. Dave played a few chords, tuned the guitar and asked if they wanted him to do it solo or would they join in. They said for him to start and they would pick it up as he went on.

Dave started the opening bars then let rip. The band didn't join in they just watched in amazement.

"That was brilliant. You've obviously done this before and by the sound of it probably professionally. I hope you don't mind but how old are you?'

"I'm younger than some of you guys and that's for sure. I'm twenty one. You don't think I fit the image right but you think I'm brilliant so how do we work that one out?"

"Well, yes and yes and I must admit you're a bit scary and we wouldn't want to lose control."

Dave actually smiled. "What's the band's name?"

"We call ourselves Einstein's Rejects."

"Ok, how about I promise not to scare anyone or try to take over. I just want to play and sing. I know I don't fit your image but you do kind of look like every other band out there so why don't you call yourselves Einstein's Rejects and The Suit?"

They huddled around and he could hear them muttering. After a couple of minutes the leader said, "Done, we love it."

Dave's musical desires were satisfied and he didn't disappoint. The band members were good musicians and whilst he generally remained aloof he collaborated on ideas and song choices when asked. They played mainly current rock and occasionally retro to audiences of students on campus. They were all too busy with their studies to take it elsewhere which again suited Dave. He now had music and less time to think about the horrors of life.

At his first visit to his psychiatrist after joining the band, Dr Marks was pleased that Dave had a new interest.

"Does this mean you're making friends?"

"No, not at all, we talk about the music and that's it."

"Don't they try to converse with you?"

"They tried once or twice but I made it clear that I didn't do that stuff, so they backed off."

"I find it odd that you can stand in front of an audience and sing yet you don't talk. Does the singing do anything for you?"

"I get to choose some of the songs and I choose those that mean something to me. I can stand in front of a hundred people and tell them my hurt through someone else's words and they don't know. Singing again also makes me feel that I'm not alone in the world. Just about everything I feel, someone else has written about."

"Yet you still won't let anyone get close to you."

"No, I just couldn't answer their questions."

"Your guilt is a heavy burden and it would help if you could share it with someone."

"Never."

CHAPTER TWENTY SEVEN

At the end of his first year at LSE he had to face a three month break. He worked at the casino full time but the problem was it was only open from six pm to two am. He set about doing research on the competition by visiting their establishments and observing what they did well. His dad's operation was tin pot compared to most. The successful casinos stayed open twenty four hours, so he had plenty of time to learn from what he ranked as the best. He was surprised to discover that the punters didn't seem to discriminate between night and day and the places were always busy.

He told his dad what he'd been doing and suggested they extend their opening hours until four am. George agreed and was pleased to see his business grow and was impressed with Dave's business sense.

Their casino looked like a church hall and had windows that let in daylight. Dave suggested that they black them out and open earlier at four pm. They did and again the business grew. Within two years they would be open twenty four – seven.

Dave had kept himself busy and his natural talent for business had been pleasing. On his return to University he decided to join the football team. He played in defence and was an intimidating sight to the opposition. He enjoyed training and playing but didn't socialise with any of his team mates. After the game he would change his boots for trainers and leave without showering. The others thought this odd but didn't remark about it in his presence.

Life settled into a busy routine. He had his studies, music, football, his work-outs, the casino and church on Sundays. He had little time to sleep but that was something he did only as a requirement of life. He would sleep about four hours a night and would often wake in a hot sweat. How he wished the dreams would stop haunting him.

One Sunday as he was leaving the Oratory a priest approached him. They chatted for a while and the priest, Father O'Connell, said he noticed that Dave didn't take communion.

"I've not been to confession father."

"Well maybe you should think about that."

Dave scrutinised the man before him, in black robes and a dog collar. He had a kindly face and a soft spoken voice and Dave thought about what Dr Marks had said about sharing his load with someone. Maybe he should go to confession, it might help.

"I will Father."

"You will think about it or you will come to confession," the priest said with a warm smile.

Dave hesitated "I will come to confession, when I have time."

"And where are you going now?"

Dave stomach started turning. He wanted to lie but this was a priest.

"I'm going for a walk and then I have to study and later work."

"Well young man why don't you take a short break from your busy schedule and we can do it now."

Dave blushed, he could feel his ears burning and his breath shortened.

"Come along my son let's go back into the church.'

Dave followed like a lamb his ears ringing and panic rising.

"Do you want to do this in the sacristy or the confessional?"

Dave wondered what the fuck he was doing and said "We might as well do this face to face as you know who I am anyway."

The priest gave him his kindly look and said he could get another priest and he could do it in the confession box if that would make him more comfortable.

Dave thought for a while and wondered why he had agreed and started to doubt if he could actually do it. He made up his mind and stuck with Father O'Connell.

The priest led him to the sacristy and they sat face to face across a small table.

Dave started immediately with the preliminaries. It had been four years since he'd been to confession and had sinned. He stopped there. He wanted to leave he wanted to run out of the church. He didn't want to say those words. He'd only been able to tell Dr Marks a bit at a time and then over a period of three months. This priest wanted to hear it all and now.

"Take your time," Came a gentle voice.

"I'm not sure I can do this, I'm sorry."

"You know it does help to know that even if you think mankind can't forgive you, God will."

Dave looked at the floor and told his story. It was hard, very hard. When he had finished Father O'Connell asked him if there were any other sins he wished to confess. Dave wondered if this priest had heard what he had said. He confessed the standard stuff which was in his case, to his own amazement, very little.

The priest gave him absolution and his penance, which was a paltry three Hail Marys.

Father O'Connell was concerned by Dave's reaction. He was as white as a sheet and when he stood up he seemed unsteady on his feet.

"Come with me." He took Dave out of the church to his own quarters. He made him sit down and he brought him a strong cup of tea. Dave's head was swimming. He sat there for what seemed an age. He managed to drink the tea, his blood started to circulate once more and he could feel his senses returning. He asked why his penance was so meagre and the priest said that he had suffered enough already and it wasn't his job to add to that.

Dave started to feel better and said he should go. They walked out onto the Brompton Road together and said their goodbyes. Dave stopped and turned back into the church and knelt and said his three Hail Marys.

He walked home and went straight to his bedroom. He collapsed onto his bed. He wanted to cry but the tears wouldn't come.

He didn't go out for the rest of the day, avoiding being seen at the casino. His head didn't seem right. He tried pushing weights but had lost all of his strength. He lay down on the sofa and fell asleep. He woke up screaming. The dream had come back with a vengeance. It was more vivid than it had been in a long time and so real.

He sat up shaking. He knelt in prayer like a child and asked God to stop the horror. He said his three Hail Marys again then kept on going until it became a mantra. His head cleared and he felt a little stronger. He got up from his knees and went to the bathroom and had a long, long shower.

The next Sunday he went to communion. He wondered if confession had made him feel any better. After the initial horrors of bringing it all back, he thought it had. He wanted to tell someone that mattered, someone who would forgive him and still be there, someone who cared. He wondered if there was anybody who cared. Dad, he couldn't ever tell him. His sister Carol, she didn't even want to talk to him. It suddenly dawned on him that even if he wanted to confide in someone, he had nobody who really cared about him enough to understand. What was just as bad was that he had nobody for whom he cared or loved. Maybe it was better that way and maybe it should stay that way. He was a piece of filth and no one need ever know.

There were a few incidents of girls coming on to him at university and he found himself having coffee with one or other. He even took one to a concert but once she started asking questions he backed off.

He continued putting great efforts into his studies which he enjoyed. Studying immersed him into a world in which he was safe and in control.

He achieved a first and without his knowledge it was a remarkable achievement which came to the attention of Dr Gordon, the head of economics.

Dave got a call from Dr Gordon's office during the summer break asking him to drop by and see the professor. He wondered what it was about and went with a certain amount of trepidation.

The outcome of the meeting was a request for Dave to change his MBA course to a master's in economics. He was told that he had a rare talent and could easily go on to achieve a doctorate. Dave was amazed and flattered but declined. He explained why he wanted to do business studies. He could use the knowledge to grow his father's business and it would be a real, live and hands on task that he could judge himself against.

Dr Gordon was a little disappointed but understood. He wished him luck and told him he'd be following his progress with interest.

Dave sailed through his MBA course.

CHAPTER TWENTY EIGHT

Dave was now twenty four and ready to apply his new found knowledge to his father's business. He negotiated a modest salary coupled with a profit sharing agreement. George thought this all a bit formal for family but went along with it. He started work in the family business on the Monday following his final exam.

George felt a great sense of pride in his only son. He had always wanted him to take over the business when the time was right. He had shown he was smart and the casino was raking in a lot more money because of the changes he had implemented. Dave took over the business, including the betting shops, and embarked on an amazing business renaissance.

After two years at the helm the casino's profits had quadrupled and the betting shops doubled. George took a back seat during this period but was still officially the managing director. Now it was time to hand over the reins completely.

George announced his intentions and asked Dave what he wanted by way of compensation. Dave was not entirely surprised as George had been hinting at full retirement for some time. He knew exactly what he wanted and told his dad the amount of salary, an increased share of the profits and as the flat above his had just become vacant he wanted to purchase that in the company's name. It would be a good investment and they could keep it vacant so George and Stella could use it when they were in town and also Carol and her family when they were in England. Most of all he wanted his flat to be put in his name, a place that would be truly his.

He thought that George would try to negotiate him down but much to his surprise George agreed to everything without batting an eye. He went further by insisting that Dave be paid twice what he had requested and the company would buy him a Mercedes to match his new position and then came the crunch. As part of his retirement plan George would take all the excess cash out of the business for himself. Dave knew this would frustrate his improvement plans but as he had been well taught, he shouldn't look a gift horse in the mouth. Besides his father was a generous man not a Trojan.

The deal was done and Dave was the proud owner of his own home. All major decisions were to be passed by the board of directors of which George was chairman and the day to day operations were Dave's totally unhindered.

Some months later at a board meeting, George did something surprising. He announced that he was very proud of his son, a true business man made from his own mould. He stood up and shook Dave's hand.

"I'm really proud of you son."

Nothing else, just that, no hug but it pleased Dave immensely. George was also pleased as he'd just been given a cheque for seventeen million pounds.

Dave had an appointment to see Dr Marks that afternoon. When he entered the consulting room the doctor said" Well someone isn't scowling today. Did something good happen?"

Dave explained briefly about his new position and yes he was pleased.

"Dave what do you see when you look in the mirror?"

He thought about it for a minute before replying.

"I see an almost twenty seven year old man, who looks much older. He has bags under his eyes and a scar down the side of his face. Why?"

"Is there anything you might want to do to change either of those things?"

"I don't sleep much. In fact I don't mind that anymore. The fact that I look older means I get more respect. The scar, I suppose I could get rid of that and you'd say it was a constant reminder and I should."

"It's not what I say or think that matters."

"Do you think it would help if I got rid of it?"

"Well if nothing else it might make you look a little less intimidating and more approachable."

Dave lowered his eyes. "I don't mean to be intimidating. It's self -defence and I'm not sure I want to be more approachable. It is ugly though isn't it?"

The next day he made an appointment to see a skin specialist. Within six weeks the scare was only visible up close and nobody was going to get close.

Dave stood looking in his bathroom mirror. He definitely looked better. He was never going to be handsome but it was an improvement. He sighed as he thought how great it would be if they could erase the scars that you couldn't see. He checked himself and reminded the Dave in the mirror that self-pity, just like guilt, served no useful purpose.

He immersed himself in his work and really enjoyed it. Making money gave him a great sense of satisfaction. It wasn't the money itself as it served little purpose for him as he had nothing much to spend it on. It was a measure of his success and each year he set ambitious goals for the company which meant he had to work hard to achieve them. That's what he wanted, to be stretched to fill his time with a purpose. His own bank balance was substantial and he'd started investing, another thing he found he had a talent for. His investments were like a personal game of monopoly for him and after a few years he had a diverse portfolio which gave a good return and turned out to be almost recession proof. Business suited him it was his substitute for personal relationships of which he now had little need.

There was one thing he wanted to change and that was the location of the head office which was in Shepherds Bush. He told George that he wanted to relocate to Soho. He said that it would be better for the company image, branding, PR and prestige. George didn't get it but agreed anyway.

Dave found just what he was looking for just off Berwick Street and they would be fully installed there by the following year, March 2008.

To coincide with the move he decided to change his image. He dumped his city attire for up-market designer suits. He looked like something off a magazine cover. He became meticulous about his appearance and it made him feel even more confident. He had a look for every occasion. He still looked older than his years and the bags under his eyes were still there but he felt better about himself.

After mass one Sunday he stood outside the church talking to Father O'Connell and asked him who the lady was to whom he had just been speaking as she looked familiar.

"That's Lady Worthington but you probably know her better as Dolly Mellow the actress."

"Of course, I saw her once on stage and of course in films and on television. She looks almost regal in the flesh."

"She's a fine person. She does a lot of work for homeless people. She set up a foundation and she's always working to raise funds. Avoid her or she'll empty your pockets and believe me she can be very persuasive."

Dave thought for a bit and then said, "I wouldn't mind helping out a bit, financially. I've just moved my office to Soho and I often work late and I see a lot of homeless people. It's a disgrace to think we can stand by and watch people sink to such a degree of hopelessness."

A few weeks later Dave's P.A. put her head round his office door and told him that there was a lady to see him. Before he could respond the lady in question had brushed past the announcer and taken a seat opposite Dave.

Dolly always took the character of one of her stage roles when she wanted something. Today she was Lady Bracknell. She started by scolding him for corrupting people's morals by encouraging them to gamble and told him that he should use his ill-gotten gains to give back to the community. She went on and on in that vein.

Much to Dolly's amazement and without saying a word Dave wrote her a cheque for fifty thousand pounds and bade her goodbye. She took the cheque and looked at Dave puzzled, then left. Dave thought she was worth it just for the entertainment value.

The next Sunday at mass she approached him on the way out.

"Young man, I didn't thank you properly so let me do that now. She stood on tiptoe and kissed him on the cheek and said, "Well now that's done, let's talk business. I understand you're some sort of financial whizz-kid. Our foundation needs someone like you to help us raise money. You must come to our next committee meeting."

Dave asked where and when. She told him and he looked surprised.

"I thought your foundation was in Baker St."

"Oh that, it's just a plaque outside a friends office, we have to have an address you see, so we use that. We meet at different people's houses, not ideal but needs must."

Dave thought for a moment, "If you want me to help, I'm afraid you'll have to hold your next meeting at my office. I'm extremely busy you know."

Dolly agreed and told him that there were twenty committee members but only half usually turned up. He was instructed to lay on tea and biscuits for everyone, to which he agreed.

The meeting was for the following Friday at six thirty in the evening. When the committee members arrived they were greeted by a receptionist who asked them to wait until all their party had assembled. After about fifteen minutes Dolly assured the young man that they were all there. A phone call was made and Dave came to greet them and led them to a sizable meeting room.

Before they started, Dave asked them if they had noticed anything when they arrived. They all looked blankly at each other. Dave held up a sign, a rather splendid one that had the foundations name on it.

"There is one exactly the same as this at the front of this building and this one is to be put on the door to this room. You need a proper home if you're going to be effective so I'm offering you that home. We can't have a foundation for the homeless being homeless now can we? I'm offering you that home."

Dolly let out a squeal of delight and everybody clapped. There were many thanks and much praise for Dave and eventually they got down to business.

Dave asked to see their accounts and they were produced by the treasurer. He studied them carefully and pointed out that it must be very hard to be effective when the source of income was haphazard donations. They all agreed.

Dave thought for a while and then made the observation that everyone in the room was well dressed. They took that as a compliment. He then said that obviously none of them were on the bread-line and they agreed. He went on to suppose they all had connections with well-off friends and acquaintances and again they agreed.

Dolly piped up, "Where's this going and where's the tea and biscuits?"

Dave gave her a stern look, "Lady Worthington, this is a business meeting and you'll get nothing until the business is concluded."

Dolly felt a little intimidated and shrank in her chair.

Dave continued by suggesting they organise a fund raiser. They could arrange a dinner at one of the Park Lane hotels toward the end of the year. They would need 200 guests each paying one thousand pounds for the privilege of being there and that included the committee.

Dolly looked dismayed. "And where do I find two hundred mugs to pay one thousand pounds each. If only it were that easy."

"Lady Worthington, you don't. There are twenty people on your committee, excluding me, which means that after you and your partners have purchased tickets, you only have to sell eight each. You've already said you have access to wealthy people so that shouldn't be too hard."

There was a buzz around the room and lots of conversations going on at the same time. Dolly banged the table and got every one's attention.

"First of all will you stop calling me Lady Worthington, my name is Dolly and I'm sure you're right we could sell the tickets but won't the dinner and venue be very expensive?"

Dave looked at her with a poker face, business like expression. "My company will pay for that, it will be our donation."

More buzz, "Oh, that's very generous of you and we'll certainly try."

Dave slapped the table. "That's not good enough. Either I have your full commitment or we don't do it. This is not a social tea party. It's going to be a real fund-raiser and your foundation will make a minimum of two hundred thousand pounds from it."

"We commit, if we can't sell a measly eight tickets each then we shouldn't be here. We'll do it" announced Dolly to applause.

Dave continued, "As an added incentive, my company will take a full page add in Tattler thanking everybody who bought a ticket by name. We'll also invite all the glossies including Tattler to the event so your guests will be seen to be charitable."

"That's a little cynical Dave but I have to concede it does have merit. You'll have no problem getting the magazines and press to turn out when they see the guest list."

"That's better Dolly. We need to organise this soon. If we can select a range of dates today, I'll get started with the arrangements. The rest we can decide later."

The end of November was agreed upon and tea and biscuits were served.

The arrangements were all firmed up and the ticket sales were going well. At the end of a subsequent meeting Dolly pulled Dave to one side. You are truly marvellous. Thank you for everything you've done. I just wish you'd look happy about it. You're always so serious."

Dave snapped back. "You want happy or money" and he walked off regretting his reaction.

Dolly said to herself, "Both would be nice."

November arrived and the event was a big success. Dave gave a speech as the sponsor and encouraged voluntary donations to be made at the end of the evening. The foundation raised almost a quarter of a million pounds from the dinner which was almost the year's target they had set themselves.

Dave became the treasurer but declined the invitations to meet the homeless.

The dinner was to become an annual event and part of the social calendar. The foundation's coffers grew thanks to the advice from Dave. Dolly frequently invited him to parties, dinners, theatre and the like but he always declined, much to her relief.

On a visit to Dr Marks he told him about his involvement with the charity and the doctor was pleased.

"You say you're treating this like just another business but there's more to it than that, isn't there?"

Dave looked at his feet and nodded. "I have so much money that it just seems the right thing to do."

"It's more than money though you're giving your time and expertise. Does it make you feel good?'

"I suppose, in a way. Maybe it's the god thing but I needed to do something, the three Hail Marys never seemed enough."

The doctor sighed, he wasn't big on god. "Do you enjoy the social side of it?"

"The meetings are business and the charity event a bit stressful but I suppose so, it fills my time.'

"When you're not working you do nothing that really interacts with people other than this and you treat the foundation as a business. What about you, when you're not working don't, you feel lonely?"

"What's lonely? I'm the only person in my head and just like you that's what I live with. I've seen many relationships go sour and watch what that does to people. I don't want or need any of that I'm fine."

"Dave you've made a lot of progress and your visits are far less frequent. Do you think it might be time to let someone in, maybe just a little? The consequences can't be as bad as what you've already suffered and you might find a friendship might give you some comfort."

"Who would want to be my friend and when would I find the time? I'm good and I am much better than I was. I still have shame and guilt to deal with but that's mine and I live with it. You do help and thank you for that. At least I don't have to avoid anything with you, so thanks."

CHAPTER TWENTY NINE

The company was still doing well despite the recession. Dave had hit his targets every year and by the year 2010 he owned half the company. That was the limit his employment contract permitted. George was happy to leave Dave with full responsibility and had watched his son with amazement grow the business and turn the casino into a world class venue.

The casino was now operating on both floors of the two storey building it occupied. The gaming tables were on the upper floor and the gambling machines on the ground floor. Also on the ground floor there were two bars, one small quiet one at the rear and a larger one with a stage on the side of the building. They had live music from Thursday to Saturday and a resident band on those nights. It had become a place to be seen vying with some of the well-known West End clubs. Dave occasionally played and sung with the band and was welcomed into that fold as someone that brought them added variety.

Dave had even started playing football with the office's local pub team. He'd been asked as a joke, by one of his managers and, much, to every one's amazement, he had accepted. They played Saturday mornings and went to the pub for lunch, unwashed and often muddy. It was all easy going and Dave enjoyed it.

George died of a massive heart attack in 2011. He left his half of the company to his wife Stella and his daughter Carol. Dave knew this would be the case as George had mentioned it. Dave was left their weekend house in the Cotswolds and the rest of the assets were to be split evenly. The house in Esher was in Stella's name so that was hers. The death duties were quite substantial mainly due to the value of the company but manageable for Dave who knew all there was to know about such matters.

Dave's life had become almost pleasant and certainly busier. He was having fewer nightmares and although still sleeping just a few hours a night he felt more rested. He interacted with many people but didn't count any of them as friends. When his dreams returned he would fall into a black mood and everyone would avoid him not knowing the reason.

Although he had not seen much of his dad whilst he was alive, he missed him. Carol avoided speaking to him and when she did it wasn't to say anything pleasant. He saw Stella when she came to town but she was always on a mission, usually shopping, so he didn't spend much time with her.

He worked out every day maintaining his muscle mass and his scary look.

He wasn't spending much time at home what with work, the foundation and football. He still managed mass on Sunday mornings and a long walk afterwards. He usually ended up in Holland Park where he would find a secluded spot on the hill and enjoy the sounds of the birds and the general tranquillity of the place. It was like a little haven where he could work out his business issues in peace. He sometimes thought about himself and when he did, it didn't seem quite so desperate in that place.

It was early February 2013 when he twisted his ankle playing football and ended up on crutches for a week.

The football team had scheduled a meeting in the pub for the following Tuesday. That was unusual as they normally had it after the game on Saturday but due to Dave's injury and that of two other team members, inflicted during the game against a bunch of animals, they had postponed it. It was to be a fateful day for Dave. When the meeting was over he picked up his phone and aimed it at the bar. The young barman came over and wiped the table and cleared the glasses. Everyone had left except Dave. The barman asked him if he would like another beer but he declined. Dave stood up about to go when the young man approached him again. "Do you have far to go only it's snowing outside and probably slippery. You don't want to hurt the other leg do you?"

Dave replied without as much as a glance at the voice's owner. "My driver's off tonight so I'll get a cab."

"Why don't you take a seat and I'll go and find you one. Where are you going?"

Dave sat down and the young man returned after about ten minutes still in his shirt sleeves looking frozen but pleased with himself.

"It's outside let me help you." He opened the pub door and the taxi door and Dave slid into the cab and took a ten pound note out of his pocket and offered it for the service. The young man shook his head and gave a sad smile and shut the cab door.

"Fuck you then" Dave said loud enough to be heard by the recipient of his oath. The taxi proceeded to the casino.

When he got home it was about two thirty in the morning, a little earlier than normal. He'd left early because something was bothering him. He got into bed and opened his phone and a cold chill passed through him as he said out loud. "What have I become when everything must have a monetary value, even a little kindness, oh fuck, fuck, fuck?" He thought of the young man and the sad smile and resolved to apologise. He felt cold inside, an emptiness he imagined would stay with him all his life.

Jonathan watched the taxi pull away. He thought the man on crutches must be rich. He wore very expensive clothes. He knew that because he'd seen the label inside the jacket as the man stood up, Valentino. He wondered if rich people all thought they had the right be rude. Most that he'd met had been but not all and certainly not that rude. He was going to be a successful barrister and that would earn him a lot of money so would he become like that? He resolved always to remember that man, who was probably a gangster, and never to be like that, yet there was something very noble and sad about him. Maybe he was just having an off day.

The next night it was snowing again. Jonathan hadn't used his bike all week, the roads were too treacherous and with all the mad drivers in London it wasn't worth the risk. He'd been using the tube to LSE and walked from there to the pub in the evening.

There were only two customers that night, the snow had sent the normal punters home early. It was very quiet. At nine o'clock the man on crutches hobbled through the door. He walked over to Len and said something and he wondered if he was going to be in trouble.

Len picked up a stool from one of the high tables and brought it over to the end of the bar where Jonathan was putting away glasses. The man followed and sat down.

"A pint of Carlsberg please."

"Coming up, you must be special."

"Why's that?"

Jonathan half smiled and told him that stools weren't normally allowed at the bar. He poured the beer and handed it over.

Dave looked at the young man and offered his apology.

"I'm sorry that I was rude last night."

"That's Ok, it was generous of you to offer, thanks."

"Then why didn't you take it?"

"All part of the service sir. Will you need a taxi tonight?'

"No I have a driver waiting outside."

Dave thought that hadn't been so hard. Jonathan looked at him intently and then flashed a smile of perfect white teeth.

"What's funny?" Dave asked not getting the joke.

"You are. You're big and scary, probably very rich and there you are apologising to me."

Dave screwed up his mouth in thought, strange, bold young man. They chatted about the snow and the state of the roads, Jonathan saying it meant he couldn't ride his bike. Dave asked him how long he'd worked there as he hadn't seen him before last night.

'About a year and a half, I like it here, Len's a good boss and it's all pretty mindless. I work Mondays to Fridays and before last night I'd never seen you."

"Then that's why we've never met I only come here on Saturday lunch times in the football season. Bit of a dead-end job though isn't it."

"I suppose so."

"Then why do you do it?"

"It fills the time and it pays, that's about it."

"Why would you want to fill your time with something mindless?"

Jonathan gave him the same sad smile he'd seen the night before and shrugged. There was something different this time there was a look in his eyes that he recognised. Why was he talking to this young man, he didn't have conversations of this nature. He needed to change the subject.

"You get a lot of gays coming into the pubs round here; you must get hit on a lot."

"Why would anyone hit on me, I'm invisible?"

Dave scrutinised him, looking him up and down. "Under all that curly hair and stubble, you're a really good looking kid."

Jonathan returned the scrutiny. "Do they hit on you?"

"Definitely not."

"You might be big and scary but you're very handsome. If you had a beard you'd look like one of the statues of Greek gods in the British Museum."

"Well thank you but I've never been accused of being good looking before. I'll have to grow a beard then. No one hits on me; I'd tear their head off if they did."

"Is that what you're doing?"

"What?" Dave was not expecting what came next.

"Hitting on me?"

Dave felt his face and neck redden. Was it anger or embarrassment, he wasn't sure. He grabbed his crutches and left the pub in haste.

Dave was too late, Jonathan had seen the blush. The man had left without paying for his beer so Jonathan paid out of his own pocket. He realised that he'd done something that upset the man but it was more than the stupid comment he'd made. There was something about him that made him hope he'd come back sometime so that he could apologise. How stupid could he be? He never got into conversations with customers but this man was somehow like him but he didn't know how or why.

Dave got into his car feeling very agitated. He didn't understand what had happened. Why had he gone back? Why had he got into a conversation? What was it about the young man that disturbed him? He didn't know but he was sure of one thing, he wasn't going back.

It was Tuesday of the following week when he went back again. The snow had gone with the end of February and there were a few more customers tonight.

Dave was without his crutches but still limping. He saw the young barman and stood at the bar at the point where he was serving.

"Would you like a pint of Carlsberg sir?"

"No, I left the other night without paying, how much?"

Jonathan looked at the pained expression on the man's face and knew then what he had seen the previous time and wondered if he looked like that. "That's Ok I paid. Sorry for embarrassing you. It was meant to be a joke obviously in poor taste. You don't take kindly to jokes at your expense, do you?"

"I don't get jokes. How much do I owe you?"

"Nothing I told you."

"I want to pay."

"Well sorry you can't. Will you beat me up or something for not letting you?"

Dave thought the kid was messing with his head. The young man smiled and asked if he would like a beer. Dave nodded and paid immediately.

Just then a man came up to the bar and asked Dave if the place was a gay bar. Dave told him that you get some.

The man looked him up and down, "Are you a fucking poofter then?"

Before Dave could reply Jonathan said, "That's enough, I think you should leave right now."

"You going to make me then?" he laughed. Jonathan walked around the bar and positioned himself between the man and the bar. In a very deliberate move the man pulled his head right back and aimed a head butt at him. The next thing he knew his head had hit the bar and then his arm was pushed up his back and a hand had grabbed his collar. Jonathan had side-stepped the head butt and used the momentum to connect the head to the surface of the bar. He frogmarched the cretin out of the pub and gave him an almighty shove.

When he came back he said to the gangster, "The guy asked me to apologise for him."

Dave was laughing. "Neat move kid, where did that come from?"

"Judo, I can look after myself but I don't think that would work on you."

"Good then I can pay for that beer"

"Well, you can't."

Jonathan had to serve other customers and when he had a spare minute he went back to Dave. He looked at him long and hard.

"What now kid?"

"You don't sleep much."

Dave shook his head. Then Jonathan said for no reason he understood, "How can I, then, return to happy plight, that am debarred the benefit of rest?"

Dave replied to Jonathan's astonishment. "And it ends –

But day doth daily draw my sorrows longer, and night doth nightly make grief's strength seem stronger. I could recite the whole fucking thing if you want. That surprised you. What do you think I am some sort of Philistine? Good then it works."

"Yes I did."

"You did what?"

"Think you were a little less versed in the works of Shakespeare. Sorry that's so judgemental. You can punch my lights out now."

Dave looked him in the eye and held his gaze. He shook his head, got up and left.

Dave slumped in the back of the car whilst being driven to the casino. His thoughts were jumbled. He wondered why this young man made him feel so uncomfortable and yet at the same time the opposite. It was as if he looked at him and knew his pain. He straightened up and told himself he was being fucking stupid and wouldn't be going back there in a hurry.

He left the casino at three and went straight to bed when he got home. He had the strangest dream. He was in court standing next to a judge and there were thousands of people watching. The judge read out the charges of which there were many. The crowd jeered and booed. The judge said how do you plead? Just then the young barman stood up and said "Not guilty" The crowd evaporated the judge nodded and left and the young barman gave a flashing white smile and disappeared.

Dave woke up but not in a panic. He looked at the clock and it was four thirty. He lay on his back and drifted off. He woke up having heard a noise. It was light. He looked at the clock and was surprised to see it was eleven twenty. He had slept a dreamless sleep for almost seven hours. That hadn't happened since he was a teenager. He felt different.

Jonathan had seen so much pain in the man's eyes and he felt awful. He needed to tell him but tell him what? You can't apologise for someone's pain, he knew this from experience. He'd already said he was sorry for his false assumption. He felt so bad. The next time he comes in he'll keep his mouth shut and just be pleasant, only he didn't come back.

Wednesday of the following week he asked Len who the man on crutches was.

"That's Dave Wilson he's got an office across the road."

"Then he must work late if he comes in here at nine or ten"

"You might say that but until a couple of weeks ago I'd never seen him in here on a weekday. I think the office is his part-time job. When he leaves his office he goes to his casino and stays there until the early hours most days, doesn't sleep much our Dave."

Jonathan asked where the casino was situated and was given the address. It was on the border of Paddington and Bayswater and Jonathan knew more or less where that was.

When all the clearing up was done and it was time to go Jonathan rummaged through his back-pack and found what he was looking for. He set off on his bike.

Dave was sitting in the security room scanning the monitors when one of the bouncers walked in.

"There's a kid outside and he told me to give you this and if I didn't you would tear my head off when you found out." He had a big grin on his face when he handed Dave a Crunchie bar.

"What's this kid look like?"

"Well, scruffy like, black curly hair about six foot and he's on a pushbike."

"I'll come down."

He went outside and saw the young guy sitting on the kerb.

"Trying bribery now are you?"

Jonathan looked up and said "Well it's the only thing that works with riff-raff like you."

Dave smiled a genuine, open smile. "You've got balls kid. Come inside."

"I can't leave my bike, there's nothing to padlock it to."

Dave pointed to the bouncer. "He'll take care of it."

As they were about to enter the bouncer said that Jonathan couldn't go inside dressed like he was, dress code and all that.

Dave looked at him in disgust. "Who sets the fucking dress code? Look after that bike and if anything happens to it, it's out of your wages."

Dave lead the way through a large hall full of gaming machines, the place was crowded, and it was well after midnight. The punters were unseeing of their surroundings, intent only on their tasks of winning small fortunes. They were pouring money into the bottomless pits in hopes of a better tomorrow. There was a steady hum in the palatial hall but it seemed to Jonathan that the sight before him was not of excitement but generally of desperation with an air of sadness.

They entered a small bar at the rear of the hall, which was deserted save the barman.

"What do you want to drink, I owe you one.

Jonathan declined saying he had to bike home.

"Where do you live?"

"Portobello Road."

"Well that's not far, I'll tell you what, you have a beer and I'll get one of the guys to put your bike in the four wheel drive we have parked out back and he can drive you home when you're ready."

"Sounds good, our lecturer is off sick so I don't have to go to Uni tomorrow."

Dave ordered two beers and told the barman to sort out the bike. "You're a real wind -up merchant, you are."

"What do you mean?"

"First you turn down a tip then you embarrass me. Then on top of that you protect me. You quote Shakespeare at me and think I'm less educated than you, as you put it. You wouldn't let me pay for a beer and now you bribe me with a Crunchie bar. When I said you had a dead-end job you didn't say you were a student. All that and I've only met you four times and probably less than an hour in total."

"You didn't ask if I did anything else, like me, you made an assumption."

Dave nodded. "So did you come here to apologise again?"

Jonathan grinned, "No I didn't I just thought I was your hero."

"Why are you really here?"

"It seems that I can't open my mouth without upsetting you, so I thought I'd try and see if I could cheer you up instead and keep you company."

"You're weird."

"So I've been told. I think we're alike in some way, which means you must be weird too. I bet you don't really know much about any of the people around you because it doesn't interest you. I know because I'm like that and something about your faux gangster character tells me you're hiding behind a fake façade, much like I do."

Dave gave him a look of disbelief. "Who the fuck are you, some sort of shaman?"

"No, I'm Jonathan Martinez and I'm afraid my only claim to fame in that area is that my grandmother is a gypsy."

"Well Jonathan Martinez why are you really here?"

"So you're also a disbelieving cynic. I told you why I came, there's no other reason."

Dave felt totally bemused and laughed. "You really are something else. Do you stalk all of your customers?"

"I don't follow anyone. I don't even really talk to anyone much. Apart from the communications I'm obliged to partake in at Uni and of course my mum, you're the only person I've had half a conversation with in almost two years."

"I'm honoured then."

Jonathan took a deep breath and looked Dave directly in the eye. "No, I'm the one that's honoured. Thank you for allowing me to be here."

Dave sighed and Jonathan knew he'd been right.

"You obviously know who I am but just in case, my name is Dave Wilson, I think I might be pleased to meet you Jonathan Martinez." They shook hands.

"Now tell me where do you go to Uni?"

"LSE I'm studying law."

"Well that really is a coincidence, that's where I went."

Jonathan flashed one of his rare brilliant smiles.

"You smile a lot and it's infectious."

"I don't usually, in fact people think I'm too serious but there's something about you that brings it out. You also make me feel stupid, inconsiderate and interested."

Dave didn't comment. They spent the next hour talking about LSE and they had a second beer. At two o'clock Jonathan said he should go.

"OK kid I'll call the car."

"Can you stop doing that please?"

"What?"

"Calling me kid, I'm twenty and I'm not a kid."

"You're right; you're very mature and perceptive even if you are only twenty. Sorry Jonathan I won't do it again. How old do you think I am?"

"Well you look like you're pushing forty. It's the hair and the bags under your eyes that do it but you're thirty two, thirty three."

"How do you know that?"

"From what you told me about LSE it wasn't hard to work out."

"What's wrong with my hair?"

"You have it slicked back like a gangster and it looks old fashioned and makes you look older."

"You're nothing if not fucking honest."

"Did you want me to lie to you?'

"Why not, everybody else does but maybe not. Anyway the image is intact then.'

"I know what that means."

"Is that what you do, hide behind that hair and those scruffy clothes? What are you hiding from?"

"That's a very direct question. Be careful I might ask you the same."

"OK sorry no questions."

"Good at least not personal ones. I do want to ask you something though.'

"Fire away.'

"Do you work at weekends?"

"When I have nothing better to do, yes."

"And I suppose that's most of the time."

Dave shook his head in disbelief yet again. How did this young man seem to know him so well?

"Yes most of the time but I must add by choice."

"I thought so. Can you give yourself Saturday afternoon off?"

Dave wondered where this was going but he wanted to know.

"I suppose so, if I had anything I really wanted to do."

"Can we meet up then and take a walk, get a bite to eat and maybe have a beer?"

Without having to think about it, Dave answered in the affirmative and asked what time.

"I do stuff in the morning but I could make it for say two, is that ok?"

"What do you do in the morning?"

"I play rugby quite early and other stuff."

"You don't look like you'd have the stuff for rugby."

"I'm six feet and pretty buff under the rags."

"I believe you after how you handled that jerk in the pub. You're going to change, so no rags on Saturday?"

"Sorry to disappoint but I change my rags for more rags. I do shave on Friday nights though otherwise I get grief on Saturday from one of the other dance instructors. Is that a problem?"

"No it's not but now I'm intrigued. You're a dance instructor?"

"I've been dancing flamenco for as long as I can remember and I'm pretty good so I help out with teaching kids."

"You dance flamenco? Well you seem to have many talents. You live on Portobello so shall we meet at Notting Hill Gate station, north side?"

"Sure if that's convenient for you."

Dave said that he lived just around the corner from there so it was good for him too.

The bouncer came and told them that the four wheel drive was at the front with the bike inside. Jonathan was chauffeured home.

Dave sat at the bar a little longer and to the surprise of the barman had a third beer. Dave rarely drank at the casino and when he did it was just usually one pint. He asked himself why he felt so good and thought fuck it, don't ask just enjoy it, it wouldn't last long.

He got into bed that night and went straight to sleep. It wasn't exactly a trouble free night but an improvement on most. It must have been the beer.

CHAPTER THIRTY

Jonathan was really busy at the bar on Friday night as usual. He didn't notice Dave come in until he waved his hand in front of his face. Jonathan asked if he wanted a beer. Dave shook his head. Jonathan had a sinking feeling, he'd come to say he couldn't make it the next day. Dave shouted over the noise of the crowd saying he just wanted to check that they were still on. Jonathan's relief prompted a huge grin and he shouted, absolutely.

They met as planned. Dave had booked a table for lunch at the Belvedere in Holland Park but hadn't mentioned it. They crossed the road and started walking west. About a hundred yards on Jonathan stopped and opened the door to a French café.

"I'm starving let's eat."

Dave was just about to object but stopped short. They went in and sat down. They ordered from the menu and to Dave's surprise the food was good. Dave had ordered three items and he ate everything. Jonathan watched him with amusement.

"Wow you were hungry.'

"I have to eat a lot to keep the body shape. I'm always hungry or I think that's what it is."

"What else could it be?"

"Maybe I try to alleviate this constant sinking feeling. By the way the two young waitresses haven't taken their eyes off you since we came in."

Jonathan shrugged. "Why would they look at me, have I got something on my face?"

"They're looking at you because you are extremely handsome now the stubble has gone."

"But you saw through the stubble." Jonathan laughed.

"You must get this all the time so you must have dozens of girlfriends."

"You don't listen very well do you? I don't have friends of either sex and if as you say I'm good looking then it's of no consequence to me. Do you know that this is the first time in my life I've ever had a meal out with just one person who wasn't my mum or dad?"

"You have a gift and you choose not to use it, why?"

"I did once I suppose but that ended in disaster, so what's the point. The real gift I have is my brain. I want to be known for what I do not how I look."

Dave smiled.

"Jonathan this was a good choice. Now let me get the bill."

"I'm paying. I asked you and please don't give me the poor student bit. I'm not poor ok, I just look it."

Dave thanked him and admitted to another misconception. They left the restaurant and walked down the hill to Holland Park Avenue.

Dave asked if Jonathan had to be anywhere that evening. Jonathan told him that he usually had dinner with his mum on Saturdays as it was the only time that they were home at the same time but his mum begged off tonight as she was going to see a show with her sister, so he had no commitments.

"Good, so I thought we could take a walk, grab a beer or two and maybe you'll let me return the compliment and buy you dinner later."

"Sounds good."

They walked along the avenue and turned off at Holland Walk, up the steep hill, pass the school and into the park. Jonathan had only walked through the park before with Gabriella and hadn't really been aware of his surroundings. He was amazed at what he'd missed. They walked down one hill and up another and it was almost like being in the countryside. They sat for a while in the Japanese garden and then had coffee in the little park café.

Time passed so quickly that they were both surprised when it started to get dark. It was early March and the light was fading fast at six o'clock.

Dave suggested they walk along High Street Ken and see what was on offer. They found an Indian restaurant and both plumped for a hearty curry washed down with Kingfisher beer. Dave ordered a double potion for himself and ate with gusto.

It was cold when they left so they walked briskly through the side streets back towards Holland Park Avenue and stopped at the Winsor Castle. They found a seat in the garden under a heater. Jonathan had seen the pub many times before as it was very close to where Gabriella had lived. He had avoided that neighbourhood since that fateful night but felt no discomfort being there now.

"Dave, will you be playing football tomorrow morning?"

"No the doctor told me I shouldn't for the rest of the season. Anyway football is Saturday morning not Sunday."

"What will you do tomorrow then, go to the casino?

"I'll do what I normally do, go to mass, take a long walk and then go to the casino."

"I thought the age of reason dismissed god as a myth two hundred years ago."

"That was also a book by Satre which I never enjoyed."

"I'm in the presence of an intellectual who dares to criticise a fantastic book."

"I didn't say it wasn't good I just said I didn't enjoy it."

"I really liked it. So you didn't read the other two then."

"I did but I didn't like them much either. I prefer a good who dunnit, not intellectual ramblings dressed up as stories."

"Wow that's the first thing we've disagreed about, what other dark dislikes do you have?"

"Manchester United.'

"Me too, and it looks like they're about to win the title yet again and my team's going down. How we resent success in football when it's not ours."

"You're right, who's your team?"

"QPR says it all doesn't it."

Dave laughed and changed the subject. He asked Jonathan what sort of books he read.

"Only law books, I'm not really interested in other people's stories or theories anymore."

"Why's that? Something in your past I guess."

Jonathan shrugged.

"Fuck the past young Jonathan let's not spoil a good conversation."

"Agreed, what time do you go to mass?"

"When I can I go to eleven o'clock at Brompton Oratory."

"There are churches closer so why there and then?"

"They have sung Latin mass and I find it soothing."

"Can I come?'

Dave looked surprised and asked if being an atheist didn't preclude him from such rituals, unless he was a catholic.

"My mother's name is Mary and my family name is Martinez, so of course I'm a catholic. I'm a catholic atheist."

Dave asked him why he would want to go to mass if he didn't believe.

"For the music, I heard from a good friend that it's pretty good and that good friend is going. Good enough reason?"

Dave looked surprised but didn't reply.

Jonathan waited for a reply but it didn't come so he asked what the matter was.

"You said I was your friend."

"Was that presumptuous? I've never had a proper friend but I feel like this is what it must feel like, sorry."

Dave was about to tell him to back off but when he opened his mouth something else came out.

"I hardly know you."

"I've insulted you three times and we're still talking so that says something. It's really easy to talk to you. We've been talking for hours and it's been great and natural. That's never happened to me before, at least not with a guy. What more do you need?"

Dave chuckled, took a deep breath and said "I like the idea of you being my friend we seem to be on the same wave length, a pair of weirdoes."

"Good then I can come."

"Yes you can and you can consider yourself fortunate or not to be my only friend."

They raised their glasses to being each other's only friend and talked some more. They left the pub at closing time and swapped mobile numbers and arranged to meet at the same place at ten o'clock the next morning. When they reached the bottom of the hill they went their separate ways.

Dave strolled home slowly, feeling better than he had since he was a teenager. He'd had the kind of day which most normal people experience but for him it was exceptional. Jonathan had seemed so easy to be with and non-intrusive, he had just enjoyed his company. What was it about him, he seemed like a genuinely good person and Dave wasn't going to be his usual cynical self and spoil his own day.

That night he slept a peaceful dreamless sleep without waking once. That was the first time in fourteen years.

Jonathan arrived home to find his mother still up. He asked her if she'd had a good time.

"Lovely, I just love the theatre and the play was great. What's up with you, you look like the cat that got the cream."

"Nothing's up, I just had a surprisingly good day."

"Let's hope it lasts son."

"I think it will mum, I think it will."

He went to bed contented, like his mother had said, the cat that got the cream.

Dave woke up and stretched. He lay in bed for a few minutes wondering if he should go back to sleep. He decided against it. He got up and opened the curtains. It was raining outside and that was why it had still been dark in his room. He walked to his shower room and glanced at his bedside clock on the way. It was ten fifteen. Oh fuck, how did that happen, he was supposed to meet Jonathan at ten. He picked up his phone and punched in the number.

Jonathan arrived fifteen minutes early at nine forty five at Notting Hill Gate station. He'd been caught in the rain and was very wet and cold. Ten o'clock came and went with no sign of Dave. He was starting to feel anxious when his phone rang. Dave explained what had happened and apologised. He said he'd throw on some clothes and be there in fifteen minutes. They could get a taxi so they wouldn't be late for mass. Dave could hear a sense of amusement in Jonathan's voice when he replied. "Mr Perfect is going to throw on some clothes. I wouldn't want to damage your image. Look I got up early this morning to finish an assignment but I still have some stuff to do and I'm also a bit wet so I'll go home and dry off and work on my paper. I'll call you when I'm done and if you're free I'll buy you dinner. In the meantime you chill out and enjoy it."

"You're not pissed off with me?"

"Not at all, I'll call you later, OK?"

Dave went down to the kitchen and made himself a very large breakfast and read the newspaper from cover to cover.

At four o'clock his phone rang.

Dave suggested they meet at Jamie's in half an hour. He didn't want to be late again so he arrived in good time. As he was browsing around the cook books he felt a tap on his shoulder. They exchanged greetings and decided as it was a bit early to eat and it was still raining they'd go a watch a movie.

They crossed the road to the Gate Cinema which was showing an independent British film.

Two and a half hours later they emerged and the rain had abated. Dave asked if Jonathan had enjoyed the film. Jonathan bit his bottom lip and said he hadn't been to the cinema for a few years and would probably wait another few years before he went again. Dave laughed and said it was the biggest load of crap he'd seen in a long time. Jonathan nodded in agreement with a big smile on his face.

"It was a load of shit but that's OK. Let's go and eat. I would like some comfort food so let's go to Pizza Express."

Whilst eating, Dave apologised again for being late and for the lousy movie. Jonathan asked him if he always felt responsible for what fate sent.

Dave mumbled through a bite of pizza that he did when it was his fault.

Jonathan leaned back in his chair. "You overslept this morning and normally you hardly sleep, that's amazing. We, not you, chose a bad movie. So do I have to apologise for keeping you up late last night and my part in choosing the movie?"

"You weren't upset when I didn't turn up?"

"I was getting a bit anxious but when you called I was fine. I'm glad you slept well."

Dave looked across the table and saw a young man with longish black curly hair, two days stubble and lacking any sartorial elegance. His big brown eyes almost twinkled with what looked like happiness. He could be a fucking angel. He shook himself and asked what time Jonathan had to get up in the morning. As that had to be seven thirty and it was now nine he suggested they head home. Dave said he'd drop by the pub in the week and they parted company.

It was Thursday before Dave dropped by the pub. He'd have done it every day but didn't want to seem too enthusiastic. The pub was crowded so when they could they snatched a few words. Dave asked if Jonathan had plans for the weekend and had to hide his disappointment but Jonathan said he had to study as he had exams the following week so he also wouldn't be working at the pub the following week. Dave asked him to call when he was done and maybe they could meet the following weekend.

Dave spent the weekend at the Casino and missed mass. On the Monday of that week he received a very disturbing phone call and on the Thursday he had an even more disturbing meeting. He worked extra hours that week trying to fill his time and his mind. He'd enjoyed his time the previous weekend and had looked forward to a repeat but now he felt that the interest had been more on his side. He knew it was stupid but he felt disappointed and now his thoughts were on something equally disappointing.

Jonathan didn't find the exams much of a stretch. As usual he'd prepared well and it paid off. On Friday he finished Uni at twelve. Before he left for home he called Dave and asked him if he had any spare time and could they meet for lunch. Dave suggested The Flag in fifteen minutes.

When Jonathan arrived Dave was sitting by himself at a table with a pint of beer. Jonathan wheeled his bike in and parked it in the rear, got himself a glass of water and joined Dave. He sat down smiled a huge smile. Dave nodded in response but looked agitated. He obviously hadn't been sleeping well again.

Neither of them spoke for a while until Jonathan asked, "What's happened? You don't look too good; you're not sleeping well are you?"

Dave said Sunday had been a one off half laughing through very sad looking eyes.

"Dave what's happened?"

"I don't really want to talk about it right now."

"Then why am I here?"

"I don't know. I suppose I just needed company. Go if you're busy."

"Are you?'

"Am I what?"

"Busy or can we go somewhere else. I'm free now until Monday. My mum's going to Spain tomorrow and I've got no studying to do absolutely no commitments."

Dave looked up at the ceiling and said. 'I'd like to get as far away from here as possible. I'm busy but fuck it, I'm sick of it."

"Great, not that you're sick of it, great you're free. I'm going home to pack a bag for two nights. You do the same and I'll meet you at Notting Hill Gate station at three o'clock."

"Hold on, hold on. Where were you planning to go and what makes you think I want to go with you?"

That big grin spread across Jonathan's face again. "We're going to Brighton for the weekend and that will take you far away, as you wanted and I'll be with you to distract you from whatever crap is upsetting you."

"You're too much, you know that?"

"No I'm not but you're a bit dim sometimes. You said what you wanted so let's do it. It'll be great. Well are you going home to pack now or when you've finished your beer?"

Dave smiled and shook his head. "Looks like you've made my mind up for me. One condition though. We won't go by train, we'll drive. What's your address? I'll pick you up at two thirty, that way we'll miss the rush hour traffic in Brighton. Is that OK?"

"More than ok."

"Wrap up well though, it might be a bit cold on the way."

CHAPTER THIRTY ONE

Jonathan was standing outside his flats with his bag when Dave drove up in an open top Morgan. Jonathan threw his bag in the back and got in.

"Wow what a nice car, no wonder you said to wrap up well. I thought you had a Merc?"

"I do but I've had this since school days. Dad bought it for my seventeenth birthday. I think the insurance cost more than the car. It's a sunny day and quite warm so hold tight."

It was one of those beautiful spring days when the blue sky and bright sunshine masked the chill in the air. They took the M4 and the M25, which was moving smoothly at that time of day. It took just over an hour before they joined the M23 and a straight run into Brighton.

The rushing air made it difficult to hold a conversation until they slowed at a junction. Dave suggested they try the Grand Hotel but Jonathan told him he'd booked on line at Premier Inn. Cheap and cheerful and he'd already paid. They wouldn't be spending much time in their rooms so they only needed a bed and a shower and the pictures on the website looked fine.

Dave had no objections but as Jonathan had paid for the rooms the rest of the expense was on him.

They reached the hotel just after five, dumped their bags in their respective rooms and met in the lobby ten minutes later.

It was still light and although breezy they went for a walk along the sea front. They walked east, admiring the regency architecture that made Brighton special, until they reached Black Rock where they found a taxi to take them to the Marina. There they found a nice looking Italian restaurant where they were given a table without hesitation as it was still relatively early for the dinner crowd.

They ordered their food, a beer each to be followed by a good bottle of Barolo. They decided on antipasti to share and cannelloni for main course. Jonathan put down his menu and bit his lip trying not to smile. Dave asked what the joke was and Jonathan pointed out that as Dave had skipped lunch he might want to order something extra for himself. Dave got the joke but it didn't deter him from ordering a large, rare steak with chips and assorted vegetables. Jonathan said he'd help with the vegetables and he couldn't hold back his smile any longer.

As they drank their beer awaiting their food Jonathan said "Ok let's get this over with so that you can enjoy your weekend. Now let me see if I can guess what's bothering you. It's not family because you don't have parents and you don't really talk about your sister so it's probably nothing to do with her. Your best and only friend is in rude health and as far as he knows has done nothing to upset you. Therefore it must be your first love."

"Ok smart arse, what's my first love?"

"Your work of course, it fills most of your waking day and you love it. "Now let me think, it can't be that you have financial problems because you're far too astute to let that happen and if it was a robbery or anything like that, you'd sort it out without too much fuss. Now I'm lost what could it be?"

"Well Mr Detective you're right so far. I got a call on Monday from a big, American company that owns casinos and other gaming businesses around the world but not in UK. They're interested in buying us out. I said I wasn't interested but they asked me check with my board before declining what they said would be a very generous offer. I didn't do that but I did meet with them on Thursday and they gave me a number which whilst it seemed a lot wasn't anywhere near what the business is worth, so I told them to get lost. That's always the way when negotiating take-overs. They ask me to come up with a number but I don't want to do that."

Jonathan understood why Dave wouldn't want to sell his business but didn't understand why he couldn't just say no.

"I don't own the whole company. I have a fifty per cent share. My step mother and sister own a quarter each so I'll have to inform them and I know what they will want to do. They have no interest in the running of the business and when faced with the prospects of millions of pounds in cash, they'll jump at it. My dad spent his whole life building the business and that should mean something but those two wouldn't understand loyalty.'

"So what will you do?"

"I have a good handle on what the business is worth so I'll ask for more and see if I can frighten them off before having to tell my partners."

"That must be tough given how much you've put into it as well. About how much do you think its worth?"

"The business itself is worth about a hundred million but we also have a lot of assets in the form of property so all in all I'd say one forty to one sixty."

"Bloody hell, half of that is yours so you're almost as rich as me."

"I could never be as rich as you Jonathan you have stuff money can't buy."

"What would you do if you had to sell?"

"It doesn't bear thinking about."

"You'd make a great fireman."

"Well that's my future sorted then."

Dinner was good and Dave mellowed the more with each sip of wine. They finished the bottle before the food so they ordered a second. At eight thirty they settled their bill and asked the waiter to call them a taxi.

They went back to the town centre and wandered around for a while then found a pub where they planned to drink a cleansing ale. The one turned into three and the conversation flowed as freely as the beer. They left just before eleven and walked back to the hotel.

Jonathan declared that he wasn't used to drinking so much but he was feeling fine at that moment but wasn't sure how he'd feel in the morning. Dave took out his phone and keyed something in.

"Well you might feel a little out of it in the morning but I know the perfect cure. Tomorrow is going to be another sunny day and warmer than today so let's go for breakfast at say eight. I'll knock on your door in case you're tempted to sleep in."

"Yes sir" and they parted company.

Dave undressed and got into bed and fell asleep, the sleep of the righteous. Jonathan did the same but his wasn't sleep, it was unconsciousness.

Dave knocked on Jonathan's door at precisely eight. Jonathan answered almost immediately, dressed and ready to go. They had breakfast, Dave eating enough to keep him going until lunch time and Jonathan plumping for just coffee.

They went down to the garage and retrieved the Morgan and headed north along Dyke Road. They reached an open countryside area and after about ten minutes drew up into a pub's car park. They were on the top of the South Downs looking out across East Sussex. It was a clear morning and the view was pleasing even if one party was feeling a little fragile.

Dave gave his friend some encouragement and promised he'd feel better soon. He led the way to a path that was signposted to the Devil's Dyke. They walked along a path for about fifteen minutes and stopped at the top of the Dyke. They sat and looked down into a very large valley that seemed to come to a sudden halt just below where they were sitting.

The sun felt warm, the sky was as blue as a summer's day and the air was still. They sat for a while not talking until Jonathan broke the silence.

"It looks like nature never finished her work."

"How are you feeling, you're looking a bit better."

"I'm feeling better but please don't suggest we walk to the bottom, you might have to carry me back up."

"I was going to but this will do. Nature didn't make that big chasm it was made by the devil. One dark night he decided he would flood the land by digging a gulley right down to the sea. There was an old lady who lived up here and she was woken by the noise. When she saw what the devil was doing, she lit a lamp bright enough for him to see below. He thought it was the sun rising and he ran away not finishing his planned destruction. That's why it looks like this."

"Nice story but I'm still not walking to the bottom."

They sat quietly looking at the scene below. There were sheep grazing on the slopes and some walkers exploring the devil's work.

After about ten minutes of mostly silence Jonathan started to talk, still looking out at the view.

"I told you I've never really had a friend but that's not really true. I was in love once with the most beautiful girl I'd ever seen." Dave turned to look at the giver of news but didn't say anything. Jonathan continued and told the whole story of Gabriella.

When he had finished they were silent again until Dave asked if he still loved her.

Jonathan looked extremely sad and Dave wished he hadn't asked.

"Yes I do and always will but I know well enough that she's never coming back. If she did it would probably never be the same but I think we should hold on to the good memories we have and dump the crap. I don't want to forget what we had. That's why I took the job in the pub. If you remember I told you that the job was mindless. That's what I wanted. I didn't want to shut her out, have her memory slip away through my immersing myself solely into my studies. It's funny though, the emptiness I was feeling slowly started to disappear and as much as I tried to bring her into my thoughts, it all started to fade. I suppose that's what happens with time. I don't know if you'd understand that?"

Dave looked down at the grass between his feet and mumbled something.

"Sorry what did you say?"

Dave took a deep breath. "I said I've never felt love."

Jonathan didn't reply he was lost in his thoughts. They sat in silence for another ten minutes then Jonathan stood up. Dave was seeing pictures in his mind of a desperately sad Jonathan wandering the streets of Madrid and it made him sad too just thinking about it. What must this poor boy have been feeling?

"Come on my oversized friend needs feeding and it must be lunch time. Sorry if I bored you but I wanted you to know. I've never told the whole story to anyone."

"Then I'm honoured, thank you. You're right it's time to go and we have time to eat before our next port of call."

They walked back to the pub and had a non-alcoholic lunch after which they set off to the A23 back towards Brighton. After a short while they turned off to the left and drove up a hill. When they reached their destination they found a space in a very busy car park. It only then dawned on Jonathan that they were at a race course.

"Ever been to the races?"

Jonathan said he hadn't and he seemed to brighten up.

"Isn't this a bit like coals to Newcastle?"

"I'm usually on the other side and I know only too well that the bookies always win but who cares. Let's go and pick some winners."

To his surprise Jonathan found the experience exhilarating especially when one of his horses won. He found himself jumping up and down encouraging his horse to go faster.

Dave didn't have any luck but the one winner they had was long odds and it almost covered their losses.

They returned to the hotel where they showered and changed. Dave remarked that Jonathan looked half way decent, no hoodie and he'd shaved. They wandered the lanes and then made their way back to the sea front and the Grand Hotel.

"Jonathan I think we should have booked. The restaurant here is pretty popular especially at weekends."

Jonathan half closed his eyes pressed his lips together in a superior way and assured Dave they wouldn't turn them away. Dave followed him into the hotel and to the restaurant and soon discovered that they had a reservation.

"Pig you didn't tell me. This place has a good reputation even though it's expensive."

"It's expensive for most people and it's going to cost us an arm and a leg with the quantities that you eat. What do I care, you're paying."

With that they both started to laugh and the evening continued in a light enjoyable vein.

As they were leaving Dave said he needed a leek so Jonathan said he'd wait across the road so that he could get some fresh air.

The wind had started to blow and the sky was starless and black. Jonathan listened with fascination as the waves rolled in and retreated with a roar like a Wembley crowd. The pebbles slip across each other in swathes making a tremendous noise. He didn't hear the menacing looking man approach him from behind until a voice told him to turn around and empty his pockets. He obeyed the first part of the command and told the mugger that his pockets were empty. The mugger waved his knife in front of Jonathans face.

"Give me your fucking money."

Jonathan stayed calm and told the mugger he should leave before he got hurt and he said it with a big smile on his face. He looked over the muggers shoulder and said, "This nice man is keeping me company while I wait for you."

The mugger swung around and saw a very large muscular man who said, "Fuck off sonny before you get badly damaged."

The mugger waved his knife at Dave who also smiled which was now making him extremely nervous but he stood his ground.

"You can empty your pockets too. Even big gits like you bleed."

Dave sighed. "Jonathan take that knife off him please."

Before the mugger could turn back to his original victim, Jonathan landed an almighty kick to the back of his knees. The mugger crumbled and Jonathan calmly picked up the knife which had dropped at his feet. Dave put a foot on the would-be thief's chest.

"I weigh seventeen stone and if I put both my feet on you and bounce up and down I'll be able to hear your ribs crack and I tell you that really hurts. Now before you stand up empty your pockets."

The mugger struggled to do as he was told and Dave let him stand up and then checked he had nothing else on him. Dave opened the wallet he'd been given.

"Oh I'm Dave as well and you live on Race Hill road. Funny we were up there today. You'll probably be hearing from the Old Bill but in the meantime fuck off and behave yourself."

They let the guy leave, which he did in a hurry, and crossed back to the Grand Hotel. They gave their stash to the concierge and told him what had happened. They explained that they didn't have time to go to the police station but left their names and addresses, never to hear of the matter again.

They left Brighton at 10.30 on a grey wet Sunday morning. They put the roof up on the Morgan and had a clear run back into London. It was two o'clock when Jonathan was dropped off at his flats.

Dave parked his car and walked in the rain back to his home. He had lunch and read the Sunday paper. At about five thirty he went to mass at St Francis. When he got home he checked his phone, which he'd left on the kitchen table and noticed he had a missed call from Jonathan which made him smile. He called back immediately.

"You called, what's up?"

"I was wondering if you were still in a good mood.'

"I am. I just went to mass and I'm feeling blessed, why?"

"A real Holy Joe aren't you. Anyway that's good and there again that might not be so good."

"Stop talking in riddles."

"Well if you'd slipped into a glum mood I'd have an excuse to see you and cheer you up and all that."

"Is that what you do, feel sorry for me?"

"No I don't feel one bit sorry for you but I don't like to think of you being one bit miserable. You see it's for me, selfish uh?"

"Ok then young Jonathan, you might be surprised to know that I'm hungry and I can't be bothered to heat something up from the freezer, so will you join me for dinner? I'm inviting so I'm paying."

Over dinner Jonathan thanked Dave for having listened to him prattle on about his broken heart. Dave in turn said he was welcome to bend his ear anytime he liked but there was something he wanted to ask him about it.

"That must have been really hard but you don't seem to be carrying around a lot of baggage. How do you do that?"

"I was in shock at first and my mum even sent me to a psychologist because she was worried. When I got over the initial shock, as I told you, I filled my time and as it turned out it really helped. So I'm left with memories of having a great time with someone I loved very much that came to an abrupt end. As Tennyson put it:

> I had it true whate'er befall;
> I feel it when I sorrow most
> 'Tis better to have loved and lost
> Than never to have loved at all.

I suppose the other side of that is the old maxim, what you've never had you'll never miss.

"Mum still worries about me because I don't have friends and when I go out it's only to classes or the library. She forgets that was what I was like before I met Gabriella and up until now thought no one would ever interest me again."

"You're very secure in yourself. That must be a great feeling but what did you mean up until now?"

"This is going to sound soft but I don't know how else to put it. When I first met you I was kind of disturbed. There was something about you that was like me. I didn't know what it was then but now I know I was right. I must have a huge ego because I like you because you're like me. You're the only person, other than my dad, whose company I've ever enjoyed for that reason and that reason only, if you get what I mean."

"A bit convoluted but I know what you mean and I really enjoy your company too, so cheers to that" he said raising his glass.

"When are you going to tell your sister and step mother about the offer?"

"I was going to wait until after I give a price to the Americans because if I do have to sell then at least we'll get a fair price. If I told them now, they might jump at the first offer as that was still a large sum of money. I'll do some work on the PE ratios, asset values and the rest this week so I be prepared when they come back."

"Do you really think they will make you sell?"

"Absolutely so I have to save them from themselves. It doesn't seem so bad now, especially as I now know my next career move. I quite fancy being a fireman."

CHAPTER THIRTY TWO

March slipped into a traditionally wet April. The friends had settled into an easy routine. Dave would go to the pub a couple of times a week and they would spend most of the weekend doing something together. Neither of them minded when the other had something that took priority such as business meetings or studies. The relationship was set fair.

During this period Jonathan, with the help of a fellow student, researched Dave's past. What he discovered answered a lot of questions but he wasn't going to tell Dave. He thought it better that he told him, himself, when he was ready as having gained the knowledge left him feeling guilty. It now seemed wrong somehow to have pried into his friend's personal life. He kept mum.

It was the last weekend in April and Jonathan had an exceptional amount of studying set before Monday. They were only able to meet for a couple of beers on Saturday night.

Dave would have liked to spend some time on Sunday with his friend but didn't like to make that seem like an obligation on Jonathan's part. An idea struck him and he went for it.

"I know you have to study tomorrow and I was wondering if you'd like to bring your books round to my place and do it. I wouldn't disturb you other than to offer refreshments and it's about time you saw where I live."

Without hesitation Jonathan said he thought it was a great idea and asked what time he should be there. Dave suggested the earlier the better, then he could cook him breakfast and then read the Sunday paper whilst he studied. As they were both normally early risers they settled on eight o'clock.

At eight sharp the doorbell rang and Dave opened the front door to see Jonathan who was carrying what looked like two very heavy back packs full of books and a laptop bag.

Dave lightened his load and apologised for not thinking to collect him in his car but Jonathan grinned and pointed out that he wasn't a ten stone weakling.

Inside the main front door were two other sturdy looking ones. They took the one to the left as the one in front of them was to the upstairs flat which was vacant. They were now in the small hallway and Dave hung Jonathan's coat on the hall coat stand and led the way down to the lower floor which was obviously the living area as through open doors could be seen a lounge and a kitchen. They entered the kitchen which was also a dining room separated by a serving counter. To Jonathan's mind the area was huge.

Above the kitchen sink was a window that looked out onto the small front area and the street beyond, which was just about at eye level.

"Are you going to show me around?"

"Not until you've finished studying. That's why you're here, remember. I always use the dining room table when I have work stuff to do but there's a small office at the back if you prefer."

"I do all my studying at the kitchen table so this will do just fine" and he emptied his bags onto one end of the table which was big enough to seat at least twelve people. He wondered why Dave would have such a piece of furniture given that he lived alone and had no friends and little family so he asked.

Dave gave a little laugh and said he lived in hopes. The truth was the room was so large anything smaller would look lost. He'd been at an auction with his father where he found it, end of story.

Jonathan set about his studies and Dave cooked breakfast which they ate on a small round table in the kitchen area. Dave ate lots and continued his morning feast long after Jonathan had returned to his books. He then parked himself at the other end of the dining room table and read the paper.

At about ten thirty, Dave stood up as about to leave. Jonathan asked him if he was going to mass but no he was going to have a shower and change.

He was gone for an hour and returned looking fresh and spruce.

"I know you're big but an hour to shower?"

"I pushed some weights for a while first, I have to keep in shape otherwise it'll all turn to fat. Now get back to your books. I'll make coffee."

Jonathan obeyed and immersed himself once again in the law of the land. Dave brought the coffee and sat down to tackle the crossword. Apart from his somewhat remote family, he'd never invited anyone and it felt very natural and comfortable sharing the table with his friend.

At one Dave conjured up sandwiches and more coffee and sat down to read a book. After a while he told Jonathan that there was prepared food in the freezer and gave him options. His house keeper, Mrs Hayes always cooked extra meals on Fridays in case Dave wanted to eat in, so there was plenty to choose from. He also suggested that they could eat out. Jonathan looked out of the window and saw that it was raining heavily so they agreed staying in made more sense and settled on Lasagne which was extracted from the icebox and placed in the microwave to defrost.

Wine was chosen from a glass fronted wine storage unit, something light was in order so a bottle of Frascati fit the bill which was put in the fridge to cool.

Jonathan closed his books and stowed them into his back packs.

"I'm done, now can I have the guided tour."

At the rear of the lower ground floor was a large lounge with French windows that opened onto a small garden. Beyond the garden there was a gate leading to the large communal garden which was for residents only. It was too wet to explore so they continued indoors. There was a large open fireplace and the lounge was tastefully decorated and the furniture was traditional rather than modern. The room had a friendly comfortable feel to it. On the same level, there was a utility room and a windowless office cum library with bookshelves covering one wall.

The upstairs consisted of three rooms. One had a bed with a bare mattress so it was obviously a guest room. Then there was a bathroom. The second room had been converted into a gym. There were weights, a bench, an exercise bike and a treadmill. There was also a free standing punch bag which looked as if it had taken many a beating. Jonathan asked if that was where Dave loosed his frustrations and got a slight nod in response.

The third room was the biggest, and obviously Dave's bedroom, which overlooked the garden. Everything was white except a series of brightly coloured abstract paintings that hung on the walls to maximum effect. There were two other doors in this room and Jonathan discovered behind one was a standard bathroom and the second held a very large shower room. There was a huge shower head attached to the ceiling and three shower jets either side.

"Wow this is neat."

"It's my monsoon shower. It used to be a small fourth bedroom and I had a door knocked through and closed the entrance in the hallway."

"Why so many shower heads?"

"It feels great and it makes me feel clean" and then almost under his breath "at least for a while."

Jonathan heard and had a good idea what he meant. All of a sudden he felt very guilty, a rare emotion for him.

"Are you a neat freak? You've made your bed and everything is so tidy. In fact the whole house is just like you, neat and perfect. You're not OCD are you?"

"You're very insulting you know. Nobody talks to me like that."

"Only me, right? If I heard anyone talking to you like that they'd get their heads kicked in" he paused "by you of course."

A wicked grin appeared on his face.

"Now I'm really going to upset you."

He jumped onto the bed and pulled the duvet over himself.

"This is so amazingly comfortable, goodnight."

Dave left the room with a big intake of breath. Jonathan chuckled to himself, got up and straightened the bed. He found Dave in the kitchen making tea.

"You really meant it when you said you like detective novels. There a loads on your book shelves. You've also got a thing about antiques and of course business. You have some very interesting history books and even a collection of classical novels, some of which look very old."

"How can you have seen that? You were only in the office for half a minute."

"Easily Mr OCD you have everything in neat sections so one glance would tell anyone what you have in there. I'd like to look at your history books sometime. I love ancient history and I spend hours in the British Library thumbing through their wonders. I know I said I only read law books but I do have other interests you know, or used to. I love that place and I also sometimes go to the British museum and sit among the ancient Greeks. That's where I first saw you. I remembered after I told you that you could be a Greek god. There's a statue of Poseidon that would look just like you if you had long hair and a curly beard. Heaven forbid that our Dave would entertain such a thing. I've also read some philosophy, hence Satre, who is not your favourite."

"Apart from those things you also like Elizabethan plays and treasures of the world."

"Oh fuck have I told you this before, I'm repeating myself. I must have run out of things to say or are you a mind reader Mr Dave?"

"You said we were alike, well in one respect you're right. Forget philosophy but I also used to spend my spare time as you do in the British Library and if ever I have an hour or two spare I still do. I also find treasures in the same reading rooms that you explore, that's how I guessed the rest."

Jonathan's big smile broke out as if he'd just received a long wanted present. Dave laughed.

Over dinner they spoke enthusiastically about their discoveries in the halls of information and mysteries and didn't notice the time slip away. It was after midnight when Jonathan stood up to leave. Dave said he couldn't let him carry those heavy bags all the way home in the rain so he told him to wait whilst he went to fetch his car. Jonathan was standing under the front door when Dave pulled up minutes later in his very plush Merc.

On the Tuesday of that week Dave had an appointment to see his psychiatrist. When he walked into the consulting room Dr Marks smiled at him.

"Well something's happened. Tell me Dave has a miracle occurred?"

Dave told him about Jonathan, how they met and how the relationship had developed.

"What's Jonathan like, what's his background?"

Dave told him as best he could but he realised there were still gaps in his knowledge which disturbed him.

"Why do you think this young man is interested in you? What does he want?"

Dave felt relieved and he told the doctor what Jonathan had said when he had asked the same question.

"We really are alike in many ways. It almost like he's known me for years. Also he has a great way of seeing things, nothing is complicated there always seems to be a simple answer even if it sounds flippant some times.

"When I told him that I might have to sell the company, he asked what I would do after. When I said I didn't know he said without hesitation that I'd make a great fireman. I knew he didn't mean that but what he did mean was there were many options I could explore and it opened up my mind. I do have dreams beyond owning a gaming company and he made me realise that with a simple statement. I don't know how he does it but he makes me see things differently without giving advice just by simple statements."

Dr Marks raised his eyebrows.

"It seems that this young man talks to you on two levels. It sounds like you've opened up your unconscious mind to him. You've been seeing me for years and this person comes along and effortlessly does what I haven't been able to do. I know that there are people in the world that have a natural way of connecting but I've never met anyone like that. You might want to be careful. He could manipulate you."

Dave laughed. "Dr Marks there isn't a bad thought in Jonathan's head for anyone. If he wanted to manipulate me I'd let him because it would only mean I'd become a better person."

"Then you should tell him what you need to tell, as you put it, a real person who could understand and forgive you."

"I will but not yet. I will."

CHAPTER THIRTY THREE

Jonathan cycled home as soon as his lecture was finished. It was the first of May and Mary was due back from Spain. She was in her room unpacking when he arrived so he made her tea. Mary slumped into a chair at the kitchen table after giving her son a quick hug. She looked tired and something else that he couldn't quite put his finger on. Mary was hard to read. She was very good at keeping her emotions in check.

He asked if she had a good time and told her she had a nice tan. She lied by saying she had because there were things she wasn't ready to tell him. She took a deep breath then looked him up and down and asked if he had been taking good care of himself.

"Well you haven't lost weight through starvation which is good to see and you're not looking down in the dumps. Do you have a new girlfriend?"

"No but I do have a friend."

Mary was visibly taken aback. Apart from Gabriella, whom he never called a friend, Jonathan had been a loner. After she let the thought settle she enquired about the friend.

Jonathan gave a quick précis of Dave and described how they met, leaving out the conflicts. He told her about how similar they were, how Dave had gone to LSE and how they had lots of interests in common."

"I never thought I'd see the day when you said you had a friend. About your age is he?"

"No he's a bit older, 32."

"You never did have much time for people of your own age but what's his interest in you?"

"For the same reasons I'm interested in him. We're alike in so many ways yet different in others. When we got talking it was just easy and natural. I don't have to think of things to say and nor does he. We're interested in different things, he's finance and me law, but he listens to me and he's interested in what

158

I'm learning and he tells me about what he does and it's fascinating. I've even been going places with him, wonder upon wonder."

"Well if it gets you out and about then that has to be good. I'm glad to see that passive look disappear. Do you know you almost look happy?"

Life at home settled back into the old routine with the exception of Jonathan's sometimes absences, which were hardly noticeable as Jonathan was rarely at home anyway.

May was a much better month altogether. The rain was intermittent and there were some glorious days when the sun shone out of clear blue skies and the air was spring fresh.

It was on such a day that Jonathan finally got to go to mass with Dave to Brompton Oratory. On the way Jonathan was very chirpy and he told Dave he had a great idea and they could talk about it over lunch. After mass they walked east along Brompton Road and stopped at a small restaurant opposite Harrods. Jonathan's mood had changed radically he was very quiet and Dave didn't want to ask why. They ate in almost silence until it was too much for Dave.

"Is there something wrong, has something upset you?"

Jonathan sighed, "Yes and no. I see what you mean when you said the music and singing are soothing. It was also very moving. When you were praying after communion you were saying a prayer over and over like a mantra but I've never heard it before."

"I didn't realise I was saying it aloud. It's an ancient non-sectarian Indian prayer. It seems to encapsulate everything one could wish for in just a few words."

"I didn't catch it all, how does it go?"

"It goes

From the unreal lead me to the real
From the darkness lead me to the light
From death lead me to immortality.

That's it and for me it says everything. My interpretation of immortality isn't living forever it's just being good enough to be remembered in some people's hearts. It might sound daft but I find it comforting."

Jonathan fell back into silence. When they had finished their coffee he looked very agitated.

"Too much caffeine?"

"Dave can we go somewhere quiet to talk, there's something I need to tell you?"

"That sounds like a good idea because there's something I need to tell you too." Dave had decided to tell Jonathan everything even if it meant never seeing him again. At least the unreal would then be real.

They walked through Kensington Gardens but it was very crowded. There wasn't an empty bench or a patch of grass where sun worshippers weren't sprawled out or there were ball games in progress. They headed towards Holland Park and found a quiet secluded bench beneath a cover of spring leaves on the avenue of lime trees.

They sat in silence for a while neither knowing how to start. The park was a stark contrast to Kensington Gardens. There was a distinct lack of humanity here, only a few people ambling slowly up the hill. The sunlight made patterns on the pathway that danced as the gentle breeze disturbed the leaves.

"Dave, can I go first?"

Dave nodded and he began and all the time he spoke Dave listened without once looking at him or interrupting.

"I've done something bad. It wasn't my intention for it to be bad but I think it's turned out that way and I feel terrible about it."

He got no response or reassurance so he continued hesitantly.

"It started off by me asking my contract law lecturer if he knew you as he seems like a permanent fixture. This was in late March. He did know you and he told me how the whole faculty thought you one of the most brilliant students they had the privilege to teach. He said you were one in a million. He also said you were unsociable, surly and totally withdrawn from student life. He said he found it odd that you'd fronted the schools rock band and still nobody seemed to know you. He thought most of the students were afraid of you given your size and attitude.

"I then did some research through the newspaper website that gives you access to just about everything written but I could only find recent stuff about you. What I read made you sound like the new wunderkind of business.

"I then researched your dad and found a very short article dated 1999 saying that George Wilson's son had been sentenced to a year's imprisonment in New York for GBH. I couldn't find any more about it but by this time I felt like I was on a mission.

"There's an American student on a year's exchange and I'd seen him in an international law lecture and I sought him out. Through his connections in New York, or should I say his father's, we were able to find out a surprising amount. It turned out that you hadn't been listened to at the trial and you had a lousy lawyer. Your conviction was overturned on appeal and you were released but had already spent three months in jail.

"That's all a matter of public record but what we also found out"

He stopped and took a deep breath and hung his head.

"We found out that whilst in prison you were badly beaten and raped by three hardened inmates. You spent two weeks in the prison hospital so it must have been bad. It must have been awful.

"I'm really sorry for not telling you that I was researching you. That was very wrong. I'm also really sorry for what happened to you and I can understand why you wouldn't want to talk about it. I'm sorry but I had to tell you and if you want me to leave I'll go but not willingly."

Dave sat for a while before speaking.

"Well you've saved me telling the easy part of the story. What happened when I was returned to the prison cells haunts my every day. I'm a real low life and if you leave I'll understand your being disgusted by me but here goes.

"The guard came to collect me from the hospital and told me they were putting me in a cell with one of the hard men and he'd make sure nobody hurt me again. I was really relieved at the time but I didn't know there was a price to pay. The very first night in the cell this six foot four monster of a man gave me an option. He could either throw me to the wolves or I could be his boy. He fucked me every night and made me do just about everything you could imagine and then some. I did it and pretended that I liked it and him. I was disgustingly submissive I should have fought back even if it meant I died. Dying might have been better than the living hell I went through. I know I'm a piece of scum and I don't deserve the droppings of people's noses.

"I couldn't tell my dad because he would have said I should have fought and died rather than to submit willingly. I've told two people this, the psychiatrist and Father O'Connell at The Oratory, neither of them count, as they both get paid to listen.

"When I first got back to London I didn't talk for a month, that way I didn't have to answer any questions. The shrink told my dad that if he stopped asking questions I'd talk. He did and I did.

"I was pretty slim in those days and I spoke with a public school accent and I decided to change all that. I kitted out my room with weights and started taking whey supplements to beef up. I listened to dad and the people at the casino and developed a West London accent all to make me look and sound hard. Nothing like that was ever going to happen to me again.

"Now you know it all. Now you know why I beefed up and why I talk like a hardened Londoner. I developed a defence mechanism that ensured nobody would ever mess with me again. I'm a scum bag so go and don't get contaminated."

Jonathan didn't say anything he just sat there with his head down. Dave stood up as if about to leave. Jonathan raised his head and a tear rolled down his left cheek.

"Where are you going?"

"For a walk, home, who knows?" Dave sighed deeply.

"On the way to church I said I wanted to ask you something and I still do, so can you sit down please." Dave obliged.

"Before I ask you, am I forgiven and don't ask any questions just say yes or no."

"Yes but I don't know what for."

"Good, then I can ask you. I'm off soon for the summer break for three whole months and I was wondering if you could take a couple of weeks off and we could go somewhere."

Dave didn't know what to say. After a minute or so he shook his head.

"Didn't you hear what I just told you?'

"I'm neither deaf nor stupid unlike you. You're a big stupid oath sometimes and I'm not going into your irrational guilt trip. You did nothing that anyone other than a martyr would have done. You're a good man. No you're not you're a great man so get over it. Now can we go on holiday or not."

Dave nodded. "Yes we can but do you mind if we discuss it later. I need to go home."

Jonathan gave him a wicked grin and said that was fine. They left the park at Holland Walk and headed down the hill. They crossed at the lights on the corner of Ladbroke Grove and when they reached Dave's turn off, he said he'd give Jonathan a call in the week or drop by the pub.

"Great, you do that. You don't think you're going home alone do you? I'm hungry and you have food in your freezer and don't do a Greta Garbo on me please, you big fucking wooz."

Dave went to bed that night and thought of the day's events. Was it really that easy to forgive, more to the point did he feel forgiven. No he didn't. For the first time since it had all happened he didn't feel like he needed forgiveness, he hadn't done anything wrong.

He picked up his phone from his bedside table and called Jonathan.

"I just realised what you did you little shit, spying on me like that. The next time I see you I'm going to punch your lights out."

Jonathan laughed and said. "Good, so Italy and a rented car it is."

Dave closed his eyes and wondered how this magical young man did what he did. Dave's guilt melted away like ice in the spring. He would still have bad dreams about the rape and beating but not very often.

He was looking forward to seeing Dr Marks, not to validate anything but to thank him and hopefully say goodbye. The day came, it was the first Monday in June and as he stepped into the consulting room Dr Marks said he looked as bright as the sunshine outside. Dave told him what had happened and the doctor listened with great interest.

"I had thought all this time that I needed forgiveness but it wasn't that at all. Jonathan made it go away by brushing it aside as though it was just a thing that happened that was beyond my control. A big deal maybe but not something that defines who I am, he didn't even use that many words."

"Now I think I need therapy. I've been seeing you for twelve years and you and your father have paid me probably twenty thousand pounds. What I couldn't do in all that time a young man does in a matter of a few months. He must be remarkable."

"He is but not that many people would ever know. He's a total introvert and never boasts or thinks he's special but of course he is."

Dr Marks looked at Dave and recognised something he should have seen the last time they met.

"Dave, are you in love?"

"Do you mean do I love Jonathan? Well yes I do in so many ways. He's given me my freedom and the possibility of a future beyond what I have now. I'd like to think he'll be in my life forever. But I know what you mean and it's not a physical thing. I'm straight and so is he."

"Does he feel the same?"

"I think so. He knows how I feel and we're good, we're friends, nothing else."

"Be careful Dave you could end up feeling more, the physical side is the last barrier and even if you don't feel that way, what if he did? Then you might lose that friendship."

"I doubt that but if I did at least I will be able to look back and say I had something special. That would still be a reward."

"That's a very philosophical view. Where did that come from?"

"A very wise young man."

"I'd like to meet this magical young man."

"Really? He's outside I'll ask him to come in but beware he might make you feel good about yourself."

Dave got up and went to find his friend. When Jonathan walked in Dr Marks was surprised, he wasn't anything like he expected. Here was a scruffy unshaven young man with longish black curly hair hiding parts of his face.

Jonathan held out his hand and they exchanged greetings. Jonathan sat down and pushed back his hair.

"Dave has told me a lot about you and how you've helped him."

Jonathan shook his head. "I didn't do anything. Dave did it himself with your help. I know you've been telling him for years to learn to trust again and only then would he be able to share what was bothering him. He's really thick sometimes and it's taken that long for it to sink in. I just happened to be the person around when his unconscious mind got it. I'd really like to thank you for helping my friend. You're great. Thank you."

With that Jonathan smiled. "I'll leave you two to carry on. Thanks again Dr Marks." He touched Dave on the shoulder and left the room.

Dr Marks sat back in his chair and looked up at the ceiling then at Dave. "Your friend is hiding something."

"I know and so does he. He doesn't like the attention he gets when he's not in disguise. I understand that. He wants to get noticed for what he does not how he looks. It's not a psychological thing. It's a conscious choice."

"Good but I think if he's for real then you've stumbled across a very special person. Not only does he look like Jesus Christ he has the humility to go with it and you're right, I do feel better for that brief encounter. He has a real gift."

Dave laughed. "Something just occurred to me, his mother's name is Mary and his father was Joe. He's for real. He just doesn't have any interest in the materialism and the obsessions of this world. He's magic."

"Dave I'm happy and sad to say we're done. If you're in the area any time, drop by and say hello."

They stood up, shook hands and said their goodbyes.

CHAPTER THIRTY FOUR

Jonathan finished his exams and Dave insisted they celebrate. They had dinner at The Ivy and went to a cocktail bar afterwards. They had one drink there and left as neither of them appreciated the sophisticated ambiance of the place. They found a pub that stayed open late and got drunk. Dave's driver picked them up at three o'clock and took them home to Lansdowne Road. Once inside Jonathan made a bee-line for Dave's bedroom and collapsed on the bed. Dave had sobered up a bit and he looked down at the young man sprawled across his bed and felt good about everything. He removed Jonathan's shoes, folded the duvet over him and switched off the light. He couldn't be bothered making up the bed in the spare room so he grabbed a duvet from the airing cupboard and crashed on the sofa in the lounge.

Jonathan literally rolled out of bed sometime after ten o'clock. He made his way gingerly down to the kitchen and found Dave looking chirpy with the sun shining brightly through the window behind him.

"Oh God everything looks so normal and I feel like the world just ended."

This provoked Dave to smile. Jonathan then went deadly white and ran out of the room and up the stairs. Dave followed and found him on his knees slumped over the lavatory bowl relieving himself of the previous nights intake of food and alcohol.

"I think I'm going to die."

Dave rubbed his back and handed him some tissue. Eventually his vomit was replaced with air as he retched to no avail. Dave led him back to bed and went to fetch him a glass of water. He made him sit up and drink the whole glass. Jonathan meekly obliged and then collapsed back onto the bed begging Dave not to leave him alone to die. He then closed his eyes and fell asleep.

Dave grabbed a book that was at his bedside and sat in his armchair reading. After about an hour Jonathan woke up.

"Am I alive?"

"Yes stupid. I'll go and get you some coffee it might make you feel a bit better."

Jonathan drank the coffee but still felt very wobbly.

"Have a nice long shower and it'll do the trick. I'll get you a towel."

Jonathan swung his legs off the bed and started to undress. Dave gave him the towel and said he'd leave him to it.

Jonathan looked at him in alarm. "Please don't leave me on my own, I feel very shaky and I might fall and hurt myself and you won't be here to help me."

Dave opened the shower room door and turned on the taps. When he went back in the bedroom, Jonathan was gingerly approaching stark naked.

Dave focussed on his face and stood aside. "Come on, in you go."

Jonathan stepped under the water jets and Dave was about to close the door when Jonathan pleaded "Don't close the door and don't go. Just watch and make sure I don't collapse or something. I still feel horrible."

Dave sat on the bed and watched Jonathan as he moved around under the Monsoon rain. The steam was building up and it was like watching an angel come and go in a thick jungle mist. He didn't want to watch but even if he tried he couldn't have averted his eyes. What were his real feelings for this young man? He didn't want to analyse that one. It was a sudden wake up call for Dave, how young Jonathan seemed in his need to be cared for. Of course he was still only recently out of his teens nevertheless he stirred unwanted feelings.

Jonathan switched off the taps after what seemed an age and Dave handed him his towel.

"I'm so lucky to have a friend like you Dave Wilson. Thanks for, well just thanks."

"Do you want some breakfast or should I say lunch?"

"I could probably manage a piece of toast."

Dave made fresh coffee and put the toaster on the kitchen table together with plates, knives, butter and spreads. Jonathan appeared five minutes later, hair wet but fully clothed.

"Where did you sleep last night?'

"On the sofa"

"Sorry I took your bed."

"That's not a problem."

"Thanks pass the marmite."

By one o'clock Jonathan was feeling almost human so he went home declining Dave's offer of a lift.

Dave was feeling a little tired so he had another cup of coffee and then a very long shower. He dressed and was about to go out for a walk when his mobile rang.

"Hi Jonathan, feeling better?"

"Yes thanks, much, what are you doing?"

"I was just about to go out for a walk."

"Good I'm sitting on your steps."

Dave went upstairs and opened the front door. Sure enough He was sitting on the steps looking up at the sun with his eyes closed.

"You were quick. I see you've changed so you've been home and back again."

"I got home and decided I didn't want to stay there. I felt I needed you to take care of me as you were the one who made me ill in the first place."

"Ok then let's go for a couple of beers."

"Fuck off you sadist. Do you want to kill me?"

"Just maybe I might, I'll think about it whilst we walk. Here you better have this"

"What's this for?"

"It's my front door key, so you don't have to park yourself on my doorstep making the neighbourhood look untidy. Come on let's go for a walk."

June was looking like summer, not exactly flaming June but pleasantly warm and reasonably dry.

Dave had been very busy with the extra work caused through his negotiations with the Americans. His step mother and sister were both happy at the prospect of receiving a large sum of money although neither of them was exactly destitute. Stella had a steady income from the investments George had left her and Carol was married to a multi-millionaire and of course they both received generous dividends from the business.

The friends hadn't met all week and had arranged to have lunch at Dave's on the Saturday. Jonathan went straight from his Judo class so he arrived at two. Dave was looking troubled.

"Hey, what's happened you don't look too happy?"

Dave was beyond asking how Jonathan knew these things at just a glance.

"The buyers have arranged a meeting in New York for next Monday. Carol's already there of course and Stella wants to go just because she loves New York."

"And you don't want to go for obvious reasons."

"Right and I'm having a visa problem because of my conviction. The embassy said it would be alright but couldn't guarantee it would be ready in time."

He sat at the table and put his head in his hands. Jonathan felt so sorry for this huge brut of a man who just saw his bogie man. He stood behind Dave, leant over him and put his arms around his neck. Dave reached for the comforting hands and held them.

"You do help more than you know Jonathan."

Jonathan released his grip and as he straightened up he kissed Dave on the head. Dave felt a warmth course through his body.

"Getting a bit soppy up there?"

"So, but that stuff you put on your hair doesn't taste too good. Now Mr Dave you've got to face up to your fears someday which means you should go. It's only been a short while since you got your head around what happened so the timing's not right. I offer this suggestion. Tell your step mother and your sister about your visa problem because they know what happened so will understand. Then you tell the Americans that you have to postpone through unforeseen circumstances and get them to come here."

"You're probably right. I could do that.'

"Ok then do it."

"I will. I'll do it on Monday.'

"I haven't seen you for a week and if you don't do it now you're going to have it on your mind the whole weekend. So come on here's your phone."

The meeting was arranged for the ninth of July. The buyers had considered Dave's asking price and came back with a new offer. After some haggling they agreed to more or less everything Dave had asked for including signing over the flat above Dave's to him. The buyer's had a condition of their own. Dave was to continue running the business until the end of 2014. They offered a salary which was double what he was getting plus a bonus when he finished. Dave had presupposed something like this as they would need to orientate one of their own which takes time. He agreed with the proviso that his company car was also signed over to him. All was agreed so the process of due diligence would commence once the relevant documents had been signed. The completion of the sale would be year end and they would be up and running under their own name by the first of January.

Dave didn't want the rumour mill springing into action giving out misleading information so he composed a detailed email and sent it to the respective heads of departments and the managers of the betting shops. In the email he promised to visit every location before the middle of September.

He was going to be really busy and he hoped Jonathan would understand and maybe even to offer to travel around the country with him.

"Dave you do what you have to do. You're going to be lying in bed one night and remember that you promised to go on holiday with me. I'm not reminding you to make you feel bad, quite the opposite. I understand that you have no choice and anyway when you've finalised everything you'll have bags of time." He was really hoping Dave would ask him to travel around the country with him but he didn't.

Dave couldn't help himself, it just slipped out. "Will you miss me?"

"I will. You'll have the odd day here and there so it's not as though I won't see you at all. You must do what you have to do. I have my last year's course outline so I'll immerse myself in law books and spend lots of time in the British Library. I still have my job at the pub remember so I'll be busy." He didn't say that he'd cancelled his time off just in case an opportunity arose for a break later.

He did miss Dave and it bothered him. Dave called him every couple of days and he was glad of that and he saw him on the odd days that he returned to London. The problem was the uncertainty. He couldn't just see him when he wanted. It was an odd feeling and it left him feeling as if he'd been deserted. He thought it through and logic told him he was being juvenile.

Dave would take his crew out for dinner in every location so he would get back to his hotel late and tired. He told himself that it was just as well that he hadn't asked Jonathan to tag along as that's pretty much what he'd have had to do, just tag along. All the same he would still rather he'd been with him. He shook it off as nonsense.

It was the first week in September when Dave finally finished his rounds. They had dinner at a local restaurant and Dave said it had all gone well and the fact that he had taken time to be seen in person had been appreciated.

They started talking football as the new season was underway. QPR was the main topic of conversation as Jonathan had been a life-long fan. Dave said he quite liked QPR so suggested they go some time and the following Tuesday Dave dropped by the pub an announced he had tickets for Saturday's match.

On Saturday morning, Mary woke with a feeling of anticipation. She was going shopping with Karen and lunching out at Fortnum and Mason's. She went down to the kitchen and found Jonathan at the table reading a book.

"You're up early. What are you reading?"

"A law book as usual."

"University doesn't start again until the beginning of October so why don't you have a break. You didn't even have a summer holiday. You know what they say about Jack. You'll grow up to be a crashing bore."

"I'm off to dance soon and then Judo. After that I'm meeting my friend and we're going to the Rangers, OK?"

Mary smiled, "Well you haven't been to Rangers since your dad died, it'll do you good. Who are you going with?"

"Dave."

"It's good that you have a friend, you've never had one. Are you coming home for dinner?"

"Yes of course. I wouldn't want to deny you the pleasure of lecturing me about getting a life."

They both laughed.

"Why don't you invite this Dave for dinner, I'd like to meet him. He's probably got something to do but ask anyway. I'll cook enough for three and if he doesn't come then there's more for us."

"Are you vetting my friends now?" he said with good humour.

"I'd like to but you don't have any. What do you want for breakfast?"

Jonathan ate and then went to his classes. He came home showered, changed and searched for his old Rangers' scarf. He walked up Portobello which was crowded. Saturday was the mainstay of most traders as flocks of tourist descended buying all the tat that was on sale. They ate the plethora of food on offer and ambled up and down the lane munching away happily.

Jonathan walked up as far as Westbourne Grove where the crowds petered out. He headed for Ladbroke Grove and at the point where it met Holland Park Avenue he entered The Mitre.

Dave was at the crowded bar waiting his turn. He saw Jonathan hovering at his shoulder and asked what he wanted and a pint of Stella was duly ordered. They stood outside the pub with what seemed like a thousand other drinkers. It was a pleasantly warm day and the populace were sun worshipping as usual.

They spoke about the game and Jonathan was genuinely excited at the prospect of seeing, what was always his and his dad's team play.

Dave offered another beer but Jonathan declined saying he didn't want to have to use the bogs at the ground. They walked down The Avenue to Shepherds Bush where the fans started to be noticeable. They crossed Wood Lane and now the crowd had built to the size where everything slowed down.

Jonathan had told Dave that he and his dad always sat on the South Africa Road side near the centre and Dave had managed to find seats just about there. As they were walking up the steps to take their seats, Jonathan notice a group of men off to his right standing at their season ticket seats. One of them looked out at the pitch and said, "Joe's looking good today." Jonathan stopped at their row just at that moment and with a big smile on his face offered, "Joe's looking great today." The men turned in unison towards the voice. It took a few seconds for it to dawn on them until one of them recognised him. "Jonathan? Are you Jonathan? Of course you're Jonathan you're the spit of your dad."

They all left their seats and joined him on the stairs giving him big hugs and causing a major jam. They quickly arranged to meet after the game at the pub on the corner of Wood Lane as the half time scramble wouldn't be conducive to conversation.

Dave had already taken his seat and Jonathan joined him. "They're my dad's old football buddies and they want to catch up after the game. I hope you don't mind? What are you planning for dinner?"

"No I don't mind and I thought we could have a pint or two, which seems to be settled already and then have dinner somewhere. What was the Joe reference?'

"Joe was my dad and I'll let them explain that in the pub. I only eat with my mum once a week and that's on Saturday's so you're invited. You don't have to come, it's truly not obligatory. If you do then you need to be warned, she's very, how do I say it, probing and perceptive. She's a witch."

"How can I refuse an invitation like that?" He wasn't at all sure he meant it.

Rangers won one nil much to the delight of seventeen thousand fans. They made their way to the pub and there they were, five middle aged men, looking at the door waiting for Jonathan to arrive.

After more hugs Jonathan introduced Dave to his dad's old gang. "Dave, now let me see if I get this right. This is Alan, Alex, Bob, Eric and Walter."

"Some memory you have there. You were what, eight the last time we saw you? We did call your mum many times to see if you wanted to come with us but she said you wouldn't go without your dad. How could you possibly remember all our names after all this time?"

"Dad taught me a mnemonic, which kind of stuck."

"So what was it?"

Jonathan grimaced and asked if they really wanted to know. They all nodded. "Ok here goes. All Arseholes But Extremely Wonderful."

There was a lot of laughter and they all agreed that was typical Joe.

"Dave wants to know why Joe was looking good today. Can you tell him?"

Bob was volunteered to tell the story as he was the one that made it possible.

"Our friend Joe was cremated and we didn't like the idea of him sitting in an urn doing nothing year on year. That wasn't Joe he was more an action man and we knew he wouldn't like that. Well as it happened the ground's man at Rangers at that time was an old friend of mine so I twisted his arm for a favour. That summer when they dug up the old turf we got him to spread Joe's ashes on the soil. They then laid the turf on top of him so he feeds the grass. Because he's under the turf it doesn't matter how many times they change it, he'll always be there."

"That's a great story. What was Joe like? Jonathan doesn't really talk about him that much and he was very young when he died."

"Before he met Mary he was a real Jack-the-Lad. Always had girls hanging round but he wasn't one to settle down. He was a really good looking man, movie star looks and he knew how to use it. Jonathan looks a lot like him only…."

He broke off and took a hard look at his friend's son "only if anything he's better looking than his dad. You really are a handsome young man the girls must swarm around you."

"Not interested, I have too much studying and no time."

He told them he was going to be a barrister and they were truly impressed. Alex suggested he could be their lawyer and help them when they got into a bit of bother. Jonathan accepted the offer with a laugh and good grace.

Alex was looking at Dave, "I'm sure I've seen you before. Are you from around here?" Dave gave them a potted history of his upbringing and as it happened Alex had known his dad but didn't want to go into how.

They parted company and promised to do it again. They took a leisurely stroll to Portobello taking the back streets through Notting Dale. Dave pointed out where his Dad was born on Clarendon Road and Jonathan where his Grandmother was from.

Dave asked what sort of wine Mary drank and was informed anything as long as it was red and Spanish. They stopped at an off-licence and purchased two bottles of the finest the shop could offer which wasn't much as it happened.

"My mum's very direct I hope you don't get offended."

"I won't. Does she answer questions?"

"Yes she's very honest so she won't lie but if you broach a subject she doesn't want to talk about she'll change it."

"Ok then I'll take a leaf out of her book and do the same."

Mary greeted them and ushered them straight into the kitchen where they ate dinner. Jonathan related the meeting with Joe's old football buddies and passed on their messages. Mary was genuinely pleased more for Jonathan then herself. She established that Dave was from the same area as she. Then she posed the questions.

Where exactly did he come from and what was his family name.

"Wilson, my dad grew up in the Dale and so did my mum."

"What was your dad's first name?"

"George, why did you know him?"

"George Wilson, it sounds familiar, what did he do?

"Back in the day he had a betting shop on Ladbroke Grove."

"Of course, I know it. It's still there. I didn't know your dad personally but I heard some things about him."

"Mum, maybe that's too much." Jonathan said getting the inference.

"No, that's ok dad was a bit of a villain in his younger days so that's probably what you meant Mrs M."

"Well he did have a bit of a reputation and I know people that knew him so I heard a few stories."

"Dave laughed. "I've heard all the stories straight from the horse's mouth. He was proud of his little antics was my dad."

Mary related how she remembered the good old days and they discovered that they knew people in common.

Mary was enjoying the wine and the conversation and likewise Dave. Jonathan listened with interest and noticed Dave hadn't offered any information about himself then came the personal stuff.

Mary scrutinised their guest. "You sound London but there's something else there. Did you ever live anywhere else?"

"Mum died when I was seven and dad did his best but neither of us was coping well so he packed me off to boarding school."

"Where was that?"

"Oxford then Harrow."

"Wow then why aren't you posh?"

"That's another story for another time Mrs M."

"So you must have gone to University then."

"I did but not straight away. I took a couple of years off."

Jonathan was desperately hoping she wouldn't probe around that and to his relief she didn't.

"Which university did you go to?"

A big smile came over Dave's face when he told her. "LSE, that's one of the reasons why Jonathan and I have a lot in common. I didn't study law though, I did economics and then an MBA and before you ask how I did, I got a first."

"I tried to get Jonathan to take a gap year, given the state he was in but he wouldn't."

"Mum, don't go there."

"What did you do with your two years off then Dave?"

Jonathan held his breath but Dave calmly replied. "Not much."

Mary's instincts were aroused. She saw pain in his eyes and she thought she should say something.

"Whatever not much was, it obviously didn't do you any good. I doubt that it was anything as bad as this one, he ended up seeing a psychologist and not for the first time, now I don't suppose you've done that."

Jonathan was now feeling she'd over stepped the mark. "Mum the first time I saw a psychologist was when I was very small and because you made me. The second time was after Gabriella disappeared and both times the doctor said I was fine. My mum has a problem getting it into her head that I just don't have a need for friends and she made me go both times. I wouldn't mind but after meeting dad's old friends today, from what they told us I must get my introvert personality from her."

Maybe it was the beer and the wine that did it but something was urging Dave to respond to the original question.

"I haven't seen a psychologist but until very recently I was under a psychiatrist for about twelve years."

"I'm so sorry it must have been something bad. Let's change the subject."

Both friends were relieved but more was to come.

"So how old are you Dave?"

"Thirty two."

"Do you have a girl friend or a boy friend?"

"Mum!"

"That's ok Jonathan and the answer is neither, in fact Jonathan is the only person I've spent social time with since I was eighteen."

"Two fucking broken souls you both need a fucking good shake."

She got up from the table and stormed out of the room. Jonathan was dumbfounded. "I've never heard my mum talk like that before and she doesn't swear. What just happened?"

"I don't know she's your mum."

They sat in silence for a while then Dave let out a big sigh and said he should leave.

"No you shouldn't." Mary had come back into the kitchen.

"I sorry for my little outburst, it's just that I thought how good it was for Jonathan to have a friend instead of a fellow nutcase but you two are probably perfect for one another."

"In what way mother dear?"

"No one has interested you for most of your life. You've had two soul mates, one died and the other left and you seem more alive since you met Dave so I am thankful for that. I hope you help him. You two should get it all out with one another it's good for the soul and all that."

"Mrs M we've already done that and you're right it is good for the soul. Jonathan was able to give me what a psychiatrist and a priest couldn't and I'm indebted to him for that."

"Dave knows everything about Gabriella and although I didn't know it, unlike my wise mother, I realise I was carrying a lot of baggage around. Dave lifted my unseen burden and I feel great."

Dave felt almost loved by those words and he smiled at his hosts.

"Now it's my turn Mrs M so will you sit down please."

Mary returned the smile and sat. "Sorry love."

"That's ok, now tell me. You're a very good looking woman and I guess with Jonathan being twenty that would make you forty to forty five, right?"

"Oh what a wonderful man you are, keep going."

Dave gave Jonathan a questioning look.

"You just made a conquest, she's fifty five."

"What?" Dave was genuinely surprised. Mary fluttered her eyelashes and they all laughed. The atmosphere had lightened to everyone's relief.

"Well anyway you are an attractive woman and Jonathan tells me you keep nipping off to Spain, so is there a man in your life?"

Mary looked at him as if he'd said nothing and said, "Come on you boys, Mrs Brown is on the tele and I think we all need a good laugh." and that's exactly what happened.

At ten o'clock Mary retired saying the wine had made her sleepy. She gave Jonathan a peck on the cheek and Dave a big hug and told him that he must come again and Dave assured her he would. Dave suggested a quick beer before the pubs closed so they went to the nearest pub on Portobello Road.

There found a seat and sat quietly for a few minutes.

"Do you think your mum is Ok with me?"

"I think so, she did apologise which is a big thing for her. Why would it bother you if she wasn't?"

"Yes it would. Anyway I wanted to ask you something. You've still got two weeks before lectures start so do you think you could get some time off from the pub?"

"No I couldn't do that, why?"

"I thought we could make that trip to Italy but if you can't go then you can't go."

A wide smile lit up Jonathan's face. "Who said I couldn't go?"

"You just said you couldn't get the time off."

"I can't get the time off because I don't work there anymore. I resigned a couple of weeks ago and yesterday was my last day. I told Len that as it's my final year I need more study time but I'd help out any time he was short of staff but I'm free to go to Italy so let's do it, when?"

Dave leaned over and punched him on the arm. "Do you always have to wind me up you bastard?"

Jonathan feigned an ouch and laughed.

"Ok then, I have to go to the office on Monday to sort a few things out, so we could fly to Rome on Tuesday and come back say Friday the week after. I'm not getting into a discussion about who pays for what so you arrange the flights and you can pay for the car rental and I'll pay for everything else."

"Sounds good, are we flying back from Rome or somewhere else?"

"It's easier if we do come back through Rome. It doesn't matter where we end up, we can always leave the rental car and get a domestic flight back to Rome and we can sort that out when we get there."

"Sounds like a plan, I'll book the flights when I get home but I'll need your passport details."

"I'll text you when I get home. Are you coming to mass tomorrow?"

"Sure. Shall I come round to your place first?"

"Yes, why don't you do that?"

They finished their beer and had a second after which they parted company with a nod of their heads.

On Sunday they went to mass and lunched together. Dave had to go to the Casino so they parted company at three and arranged to meet on Tuesday to go to the airport.

CHAPTER THIRTY FIVE

The Rome sunshine brought out the warmth of colour in the ochre buildings. They wandered the sights, drank coffee in the piazzas and dined at some of the finest restaurants. Luckily, he had packed a jacket and some shirts so whilst still ill groomed he was able to make himself presentable enough. Dave never commented. At the end of each day they had a beer and retired to their rooms exhausted.

At breakfast on the fifth day Jonathan asked when they would be leaving Rome.

"Had your fill then, we can go anytime, today if you like."

"Well that's the problem. There's so much still to see and it seems a bit of a waste being here and not exploring the stuff off the beaten track as well as the sights."

"So you don't want to go to Naples and Pompeii or see the blue grotto of Capri or any of the beautiful sights on the way?"

"I do but I don't want to feel like I rushed everything. This city is so beautiful and well…." He cut his sentence short and sighed.

"I'll tell you what, why don't we stay in Rome and do the rest another time? Would that suit you?"

Jonathan smiled and thanked him and asked if they could still stay in their hotel. Dave confessed to having booked the hotel for the whole ten days because he thought this might just happen. Jonathan felt even happier that his friend knew him so well. There was only one thing that could make him happier.

On their return they fell into a routine. Jonathan would spend his days at lectures and the library. Dave adjusted his schedule so that they could meet a couple of evenings a week and on those days Jonathan would study at Dave's house. Weekends were judo and dance lessons, football when possible and church on Sundays.

Dave was sleeping better but it was probably out of habit that he never slept enough. The dreams still came occasionally but seemed to have lost their intensity and to his alarm he sometimes dreamt about Jonathan in a very intimate way. He awoke one morning to a wet patch in his bed.

"Oh Christ what am I doing. What's wrong with me?" He sat up in bed and decided to talk himself through it honestly. He had met a young man by accident and they had developed a close friendship which had developed into a trusting relationship. Jonathan had eased his pain and he was now just transferring a fantasy he had of love, it wasn't real. That pleased him for about a minute. He then put his head under his pillow and shouted out loud. "I'm a fucking liar, I love him."

There was no Rangers that Saturday and Jonathan suggested they meet anyway and have a stroll, a beer and dinner. Dave declined and lied when he said he had promised to visit his stepmother for the weekend. Oh how he wanted to be with him but that was the problem, it seemed his feelings were getting stronger, so he thought he should back off. He stayed home all weekend reading or working on some financial projections and even gave some thought to what he would do after life at the casino.

On Sunday evening his phone rang and Jonathan's name appeared on its display. His heart skipped a beat but he answered as casually as he could.

"Hi Dave, are you back?"

"Yep, how you doing?"

"Good, I have a late start tomorrow so would you like a quick beer?"

They met at the Mitre and Dave attempted to steer the conversation away from the weekend activities as he didn't want to compound the lie. How he hated lying to his one and only friend but he justified it by telling himself it was for his own good.

They chatted for a while and Jonathan said Len had called and asked him to help out at the pub so he had obliged willingly as he had nothing better to do.

"I worked from two until midnight and we were run off our feet but it was good to be able to help, Len's a good man."

Then out of the blue he asked Dave to tell him a lie. Dave was puzzled but Jonathan told him they were doing something about watching for signs of lies on his course. Dave told him an obvious lie.

"Good, now tell me what you did at the weekend."

Dave repeated his story and Jonathan shook his head.

"How could you know I didn't?"

"Because you're such a poor liar but why did you lie? What did you do?"

Dave grimaced. "I stayed at home, it's just I thought maybe we were spending too much time together and I needed some time to myself."

Jonathan laughed, not unkindly.

"I'm really transparent it seems. I should know not to lie to a gypsy."

"Look, you don't ever have to lie to me, why should you but you needn't answer that one. There is another lie I found out last night at the pub from one of your football team. It's more a lie of omission you're a fucking Chelsea supporter."

Now they both laughed and Dave felt the tension ease from his body and mind. "I shall now confess my other sins as you found out the worst one." Dave let himself enjoy the moment and he felt happy although incomplete when they parted.

The next few weeks went by in the same vein as before. When not working or studying they went to football, a movie, the odd beer and dinner out a couple of times. Dave was getting to know Mary and they got on well. Jonathan said he learnt more about Dave by listening to his conversations with his mother than he did talking directly to him. Neither of them ever really probed for information, they just let it come as a natural course of conversation. They never ran out of words to say and their relationship was on the surface very fraternal.

Dave was heavily involved in the sale of the business and hadn't been able to see Jonathan for three days and was aware how much he missed him. To his surprise Jonathan verbalised the same emotion of separation.

It was Friday night and after they parted Dave walked down Holland Park Avenue towards home. The plane trees had a few leaves hanging on in desperation but now you could see the skeletons of guardians of the Avenue. The lack of foliage unmasked their true height and the street lights spread a glow about them which made them look beautiful and almost surreal. Their strength and constancy is Holland Park. Without them the small rich conclave would lose much of its magical grandeur.

Dave wasn't ready to sleep, what Jonathan had said about missing him was playing on his mind so he went through his small garden and sat on a bench in the deserted communal garden. The garden rarely hosted more than a few people at a time and Dave often wondered why the residents didn't utilise it more, maybe like him they were just too busy.

Why had Jonathan said he'd missed him? He was certain of his love for the magical young man but was such a relationship possible? The answer to that was no, so what should he do? He always felt so much better, happy even, when that warm voice spoke to him, that indescribably beautiful visage looked his way and sheer joy ran though his veins when the smile of an angel lit up his face.

How should he progress? Then he thought "Oh fuck it I'm not going to lose him so I'll just have to live with it."

He now knew he must be gay but men didn't turn him on nor did women for that matter. If loving Jonathan meant he was gay so be it. He reasoned he'd be doomed to celibacy for the rest of his life which was a much better option than losing the one thing that made him happy.

A fox sauntered across the grass, stopped and gave him a defiant look and then slipped into the bushes. "That's me" he said aloud "putting on a show."

After football on Saturday, Dave bought three bottles of what he's discovered was Mary's tipple of choice. He wanted to get her tiddly so she would open up a little more and he did and she did.

Dave wanted to know more about Joe. Mary told the story of how they met and a brief account of the marriage. She looked sad when she recounted the night he had died and said she found it hard to believe that it was a random mugging.

"Do you know I was never really sure what Joe's real job was? I know it was something to do with security for the foreign office but it used to upset him when I asked too many questions. He said he couldn't tell me because he was bound by the official secrets act. It did upset him because I think he wanted to tell me and I played the bitch by getting upset about it.

"Poor Joe he wasn't the luckiest of men when it came to being injured. That's how we met, he was in a bad car accident in Germany and when he was well enough they brought him home and I nursed him. Oh he was a handful at times but so charming and handsome."

It slipped out, "Just like Jonathan."

"No, not at all, Joe was an extrovert and had time for everyone unlike Mr Head in the Clouds here. Jonathan looks a lot like him but softer.

"You know he never had to work in that pub? Joe left him enough money to pay for everything and that boy has hardly touched a penny. He's probably worth twice what his father left him. He won't spend it because he says it's really mine but I don't touch it, I don't need to, Joe left me well provided for. I even get a pension from the foreign office. I hope he pays his share when you're out."

"Yes always he insists. He's a bit of a pain in the arse about it to tell you the truth but I think we've worked it out. I hope you don't mind me asking but how much did Joe leave you?"

"No I don't mind. He actually didn't leave that much because he transferred half of this flat to me and made his bank account into a joint account when we got married and when Jonathan was born he put the other flat and the rest of his savings into a trust fund. When he died there were no death duties but the solicitor said we were worth over a million pounds and that was twelve years ago. There are also some shares but I don't get anything from those. I get a statement every now and again but I don't really understand what it says."

"Smart man your Joe, he must have saved a lot before you got married because government departments don't pay that well."

"He got paid more than we needed to live on.

"You know sometimes I used to think he was really a spy or something."

"He sounds like he was quite exciting to be around, James Bond type was he?"

"Quite the opposite, he spent every spare minute with his beloved son and the rest was television, dinner and the occasional trip to the pub. I wasn't always as grateful for what I had as I should have been though. We used to go to Spain every year for our holidays and stay with his relatives and I must say that was the highlight of my year. He was a good husband and a great father and after we got married he discovered he'd got an introverted bitch for a wife."

"Mum, you weren't like that. That came much later."

Mary threw a piece of bread at her son and the mood lightened again.

"So your Joe really was a bit of a mystery man and a relatively wealthy one. The question is where did the money come from? This is great a puzzle to be solved."

"Oh don't do that or we might have to give the money back." She laughed.

"Now Mr Dave tell me why you have a London accent after going to posh schools."

Dave was only prepared to tell half the truth.

"When I went to work with my dad I just thought I should talk like him and the rest of his crew. Like you they would say I was posh and I don't think I would have got respect."

"Can you turn on a posh voice still?"

"I used to speak much the same way as Jonathan, no affectations I'm afraid." He said in a neutral BBC voice.

"Bit of a fraud then really aren't you?"

Dave thought if she only knew.

"Suppose I am really." He didn't mean it but his voice sounded very sad. Jonathan heard the pain and reached out and touched his arm.

"So now the important stuff, when was the last time you had a girlfriend?"

"When I was eighteen."

"Same as him but that was a long time ago for you, why such a long time?"

"A bit complicated."

"So mind my own business." And she did.

After much mirth courtesy of Mrs Brown, Mary retired to her room and the friends to the pub. Jonathan felt uneasy about that evening's grilling of Dave and offered his apologies.

"That's fine I wasn't offended and you had warned me. As you must have noticed, I side stepped the awkward questions and she was gracious enough not to pursue them. What do you remember about your dad?"

"Dad was always with me when he was at home. He spoke only Spanish to me when mum wasn't around and that's why I'm fluent, in fact I understand that my first words were in Spanish. He taught me to read and write and to love learning. He was a very dextrous person a trait I didn't inherit. He recognised that and never made it an issue. He told me that we all have different gifts that it was our duty to hone those and not waste our time on things we would never be good at. In short he taught me to focus.

"He used to make me laugh and he'd tell me fantastic stories about his family. I'm not sure if any of them were true but it didn't matter then and still doesn't."

"What sort of stories did he tell you?"

"We have a chest at home which he said had been handed down the generations that once belonged to a very rich powerful man. In short the chest gives its owner a certain power and when one of my ancestors stole it the rich man lost everything and died in poverty. So I must treasure the chest because one day it will give forth its' secret. It was his way of telling me it was important to him and I should look after the family heirloom. Of course the way he told the story was far more exciting than I ever could."

"His friends say he was very popular, were you aware of that?"

"I was but when I'd be out with him people would often stop and want to talk but he'd look at me and smile and tell them he had something very important he had to do and said he'd catch up another time."

"And you were the important thing. He used to travel a lot so must have missed him when he was away."

"I didn't because he'd always set me a challenge that I had to complete before he came back. It was mostly about learning or reading something. When I was seven he gave me Don Quixote to read in Spanish. He gave me a marker pen so I could highlight anything I didn't understand. It was hard because the language wasn't exactly everyday Spanish. I had to look at my Spanish dictionary so often but I got there one day before he was due back. I so didn't want to disappoint him that I'd take it to bed with me and read with my torch under the covers. The time went so fast that it seemed he was away no time at all but then I suppose that was the point."

"So how often did you have to use the highlighter?"

"That was never going to happen."

"That's where you must get it from. The ability to let someone feel they can do anything."

"Do I do that?"

"Yes you've helped me so much so I have your dad to thank for that. Thank you Joe." He said looking up to heaven.

"When I'm at your house you never seem to really talk to your mum, is that because I'm around?"

"No, it's always been that way. When I was small dad always did everything for me and mum willingly let him. She thought I was odd and didn't really know how to talk to me and in a way still doesn't. She's my mum and of course I love her dearly and I wouldn't have it any other way. She would have preferred that I was a girl. When Gabriella was around she'd light up and they would talk endlessly. They'd go shopping together and nip off at any excuse. Gabriella didn't have the best experience with her own parents and I think they fulfilled a need in each other. It was nice to watch."

"Didn't that get in the way of your relationship?"

"No, we still had time alone."

"You've had two very special people in your life and although you've lost them both you've experienced something I never have."

Jonathan was silent, letting that comment sink in.

"I told you that I'm aware and grateful for what I've had in my life but you're wrong about one thing. I've had three special people in my life and one is sitting opposite me.'

Dave shook his head. "You do know how to say the right things."

"I wouldn't bother saying them if it wasn't worth saying."

Dave knew this to be true and at that moment he wanted so much to tell him how he really felt but common sense got the better of him.

Two weeks passed and football Saturday ritual kicked in. Joe's old friends passed on information about their escapades when young over after football beer and dinner at Jonathan's followed.

They arrived to a warm welcome from Mary, she giving Dave a big hug and a peck on the cheek. Whilst she was laying the table for dinner she declared that she'd forgotten to buy ice cream and asked Jonathan to go to the shop which he duly did. Dave was left alone with Mary.

"Jonathan showed me a newspaper article about some Americans buying your business. How do feel about that?"

Dave related the events of the past few months and said he had come to terms with it, thanks in no small part to her son's support. Mary asked if he was disappointed that his sister hadn't taken his side. He explained that it wasn't unexpected as they hadn't really got on since she had married and left to live in New York.

"Such a complicated life you lead. Tell me, you're thirty two and Jonathan is twenty, why are you friends?"

Dave wasn't going to lie. "I don't know from his point of view but for me it's clear. He's so easy to talk to and he makes me feel better about myself than I have for many years. Jonathan is a very special person. Does that answer your question?"

He knew immediately that she could see beyond that and all of a sudden he feel very uncomfortable.

"I used to think there was something wrong with my son and still do sometimes. I had him checked out for autism and a bunch of other things when he was little. He wasn't interested in other kids or the things all boys do except football. The doctors said he was very intelligent and didn't need the same stimulation other boys of his age needed. When his dad died he lost his best friend. Then there was Gabriella she was so good for him but that ended in disaster.

"Since then he has filled every minute of his day with studying and working at the pub. Then you came along and he's as happy as I've ever seen him, if not happier. Something bothers me though. You can't hide your feelings very well. I don't know if he's noticed but it's the way you look at him and that tells me it's more than friendship. Are you two, well you know?"

Of course he knew and he reassured her that nothing of the sort had happened.

"But you'd like it to, so just be careful. You've both very vulnerable, you more than him and I don't want to see either of you hurt. Jonathan, and I suspect you, have suffered enough and he is still very young, to have to go through anything like that again. Ok?"

He felt sick, was it so obvious. All he could say in response was "Ok."

Jonathan returned with the ice cream and was aware of an atmosphere and asked Dave if something was wrong. Dave dug deep and smiled and said everything was fine and it was just he had a lot on his mind and a whole bunch of things he still had to do for work and the sale. He apologised for letting his mind wander and did his best to stimulate conversation sticking mostly to football. He told them that he would have to forsake Mrs Brown as he had to go to the casino that night and would have to more or less eat and run. He also wouldn't be around for a couple of weeks due to his work load.

Mary helped by saying, "Of course love we understand you've got to do your duty."

Jonathan walked to the door with Dave and asked if he would like him to go with him to the casino. Dave declined graciously and when they parted said goodbye, not see you or ciao or later or anything that would indicate a further meeting, just goodbye.

Jonathan closed the door and went straight to his room. He lay on his bed and thought about the evening's events and it was obvious that something had happened whilst he was out and left the thought to percolate.

He lay on his bed thinking and then picked up a book. Mary came in about half an hour later and sat on his bed.

"I'm going to Spain two weeks today but not to worry I'll be home well before Christmas."

"That's the third time you've been this year. I think Dave was right, you have got a boyfriend."

"None of your business," she said on her way out.

Jonathan went back to his book and woke at three o'clock with it balanced on his chest. Never lie down to read. He thought about calling Dave because he knew something was upsetting him. He decided to leave it as if he woke him it would deprive him of precious sleep.

Dave walked to Westbourne Grove and hailed a passing cab. He stayed at the casino until four o'clock and was driven home by one of his staff as he hadn't got his own car with him and it was pouring with rain. It was early November and Dave remembered it would be Guy Fawkes Day on Tuesday. Didn't it always rain on Guy Fawkes, well then it was likely to rain for a few more days if not weeks. He shook himself and reminded his fragile being not to get cranky, be positive.

When he got home he went straight to bed but sleep was fitful. There was nothing specific just one of those crazy mixed up nonsensical group of images that fill restless sleep. He got up at eight and showered and thought about going to mass but decided to go back to the casino instead. He sat at the kitchen table and noticed a circular stain that his coffee cup had made so he got a cloth and cleaned it. How ordinary on a day of extraordinary pain. He had to clear his mind and understand that separation was the only solution. It was better than Jonathan finding the truth and really hating him. He resolved to be stoic.

Jonathan waited until Wednesday before he called. Dave answered almost immediately and without waiting for Jonathan's greeting he apologised and said he couldn't talk and he would call him back when he had time.

Jonathan heard that familiar desolation in his voice but left it at that. By the middle of the following week they had still not contacted one another. Dave had rehearsed what he would say when the call came.

Jonathan didn't know how to handle the situation. He wasn't sad or angry, just worried for his fragile friend. He made the call and was greeted with an abruptness that surprised him.

"Jonathan, please don't call me again, just leave me alone ok."

"Ok but should you need me anytime night or day I'm here."

"Oh fuck off and leave me alone."

He hung up and his stomach turned to jelly. He made his way as sedately as he could to the bathroom and emptied what little there was in his stomach. When he came out of the cubicle his floor manager was standing outside the door.

"Dave I thought it was you. You look terrible. We'd better get you home."

Dave didn't have the energy to argue and was promptly driven home. Mrs Hayes had just started her holiday, two weeks in the Canaries, so he was alone. He spent the next few days doing his best to distract himself and was to some extent successful. He could easily justify what he did and he knew he'd done it for the greater good. He went for short walks always ending up in a church of any denomination where he would say a prayer asking for forgiveness for the carnal thoughts he'd had for Jonathan. They say guilt is taken to extremes by Catholics but Dave had more than his share. He wondered what Jonathan would do if the roles were reversed but that made him feel worse. He wondered what Jonathan was doing.

It was Friday night, the only good thing in his life had gone and there didn't seem any point in living. He wanted to die. He'd had his share of crap in life but this was worse than everything combined. He considered suicide but his strong catholic principals won out. He resorted to the whiskey bottle. He had two glasses and realised that wouldn't help. He stripped down to his boxers and his under vest and went upstairs and pushed weights. He'd been told on many occasions that whilst you're exercising you can't feel depressed so he went for it in a big way. He continued for almost three hours and was dripping wet when he went back down to the kitchen. He made tea and nibbled some toast. He picked up the newspaper and looked for the crossword. He kept himself occupied this way until finally at four o'clock in the morning his eyes started to feel heavy. He got up and went into the lounge and lay on the sofa.

He closed his eyes and knew beyond doubt that it would get better. He fell asleep about an hour later having lost that argument.

Jonathan closed his phone. He tried to work out what was wrong. He knew Dave hadn't meant what he'd said but what would make him say those words.

The following days he went about his day as usual, lectures, library and when he got home he studied but for the first time in his life he found it hard to concentrate. He was getting increasingly worried about Dave and on Friday night lay on his bed thinking about the situation. He knew Dave very well and the only thing that kept popping into his head was that somehow this was supposed to be for his good, but why? What could he think he was doing that would benefit him and at the same time cause himself so much pain. He closed his eyes and remembered what had happened the last time they met. His thoughts were jumbled. He picked up a book and started to read. He read the same page three times without absorbing one word. He had an ache in his chest and a big hole in his stomach. He tried to read the page again and a teardrop wet the page. Suddenly he was convulsed with grief. He cried like he was a child and sobbed into his pillow

He looked at his clock and it was already five in the morning. It seemed that he'd been awake all night but must have dozed now and again or time had entered a new dimension.

He got up, dressed and went to the kitchen and made coffee. He sat at the table with the coffee pot close to hand to help him revive when the sinking feeling of exhaustion visited his tired mind. That's where Mary found him. The minicab was picking her up at seven thirty so she had set her alarm for six.

She asked her tired looking son why he was up so early but got no response. She made herself tea and toast and then went to finish packing and getting ready. She came back into the kitchen at seven and Jonathan was still stuck to the chair.

"Football today?"

"No, Dave doesn't want me to bother him any more so I have no one to go with."

"Oh, maybe that's for the best. You look terrible, have you been crying?"

"Yes I have been crying, all night and why is it a good thing?"

"Well you don't have much in common, do you? He might be clever but he's a bit rough and well, his business is a bit shady. You'd be better off having friends of your own age who are more like you."

"Mum, I'm twenty and before Dave came along I'd never had a friend in my whole life. I miss him so much. We are alike in so many ways. He gives me more than anyone in this world ever has and he filled a space in me I didn't know was empty. He's not what he seems, he hides himself the same way I do. He needs me, he's the only person that has ever needed and I need him to need me, if that makes sense. I can't concentrate, I feel like half of me is missing. Mum, I was the one that started this friendship. He understands and I love him so much. Why has he done this?"

"You love him? How can you love him, he's a man. I thought you loved Gabriella."

"I did, and still do, love Gabriella but this is different. I know you loved Gabriella she was the daughter that you wish you had. I was always a disappointment to you. You thought I was odd, different and you still do. Well mum that's me and Dave get's it."

"Have you had sex with him?"

"No, he's never shown any interest in me that way but I want to have sex with him. I want to go to bed with him every night and wake up next to him every morning for the rest of my life. I feel so much pain. It's not just my pain, I can feel his too. I know he's somewhere feeling terrible. The guy's had a real shit life and now something's happened and he's hurting badly. I can feel it. He won't talk to me, I don't know what to do" With that he burst into tears again.

Mary had never seen him like this before. He cried when his dad had died and he was frantic when Gabriella left but this was different. This was so intense. What had she done?

Mary sat down at the table and took a deep breath. "He loves you too. It's obvious and I thought it was one way. The last night he was here for dinner, I sent you out for ice cream. That was a ruse to get you out of the way. I had a heart to heart with Dave."

She related almost word for word the conversation they had that Saturday night. Jonathan listened and when she was finished she added. "It's more than friendship he loves you and that just won't do will it or that's what I thought. I'm a stupid interfering woman."

"Thanks for telling me mum".

"Well are you surprised or something?"

"What that you're a stupid interfering woman or that Dave's doing this because he loves me? In either case I'm not surprised but I'm just so relieved"

"Jonathan you're right, I've never understood you. You speak in riddles sometimes and maybe I did want you to be different but you're my son and I love you, so do what you have to do with my blessing."

Just then the doorbell rang and Mary started her journey to Spain. Jonathan kissed her goodbye, hugged her and thanked her. In passing he said

"What you said to him has actually made everything right." She shook her head in disbelief as she ducked into the back seat.

Jonathan went to his room and packed the books he needed, two days change of clothes and some accessories. He brushed his teeth and splashed his face and set off to Lansdowne road.

When he arrived he thought better about ringing the door bell so he let himself in with his key. He dropped his bag in the hallway and hung up his coat. He looked into Dave's bedroom and his heart sank. The bed had not been slept in. Never mind Dave had to come home sometime. He went downstairs to the kitchen which whilst not exactly a mess was a war zone by Dave's standards. He went into the lounge and saw his friend asleep on the sofa dressed only in his underwear and smelling like the zoo. There was a throw on the back of the armchair and Jonathan lifted it gently on to Dave's putrid smelling body. He crept out of the room and set about making coffee and tidying up the kitchen. When he was finished he poured himself a coffee and stood by the kitchen sink looking out of the window at the occasional headless body passing by. He was about to pour himself another cup when Dave's voice broke his reverie.

"Jonathan what are you doing here? You should leave."

"Good morning Dave. What a perfect day and as to your question, I live here and I was cleaning up your mess because I don't like a messy home."

Dave put his hand to his head. "I don't understand what you're saying will you please go?" He looked at Jonathan and saw his eyes were swollen. "What happened to you, you look terrible but please leave."

"I've been crying all night because I thought I'd lost you and if I thought you half meant that I'd be out the door like a shot but you don't. I managed to get my witch of a mother to tell what she said to you when she conveniently forgot the ice cream."

"And what did you learn from that?" he said just audibly.

"That you're a fucking pervert and you want my body."

Dave had been standing on the other side of the kitchen counter and now he had to hold onto the worktop for support. He felt a million emotions and none of them good.

"That's ok though because I want to be a fucking pervert with you."

"Jonathan are you some kind of idiot. You're saying you want to have sex with me?"

Jonathan gave Dave a look that would have melted anyone's heart.

"Come round here and sit at the table I have something I need to tell you and I think all this is my fault because I'm as guilty as you in the trying to protect arena."

Dave slowly moved around the counter and sat down as instructed and accepted the cup of coffee proffered in silence.

"Mum thinks there's something wrong with me and always has. I don't have the same needs as mister average, in fact I've never felt that I've needed anything really or anyone. Gabriella was a teenage thing and very intense but I think that just happens when you're young. I did love her and probably always will but that's little more than a memory now.

"When we first met you moved me and I didn't understand what was happening. You seemed to find something in me that nobody else has been able to. I feel different when I'm with you. I feel important and needed and that's not a feeling I've ever experienced before.

"I love being with you, it's all so easy. You're smart, you're magnificent and over time I've come to need you and love you very much. I can't imagine life without you. There's no one in this world that could make me feel like that, just you. I do things with you that I never thought would interest me. I even enjoy going to mass with you and I'm a fucking atheist.

"I've wanted to get into your bed for a while now. I didn't know it then but I think it was in the back of mind as far back as Brighton. I wanted to say something but I wasn't sure you were ready to hear it. When you said we could go to Rome I was hoping we'd share a room but that wasn't to be."

"Jonathan you want to have sex with me, why?"

Jonathan feigned a shy look and said. "Because I love you and I know you love me just as much so making love is the next logical progression to cement the relationship. We've done the most intimate thing and that's getting into one another's minds so the physical bit is just icing on the cake so to speak."

"Jonathan that was doomed from the start. You're only twenty and I'm thirty three. Have you ever had sex with a man?" Dave hid his face in his hands and stayed that way. Jonathan watched him and wasn't sure what to say. They sat like that for about five minutes.

"Look at me Dave."

Dave shook his head and said without looking up, "Just leave will you, this could never work, you're too young and I don't think you understand what you're asking for, so go."

Jonathan thought for a while and Dave remained with his hands covering his face.

Jonathan stood up and said in an angry loud voice, "You patronising cunt."

Dave's head jerked up and he couldn't work out what had just happened as Jonathan had a smile on his face.

"I thought that would get your attention and now you're looking at me.

"Now I'll answer your question, no of course not. I've never had sex with a man, have you?"

"You know I have so don't talk like an idiot."

"Right so when we have sex I can expect to be beaten to within an inch of my life, raped, coerced into giving you exactly what you want and generally abused."

"How could you even think that?"

"How could you? Now David Wilson have you ever had sex with a man?"

Dave took a deep breath, "I suppose not."

"Sorry but that's not good enough."

"No I've never had sex with a man." Having said it he somehow felt better. "You little creep, you've done it again."

Dave felt a calmness descend. Jonathan had that effect on him. He was logical without being dispassionate and just the sight of him brought warmth that flowed through his body. Did he have a right to love such a perfect being when he was damaged goods? Jonathan had said he loved him and those words were still ringing in his ears. He closed his eyes and tried to think clearly. Jonathan was different; he was close to being a genius. He reduced problems to their simplest form and made them go away. Why should he doubt his sincerity and his certainty? He realised he doubted himself but why? He would never hurt Jonathan, he could only love him and that's what they both wanted.

"Jonathan using your logic and knowing how I feel about you I can honestly say I never thought it possible for me to love anyone but I do. I love you more than life and I've never had sex with a man and I'd like to discover what that would be like but only with you. There will never be room for another person in my head; it's full of just you."

Jonathan gave him the warmest smile and said. "Good I thought not but I can help there. I know more or less how it's done. Don't say a word and can that be the end of the stiff upper lip adult conversation?" Dave had opened his mouth but now sat silent knowing something magical was about to happen.

"When you said we could go to Rome I had all of the Monday before to do research whilst you were working. I went to the British Library and looked at books on homosexual love and most of them were unhelpful but then I found one that gave a step by step description of what to do and how to do it. I memorised that, thank goodness there weren't pictures of real people that would have grossed me out but there were drawings. It all looks pretty straightforward. There was one problem though, it said you had to apply a lubricant but it didn't say how much. Living in hopes of getting into bed with you for ten days I went to the chemist and bought a few tubes to be on the safe side."

At this point Dave could hold it in no longer,

"Jonathan I love you so much it hurts."

"Is that what the pain in my stomach is, love? Stand up. We can learn how to do this together. Step one we have to caress so hug me. Fucking hell don't kill me."

Dave had held him tightly but obviously too tightly. They stood holding each other then Jonathan whispered "Now we have to kiss."

They kissed gently and then with a bit more passion. Jonathan slipped his hand up the back of Dave's vest and gently moved his hand up and down his spine until he reached the waistband of his boxer's. He put his hand inside and held his bum, all the time kissing. With his hand still on Dave's bum he pulled his head back and said "That's step three but I couldn't tell you because I didn't want to stop kissing you. Why does your bum feel so soft when the rest of you is rock solid?"

"I'm also soft in the head,"

"There's something I forgot in my eagerness to get to your good parts. It said we have to be clean and you smell like a bear that's been rolling in shit, so let's go and have a shower only this time we have to do it together so that I can be sure you're clean. It says that in the book and by the way I have ten tubes of lubricant in my backpack upstairs."

Dave hugged him and kissed him with difficulty as he was laughing. They headed hand in hand to the kitchen door when Jonathan suddenly stopped, looking puzzled. "When did you become thirty three, did I miss your birthday."

"No you didn't, it's today."

"Well happy birthday Dave let's celebrate."

CHAPTER THIRTY SIX

Jonathan woke up disorientated. He had to think for a moment as to where he was. The large arm around his waist reminded him. He looked at the bedside clock; it was four in the afternoon and very grey looking outside. His first reaction was to pull the covers over his head and go back to sleep but he thought better of it. He turned to face the owner of the arm who was sound asleep.

He slid out from under the appendage and slowly got out of bed so as not to disturb. He slid on his undershorts and went down to the kitchen. The coffee was still on the hot plate so he poured himself a cup of the stewed brew. It tasted bitter but he drank it anyway as an aid to revival of his, wanting to go back to bed, body and soul.

He searched the fridge for food but everything in there was stuff that one had to cook and that had never been a skill he'd acquired. He found bread, butter and rifled through the cans in a food cupboard until he found sardines, a little fish to which he was partial. He toasted the bread and made himself a sandwich. He was about to take a bite when he realised that Dave would awaken starving. He ate whilst making three more and a fresh pot of coffee. He put the fare onto a tray and carried it up to the bedroom. He bent over and kissed Dave on the head and gently suggested he wake up. He got no response so he tried a little shake but still nothing. He then resorted to pulling back the bed clothes and a semi-violent shake. That did the trick. Dave woke up with a start. When he gathered his thoughts and recalled the previous events of the day he smiled at Jonathan and said, "I'm starving."

He ate with gusto and then suggested they stay in bed all day as it looked so miserable outside.

"That's not why you want to stay in bed. You are going to get up and shower and then you're going to the casino to show everybody that the boss is fine. Whilst you're doing that I will do my studying. It's almost five o'clock so what time will you be back?"

"You're very bossy." He grabbed Jonathan and pulled him down onto the bed. "What if I don't want to go to the casino? What if I want to stay here with you?"

"Dear Sir, we must start how we mean to continue so get up."

At six Dave got up and Jonathan awoke and followed him into the shower. Dave was hungry again so they aborted Jonathan's plan and went out to dinner instead. Jonathan had seen Dave eat large portions but that night he surpassed himself.

"I've hardly eaten these past two weeks and my stomach feels like a bottomless pit."

"I love to watch you eat, it's incredible how much fuel your large frame needs." He raised his glass and said "Happy birthday Dave."

Dave raised his glass and offered no reply other that a smug grin.

They went straight to bed when they got home and after following Jonathan's steps to sex, fell into a deep sleep.

Jonathan woke up at six and it was still dark. He needed the bathroom so he got up without waking Dave and relieved himself. He threw on his clothes and went downstairs. He made some coffee and sat at the dining table and sorted out his books. It was cold so he put on his coat which he retrieved from the hall but he still felt cold. He tried the office which felt marginally warmer and settled at the desk to work.

Dave stirred at nine thirty then turned over to find the other side of the bed empty. He sat up and listened but couldn't hear anything. He got up and checked the shower and the bathroom then on his way down to the kitchen he noticed that Jonathan's coat was missing from the coat rack. The coffee pot was hot and there were signs that life had existed but where was it? He thought maybe books had been required or something and he went back upstairs to retrieve his hand phone. He called Jonathan's number and a phone rang in the bedroom, it was Jonathan's. He went back downstairs and poured himself a coffee and searched the refrigerator for breakfast materials. He found eggs, sausages and bacon and set about cooking. It was then he heard a noise over the sizzle of the bacon and went to investigate and found Jonathan in the office.

"Why are you in here?"

"It's freezing this was the warmest spot I could find."

"Sorry, I'll switch the heating on. I'm cooking breakfast come and eat and you can carry on with your studying after breakfast."

"I've just about finished. I've been at it since six."

Dave felt a little guilty, something he was good at, and apologised for distracting him the day before.

"I get up about six most mornings, I have an internal alarm clock and as for the distraction bit, I hope you have to apologise every morning. Go cook and I'll be with you in a minute."

After breakfast they had a quick shower and went to mass. Jonathan was surprised that Dave went to communion. He knelt with him when he returned to listen to his mantra but it wasn't forthcoming. Dave said whatever prayer he had needed to in his head.

When they left the church Dave quickened his pace and Jonathan fell into step.

"What's the rush?"

"The priest just waved and he's talking to the Worthingtons and I don't want to get caught up in a half hour conversation and then have to decline a lunch invitation."

"Why?"

Dave had a thoughtful look on his face and he looked up at the clear blue autumn sky and said he didn't know why anymore, it's just what he always did.

"Maybe we should go back and I can introduce you."

"That might look a little odd, next time. You didn't say your little Indian prayer after communion."

"It's redundant."

"How so?"

They entered a small restaurant and sat at a window table and ordered.

"From the unreal I have already found reality, the world is bright and I'll make my immortality through you."

"Sounds like a heavy burden."

"It won't be you'll be my inspiration that will let me create something meaningful that will outlive me."

"What will that be?"

"The thoughts have been coming together since I realised I wasn't really cut out to be a fireman but they need time to brew, like this coffee that's just about to arrive."

After lunch they walked along Knightsbridge to Hyde Park corner neither of them suggesting where to go. They walked under the subway to Piccadilly and bypassed the queue at the Hard Rock. They crossed over and walked through Green Park waved to the queen and entered St James's Park where they sat and watched the children happily feeding the birds.

"You went to communion?"

"I did indeed and I can honestly say I have never felt more worthy. Do you think I shouldn't have?"

"No, I was surprised that 'Mr I'm Guilty For Everything' didn't see us as a sin."

Dave lifted his head back and breathed in deeply and exhaled with a smile on his face. "God sent you to me so how could that in anyway be anything but a blessing."

Jonathan stood up and faced Dave who remained seated.

"You're amazing and I'm getting a bit cold sitting so let's walk."

They walked across the park and through Horse Guards Parade to Whitehall. The number of tourists was increasing the closer they got to Westminster Bridge. They crossed the river and walked along the South Bank. They conversed most of the time and only paused when they stopped to look at something. They arrived at the Tate Modern and went inside to see what was on but there was nothing much of interest to either of them so they went up to the top floor restaurant and had tea. It was Jonathan's suggestion as he was thirsty and he knew the Hulk would need feeding at any moment and sure enough he had two sandwiches and a large piece of carrot cake.

They exited the gallery at four and crossed the millennium bridge and caught the tube home from St Paul's.

Once home they found warmth and comfort under the duvet. It was dark outside and Dave woke up at five thirty and closed the curtains and lit his bedside lamp. Jonathan was asleep so he got back into bed and picked up a crossword book that was on his bedside table. Jonathan awoke at six thirty and snuggled into Dave.

"Wow its six thirty, what are we going to do for dinner? Shall we order in a pizza or six?" Dave thumped him.

"No, there's food in the freezer so I thought we could sort something out and bung it in the microwave." And that's what they did.

With all the happenings of the last thirty six hours Jonathan had forgotten to ask Dave how the sale of his business was going and Dave hadn't mentioned it and it seemed like an opportune time to ask.

"There's one document still to sign and then we're done. My step-mother has signed and we just need Carol's signature and she's coming over in a couple of weeks time so it's more or less done."

"How do feel about that?"

"If someone had asked me that question last week I'd have said it was shit and so was life in general. I'd lost something I'd built, I'd lost you and I just wasn't functioning well. In fact I thought I was going crazy but now it seems the right thing to do and life is almost perfect."

"Only almost, what would make it perfect?"

"Dinner, so come on get yourself out of bed and let's go and raid the freezer."

"So life is going to one long competition for your affections, it's me versus food, what a life."

"We could stay here and I could starve to death if that pleased you."

"It just might."

Dave jumped out of bed and dragged Jonathan with him.

"Food here we come and do you know we've slept three times since yesterday morning and I've not dreamt once."

Over dinner they decided that Dave would drive Jonathan to LSE in the morning and pick him up at four. He had to go to the casino that evening but not until nine and that worked for them both. Jonathan didn't ask how long he would be gone because that was Dave's life and not a thing to be questioned.

For the next three weeks Dave spent his days and some of the night as usual at the casino and when he returned home in the wee hours there was a warm body waiting for him in bed. On Wednesday evening of the third week, something very strange happened to Jonathan but it wouldn't be until the following Monday he would understand why.

On Friday Jonathan announced that he was on study leave the next week and had a lot to do. Dave played with an idea and offered a suggestion.

"I've got an idea but please say if it doesn't work for you."

"What is it?'

"I could ask my boss for a week off and we could go to the house in the Cotswolds. It's peaceful there and I promise I won't disturb you. I'll be cook and general dog's body."

"You are the boss."

"Then permission granted. What do say?"

"Sounds great but you can disturb me sometimes. What will you do?"

"There's a lot of money coming and I need to decide how best to invest it. I can't leave it sitting around idle so it will give me time to do some research and formulate a plan to increase the already considerable sum. I still have another year to work in the business but I should start getting my head around what's next. So it will be productive for me too."

"Great, let's do it."

"Ok we'll go on Sunday and come back Friday because your mum's coming back the following Monday isn't she? That'll give you time to give your flat a clean before she arrives."

"You mean it will give us time to clean up. The place hasn't been lived in since she left so it shouldn't take long especially with the two us doing it." He put on a smug face, "Sunday it is then."

"What time does she get back?"

"I don't know, sometime in the morning, she's going to call me on Saturday to tell me so I can book her a minicab."

"You'll be at Uni on Monday so no welcoming committee for her?"

"No, my schedule has changed and I don't have lectures on Monday until the New Year, so I can be at home when she arrives."

"Why don't we pick her up from the airport?"

Jonathan smiled. "She's going to know as soon as she sees us."

"Well isn't it better to get it over with as soon as possible."

"Your right, let's do that."

They left early Sunday morning and stopped at a twenty four hour supermarket on the way for provisions.

As they drove into the village the autumn sun made the leaded lights of the immaculate houses' windows sparkle. The village looked like something out of a children's book. There was a village green and of course the compulsory pond. It all looked immaculate and manicured. They drove through the village and out the other side. There were just a few houses now dotted around and after a mile Dave pulled up in front of a double fronted stone cottage.

They took their bags from the boot and headed through the front garden to the oak door. The garden looked well tended although void of flowers at this time of year. Dave fished in his pockets for the keys and they entered a small hallway with a coat stand and a shoe rack. Dave removed his shoes and Jonathan asked if he should do the same.

"It gets a bit muddy in the country so it's best to get into the habit." Jonathan followed suit.

They entered a space with a staircase in front of them. To the left was the dining area and kitchen separated by a breakfast bar and to the right was a well appointed living room. It all looked welcoming but too grand to be cosy as Jonathan had imagined. The whole place still had a rustic charm that you wouldn't find in the city but it had a feeling of order which was Dave's trade mark.

It was a two storey cottage and the upstairs consisted of two reasonably sized bedrooms separated by the staircase at the front of the house and a larger bedroom at the back which was where they dropped their bags. Each room had its own bathroom.

Jonathan flopped onto the bed and said "Nice."

"Glad you like it, let's get unpacked and then we can sort out the kitchen."

"That will take me about a second but your bag is big enough for a six month holiday. What have you got in there?"

"I err on the safe side and bring what I know I need and what I might need, you know in case. I suppose all you've packed is tee shirts and jeans. You're just a scruff bag but I like you."

"Thank you squire, but do you really think I'm a scruff bag?"

"A clean one but a scruff bag none-the-less."

"Good then the image remains intact and hasn't been polluted by the moneyed class but do you mind?"

"Mind what?"

"Me being a scruff bag."

"I love it, the contrast makes me look so much better."

"You bastard" Jonathan said whilst punching the insult deliverer. That lead to more physical abuse and then with them ending up on the bed and a hiatus in the unpacking process.

Dave unpacked and put everything away neatly, hanging his clothes in the wardrobe and his neatly folded underwear in the drawers. Jonathan stuffed all his clothes into drawers without care.

"I bought you something." Dave said handing Jonathan a bag.

"A present for me?"

"Not a present, it's an essential for living in the colder climes of the countryside."

Jonathan opened the bag and took out the contents.

"A jumper, thanks, bloody hell it's soft."

He slipped it over his head and straightened it over his torso. He rubbed his hand over the sleeves and then rubbed a sleeve over his face.

"Wow this didn't come from Marks and Sparks I bet." He looked at the bag and read the shop's name but didn't recognise it.

"Is it cashmere?"

"No alpaca, do you like it?"

"Of course but it must have been expensive and it might be wasted on me, you know how I am with clothes."

"I bought it to keep you warm how you treat it is up to you."

"Thank you Dave. Well whilst we're into giving presents, I have something for you. I know you don't wear jewellery or watches and stuff but it's not really anything like that." He handed him a small brown paper package. Dave opened it and looked at the thing on a string. The thing was an oversized dog tag with David Wilson engraved in capital letters.

"Turn it over."

He did a big smile lit up his face. He read what it said out loud.

"If you find this person please return him to Jonathan and it's got your phone number. Come here."

He gave Jonathan a huge hug and said it was a great present. He slipped it over his head and vowed never to go out without wearing it.

Dave sorted out the groceries and cooked steaks and fries and made a salad whilst Jonathan readied his studying materials at one end of the dining table and commenced reading.

When the food was almost ready Dave went into the living room and put on some music. Jonathan got up from the table and followed the music. Dave was thumbing through a record collection stored in a large upright cabinet. There was a record playing on a deck which Jonathan recognised but couldn't put a name to. The music seemed to engulf him as the sound system was brilliant.

"It's Billie Holiday. Dad loved blues, rock and anything sixties so that's what this lot is. If you want we can go through them later. We should light a fire the logs are already in here, good" he said noticing the pile in the hearth.

They sat down to lunch and Jonathan asked where the logs had come from and why was everything so clean. Dave explained that he paid a lady from the village to come in once a week to check everything was alright and to keep the place dust free. Her husband looked after the garden.

After dinner Dave washed the dishes and Jonathan helped.

"You're supposed to be studying."

"Not today, I've sorted everything out so I'm set to go in the morning. It's Sunday Father Dave, the day of rest. When we're done here can we go for a walk and you can show me the sights?"

"It'll take a lot longer to walk to the village than it will to show you around but that sounds like a good idea."

They walked down the road on which they'd arrived back to the village. Apart from the occasional rustle of dry leaves and a lonely bird call all was silent. The trees were nearly bare except for the hollies and conifers yet there was an overall impression of greenness.

They walked around the village and Jonathan noted one baker shop and a grocer's. They passed a quaint looking pub earlier and were now heading back in its direction. The pub was equally quaint inside and they found a table and had a couple of beers. There were about twenty people other people in the small confines which gave it the impression of being full to capacity. There was a large garden at the rear but the weather didn't tempt anyone outside.

They walked slowly back and Jonathan commented on how peaceful it all was.

"Do you like it?"

"Well enough for a visit but it must be hard to live in a place like this. Maybe that's the city boy in me talking."

"I agree, nice to visit deadly to live in, half the houses are weekend residencies, that's why there aren't many shops, not good for the local economy."

"Do the locals go around protesting and setting fire to empty houses like they did in Wales a few years ago?"

"Heaven forbid, this is the Cotswolds there aren't many locals, they were driven out years ago, sad really."

Jonathan was about to comment but stopped himself anyway Dave saved him the bother.

"I told you I do some committee work for a homeless foundation and here I am leaving a three bedroom house empty. It's a bit hypercritical really."

Jonathan didn't respond.

When they got back Jonathan made coffee whilst Dave lit the fire. They sat in armchairs reading the newspapers they had brought with them and chatting about articles of interest. They finished the coffee and Dave put down his newspaper and started telling Jonathan about the new owners of the business. He was five minutes into his tale when Jonathan started to laugh. Dave couldn't fathom it, what was funny? He certainly hadn't said anything to laugh at. He shot a quizzical look at the amused party.

Jonathan composed himself. "Sorry but since we left London your accent has slowly changed until now you're full on BBC."

"Really, have I? Do you mind? Maybe I've left the source, do you mind?"

"I wouldn't mind if you spoke with a Mongolian accent, in fact I sometimes think you do."

"Fuck you."

"Now it's French."

They listened to music by the fireside and both dozed off in the warm glow of burning logs. Jonathan awoke with a raging thirst and noticed Dave had vacated his chair. He went into the kitchen where Dave was preparing food and got himself a glass of water hastily followed by a second. He looked at the clock at couldn't believe that he'd been asleep for two hours, he felt dreadful.

"You're dehydrated. Whilst we were sitting by the fire the central heating came on, that's what did it. Go and have a shower it will wake you up. Dinner will be ready in about half an hour."

"Dinner, I feel like we've just had lunch." He was winding Dave up as usual knowing Dave was probably hungry again.

"No problem, let's go for a run and you can work up an appetite. I've been pushing some weights whilst you were snoring and I feel up for a leg stretch."

"Ok then, I'll go change and off we'll go."

They ran along the lamp lit road away from the village and admired the non-existent view. By the time they got back and showered Jonathan had worked up an appetite and Dave was hungry enough to eat Jonathan.

After dinner they cleared up and sat by the fire on the sofa and did Dave's crossword together. They went to bed at ten. Jonathan was in the bathroom brushing his teeth and Dave was in bed. When ablutions were complete Jonathan turned off the bathroom light and got into bed. Dave was fast asleep.

Jonathan got up at six thirty and started his studying with a fresh pot of coffee. Dave came down at nine and made breakfast. Whilst he was clearing the dishes his phone rang and Jonathan looked up and listened to one side of a conversation.

"Hi, yes I'm fine I was going to call you later. I just needed some sleep so I'm taking a break in the country.

"I'll be back Tuesday next week but I can be contacted if needs be.

"Yes really, thanks for your concern.

"So I've been told. Is that a problem?

"You'll get used to it, can you transfer me to Marcus.

"Hi Marcus, I'm not going to be around until Tuesday next week so can you work out a roster until then so that one or other of the senior guys are on night duty until I get back. You can also warn them that it will become a permanent arrangement but we'll talk about that when I get back.

"That's exactly what it means no more burning the midnight oil for me, I've got a life.

"Ok great and can you tell Michael to email me if there are any problems with the auditors.

"Thanks. See you a week tomorrow."

"Dave I listened purposely and did I hear right, you're giving up the night life?"

"Absolutely, I have other things I'd rather do."

"Are you doing it because of me?"

"Yes and no. I started off spending my nights at the casino because it was better than sleeping, then it became a habit. I'm not really needed there all the time I can delegate, something that doesn't come naturally or didn't. I'll still do nights a couple of times a week. I never had any reason to go back to the house but now I do. Now I have a home, alright?"

"Very alright."

Jonathan continued his studying and Dave disappeared upstairs. He came down at eleven thirty and said he was going into the village to get some fresh bread and a newspaper. He'd be gone about an hour.

Jonathan was staring at him.

"Is something wrong, are my flies undone or something?" he said checking.

"Nothing's wrong, you look like someone off the cover of Country Life and your hairs floppy, no gunk and it looks really blond."

"Is that a good thing or a bad thing?"

"You look terrific, too good to let out alone, I'm coming with you"

"No you're not you're staying right here. If you mess around we're going straight back to London and I'll go to work."

"Yes almighty one, you do look great though. Wait just a sec." He picked up his phone and took a picture.

Jonathan sat at the table thinking about what he'd just seen and what he'd heard earlier. For the first time since they had met Dave looked his age. His bags were almost gone and his eyes had a sparkle in their deep blue. He'd been sleeping a lot which was new and its effects were apparent. He smiled to himself and searched his phone for a photo he had taken surreptitiously of Dave in February. The difference was astounding. He smiled and returned to his studies.

Dave left and returned with his purchases at one o'clock which he put in the kitchen. He was about to fill the coffee pot but stopped and from the back view it looked like he was admiring the view through the kitchen window. Jonathan noticed the inactivity and knew something was wrong. He got up and joined Dave at the sink. The big man's face looked so serious but he didn't ask why.

"Come and sit down and I'll make some coffee."

Dave obeyed without objection, the look having intensified. He put his head in his hands and just sat there. Jonathan said nothing and offered no comfort he had made coffee and he put a cup in front of the silent man and just sat there and watched. After a few minutes Dave sat up straight and smiled.

"Sorry about that."

"You've nothing to be sorry for. What do you think happened?"

"When I was walking back I was looking about me and everything looked so beautiful. I felt light and free and extremely happy. Then when I came in and saw you it just happened, I was dumbstruck and I'm not sure why. I think I was in a panic that it might not be real"

Jonathan sat looking into his empty tea cup, then lifted his head and scanned Dave's face.

"Pretty much the same thing happened to me on Wednesday. I was sitting on the side of the bed thinking how perfect life was when I started to cry. I fell asleep crying but I didn't feel unhappy, quite the opposite."

"You did this Jonathan, you make me so happy. I'm sure I'll still have some insecurities but doesn't everyone? Maybe I'll be able to cry one day."

"The last thought I had before I started crying, was that I felt safe for the first time and I'm not sure what that meant. You make me feel safe in a way I've never felt before and yet I didn't know I hadn't felt that. Sounds screwy I know."

Dave stood up and removed his jacket. "I'm not hungry, don't worry it won't last. You're going to take a break now so come on let's go and check the view from upstairs."

They slept until five and Dave cooked dinner. Whilst eating Jonathan said he had finished the first part of his assignment and only needed a couple more days to study. He wanted to have the next day free if the harsh task master would allow.

"I'd ask you if you were sure but you're too diligent to not know. Ok tomorrow shall we go into Oxford and wander?" which is exactly what they did.

On Wednesday afternoon Jonathan fished in his backpack for a book and came across an envelope. He was about to put it back but he thought of Dave who was in the sitting room by the fire doing his crossword. He went to join him and took the chair opposite. Dave looked up.

"Dave I have to do this some time and I'd rather get it over with now. I don't want anything coming between us and no secrets."

Dave nodded his agreement and noticed the envelope and wondered with trepidation what it might be.

"I told you that Gabriella left me a note, well this is it. I'd like you to read it."

He handed it over and Dave noted it was addressed to Juan Martinez.

He took out the contents and raised his shoulders with a puzzled look on his face. "It's in Spanish."

"Sorry of course shall I translate?"

Dave wasn't sure he was ready for this but agreed anyway.

"There's no introduction it goes straight in, here goes.

'I have to leave and I mean forever. I love you so much and I know you love me, that's something I will always have.

We've had almost two years of pure heaven and I want you to remember that. If I stayed things would change and not for the better. Our careers will take us in different directions and like most people we'd end up bored or stifled. We're just too young to make life time decisions. When you asked me to marry you I so wanted to say yes but I love you too much for that, you deserve the freedom of youth.

I want to appreciate what we had and I think you will. It will never go away but I know it will fade with time.

I will have a part of you until the day I die and you will have a part of me for the rest of your life.

I love you. Gabriella.'

That's it."

Dave had been leaning forward listening and was now silent and staring at his feet. He was trying to understand why Jonathan had shown him the letter. Wouldn't it have been better to just hide it away if he needed to keep it? What purpose had been served? He felt hurt and sighed as he looked up.

"You said before that she's inside your head and it's obvious that you'll always be inside hers. You must love her very much. It now all seems very real and I can't compete with that. What was the purpose of showing me the letter, I don't understand."

"I have it and I need you to understand how much I love you. I don't want to do or have anything that I can't share with you and I found the letter in my bag. I wasn't keeping it for a reason I just forgot it was there. I'm not sharing it to hurt you, quite the opposite. That life is over. Do you want me to hide things?"

"No of course not, the way the letter finished made it sound like it would never be over between you two. It was also a bit strange, maybe it was the way you translated it. She would have part of you until the day she died and you would have part of her for the rest of your life." Dave was hurting but he kept control as he measured his words.

Jonathan looked at the letter and shook his head.

"No that's exactly what it says. Dave I can't and won't deny that I love or loved her. I can't change the past and if I could I wouldn't. Everything we've done in life has lead us to our present, changing something would mean I wouldn't have you. I told you that you make me feel safe, you also make me feel loved, appreciated and I even think you find me interesting. You're the complete package, if I lost you, which I won't, my life would be meaningless."

He held up the letter and said, "My life is like this letter the right side is you and the left side is me and together it makes sense."

He tore the letter in two. "Now this piece is me and that piece is you now neither piece has a meaning." He screwed up the bits of paper and threw them on the fire.

"You said that when you had to think about something, you'd discuss it in your head with Gabriella. You don't do that with me."

"Are you jealous of Gabriella?"

"I'd like to say no but I'd be lying. If she suddenly turned up, what would happen?"

"When I first met you I was already losing that. I had been trying to hold on to something because I really didn't want to let go. I realised that I wasn't listening to her but just my own thoughts. I think I was just being juvenile. You're right though, I never discuss things in my head with you. You're non-intrusive yet unless I've got my head stuck in a book, you're all I think about. I don't need to ask what you think, I just know."

"You didn't answer the question about what if Gabriella suddenly turned up."

"What if she did? I'd like to think that she and I could be friends and that's about it. Nothing would change about the way I feel about you absolutely nothing."

"I'm sorry Jonathan, I know it's stupid but I'd wish neither of us had a past. You've accepted mine and if anything was hard, it was that. I'm like a fucking schoolgirl. Let's be very British and have a cup of tea."

"Dave if my life is going to be worth living I need you to be with me and I mean like forever."

"I've known you for only nine months and now you want forever?"

"Absolutely."

"Thank god, let's have that tea." All his insecurities slipped to the back of his mind and he felt good again.

The next morning Jonathan got up at six thirty and crept into the bathroom. He was brushing his teeth when he heard an alarm. It went quiet and Dave entered the bathroom looking very sleepy. He put his arms around Jonathan's waist and laid his head on his back.

"Why are you up so early?"

"Turn around and hug me for a minute."

Jonathan did as he was asked gladly and they stood in a naked embrace for a few minutes. Dave leaned back and let go.

"I've been sleeping a lot and if I don't get my lazy arse out of bed it'll be time to go home. We leave tomorrow."

Jonathan went into the bedroom and dressed whilst Dave brushed his teeth. He went back into the bathroom and said, "I have an idea. Mum doesn't get back until Monday so if we left early Sunday morning we could get back in time to clean the flat, it shouldn't take long."

"Done," Dave said through a mouthful of toothpaste. He rinsed his mouth and asked if Jonathan wanted breakfast now or later and they agreed nine o'clock would work well. Jonathan went downstairs and Dave put on his shorts and did weights for a couple of hours. He showered and put on a bathrobe and went downstairs to make breakfast.

"Have you seen the frost? It looks like Christmas outside." Jonathan got up and looked through window.

"Wow that looks so cool or should I say freezing?"

"Do you want me to turn up the heating?"

"No I'm warm enough I've got a very nice jumper. If it gets too warm I'll get drowsy."

They had breakfast and Dave put his country life outfit on and walked down to the village and Jonathan went back to his studies. After about an hour he felt a little cold. He stood up and went to the window. The frost had nearly gone and the sky looked an even slate grey. Jonathan shivered. He went into the living room and to his delight Dave had lit the fire. He fed the fire with a new log and settled in an armchair with a book. The warmth of the fire was soporific and he gradually nodded off.

On the way back from the village Dave saw a neighbour in his front garden cutting back a leafless shrub. Dave knew him by sight so he stopped and said good morning. The man looked up, smiled and returned the greeting.

"You're David aren't you, George Wilson's son?"

"Yes I am. Did you know him well?"

"You're dad and I go back a long way but I won't tell you the stories, they'd curl your hair," he said with good humour. "Are you here for a while?'

"Just until Sunday."

They chatted for a bit then an enormous German shepherd came bounding out of the open front door and stood on its hind leg with its front paws on the top of the fence right in front of Dave, who took a quick step back.

"She won't hurt you. Poor thing wants a walk but I've hurt my ankle and the doctor said I mustn't walk far for a couple of days. She'll have to wait until my daughter comes back from work.'

Dave stepped forward and stroked the dog. "Would you like me to walk her, would she let me?"

"She's a real softie and she would love that. You sure you don't mind?"

"Not at all, I was going out for a walk later anyway, so I might as well go now. What's her name?"

"Bella, this is very kind of you. I'll go and get her lead."

Dave remembered the neighbour's name, it was Jack Turner and when he returned with the lead Dave asked, "Does she have a special route for her walk Mr Turner."

Jack Turner smiled, "Just remembered my name."

"Guilty."

He told Dave where to go and asked him not to go further or deviate from the route. He also instructed him not to let her off the lead as there were farm animals around and she loved a good chase. Dave ensured him that he would do exactly as he was told and took control of the enthusiastic hound.

He walked the hundred yards to his own cottage without event. Bella was well behaved. He opened the front door and noticed immediately that Jonathan was not at his studies. He put his shopping away apart from one item and went to find the truant. He saw him slumped in an armchair fast asleep.

Jonathan was having a pleasant dream that he wouldn't remember, he rarely did. He was rudely jerked into consciousness by what felt like a wet rag being slapped on his face.

"What the hell?" he said opening his eyes to see the hound of the Baskerville's laughing in his face. He sat up quickly and blinked. The dog put its head to one side as if to say "Who are you?"

Dave started to laugh. "Bella this is Jonathan and he's been a naughty boy. He was supposed to be studying but took a nap instead, tut tut."

"What a beautiful dog. Where did you find her?"

Dave explained and said he had only come back to drop the shopping and papers. "I'll be gone for one hour I have been instructed not to exceed that, so I'll see you later."

"Creep, you know I want to come."

"But you have studying to do." Dave said with a wicked grin.

"Bastard, I'll grab my coat."

"Before you do that I want to give you something by way of an apology." He handed him a Crunchie bar and gave him a hug. "Sorry for being such a jerk about the letter, I'm glad you showed it to me."

"A Crunchie bar will get you anything as you well know. You have nothing to apologise about but if that means I have to give it back then I forgive you."

Off they went on the designated walk. They found the footpath they were told to take and followed the route. They didn't really have to look for landmarks because Bella knew exactly where she was going. She became very excited when she saw a flock of sheep but she was no match for the hulk when she pulled at the lead. The route took them to the other side of the village and then through the village. There were a just a handful of people around either standing outside of their houses chatting or like them, walking dogs. Good mornings were exchanged as they headed towards Bella's home. They offered to do the same on Friday much to Mr Turner's delight.

Dave started to prepare lunch and Jonathan set about brewing a pot of coffee.

"Dave have you ever had a dog?"

"No dad said dogs should only be on a track but I would have liked one. Have you?"

"No we've always lived in the flat and they're not allowed, although some people do have small ones. Maybe we can have one someday."

Dave pinched him on the arm and said, "Yer, let's do that. When I exit the company it will be the first thing I do."

After lunch Jonathan opened his laptop and started typing notes and Dave set about the dishes.

"Dave I need a shower to wake me up, I'm not skiving Ok?"

Dave switched on the radio and hummed to the music. As Jonathan was tidying his things he heard the DJ say "And now we have three in a row, classic ladies of the sixties."

Almost immediately Dusty Springfield's voice started singing "I just don't know what to do with myself." Dave started singing along. He drowned out poor long lost Dusty. Jonathan was amazed by what he heard so he leant on the counter and listened. He assumed Dave had thought he'd gone to have a shower as he was singing unabashedly.

Then came Tina Turner and Proud Mary, Dave picked up two wooden spoons and used them as drum sticks on the draining board as he powered out Miss Turner with a big rock voice. The Ronettes were the last of the medley. Dave tapped out the opening bars and sang using a mixing spoon as a microphone. At the end of the first chorus Jonathan couldn't resist but to sing out loud "a woh woh woh woh."

Dave turned around grinning from ear to ear and started the second verse using overly dramatic gestures. "I'll make you happy baby, just wait and see. For every kiss you give me, I'll give you three." At which point Jonathan gave him the thumbs up and watched the rest of the performance.

"Fucking hell, you can really sing."

"I told you I used to be in a band and that I occasionally sing with the band at the casino, what did you expect?"

"You know I don't know, I never really thought about it but you're beyond good you're like a pro. You can become a singer when you quit work. Do you sing new stuff when you're with the casino band or only golden oldies?"

"Are you implying something? We do mostly new stuff and I have been known to pen a tune or two. I've actually had some very interesting offers in the past but I can't just sing to order. The thought of going on the road and singing the same stuff night after night is anathema to me. The Uni band was great because we didn't do that many gigs and I more or less chose what we played."

"You've never sang in front of me before but it would be nice if you broke into song anytime. I love it."

"Go have your shower."

Dave stretched and laughed.

"What's funny?"

"I think I was a bit hasty getting up so early, all that exercise has knackered me. I think I'll go upstairs and have a nap."

"Right on old man. Do you need a glass for your false teeth?"

Dave ignored the ribbing and went upstairs with Jonathan one to the shower the other to the land of nod.

At three Jonathan stood up and switched the light on. He looked out of the window and the sky had now turned a threatening black and rain would soon be watering the already muddy countryside. He wondered to himself who could live in a place like this. He returned to his laptop and didn't hear the rain cascade down outside being engrossed as he usually was.

The door bell rang and he got up to open the door quickly as he didn't want a repeat to wake Dave. Standing on the doorstep was a women dressed for the elements carrying an umbrella.

"Oh, I was looking for the young Mr Wilson, I'm Elizabeth and I look after the house whilst he's away. Jonathan stepped aside to allow her entry. She hung her coat on the rack, removed her shoes and replaced them with a pair of slippers she took from the shoe rack which were obviously hers.

Jonathan suggested she join him at the dining room table and she took a seat.

"Dave's upstairs, I'll go and get him." She nodded her thanks and Jonathan bounded up the stairs and leapt onto the bed rudely awaking the sleeping Dave.

"You've got a visitor so get your clothes on and come downstairs."

Jonathan quickly returned to the guest who insisted he call her Lizzie, everybody else did.

"I'm making tea and coffee which would you prefer Lizzie."

"Tea would be nice, what's your name?"

"Oh I'm sorry that was very rude of me. My name is Jonathan and I'm staying here with Dave, in fact we live together in London."

Lizzie smiled for the first time and said she was pleased to meet him. Jonathan excused himself whilst he made the beverages and quickly set a tray with biscuits, cups and saucers, and the tea and coffee pots. He carried it to the table and sat opposite Lizzie just as Dave appeared.

"Mrs Ure how nice to see you to what do I owe this honour?" He sat next to Jonathan and poured himself coffee as the other two occupants already had their drinks.

"David, you're looking well. The last time I saw you, was just before Christmas last year and I said to my Maurice, that boy looks older than his years. He must work too hard now his poor old dad is gone. You look like a young boy now."

"Thank you Mrs Ure but I'm sure you didn't walk all the way here in the rain to tell me that."

Lizzie stirred her tea and sighed. "I'm sorry to have to tell you but I won't be able to look after your lovely house starting New Year as we have to move." She hadn't stopped stirring her tea and her hand had become shaky making the tea splash into the saucer. Before Dave was able respond the ever alert Jonathan interceded.

"Where do you live?"

"In Railway Cottages at the back of the village."

"Is there a train station here?"

"No luvvie, there used to be but they closed it down in the sixties. The railway line is still there buried under the grass and the station was bought by a townie, no offence, and turned into a house of sorts."

"How many cottages are there?"

Dave was wondering why he was asking all these questions and wondering where it was all going.

"It's a terrace of five, two up two down. I've lived in ours all my life and Maurice and me have lived there all our married life."

"Who lives in the other cottages?"

"Well the one at the other end to us, we live in number five and that's number one, has been empty for five years. Then there's Ann Montefiore in number two, she's a teacher and she's moving to Australia soon. Her sister lives there and she's been offered a job there. Number three is also empty, poor old Mrs Aslett died last year. Then next to us is Roma Mackenzie, she lives there with her boyfriend who works in Oxford. He doesn't like the commute and he's keen to take the money so they're going soon."

"What money?"

"The owners of the property want to build fancy cottages on the land and they own a big chunk of it around us and they don't want our scruffy little houses being an eyesore so they offered us all twenty thousand pounds each to move out, not that we really have a choice. We went to see a solicitor and he says they have every right to evict us." At this point she shed a couple of tears.

"Sorry, I'm being silly."

Jonathan was quite for a minute so she could compose herself and Dave stayed silent wondering what was coming next.

"Where will you go?"

"We've been looking at some places in Cowley, its cheaper there you know. We have some savings and Maurice can take a lump sum when he retires at the end of the year. The thing is we can't get a mortgage at our age so we can only afford a one bedroom flat or as Maurice puts it a sardine can."

"What would you have done if you didn't have to move?"

She smiled a wan smile. "We had it all planned. I worked for the local corporation all my working life, forty four years and I retired a couple of years ago and I get a decent pension. Maurice retires soon and he'll also get a good pension, better than mine. We were set for our old age and we were going to travel. We both want to go to Rome on account that we've both Catholic. We thought life was going to be so good but now we'll have to spend all our savings and Maurice will have a reduced pension if he takes a lump sum. We have to move away from here to somewhere neither of us want to go and this is home."

"How much rent do you pay?"

"One thousand one hundred a month, I'm sorry I shouldn't be burdening you with my problems."

"You're not. I asked the questions. Are all the other cottages in the village like this one?"

"On the outside as you must have noticed but none are as nice as this inside. I love coming here." And looking at Dave she said "Your dad did a lovely job."

Jonathan then asked, "Did Mr Wilson like it here?"

That prompted a real smile. "He once told me that when he was a little boy he had a picture in one of his books of a country cottage with roses growing around the front gate and wisteria around the front door. He said that they didn't have much money and he'd dreamed of living in a house like this. In the summer there are roses and wisteria. He said that it was his dream come true and a statement that he'd made it. He was such a nice man and he deserved it."

Jonathan continued. "When you move will you have a lot of furniture and things to move, I mean if you have to move to a smaller place."

"It doesn't matter where we move we won't be taking much. Most of our stuff came out of the ark and would fall to pieces if we tried to move it." She smiled again but a sad smile. "We might have to stay with Maurice's brother in Cheltenham for a while so I wanted to ask you David if we could store a few boxes in your store room for a little while. That's what a life time comes down to a few boxes."

Jonathan looked at her with compassion and said "I suppose it's a bit like parts of London here. Rich people decide they like a place and buy everything up and destroy whole communities because they don't support the local community or businesses; they don't integrate. Is that what happened here?"

"I've never thought about it like that but I suppose your right. We used to have more shops and we even had a school. Everybody knew one another and we used to help one another. It was really nice but it all started to change in the seventies when townies took over." She grimaced hoping she hadn't caused offence.

At this point Dave spoke up. Thank you for coming to tell us and I'm grateful for the good care you've taken of the cottage over the years."

"Would you like me to recommend my replacement?"

"Thank you but somehow I don't think that will be necessary."

Lizzie stood up and they showed her out.

Dave looked menacingly at Jonathan and said, "I hate you, I fucking hate you" and disappeared upstairs. Jonathan smiled and thanked him.

An hour later Dave came back down trying to look angry.

"I've asked someone to send you an email with a file attachment. You should get it in about half an hour. When you do I want you to print two copies of the attachment and don't read it ok?" Jonathan nodded but said nothing. Fifteen minutes later he handed some papers to Dave.

Dave sat at the table and read through the document and nodded his satisfaction.

"Right arsehole you need to do something. Put your coat on and walk down to railway cottages and invite Mrs Ure and her Maurice here for a glass of wine at eight o'clock and don't take no for an answer."

"Dave it's pouring with rain, can't you drive me?"

"No Mr fucking clever Dick, walk and get wet. All wishes come with a price."

Jonathan put on his coat and started walking. He got a hundred yards down the road when the Merc pulled up and he got in. Neither of them said anything and when they arrived, Jonathan got out of the car and delivered the invitation which was accepted without question. They drove home in silence and ate dinner much the same way. Jonathan had a shower whilst Dave tidied the house. He didn't need to shower but just wanted to stay out of the way for a while.

They were sitting by the fireside in silence reading the newspapers when the doorbell rang.

The Ures thanked Dave for the invitation and said it was nice when people took the trouble to say goodbye properly.

"That's not why I invited you here. I want to ask you something. Please feel free to say no. I was thinking about your predicament and I think we can kill two birds with one stone here."

The Ures looked at each other puzzled.

Dave continued. "I'm really busy these days and I won't be coming here anytime in the foreseeable future so the place will be empty. I can't sell it because as you said earlier Mrs Ure, this was dad's dream and I'd feel terrible doing that. So I was wondering if you would like to rent it."

Maurice was the first to respond. "We couldn't afford a place like this but it was nice you offered."

"I think you can afford it. At the moment I pay council tax and of course Mrs Ure to look after the place. Then there's the maintenance. With the place being empty things are always going wrong. What I'm proposing is that you rent the place and do the minor repairs yourself and I get a tenant that I can trust."

Now it was Lizzie's turn. "Maurice is right we couldn't afford a place like this."

Dave handed Maurice some papers and asked him to read them. Maurice read with interest then looked up and laughed. "There's obviously a mistake here."

"There's no mistake." Dave said.

Maurice looked stunned.

"What's wrong love?" said a concerned looking Lizzie. When Maurice had gathered his senses he turned to his wife and said, "The rent is ten pounds a month."

Lizzie took the contract and read it then looked at Dave and asked if it was some sort of joke.

"Mr and Mrs Ure I'm deadly serious. This works well for me because I know I won't have to worry about the place. I don't want any old body in here so I refuse to put it on the market for rent. I can't sell my dad's dream so I'm stuck with it. If you rent it I get responsible people I know, I also save money because I don't have to pay council tax, or for someone to take care of the place. I know you'd take good care of it so you really would be doing me a favour. If you say no then the place stays empty."

Lizzie held Maurice's hand and burst into tears. Through her tears she said "As soon as I saw this young man I had a feeling that something good was about to happen. You look like an angel and I think you must be one. Thank you David..." she couldn't finish her sentence because she was sobbing.

Dave dropped his business demeanour and offered a little information. "Jonathan is an angel but a very devious one, I don't like him one bit."

Lizzie said through her sobs, "No but you love him, who wouldn't"

"You got it one Mrs Ure" Dave said looking at Jonathan and shaking his head.

They signed the lease papers and Jonathan witnessed them and spoke for the first time.

Jonathan had kept quiet all through but there was something Dave hadn't said. He addressed himself to the Ures. "I hope you don't mind but we intend leaving the furniture here. The only things we're taking are the sound system, the record deck and Dave's dad's record collection. If you want to get rid of anything you can."

Dave gave him an exasperated look.

Almost at one the Ures said "You're leaving all this beautiful furniture and things behind?"

It was Dave's turn. "We haven't got room for any of it, so yes. We don't have room in the car to take the records and stuff so I'll get a couple of guys to come and collect it next week."

"I'll do that, it's the least I can do and I'll install it at the other end, dab hand at electrics me" Maurice said proudly.

"Shall we all go to the pub and celebrate?" Jonathan suggested.

Maurice said "A fine idea young man and the drinks are on me."

That night as they got into bed Jonathan asked Dave if he still hated him.

"Yes of course. You speak to my conscience without actually stating a case. You're a devious bastard."

"But you're happy about what you did aren't you?" there was no reply so Jonathan thought he should leave it at that and he turned over with his back to Dave who lay motionless.

Suddenly Dave sat up. "You know what the fucking problem is?"

"Well there's no fucking problem here, I think that's off the menu tonight."

"Every time I think I can't love you more, you do something that surprises me and I do."

"You do what?"

"Love you more."

"What you did today was really great and I love you. So is it back on the menu?"

Dave let out an almighty yell and Jonathan gave him half of his Crunchie bar.

Dave woke up late and opened the curtains. It was eleven o'clock. He dressed and went down to the kitchen. Jonathan was looking at his laptop drinking coffee. Dave kissed the top of his head and asked if he wanted breakfast. As he did he noticed there was a picture of a body builder on the screen.

"What are you looking at?"

"Sit down and read this."

Dave sat and read the article.

"I know and I've been thinking about it. I'm up to eighteen stone and that will be hard to shift if I get lax and start turning to fat but you're not going to lecture me are you?"

"Of course not I just wanted to know if a sustained heavy weight affected your health, so I looked it up."

"Is this another one of your mind games?"

"No honestly it's not. It says you're fine it just warns of the consequence of inactivity so maybe you need to remember that if your next job doesn't give you the flexibility you have today."

"Dr Jonathan, you'll be pleased to know that it's on my to-do list and I've already planned how to get down to sixteen stone, ok?"

"I thought you were going to use your time here to plan what you're going to do with your fifty million."

"Are you turning into a fucking nag?"

"I think I am that's fucking terrible."

"Maybe the angel is actually dumping his neutrality and has started showing concern. I can live with that. As to a hundred million pounds, I worked that out on the way here on Sunday whilst you dozed off."

"Wow, money is really easy for you. I haven't got that much and what I have got sits around doing nothing, I haven't got a clue."

"It's about having an interest and money holds no interest for you. For me it's like a challenge and it really interests me. So do you love me this morning after my little outburst last night?"

"No you broke a promise."

"Oh I did, didn't I? I'll get breakfast right away. It was your fault you kept me awake until four o'clock."

Jonathan said with a satisfied grin "It was worth it though. You need to hurry we promised to take Bella for a walk. Just bung on twenty slices of toast and a piece for me."

When they came back from their walk they ate and sat at the table talking. Jonathan had finished all he needed to do so he could relax.

They got onto the subject of Dave's life after the casino.

"I'm going to take some time off and get my head around it. I'm not going to be rushed into anything. I've already had offers from some gaming companies and I get calls all day long at the office from head hunters. I might not know what I want to do but I do know that I don't want more of the same. I've had a few ideas and I'm weighing up the pros and cons."

Jonathan didn't ask what they were because he knew Dave would tell him when he was ready. Dave also knew it was ok to keep it to himself.

"Dave you're great at what you do, you have an amazing voice but there's something you need to practice."

Dave grinned and they got up at five o'clock.

Sunday came all too quickly and they set off back to London at seven thirty and arrived at Portobello Road at ten. It was easy to park as it always was on the day of rest. Once inside the flat they set about cleaning. They started by packing the things Jonathan still needed to take to Lansdowne Road. Dave lay down on the bed.

"Jonathan, come here please."

"Dave we should finish first or we'll have no energy left."

"I don't want sex, I want to talk to you, I have something to ask you but I want you to lie down here with me whilst I ask."

Jonathan lay down with his head in the crook of Dave's arm."

"What's up?"

"I told you about the homeless charity and that I'm the treasurer right?"

"Right,"

"Well we have a fundraising dinner dance once a year. It's our main source of income so it's important and my company sponsors it and arranges everything. I have to make a speech and generally make sure everything goes smoothly on the night, well it's this coming Saturday."

"So you won't be around all day Saturday and you'll be back late on Saturday night. So we miss the football, that's ok and you have to do it of course. I'll keep the bed warm for you but what's the question?"

"I know that's no big deal and if you shut up long enough I'll ask the question."

"Sorry."

"It's a black tie affair and if you're not dressed properly they won't let you in, you know one of those sort of things?"

"Sure I'll come and I'll dress appropriately."

"I haven't invited you yet."

"But you will. Now whilst we're here I suppose we must christen my bed although technically it's not my bed anymore."

"So you'll come, even though you have to dress up like a penguin?"

"I said so didn't I. Trust me I won't embarrass you."

"There is another thing. We're on the top table in full view of everyone."

"I've never been to a big function in a fancy hotel before but I do know my table manners and I'll do my very best not to let you down."

"Now I feel terrible."

"No you don't you feel really good, so can we get our clothes off now?"

"Before that I have to warn you that Lady Worthington, or Dolly Mellor as you know her, is on our table with her family and she can be a bit of a tease and she's bound to interrogate you."

Jonathan smiled and said "I'll be fine. It will be good practice for me because these sorts of things are bound to happen in the future and I need to get my head around understanding that I should be more interested in people. Mum told you that when I was young she thought I might be autistic and I think she wasn't far off. I've read a lot about it lately and I took an on-line test. It said I wasn't but what it did say was I'm deeply introverted so I read about that. Jung said it was a matter of preference so I can learn how to display other types of behaviour without seeming like the oddball I am. I can converse and knowing I'm doing it for you will make it easier."

"You'd go through that for me?"

"I'd do anything for you but now I want you to do something for me."

After they had their fun neither of them felt like cleaning but the place was dusty. They worked out a method, or at least Dave did, that made sense. Jonathan dusted a room and Dave followed up with the vacuum cleaner and then some perfumed surface polish. Mary's room was last and when they had finished it Dave asked Jonathan if the chest it that room was the one his dad had told him the story about.

"Yes that's it. Mum doesn't like it but she keeps all her documents in it because that's what dad used to do."

"Why doesn't she like it?'

"She says it looks out of place but I know she finds it strange and it makes her feel uncomfortable."

Dave made a closer inspection and declared the piece to be beautiful.

"This is a work of art and Arabic I should think which would be possible if it originated in Spain."

"Do you know stuff about furniture?"

"A bit and enough to know this is very old and may even be valuable."

"My dad used to call it his magic box."

"Why's that?"

"I don't know he just did I suppose. It's locked and I don't know where the key is. When you open it there's a mosaic in the lid. It's a picture of a garden I think but I never took that much interest and only saw it open a couple of times."

"I'd like to take a look."

"We'll ask mum when she comes home."

They finished tidying up, loaded up the car with the rest of Jonathan's clothes and books and headed for Lansdowne Road.

Mary had called Jonathan's mobile the day before and said her flight was due in at two thirty.

"If we leave at one we'll be in plenty of time, which terminal is it?" Dave asked.

"She's not coming in at Heathrow, its London City."

"Then we better leave at eleven. We have to drive right across London and the traffic can be pretty horrendous on a week day. If we're early then we can grab a bite to eat whilst we're waiting. I definitely don't want us to be late. Your mum's a witch and she'll put a curse on me, come to think of it she'll probably do it anyway. She'll know as soon as she sees us."

"Probably, she's very perceptive but that means we won't have to tell her right?"

"You're right, let's hope she hasn't lost any of her gypsy powers whilst she's been away."

CHAPTER THIRTY SEVEN

They set off for the airport at the allotted time and the traffic was surprisingly light. They arrived just after one so they had lunch and a few cups of coffee to pass the time. The flight arrived on time so they wandered the short distance to the arrival gate. Mary came through at three. Dave hung back so she didn't see him at first. She hugged Jonathan and kissed him on the cheek. Jonathan took her bag and she walked over to Dave and repeated her greeting.

They walked to the car park and set off for home. When asked if she'd had a good holiday she replied in a neutral manner. Mary sat in the back of the car and Jonathan next to Dave.

Mary spoke at last. "Nice to see you two looking so happy, Dave you look ten years younger and you've lost that hang dog expression. I know what's happened but I don't need to talk about it. You're both adults and it's none of my business"

Dave thanked her and they left it at that but it did prompt a further comment from Mary. "What happened to your London accent?"

"I lost it with a lot of other things I realised I didn't need or want but I'll dig it up if makes you like me any better, Mrs M."

"Stop calling me that, it's Mary to you and who said I didn't like you, you silly sod? Are you coming up when we get home?"

"Sure if I'm invited."

"You don't need an invitation but will you please?"

"Of course"

Jonathan thought this sounded a bit ominous. She looked distracted and she certainly wasn't her normally inquisitive self. She didn't talk much about her trip and spent most of her time looking out of the car window.

"This is such a wonderful city" she said in a tone that suggested she was about to lose it.

"What's up mum?"

"Nothing serious, I'll tell you both when we get home."

Now Dave was starting to feel nervous. It had gone well so far but what did she need to tell them both?

Dave miraculously found a parking space within walking distance and Jonathan carried his mother's bag as they followed her up to their flat.

"Put the kettle on love" she said to Dave, which he did, making tea for three.

Mary emerged from her bedroom and sat at the kitchen table and ordered them to do the same. Dave was getting butterflies expecting the worse. She looked at them both with a half smile and asked how long they had been friends.

They answered in unison "Nine months."

Mary chuckled to herself and said "Long enough to have a baby but that's not going to happen is it."

They knew not to attempt a reply.

"What is it mum?"

Mary didn't answer immediately. She was looking thoughtful and focussing on Dave which made him feel very uncomfortable. Then she addressed him. "Dave are you serious about your, um, feelings for Jonathan and are you going to stand by him for a long time?"

Dave thought to keep it short so he responded with a yes and a yes.

"And you Jonathan?"

"Same mum, you're making this sound like you're the priest and we're getting married, in which case, I do."

Mary laughed a genuine laugh and looked at Dave and said "Well?"

Dave looked at Jonathan and said "I do."

Mary laughed again and said "What a crazy world we live in. I knew I'd come back to this but I didn't know it would make me feel so happy, it's nuts and it's all out in the open which is good but I don't want any hanky-panky in this flat 'cause the walls are paper thin."

"Mum Dave thinks you're a witch, he said so. He said you'd know as soon as you saw us and you did. He must be right, you're a witch."

"Cheeky sod, if I had my wand handy I'd turn this mountain of a man into a tiny frog" she said waving her finger as a wand at Dave. She continued, "So I can safely assume that my son is in good hands, that helps."

"I'm not a child mum so he's in good hands too."

"Jonathan I know you but I don't know Dave that well so I have to be sure ok? Well here goes, I've got a nursing job in Spain starting in January."

Jonathan looked stunned. "What, where, for how long?"

"In Malaga and I don't know for how long but I'd say for at least three to four years. I can come home every now and then but I really have to do this."

Jonathan wondered why she had said she had to do it but thought better of questioning his evasive mother. He got up in silence and made more tea. When he sat down again he nodded at Mary and said "Mum if that's what you want then you must do it. Don't worry about me, I'll be fine and I'm not exactly alone. I have Dave and I haven't told you yet but I'm living at his place and intend to carry on doing that whether you stay or go."

Dave hadn't said anything up to now and he stood up and said he should go and let them talk about it.

Mary looked up at the large frame that seemed to almost fill the kitchen and ordered him to sit down. "I need your help."

Dave obeyed and wondered what was coming next and he replied "Anything, just tell me."

"You're good with money and finances and things like that so I want you to sort out mine."

"Sure when do you want me to do it?'

"I don't know how long it will take you but I haven't really got much time. There's a whole load of papers and statements you'll need to go through. Joe kept everything in that old chest of his so I do the same but I never really look at some of the stuff."

Dave suggested that she take a day to get herself settled and he offered to do it on Wednesday morning.

"Oh Dave that would be lovely, say nine o'clock and I'll cook you breakfast.' Dave assented.

Jonathan was now very curious and said "Mum you haven't told us anything about this job other than it's in Malaga, well?"

Mary bit her bottom lip and wondered how much she could tell them without lying and then found inspiration in the truth. "It's a relative of your father's who is more or less an invalid and very unwell. Her father asked me if I would do it as I know her quite well and she trusts me. I've been spending time with her recently and I feel like it's something I must do and I really want to. I'll get paid well although I said I'd do it for nothing but the father insists."

"I thought you were in Madrid."

"I was and that's where they live. They're moving to Malaga next month because the climate's better for her, not too cold in the winter and you know how hot Madrid can be in the summer. I have happy memories of Malaga so that suits me as well."

"Do I know these people if they're related?"

"Probably but that's enough for now."

Jonathan knew that meant any more questions would be ignored so he didn't pursue it other than to say he was happy if she was.

"Jonathan I'll miss you but yes, I'm happy about it" she said in a wistful way. "I have something for you." She fished through her bag and pulled out two small wrapped parcels and gave them one each.

"Jonathan this is an early birthday present and Dave this is for you in case you have a birthday that I've missed. When is your birthday?"

"Nineteenth of October and thank you very much."

"That's the day I left for Spain. I hope this boy brought you a nice present and took you out somewhere nice for dinner."

"I had the best birthday ever and he did buy me something that I really needed. We also went out for dinner and Jonathan paid."

Jonathan looked puzzled then he got it and they both started laughing.

"Private joke I suppose, well open your presents."

Mary went to her room after receiving thanks from the birthday boys.

"Jonathan, when's your birthday?"

"December"

"Should I say oh Christ?"

"No, it's the seventh and you had better buy me something as good as what I bought you."

"That's impossible but I'll try."

Mary came back in and asked Jonathan why he wasn't at lectures and he explained saying he started the next day. He told her where they had been the previous week and how nice the place was.

"It sounds lovely but I prefer London. Driving through the city and the West End today reminded me that I haven't done much wandering around town this last year so I have some catching up to do especially now that I won't be spending much time here.

"Dave your accent, it suits you, it sounds really nice. The only problem is your name doesn't seem right now. You're more of a David than a Dave so I'll call you that from now on."

"Mary you can call me whatever you like.'

"Are you sure? Remember where I come from and some of the nicknames people had, I might just come up with a horrible one for you, how about Big Bookie?"

They all laughed.

"Now if you don't mind I'd like you two out of here, my sister's coming soon and I need to get ready. I've a lot of gossip to catch up on. Jonathan maybe you could stay at Dave's tonight and I'll see you tomorrow."

"Mum I've already told you that I don't live here anymore, I live with Dave. I'll drop round after Uni ok?"

"Of course you did. I'll see you tomorrow afternoon then and Dave I'll see you on Wednesday morning, now out of here the pair of you."

They drove home, parked the car and as neither of them was in the mood to prepare food they went out to dinner.

Jonathan had been very quiet since they had left Mary's. When they were looking at menus Dave offered an observation. "It seems like you're in shock."

"I am a bit but I'm not sure which of the things that happened today I'm most in shock about, maybe all of them. It's no good pumping mum for information the more you ask the more she clams up. First there's this nursing job with someone I should know but she's not telling. Then she wants you to sort out her finances, why? I don't think she has that much to sort out. Then, and I know you said she'd know about us as soon as she saw us and she did, but really instantly, is it that obvious? Probably only to her but I still wasn't expecting that. Then the most amazing thing of all was we got married."

"Well then we need to celebrate. I know you have lectures tomorrow but it's still quite early so we could manage a bottle of champagne don't you think?"

"That sounds like a brilliant idea but you'll have to drink the lion's share."

"Done, your mum is an incredible woman and I'm sure she knows what she's doing. She was a bit mysterious but she must have her reasons. Maybe she has a man as well and doesn't want to tell her only child that he might be getting a step father. Anyway I get to look into the magic box, I can't wait."

"I'm glad you're pleased but I can tell you now that mum does not have a man in her life that she would want to marry. If she did she'd look as happy as I do."

On Wednesday Dave went to Portobello Road to explore Joe's magic box. Mary opened the door to him with a warm smile and a kiss on the cheek. She knew he'd be punctual so she had already started preparing breakfast and they sat down to enjoy a traditional English one with lashings of toast and steaming hot tea.

"I'm glad Jonathan is staying with you because I have so much to do in such a short time."

"Mary, he's not staying with me, we live together permanently."

"Yes of course, it just takes a little time to get used to."

"Right now how much do you know about your finances and what do you want to do when we've assessed how much you're worth?"

"Not much really except how much I have in my current account. It's never really interested me. As to what I want to do with the money, well if I have enough I'll buy a house just outside Malaga."

Dave raised his eyebrows and said they had better get started.

"Let's see this magic box."

Mary took him into her bedroom and found the key in her dressing table. She opened the chest and they took all the papers out and carried them through to the kitchen and placed them on the table. Dave returned to the bedroom and examined the inside of the chest whilst Mary watched.

"I've never liked that thing but it's been in Joe's family for generations and now it belongs to Jonathan. I think it's Spanish but the writing on the tiles in the lid is Arabic. I know that because Joe told me. I've never liked the thing. It's not just that it looks out of place here it's something else that I've never been able to put my finger on. I'm just silly I know but it seems to tell me that it's not mine to touch. Joe said he got the same feeling sometimes but he pretended to love it as it was a family heirloom. Look it has a false bottom. You just press here and it pops up, just like that. Unfortunately there was no treasure in it, just empty space."

The empty space was set out in small compartments lined with silk which was frayed but still intact. It looked like it had been designed to hold pieces of jewellery.

Dave was intrigued but said he should get started on the papers. He set about his task in his usual methodical way sorting everything into relevant piles. There were birth, death and marriage certificates dating back to Jonathan's grandparents. There were bank statements, two property deeds and many envelopes that looked the same, most of them unopened from a broker in the city. Inside each envelope was a statement of activity of bonds and shares over a six month period. He sorted everything into date order and he noticed in doing so that everything except one property was in Mary's name and the other property in Jonathan's name. Jonathan's bank statements were not there. The investment account was split into two one which held a fixed portfolio in blue chip stocks and government bonds which received a credit each month from an external bank account. Dave crossed referenced the deposits to Mary's bank account. He looked up and she was standing at the sink and he asked

"Did you know that you saved money every month into an investment account?"

"That goes back to when we had a joint account and I just supposed Joe knew what he was doing so I let it continue."

Dave nodded and returned to his task. The interest and dividends from the main account were invested into the second account which had a mixture of random shares, most of which Dave recognised.

Mary announced that she was going down the lane to buy some bread and Dave asked her if she could buy the financial times if she passed a paper shop.

"How long will you be and where's the lane?" he asked.

"I'd have thought you would have known that. It's what the locals call Portobello, not that there are many locals left and soon to be one less."

Mary returned after half an hour and gave Dave the Financial Times. Dave took out a writing block from his brief case and wished he'd brought his laptop as it would have saved time.

Mary made coffee and three cheese rolls for Dave.

He was sharp on numbers and within a short space of time he put his pen down and said to Mary, "Well do you want to hear what a clever husband you had?"

Mary looked at the clock and saw it was two so she suggested that they wait for Jonathan who would be there anytime soon. They had more coffee and Dave was amazed by the seeming lack of anticipation coming from Mary. If anything she was displaying apprehension.

Ten minutes later Jonathan arrived. Dave stood up and was about to hug him but thought better of it so he sat down again. Jonathan looked over his shoulder at the pile of papers and squeezed his arm.

They all sat down and Dave explained what all the documents were.

"I think you know what most of this is but the envelopes are brokerage statements which obviously held little interest for you Mary."

"It's not that I wasn't interested, I just didn't understand them."

"Well some of these investments go back thirty years. You have a standing order each month of five hundred pounds which goes to increase the investment on the main account. The dividends and interest are reinvested at the broker's discretion, of which he reminds you with every statement, and that's the second account.

"All in all the value of the investments today is roughly nine hundred thousand pounds and of course on top of that there's the value of this apartment and your bank accounts. Your Joe was one smart man Mary,"

Mary went white and was lost for words. When she composed herself she said "I'm a bloody millionaire.'

"Yes you are. Now what do you want to do, keep it or cash it in?"

She sat still thinking for a while then she looked Dave in the eye with a determined look on her face and said "Cash in everything but keep the apartment, can you do that?"

"Mary that's easy all we have to do is fill in one of the instruction forms they send you every six months or just call them."

"Can you fill in the form for me Dave? If I call them I might not know what they're talking about."

Dave picked up one of the forms and a pen and proceeded with his instructions. A thought then struck him and he told Mary. She was lost for words and thought about it. She wanted more information and bombarded Dave with questions before resigning herself to his suggestion.

Jonathan hadn't said a word so Mary asked for his opinion.

"I just love this man to bits," was all he offered in response.

"Do you want the money credited to your bank account here or the one in Spain?"

"How do know I've got an account in Spain?"

"You made a couple of transfers this year, sorry, wasn't I supposed to know?"

Mary ignored the question and instructed Dave to have six hundred thousand Euros transferred to her Spanish account and the rest to her deposit account.

"How urgent is this Mary?"

"I'd like it done as soon as possible."

"Then it will be done today."

"One more thing Dave, I want to change the ownership of this flat into Jonathan's name, can you help with that too?"

He looked at Jonathan and said, "Your mum's still a millionaire and now so are you. Mary I'll get the solicitor to do the necessary. The papers are just here somewhere, here they are. I'll put everything back in the chest in a nice orderly fashion so it will be easy to find things in future."

When he was done he grabbed his things, patted Jonathan on the back and told him he'd be home about two in the morning and would try not to wake him.

Jonathan smiled "Wake me and call me if you have time."

Mary made coffee and sat with her son passing the time of day. "You should ask Dave to look at your money, he's very clever."

"Mum I know exactly how much I have and how much I get every month so I needn't bother him at least not at the moment."

The rest of the week seemed to pass in a blink of an eye. On Saturday morning at breakfast Dave reminded Jonathan that he had to leave early for the hotel to ensure all the arrangements were in order. Jonathan nodded and said he'd be there at seven sharp as per the invitation. He reached over to the sideboard and picked up the envelope which held the said invitation and took it out.

"Here, it says seven and dinner at eight. Bloody hell it's got the ticket price on it, one thousand pounds. Does the committee have to pay, like did you buy my ticket?"

"Well there are so many of us that it wouldn't make sense if we didn't pay for ourselves so yes, I bought your ticket but if I hadn't I'd still have had to pay for two. That's the rule and I made that rule so you didn't actually cost me anything. How will you get there?"

"I'll book a mini-cab. I don't want to get on the tube looking like a penguin now, do I?"

CHAPTER THIRTY EIGHT

At six Dave was satisfied that everything was as it should be. The hotel had provided him with a room to change so he went and showered and put on his tuxedo. He dried his hair and splashed on some after shave and looked at himself in the mirror. He was pleased with the image before him and marvelled at the change from what was really just a few months ago.

He went back down to the ballroom by six thirty ready to greet the early guests. They arrived in dribs and drabs then it seemed a host of people must have caught the same tube train as suddenly there was a line of people waiting for the ushers to show them to their tables. Somewhere amongst the throng Jonathan was waiting his turn desperate not to disappoint. When he reached Dave he gave a sheepish smile and handed him the invitation. Dave did a double take and said, "Do I know you? You look amazing."

"I take it that I scrub up well then?"

"I can't talk now I have to see to this lot. Give your invitation to the next usher to appear and they'll show you to our table."

Then he whispered, "Go for fuck's sake before I do something embarrassing."

Jonathan was ushered to the top table which was prominent by its location, just in front of the stage. All the tables were set for ten people except this one which had only eight place settings. The usher pulled out a chair and he sat down. Sitting opposite was a very regal looking woman who he recognised immediately. Next to her was an older man and the other places were occupied by two couples in their late twenties or early thirties.

All were silent until the regal woman looked at him with distaste and said, "And who are you young man?"

Jonathan stood up and said, "I'm sorry I'm forgetting my manners, I'm Jonathan." He walked around the table and shook hands with the sextet.

"Well now you know who I am who are you?"

The older lady gave him an icy stare and nodded to her party. The young lady sitting on his left offered the first introduction. "I'm Poppy and this is my husband Charles and the older couple are my parents but I'm sure they want to do their own introductions," she said with a warm smile.

The man on his right said, "I'm Robert and this is my wife Anna and Poppy is my sister." It seemed to Jonathan that Robert was suppressing a smile but he was ready to go along with whatever the joke was, even if it turned out to be at his own expense.

"I'm Lord Worthington," declared the older man, "but you must call me Dicky."

Jonathan smiled and nodded. The regal lady looked Jonathan over as though he was something unpleasant and said, "I'm Lady Worthington."

"I'm pleased to meet you all," Jonathan said politely. Poppy nudged Jonathan and leant over and whispered something in his ear. Jonathan got the message. He looked at Lady Worthington and asked "What do I call you?"

The Lady went stiff and in a haughty voice said, "Lady Worthington, what else would you call me?"

"Pleased to meet you Lady Worthington," as he said this he smiled. Everyone started laughing and Poppy said" Oh mummy I think that joke is wearing a bit thin," and turning to Jonathan she said, "She's being Maggie Smith in Downton, very theatrical is mother. So who are you tonight mummy or should I call you ma, mother, mater or old girl?"

"I haven't decided yet. I thought I might be very dramatic and be Somerset Maugham's Sadie Thompson but now on seeing this truly beautiful, exotic looking young man I think it will have to be a star crossed lover. So Jonathan how do you know Dave and how well do you know him, only he seems to have lost his lovely London accent, what happened?"

"I think that would be better coming from him."

"Oh it was wonderful, so working class you know. You don't sound working class, what's your family name?"

Jonathan knew there was a game afoot so he decided to go along for the ride but now couldn't avoid giving his surname.

"My family name is Martinez so nothing to get excited about and until quite recently I worked in a pub and still help out occasionally so I suppose that makes me working class."

"How terribly exciting to meet someone who works in a pub, Dicky works in the foreign office you know."

"That's nice and what class are you Lady Worthington?"

"Oh, aristocracy of course."

Jonathan smiled again "Oh the robber class."

"What do you mean you insolent young man?"

"I mean, if your title has been in your family pre-nineteen hundred then probably most of your wealth was stolen from the colonies especially India."

"Well said young man," piped up Dicky.

"Before we go any further you must call me Dolly, I'm tired of the lady bit. Now Dicky, what does he mean?"

"My ancestors filched most of my inheritance from India just as young Jonathan says. Real bunch of looters they were and do you know most of the valuable knick knacks that we have at home were stolen from some unsuspecting bugger in the Punjab and most of our inherited money comes from that source, bunch of thieves the lot of them."

Dolly's hands went up to her face and she addressed her children with a plea, "This is horrible. When your father and I die you must give it all back."

Everyone laughed especially Jonathan who observed, "This is like being back at school," and he shook his head.

Dolly smiled and looked for a few seconds at Jonathan before responding. "Jonathan you're right so just let's have some fun before that killjoy Dave joins us. Now tell me, you are truly beautiful are you someone we should know from films or TV or something like that?"

"No, I'm nobody, just Jonathan."

"But that face, your physic, you're pure beauty. Don't you agree?" she asked everyone.

They all smiled and nodded.

"You're a fine looking specimen young man and no doubt about it," said Dicky.

"That smile is devastating. Dicky I should have left you at home. You look so exotic, where are you from?'

"Portobello Road, there's a lot of odd people there. My dad was born in England but his parents were Spanish."

"Really, I love Spanish, say something about me in Spanish."

Jonathan obliged.

"Oh that sounded so romantic. Charles what did he say?"

Charles looked for approval from Jonathan who nodded assent.

"Well let me warn you mother-in-law dear, you're in for a rough time. This young man can see right through you."

"I don't care, what did he say?"

"He said you are a very beautiful woman and when you were younger you must have been the Helen of Troy of your day. Behind that air-brained facade is a very smart lady. It's the twinkle in your eye that gives you away. Is that about right Jonathan?'

Jonathan nodded wondering what the response would be.

Dolly gave a soft smile and said, "How splendid you are Jonathan. Now tell me how do you know Dave?"

Jonathan thought for a moment and said, "We're family."

"How come you're so dark, beautiful and mysterious and he's boring old Dave that looks like he's just done ten rounds with a pro boxer?"

"I think I'll let Dave explain that one."

Anna up to this point had said nothing than a light bulb went off in her head. "Oh something was tickling my brain and I've just got it, David and Jonathan, how wonderfully biblical." There was more laughter and Jonathan was feeling more at ease and enjoying himself. These were really nice people.

Dolly chimed in again, "So my beautiful Jonathan what else do you do?"

"I'm a student, I'm studying law and tell me do you always monopolise the conversation?"

"Always you rude boy." In Chorus the rest of the table said, "Always."

Jonathan pointed to the stage as Dave was about to make a speech.

Dave greeted and thanked the guests for their generosity. He told them about the progress the foundation had made over the past year. He went on to make an impassioned speech about the plight of the homeless in London and said that a new plague had descended on the capital. Not a disease of the body but one more dangerous, one of apathy. Nobody seemed to care anymore especially the politicians. He carried on in that vein for about five minutes and then told a very funny joke to lighten the mood. He finished by saying that if anyone wanted to make a further donation there would be a drop box at the ballroom's reception desk that would be removed at eight thirty as they didn't want anyone who might be a little inebriated to make a donation they might regret in the morning. He thanked them again and left to a loud round of applause. Jonathan stood up to applaud and the whole room followed suit.

Dolly sat looking at the stage dumbfounded. Dave joined his table to the congratulations of all.

Dolly went straight for the jugular. "What's happened to you Dave Wilson, your bags have gone, your hair is blonder, you look about thirty and you've lost your lovely London accent. You even made a decent speech and told a joke, you actually made people laugh. You invite a rude terrible young man who has insulted me more than once. He told me that everything I own was stolen, I talk too much and I'm an air brain. All that and I've only known him for fifteen minutes."

Dave laughed and said, "He's very perceptive and he's certainly got your number Dolly although I can't imagine he said you were an air brain."

Charles offered clarification on that point and agreed that Jonathan was very perceptive. Dave looked at Jonathan and then said to the rest of the table, "You should meet his mother. She knows what you're thinking before you've even thought it. It's the gypsy in her."

Now Dolly looked really excited. "Oh your mother is a gypsy, I must meet her."

The waiters began serving dinner and whilst they were eating Dolly looked earnestly at Dave and asked, "Dave what has happened to you, I'm dumbstruck by the change. Not only do you look better, good even, you've found a sense of humour. I don't think I've ever seen you smile before and it seems you can't stop, what's happened?"

He hesitated before replying. "I've been struck down by a bolt of happiness."

Dolly looked at him kindly and said, "I think you deserve it. I don't know why I think that you miserable sod but I do. Now tell me what happened to your lovely London accent."

"I didn't need it anymore."

Dolly looked puzzled and asked what he meant. To Jonathan's absolute amazement, Dave gave them a much abridged version of what had happened to him, not leaving out the really bad bits.

Everyone was silent whilst he gave his account. Dolly got up from her seat and went round to Dave and put her arm around him and kissed him on the cheek and said for all to hear, "That explains so much, I'm sorry that such ugliness could happen to anyone let alone to you," and she kissed him again and returned to her seat on the silent table.

Jonathan thought she had said exactly the right words. Anna then said, "Dave that must have left you scarred both mentally and physically, how do you cope with such things?"

"I still have some of the physical scares but the psychological ones are more or less gone. Until tonight I'd only ever told three people about this but somehow now it doesn't seem to matter so I'm surprised how easy it was to tell you."

"So what happened to make you feel better?" asked a concerned looking Robert.

Dave raised his hands palms up and turned them towards Jonathan and said, "This is my salvation."

Anna said, looking at them both "I can believe that, he looks like an angel and now I'm sure he is."

Charles said something to Jonathan in Spanish and Jonathan replied in English, "I'm in shock so I suppose so."

"Jonathan told us you were family but wouldn't explain. He said it was best coming from you."

Dave looked thoughtful and hesitated before he replied. "Family eh, I suppose that's exactly what we are, we're life partners."

Jonathan's head was swimming wondering where this sudden boldness had come from.

Anna looked from Jonathan to Dave and announced to nobody in particular, "I should have known, it seems that all really handsome men are gay."

Dolly was not going to be left out so she feigned horror. Dicky tried to comfort her not getting the joke. "It's ok darling, a bit of buggery doesn't make a man less of a man. In my days in the army there was some of that around and these were fighting men."

The whole table collapsed into fits of laughter and realising that he was the brunt of the joke, poor Dicky reddened and Dolly squeezed his arm and kissed him by way of comfort.

When they had composed themselves Dolly asked Jonathan how old he was.

"I'll be twenty one, two weeks today but will you excuse me please I need the bathroom." He got up and made his way to the door with many admiring glances aimed his way. He was totally unaware of the eyes watching him until just before he reached the door a young lady stood up and stopped him. "Are you leaving?" she asked

"No just going for a natural break."

"I'm sorry I couldn't help but notice you, you're sitting on the top table with Dolly Mellor. You must be somebody of note so how comes I've never seen you before? Who are you?"

"I'm no one but I know who you are. You're Rachael Young the movie actress."

She nodded, "Now you have one up on me, who are you?"

"I'm Jonathan and as I said, I'm nobody."

"A mystery man, that makes you even more attractive."

"I'm sure not," he said without modesty, just as a matter of fact.

"Are you in the entertainment industry?"

"Is this twenty question?" Jonathan asked and gave her a huge smile.

"Oh my god, what a beautiful set of teeth you have and your smile would melt the heart of the devil himself. You could sell a container load of toothpaste in a minute. I'll call Colgate." They both laughed.

"I sorry if I'm being rude but I'm sure there isn't a female in the room who doesn't want to know who you are. I checked the guest list but your seat doesn't give you a name, it just says guest of sponsor."

Jonathan wanted to change the subject so turned it back to her. "I've seen one of your movies, 'Love in a dark place'. It was an awful film but I thought you were the only good thing in it."

"You're right, it was awful but it got me noticed and I've been in Hollywood for the last year and I've made two films one which came out here last week."

Neither of them noticed photographers taking their pictures.

"If you're not famous, which is hard to believe, what do you do?"

"I don't have a job yet, I'm a student."

"I just noticed a number of photographers taking our pictures so beware Jonathan, tomorrow you will be famous."

He gave her another huge smile and said, "Tomorrow I will be invisible but if you'll excuse me I need to do something and I really do need the bathroom."

"So do I, I'll come with you."

Jonathan stopped at the donation box and dropped a cheque in. He had read on the invitation that you should bring a cheque book if you wanted to make an additional donation, so he came prepared.

On the way to the bathroom Rachael said, "What's Dolly Mellor like? I idolised that woman. One day I want to be as good and as versatile as her. The entertainment industry is so fickle and you have to work really hard to gain traction and be enduring. She's done it all."

"Would you like to meet her?"

"I'd love to."

"When we get back, wait five minutes after Dolly has made her speech and come over and I'll introduce you."

Rachael was delighted and she grabbed his face and kissed him full on the lips.

When he returned to the table Dolly continued

'Well twenty one young Jonathan, that's a milestone. Dicky we'll have to throw him a party. You must bring your mother but we won't invite Dave because he's turned down every invitation that I have given him, so bring your friends."

Jonathan smiled and asked whether he got a say in it.

Dave answered, "I'm afraid not, unless you look and sound like a London gangster she won't take no for an answer."

Jonathan looked at Dolly and thought this was obviously some kind of story so he said, "Thank you but I can't come. I've only ever had one friend in my whole life and he's sitting next to me and he's not invited."

Dolly opened her mouth but nothing came out, then she managed to croak, "This is so beautiful, I'm going to cry," which she did along with Anna and Poppy. The men all started laughing and the women joined them through their tears.

When they managed to control themselves Robert said, "Mother stop being so obtuse. Jonathan my mother has a Christmas party every year and it just happens to coincide with your birthday so of course Dave is invited and your mother, so please come."

Jonathan looked at Dave and said they would love to and he'd ask his mother.

At that moment Dolly saw three photographers heading towards their table. To hers and everybody else's surprise they made a bee-line for Jonathan. Dolly winked at the surprised young man. They asked Jonathan for his name and he was about to tell them his Christian name when Dolly intervened.

"Oh he's no one of interest let me tell you about my new venture."

She carried on in this way frustrating the pressmen until they became quite insistent. Then Dolly played her trump card.

"Oh if you must but please keep it to yourselves or there will be D notices flying everywhere. This is Prince" then almost inaudibly, "Charming."

Dicky had obviously played this game before so he said with a note of horror in his voice, "Dolly no you mustn't. Excuse me young men but this young man is a private citizen and of no interest to you."

The press left with what they thought was a real juicy story and the guests at that table all got the giggles.

"Nice one darling, I can see the headlines tomorrow 'The prince and the showgirl' eh what, even if the showgirl isn't a spring chicken" chortled Dicky.

At eight thirty Dave excused himself to go and help count the voluntary donations. When he returned he handed Dolly a sheet of paper. "You're up now. I prepared a note on the donations so after you've said your bit you can tell everyone how generous they've been."

Dolly stood up and in passing said, "Dave you usually do the donation bit."

"Just do it Dolly" He said forcefully and she raised her eyebrows and headed for the stage.

In her best cockney accent she opened to a cheer by saying, "Right you lot, fanks for commin," and continued in that vein for the next five minutes, telling little anecdotes and raising much laughter.

"Ok now for the money bit. Let's see how generous you tight fisted bunch have been."

She unfolded the sheet of paper most of which was type written except that evening's contributions which had been inked in after checking the donation box. Dolly began reading, "We made as usual two hundred thousand pounds from the ticket sales and I thank you all because this is our life blood. Tonight's contributions from the donation box are," she hesitated and said, "Wow three hundred and twenty five thousand which includes two individual donations of one hundred thousand each." She was obviously moved but what she read next left her speechless and a tear rolled down her eye. "Excuse me" she said to a now silent ballroom, "It's just I can't believe what I'm about to read." She looked over to Dave and asked, "Is this real?"

Dave nodded so she continued. "There is a donation in the form of a trust fund set up for our foundation and we will receive the income from it for the next ten years after which we can decide what to do with the capital. The value of the capital is nine hundred and twenty six thousand pounds and the donor is the estate of the late Jose Martinez. I don't know what to say except thank you Jose Martinez whoever you are." She left the stage in a daze accompanied by much applause, and took her seat in silence.

Anna was the first to speak. "That's amazing you must be so happy Dolly. I've known you for twelve years and I've never seen you speechless before. Dolly remained silent, she was thinking and a sudden realisation hit her and she looked up at Jonathan and before she could open her mouth he said, "Please don't." He so wanted to tell her who the real donor was but Dave had forbidden him and his mother ever to speak of it.

She gave an almost imperceptible nod and brightened up. "This has been the most amazing evening of my life and I'm very happy." She got her mojo back and kissed Dicky and whispered a thank you as she was the one who had twisted his arm to give a hundred thousand, much needed, pounds.

Jonathan saw Rachael walking towards them so he stood up and introduced her. Dolly ordered Robert to find her a seat and made Rachael sit next to her.

"I know who you are young lady and it's always a pleasure to meet a fellow thespian especially a young one with lots of talent."

Rachael spoke enthusiastically about Dolly being her icon and they started into talking about the current state of their industry when suddenly Dolly stopped and asked, "So how do you know our beautiful Jonathan?"

Before she could answer Jonathan interrupted, "We've met several times over a period of about two years." Dave understood what was happening and he pulled out his phone. Rachael looked puzzled, "I know I've seen those big amazing brown eyes before but where?"

Jonathan offered, "A bottle of Chardonnay and four glasses please." Dave said "Jonathan makes himself invisible most of the time," and he held out his phone and Rachael looked at it in amazement. Dave laughed and said, "I think he looks better that way although he looks passable tonight."

Dolly grabbed the phone and also looked amazed. "You look even more like an angel, you have a halo."

Jonathan looked puzzled and asked to see the picture and sure enough he appeared to have a halo. He was looking down as if in prayer.

"Dave when did you take this?"

"The first time I saw you. You where standing behind the bar washing glasses and there was a light behind you and I couldn't resist. I was in sore need of an angel and you looked like Jesus Christ. It's my favourite picture of you."

"You have more?"

"Only about a thousand," Dave replied laughing. Jonathan wanted so much to kiss him.

Rachael looked at the picture again and said, "I'm so unobservant, I've had this beautiful creature within my grasp so many times and I didn't even notice. It's only when I see him in an event like this I take notice. That says a lot about what I've become. This is really a wake-up call, thank you Jonathan and I'm sorry I ignored you before. You are so beautiful but you hide yourself away from the world, why?"

Jonathan smiled which sent a shiver coursing through Rachael's body and said, "I don't care how I look or what other people think of me and I certainly wouldn't want any form of fame attached to me because someone likes my face. I will be famous one day but not because of how I look but because of what I do." He said these words with an absolute certainty.

"You're like a Cinderella story, nobody notices you until you go to the ball." Rachael said with admiration painted all over her face.

Jonathan added, "Ah but I have the best life of anyone in the whole world, I have Dave."

Rachael understood immediately and looked at him wistfully then at Dave and made a request. "Dave if you ever get tired of him call me."

"That will happen when hell freezes over," Dave proudly announced.

Dolly looked at Jonathan and he knew what she wanted.

"I have just two pictures of Dave, a before and after" He took out his phone, found the pictures and opened the first one and handed it to Dolly.

"That's the most melancholy photograph I've ever seen, when did you take it and why?"

"I took it before I'd ever spoken to Dave. He was sitting in the pub and it was snowing outside and the few people that had been there had gone home and Dave was the only person left. As my grandmother used to say, he looked like he'd found a penny and lost a pound. I was moved by this mountain of a man with his leg in plaster looking so sad. He looked like a Greek god having a bad day."

She clicked onto the second picture. "It's the big man dressed up for the country, how splendid you look Dave."

Dolly's curiosity got the better of her and she said, "Tell me to mind my own business but was it love at first sight."

"It was something like that but having grunted a few words at me he ended by saying fuck you."

"Then what happened?" Dolly asked enthusiastically.

"He came in the next night to apologise but I upset him and he walked out without paying for his beer. He came back a couple of days later and offered to pay and we started talking but I upset him again and he walked out. A couple of weeks later I went to find him at the casino and we became friends."

"Only friends?"

"Dolly, yes just friends, the rest happened nine months later."

Dolly then looked at Dave who seemed to have a permanent smile on his face and asked, "What did he do or say that upset you Dave."

"It wasn't so much that he upset me it was more like he knew me. It felt like he could read my thoughts and that made me feel vulnerable and Dave Wilson was never going to be put in that position."

"So if he looked like Jesus Christ and he upset you what happened." Dolly was almost on the edge of her seat waiting for the response.

"He happened, I let him in and he made everything right, he's magic."

Dolly looked at them both and then addressed Jonathan. "I don't believe that was one way traffic, what did Dave do for you?"

"That's easy, he gave me a life and a purpose and he liked me for who I am and obviously not how I looked."

"You under estimate yourself young man, even in these photographs you can see your beauty shining through. It would take a self absorbed person like an actress not to notice."

"Ouch" said Rachael.

Jonathan laughed and said "Then the whole world must be self absorbed because nobody really looks at me."

At that point the band started tuning up.

Robert asked Dave if they were any good. "They play at your casino don't they?"

"That's right and they are very good. They've boosted our club room takings by two hundred percent and they have quite a following. They write their own music and they have records out there. Tonight though, because the audience is somewhat mature they'll be doing golden oldies."

Robert nodded in response and the band started playing and they were good. A few people got up to dance and they were followed by a few more after the next song. Twenty minutes into their set the leader of the group took the microphone and announced, "We have a guest singer who graces us with his vocals now and then and he's here tonight so Dave Wilson come on up."

Dave stood and the whole table, with the exception of Jonathan, looked at him open mouthed. As he left Dolly looked concerned and said to Jonathan, "This isn't going to be embarrassing is it."

Jonathan replied with a big grin and told her to wait and see.

Dave took the mike and told the audience that they all had to get up and move and then began singing Mustang Sally.

Dolly couldn't believe what she heard or saw. Dave was beyond good and he moved like a rocker.

"Goodness me," she exclaimed, "He can sing and some one's oiled his joints. Jonathan did you know."

"Of course, he sings around the house and I like it better when he has no music. He's great."

Dave sang a few more songs and then a slower one that was meant for one person only in the room. He sweetly sang the Ronettes, Be My Baby.

He finished to cheers and whistles and returned to his party, where he got an additional round of applause.

"Mr Wilson, well-well" said Dolly. "Can you bring that lot to my party and of course you're now invited."

Dave laughed and said he could and would and then he admonished them all for not dancing.

"Jonathan will you dance with me?" asked Rachael.

"I'd love to but I can't do that stuff."

Dolly said, "You can't dance?"

"Not like that. I've never been to a party or a dance so I've never had to but I can dance but just not like that."

Dolly continued her enquiries, "So don't tell me you do ballroom."

Dave intervened, "He dances flamenco and brilliantly."

"More surprises" gasped Dolly. "Will you dance at my party but who do we know that could dance with you?"

Jonathan said, "I'd love to and I can bring my partner and the musicians if you like but they would have to leave by eight thirty as they have a community thing at nine."

"Oh what a lovely party we're going to have all courtesy of these two wonderful young men" Dolly said enthusiastically as usual.

Rachael was determined to have her way and said, "Jonathan I can't believe that you've never been to a party or danced, not even in front of the mirror?"

Jonathan conceded that he'd done that.

"Good then you can dance, come on." He followed her onto the dance floor and once he got into the rhythm of the music he moved with ease. They laughed and danced then laughed some more.

Not to be outdone Dolly insisted Dave dance with her saying poor Dicky had a back problem, so Dave obliged. The others followed leaving Dicky to sup his wine in peace.

At ten thirty Dave went up to the stage and announced that they would have to vacate the hall in half an hour. There were boos and jeers and then a growing number of voices shouting "Sing, sing."

Dave gave them what they wanted with some Motown and Rolling Stones.

It was time to go so they all stood as to leave and Dolly said, "This is the best night I think I've ever had and it's not ending now. Let's go to the hotel bar."

"Jolly good idea, old girl," agreed Dicky.

Dave said that might not be a good idea as it closed at midnight. They discussed other options but couldn't agree so Jonathan made a suggestion. "I know a place that stays open all night and they have music in an adjoining room."

Dave nodded, "He means my casino and that's a great idea. I'll call ahead and tell them to close the small bar and we'll have it all to ourselves and the drinks are on the house."

Everyone was agreeable so off they went in their chauffer driven cars.

Dolly was on good form keeping everyone entertained and Rachael had deserted her party to tag along.

Dolly pulled Dave and Jonathan to one side and, a little inebriated, said slyly, "There's one thing I don't understand about you two, Dave you look so rested and fresh whereas you always used to look like you needed a good night's sleep."

"So where's this going?" Dave asked.

"Well," she said, fluttering her eyelashes, "if I went to bed with either of you I'd want to stay up all night long having wild sex."

When they had stopped laughing Jonathan spoke boldly. "We only do that at weekends and holidays," and the laughter broke out again. Dolly kissed Jonathan on the cheek and demanded of Dave, "Give him to me, I want him so badly and I mean that in every way."

After they had been there for about half an hour Dave asked Jonathan if he would take a look at something in the store room. Jonathan tried his best not to laugh and followed Dave who closed the door behind him. They embraced and kissed and they both said they had wanted desperately to do that all night. They quickly returned to their party.

Dave had asked the band to join them and they arrived together at twelve thirty. They mingled and seemed at ease with the party. Mick the lead guitarist took Jonathan to one side and introduced himself. He said he knew who Jonathan was and told him that the whole band was grateful to him, in fact the whole casino staff, for making Dave so happy.

He then hesitated before saying, "I want to ask you something but please don't say anything until I've finished. Of course you know that Dave sings with us sometimes but I don't know if he's told you that he also helps us write songs and he's really good at it. He said it comes from his school days when they had to learn Shakespeare and poetry. Anyway the band is recording a new album and it's looking really good but we want Dave to sing on just one track but he keeps refusing. He wrote this love song on his own and he gave it to us saying not to use his name. He sang it to us the first time and it was so fucking moving we all cried. I must tell you we're a bunch of girls with stuff like that. Anyway I've tried singing it and it sounds ok but I can't get the raw emotion that Dave put into it."

He stopped there and Jonathan said "So what's this to do with me?"

"Well you see, although he hasn't told us we all know it's about you and him so we thought you might help persuade him. Look, come with me."

He led Jonathan through the club room to a small room behind the stage where they kept their equipment. He opened a recording device and searched for the track he wanted and played it.

Jonathan listened in silence and like Mick and co, it really moved him, maybe more so as he knew what the words really meant. Without saying anything he went back to the bar with Mick in tow.

He beckoned Dave to join them. "Mick just played me a tape of you singing the song you wrote about us. He said you don't want to record it, which I get but would you mind if he gave me a copy so I can listen to it whenever I like?"

Mick looked crestfallen he had hoped Jonathan would persuade Dave to let them use it on their album.

Jonathan sighed a big sigh and said to Mick. "I don't really have anyone to tell about Dave and me and sometimes I feel like stopping strangers in the street and telling them. I want the whole world to know. Anyway I have to go and talk to Dicky. See you later. Ouch."

Dave had punched him on the arm as he departed.

Dave looked at a very disappointed looking Mick, "I hate him, I fucking hate him."

"Who, Jonathan, what has he done to upset you. I thought this was true love?"

"He takes what I think are complicated problems through my stupid emotional needs and he reduces them to the obvious."

"I'm sorry Dave I'm lost, he didn't say anything."

"He just told me that I should be proud of our relationship and should tell the world about it and of course he's right."

"I didn't hear him say that but does it make a difference."

"Of course it does. I'll record it for your new album but not with my name on it. I'll admit to writing it but not to singing. That's stuff for you guys."

Mike looked amazed. "Is that it, you'll do it?"

"I said so didn't I?" laughed Dave shaking his head.

"I still don't understand what you think Jonathan just did but if it got the result, who fucking cares?"

Mick was so excited he high fived and rushed off to find the rest of the band who quickly surrounded Dave and showed their appreciation.

At three o'clock Dave and Jonathan said their goodnights leaving the rest of the party to enjoy themselves. Once home and lying in bed Dave wondered if the motionless Jonathan had fallen asleep, so he nudged him.

"What can I do for you Mr Wilson?"

"You really were brilliant tonight and I know it wasn't always easy for you but you soldiered on like a good one. You look kinda different but the same. It's the hair cut, now you can see all of your face. The amount of attention you garnered was truly amazing and I think I understand better why you hide. You looked so uncomfortable at times. You did that for me and I saw your cheque, ten thousand pounds."

"Dave I'd do anything for you but I'd never get used to the attention, I just couldn't. Tonight was alright though because you were there, it made it easy. They were nice people but if I never saw any of them again that would be ok."

Dave sighed, "Why me Jonathan, why do you love me?"

"How many fucking times do I have to tell you? Maybe I'll try another way, how's that."

Dave laughed at the touch and pulled Jonathan to him and held him tightly. "I love you so much, Jonathan."

"Good because I have no interest in the rest of the world so it would be tragic if you didn't"

Dave felt good. Jonathan always knew the words he needed to hear in a way that was uniquely Jonathan.

CHAPTER THIRTY NINE

It was eleven o'clock and they were rudely awakened by Beethoven playing on Jonathan's mobile. He answered sleepily and Mary's voice asked if they were up yet to which her son grunted and asked why.

"It's obvious that you're still asleep but I'm coming round now, so get your lazy butts out of bed. I've never been there before but I know the address so see you in about twenty minutes."

"Who was that?" Dave yawned.

"My mum, she's on her way here and she sounded excited. I suppose we have to get up."

Twenty minutes later Mary arrived carrying an armful of the Sunday tabloids. She told them to sit at the kitchen table and to read whilst she cooked them breakfast.

"That's ok Mary I'll do it," said Dave sounding the worse for wear.

"I'll find what I need so you two sit and read."

Dave was the first to find the source of the excitement and he roared with laughter.

"Dicky was almost right," laughingly handing Jonathan the page he was looking at.

There was a large picture of Jonathan being kissed by Rachael and some smaller ones of them talking and dancing. The caption said 'The movie star and the mysterious Prince.'

Jonathan also found it amusing. All the other tabloids had much the same photographs but didn't all say he was a prince but a variety of things from new boyfriend to rich young playboy.

Mary placed two plates of fried eggs and bacon in front of them and sat down and expectantly said, "Well, explain."

They related the previous evenings events and how Dolly had purposely mislead the press.

"Dolly Mellor, you met Dolly Mellor?"

"Yes mum, look she's in some of the pictures, we were at the same table. She's the chairman of the foundation and Dave's the treasurer so we were on the top table with her."

"No wonder they thought you were a somebody."

Dave interrupted as Mary was now sounding a little agitated.

"Did you take a good look at the pictures because Jonathan was, I suppose for want of a better term, the belle of the ball. He looked magnificent and he had everyone's attention long before Dolly played her little joke. By the way, Dolly's having a party Saturday week and you're invited. She really wants to meet you."

"Me, why would she want to meet me?"

"She asked Jonathan a million questions and you came into the conversation and she thought you sounded fascinating."

Jonathan groaned, "Dave told her you're a gypsy or was it a witch or both and she's nuts so she wants to meet you."

"Oh really?"

"Really."

Dave stood up after finishing his breakfast and made fresh coffee and some toast.

"Jonathan there goes you're invisibility. You're now officially famous, what do you think Mary?"

"He'll revert to his unshaven self and scruffy clothes and no one will notice but he shouldn't go out today still looking like a prince," she said teasingly.

"Enough of this crap I'm going to have a shower and leave you two to your sniggering."

When he came down half an hour later, Mary and Dave were still reading the newspapers except now Dave had his five kilo Sunday Times in front of him. He looked up and shook his head, "No pictures of Prince Jonathan here."

"Fuck off, the jokes over."

Dave suggested they skip lunch and have an early dinner to which they agreed. "Do you want me to cook?" asked Mary.

"No I'll do it, in fact I'll cheat, we have loads of pre-cooked food it the freezer that our housekeeper makes for occasions such as this, the occasion usually being Sunday," Dave confessed.

"Jonathan show your mum around whilst I clean up here will you and show her the top flat as well."

Jonathan did as requested.

It was a typical dreary November day and they had to put lights on in the lounge. They sat around chatting and reading or just dozing off in front of the fire until it was time for dinner.

They sat down and ate a satisfactory meal which gained Mary's approval. "Your Mrs Hayes cooks well."

"Yes she does," replied Dave "There's something I wanted to ask you Mary and now is as good a time as any I suppose."

"Let me guess. It's probably about the flat in Portobello you think Jonathan should rent it out when I go, right?"

"You really are an incredible lady."

Jonathan was feeling a bit lost with the conversation so he asked what they meant as Mary still needed a home when she came back to England for visits.

"My son you are supposed to be smart and observant. I will never live in that flat again after I return to Spain and why do you think Dave asked you to show me the upstairs flat?"

Jonathan sat with a blank look on his face.

"I'll stay in the upstairs flat when I visit England."

"But Dave, what about your sister and stepmother?" Jonathan inquired.

"The house is now, or will be soon, wholly mine. It was their choice, they wanted to sell the business and I don't mean that with sour grapes. Now they'll have to make their own arrangements."

"What do you think mum?"

"Dave is a very bright, kind man and I would love it. If I come back permanently I'd have enough money to buy my own place so don't worry, you won't be saddled with me. The flat is self contained so I wouldn't need to bother you and I can easily slip my boyfriends in without you two seeing."

Jonathan wasn't sure he liked that statement but Dave found it amusing.

"Mum, what do you mean, if you come back?"

"Slip of the tongue. Ok I don't know, I might just build a new life there and if I did would you not be happy for me?"

"Of course I would but I'd miss you" and he gave his mum a hug.

To which she responded, "Yer, like a hole in the head."

When Mary had gone Jonathan asked Dave if he minded him asking a question, "If you do, just do what mum does and change the subject."

"I don't mind, I tell you everything and if I miss something it's only because I don't think it's important. What do you want to know?"

"Last night Dolly said that you had been seen on the town a few times."

Dave couldn't help but tease, "Jealous are we?"

"No you must do whatever you want to do. Well, maybe a bit."

"Since I met Jiminy Cricket I've taken a bit more interest in the work the foundation does, so if I'm late in the office I go walk about and see the real situation for myself. I go armed, as instructed, with lots of cigarettes to use as conversation starters and I talk to the homeless first hand. It's very humbling when you see what some of the volunteers do on a regular basis."

"Now it's my turn to say it, I fucking hate you. I should have known it would be something selfless but I did feel a bit insecure about you being out on the town without me, sorry. Do Dolly and the others do that?"

"Some of them work a weekly roster, so yes, but Dolly and the other less physically capable work in the soup kitchen two or three days a week. They all try to be hands on. They're great."

"I must live in a bubble. I don't think I've ever noticed homeless people and from what you said last night there must be thousands of them."

"You've probably seen people sleeping on park benches but you don't really notice in the day time, it's at night that it becomes more obvious and you've never gone out much have you. I'm glad I made you feel insecure for once, it's usually me."

On Wednesday, Jonathan got a call from Dolly. She announced in her Queen Victoria voice that Lady Worthington wished to converse with one Jonathan Martinez.

"It is I my lady."

"Then you are summoned for tea at my mansion at four o'clock today and I know you're free. I checked with your master."

"It seems that I have no choice then my lady."

Then in a broad Scottish accent she said, "Oo och and will you bring that ma of yours, I just gotta meet her? Will you do that my lovely wee boy?"

Then back to Queen Victoria, "Of course you don't have to do that as I summoned her myself, I was just being polite to one of my subjects." Then she hung up without waiting for a reply.

Jonathan called Mary and told her about the phone conversation and asked if she wanted to go.

"I'm not going, I'm already here. Dolly called me earlier and sent a car to pick me up at ten o'clock. I'll see you later."

Jonathan arrived at Cadogan Square at four and was shown to the drawing room where Dolly was sitting with Mary, gassing. To his surprise Dave was also there.

Dolly noticed and explained, "I'm sorry I didn't tell you your master would be here but I only invited the oath at the last minute and why are you doing an impression of a tramp?" a question she already knew the answer to.

"Tell him please," Mary said with a big sigh. "He dresses like that most of the time and only shaves once a week."

"Sorry Mary my dear but if you were there on Saturday you'd understand better why he wants to be invisible. Anyway I think he looks mysterious and gypsy-like. Look at the attention the tabloids have given him.

"I've had a million phone calls from the press and acquaintances asking 'who's the mystery man?' I just say I don't know he just floated down from heaven. This is so entertaining.

"Dave's PR called me and told me that Jonathan will be featured front page in most of this month's celebrity magazines, so we have to keep the mystery going. They're going to be bitterly disappointed when they find out that he's really only a boring, scruffy student."

It was Dave who responded. "I wouldn't have him any other way so enough of the insults."

Dolly started bouncing up and down on her chair and said she was bursting to tell something that just happened and after a little persuasion she told them that she had just got the part of Mrs Hastings in She Stoops to Conquer at the Old Vic.

They had tea and spoke about the upcoming party and after the men were dismissed, to leave the Ladies to talk more.

"Mary my dear, I'm not a complete air brain as your son suggested and I wanted to get to know you for a reason, that's why I asked you to come early. First I have to thank you for the amazing donation that you made from your late husband's estate. You can't imagine how much that helps."

Mary wanted to tell her the truth but couldn't.

"If you'd have been a real horrible witch then I wouldn't have wanted to have this conversation."

Mary wondered what was coming but stayed silent.

"Your son is extremely perceptive and those men tell me that you're even more so. Dave says you're a witch but a nice one. Are you?"

"Of course not, like Jonathan only a few people interest me so I observe and use whatever knowledge I have about them to make connections."

"Well then gypsy woman tell me something about me that nobody has told you."

Mary sighed.

"Oh dear Mary that doesn't bode well, am I cursed or something?"

Mary looked at the elegant woman sitting beside her and nodded. "You might say that but I suspect you already know."

Dolly hung her head and then looked up and smiled. "I've not seen a doctor but I've read up the symptoms but is it that obvious or is that just your gypsy powers?"

"I'm a nurse and I've seen Parkinson's quite a few times. You're obviously in the early stages and there's so much they can do now. I used to do relief work in Harley Street and I still know a couple of doctors so I'll ask who the best specialist is. I'll make an appointment as soon as possible and I'll come with you just so we understand what you're told. We don't want you playing the hero you're much too precious to this world."

"You'd do that for me? I hardly know you but somehow it doesn't seem like that. Thank you Mary but you mustn't tell anyone."

Mary gave a wan smile and assured her new friend that the secret was safe with her.

"Back to the donation, Jose Martinez was your late husband and it's such a huge legacy, hasn't he been dead twelve years? So who decided to give us such a large sum?"

"It came from his estate and that's all you need to know, Dolly Mellor."

"Mystery upon mystery, how you and your son have brightened up my life."

CHAPTER FORTY

Jonathan's birthday arrived and Dave was ready at six o'clock and sat in an armchair reading The Times waiting for Jonathan to get changed. The car had gone to pick Mary up and would then collect them. Jonathan appeared about ten minutes later.

"Ready Dave?"

"Yes the car should be here any minute. Wow you look cool. Where did you get that suit?"

"I splurged and went to Hugo Boss. I got the shirt there too. I didn't know whether to wear a tie or not but as you're not, nor will I"

"You mum will be happy."

"Are you happy that I look half-way decent?"

"I've told you many times, I don't care how you look. Mind you I'll have to stay close tonight, 'cause you look great. I hope the press aren't invited or we'll have another round of the mystery man fiasco."

"Thank you for the words of approval. I think that's the car. Let's go."

Jonathan sat in the back with Mary who was obviously relieved that her son was well turned out and she told him he looked beautiful.

"Well, look at yourself mum. I've never seen you looking so glamorous."

"I went round to Dolly's earlier and she had someone there that did our hair and make-up. I bought the dress in Selfridges in the week. I went to the fancy section and spent a small fortune. Is it nice?"

Dave turned round and told her she looked fabulous and she really did.

They arrived just before seven and went straight to the hall where the party guests were gathering. Dolly approached them and said how wonderful they all looked and then made her exit with Mary on her arm.

The men found the bar and got drinks and Dave mingled with Jonathan in tow. The only people Jonathan knew were the Worthington clan but Dave seemed to know a lot of people all of whom were connected with the foundation. Jonathan recognised a number of actor's and Poppy introduced him to a few, pointing out that he was the birthday boy.

Dolly and Mary appeared with a man Jonathan recognised immediately as Charles Levant, Mary's favourite actor and biggest heartthrob. They approached and Mary made the introductions. Jonathan gave his mother a quizzical look but she just smiled enigmatically. They chatted for a while and then Charles apologised for not being able to stay and he kissed both women on their cheeks and said his goodbyes.

"Oh Jonathan that was so lovely, I met the man of my dreams so now I can die happy. Dolly did that just for me. Poor Charles he popped in on his way to the airport and made me a very happy woman."

Dolly stood on the stage and called for everyone's attention and summoned Jonathan to join her. She introduced him as the birthday boy and proposed a toast. She handed him a present and ordered him to open it. He did as ordered and when he looked inside the small box he laughed.

"Well put it on" commanded the hostess.

Jonathan extracted a gold circular earring and Dolly assisted in attaching it to his right lobe and declared "For my gypsy boy."

She whispered in his ear and he left the stage and the hall to return a few minutes later with the flamenco troupe.

The music started and Jonathan and his partner performed a sensuous dance which had everybody spell bound. The music paused and the female dancer stepped to one side leaving Jonathan to do a solo. He seemed lost in his dance which increased in pace, until it seemed almost frenzied. He stopped as did the music and he dropped to his knees with his head bowed. The room was silent for a moment then the party went wild with applause and cheering asking for an encore.

Dolly took to the stage once more and explained that the troupe had to be somewhere else very soon so they could not give an encore to everyone's disappointment.

Jonathan found Dave who handed him a beer.

"You deserve that. I'm dumb struck, I've seen you dance but never like that, it was incredible."

"I do have some talents you know."

"I do know, very well so shall we go home now?"

"Very funny but you don't know how much I'd like to right now. Flamenco makes me feel very powerful and very in need of you."

Dave gave a knowing smile and then looked Jonathan in the eye and said something was wrong. "You've grown."

"I changed my shoes idiot, for the dance. Cuban heels look. I'll go and change them."

"Please do, I don't like you being as tall as me, I'm the big one remember?"

Whilst Jonathan was gone Dave took to the stage with the band and really got the party going. He sang a couple of sixties rock songs and some funky Motown.

Jonathan returned and was headed for the bar as dancing had made him very thirsty. As he crossed the room he saw Poppy talking to a man that looked familiar and she waved him over.

"Juan that was terrific, mother is so happy. Thanks to you and Dave everyone is having a great time. These parties are usually a bit fusty. Oh excuse my manners, Juan this is Clive, Clive, Juan and before you get any ideas Clive, Juan is taken so behave yourself."

"Thank you for that but we're only doing things we like to do so it is our pleasure. Anyway my mum would have killed me if I refused. I was just on my way to the bar, can I get you anything?"

Poppy declined but Clive said he would accompany him to the bar.

Jonathan ordered his beer and Clive did likewise.

"So Juan, you're the mystery man that the celeb mags have been raving about."

"There's no mystery to me, it's all in their imagination."

"I've asked a few people here about you but only the Worthingtons and a few others seem to know you and nobody will tell me anything other than your name and the fact that you're with the guy that's singing. Those that don't know you would like to have a piece of you even the guys. With looks like yours you could turn the straightest of the straightest. So as you won't tell me who you really are you put me at a disadvantage as you obviously know who I am."

Jonathan had started to feel uncomfortable but resisted the temptation to walk away.

"I'm sorry but I don't know who you are but you do look familiar. Let me guess, you're one of Dolly's actor friends, right?"

"You must live in a cave, young man."

"I do as it happens and a very comfortable one. I only come out on special occasions such as today."

"Why don't I believe that? I can't believe you don't recognise me. I'm Clive Osbourne, I'm a movie star. I've been in lots of films and have starred in most of them."

Jonathan shrugged. "I'm sorry but I don't go to the cinema often and I only watch TV when my mum asks me to watch something with her. I'm a bit of a Philistine when it comes to celebrity."

"Well young man, tell me about yourself."

"There's nothing to tell, I'm a student and as you said, I'm with Dave. That's about all there is."

"You're extremely handsome and obviously have talents, you should be on the big screen and I could help you there. Tell me what do you see in that singer guy? He's big and hunky for sure but lacks a bit in the looks department."

Jonathan could sense what was coming but said nothing.

"What are you doing on Tuesday night?"

"Staying in my cave with that ugly guy, why?"

"Well why don't you come round to my place for dinner and we can talk about getting you into the industry."

Jonathan looked at him and gave an ironic smile and said, "And will we have sex for dessert?"

Clive thought he had cracked it and said "So are you on for Tuesday night?"

Jonathan's temper was rising but he checked himself and just said "Umm."

At this point Rachael tapped Jonathan on the shoulder and as he turned she gave him a hug and a kiss.

"You were terrific, absolutely amazing. Hello Clive, are you hitting on the man I love?"

"You interrupted; we had just arranged a date."

Rachael squeezed Jonathan's arm and smiled at Clive. "Are you sure? I couldn't help but hear the end of that conversation and all I heard was a sound emanating from Jonathan's mouth which was definitely not a yes."

Clive smirked and said, "Oh I know it was a yes, isn't that so Juan?"

"He said umm which is not a yes but a polite way of telling you to get lost I should imagine," said a laughing Rachael.

"So what did you mean Juan?" enquired a confident looking Clive.

"Let's just say it was a substitute for what I was really thinking."

"And what was that?"

Rachael stepped in and said, "Juan is very honest so better not ask, just believe me, it was a definite no."

"Come, come I think you're jealous. I really would like to know what Juan was thinking, I'm sure it was something about Tuesday. Come on Jonathan, shock me."

Jonathan raised his shoulders and said, "You sure?"

"No problem young man, continue."

"You said Dave was not good looking, when I look at him I see something very different. His goodness shines through and I wouldn't change one thing about him, absolutely nothing. The reason that I hesitated was I was holding back my desire to punch you in the face. The only reason I didn't was I wouldn't want to spoil Dolly's party. I look at you and I see a very sad aging man who's grotesque and sordid, so you had better leave now before I change my mind and split that over stretched face of yours like a tomato. So fuck off pervert."

Clive reddened and was visibly shaken. He turned tail and they watched him leave through the front door.

Rachael held Jonathan's arm and looked up at him and said, "Well said, someone should have done that a long time ago, you're now officially my hero. I've worked with him and he pursued every male under twenty five that worked on the set.

"Jonathan my beautiful friend, I'm in a business where getting noticed is normal and some would say even necessary but you don't like it and you certainly don't ask for it. I think I understand why you like to try and hide yourself away, it must be hard."

"That man said that most people would like a piece of me and now I think everybody is looking at me, it's crap."

"Jonathan, forget it. You're amongst friends and you're here with Dave so focus on that. I'm so sorry that creep has upset you."

"Thanks Rachael, I'll live and why is everyone calling me Juan?"

At that point Dolly appeared. "Did something happen? I saw Creepy Clive talking to you then he left like a bat out of hell."

"He said some unpleasant things to Jonathan and my hero threatened to punch him in the face. He was marvellous and very controlled."

Dolly fell into fits of laughter. "Oh Jonathan dear boy I'm sorry he upset you but the thought of you punching him in his million dollar face is hysterical.

"There is something I should have told you earlier. We have a freelance photographer here. He's an old friend and a bit down on his luck so I gave him exclusive rights to tonight's party. The problem is he seems most interested in you two so you can expect to find yourselves in the gossip columns and the celeb magazines. I hope you don't mind Jonathan."

Jonathan wasn't happy but hid it and said, "Dolly it's your party and this is show biz. I knew that before I came so it's fine."

"Oh you're such a darling. I've told my lot to tell him only that your name is Juan and nothing else so you can retain some anonymity. Is that ok?"

Jonathan kissed her on the cheek and thanked her. "That does answer one question. I was wondering why Poppy and Rachael called me Juan." Dolly kissed Jonathan on the cheek and noticed he was still wearing the earring, so she reached up and unscrewed it and put it in his pocket. He smiled a thank you and she left to continue her duties as host.

Dave finished his set and found the two young people still in conversation. Rachael kissed him on the cheek and applauded his performance.

"You two are very talented you should be in show biz."

"Not our thing Rachael, we'll leave that to you," Dave offered. "What's up Jonathan, you ok?"

"Yes I'm fine but I wish we could go home."

Rachael tried to change the conversation by asking "Do you have any other hidden talents?"

"Dave can play drums on the kitchen sink."

"Jonathan what's wrong?" Dave insisted.

"He's not enjoying the attention but you know that you big idiot."

They laughed and Rachael dragged them both onto the dance floor.

At eleven thirty Dolly called Dave over and asked him to slow things down as they had to finish by midnight. Dave obliged and took to the stage and sang a Sinatra number then slowed it down further with Etta James "At last". Rachael took Jonathan by the hand to the dance floor.

"He's singing this to you Jonathan."

"Maybe but I think it would be more appropriate if I sang it for him, only trouble is I can't sing."

They looked into one another's eyes and gave movie star smiles.

Dave wound it down with "The Party's Over" and it was.

They found Mary and offered Rachael a lift which she gladly accepted and they left with lots of kisses and hugs from the Worthingtons.

Mary was a little tipsy and laughed at anything anyone said. They dropped Rachael then Mary. Jonathan helped her out of the car and up to her flat.

The car then took them home and when inside the front door Jonathan put his arms around Dave and held him tightly. Dave stroked his head and said "When you went to the gents Rachael told me what happened, I'm sorry. You can go back to being the invisible man tomorrow, ok."

Jonathan released his grip and nodded.

Dave told him to sit in the lounge, which he did. Jonathan heard a loud pop and Dave appeared with a bottle of champagne and glasses on a tray on which there was also an envelope which Jonathan opened to find a funny birthday card. Dave had written some very nice words on the back and Jonathan smiled happily.

"I couldn't give you your birthday present today but it will be delivered at eleven o'clock tomorrow, so you'll have to wait. They drank the champagne and talked into the small hours.

CHAPTER FORTY ONE

The next morning Jonathan was up first and prepared breakfast. He had to drag Dave out of bed as he was a little hung over. A shower after food put him to rights and he was dressed just in time to hear the door bell. He shouted down the stairs to Jonathan and told him to close his eyes and keep them closed.

Jonathan knew he was in for a surprise and did as requested. He heard Dave enter the room then he felt something warm and alive in his lap. He opened his eyes to see a very cute puppy staring up at him.

"It's a female German shepherd, just like Bella."

Jonathan stood up with the puppy in one arm and embraced Dave with the free one.

"Dave every time I think my life can't get better, it does, thank you so much. She's perfect."

"I've invited your mum over for dinner this evening and she'll be here about six. I thought it would be good if we had a private birthday dinner, just the three of us."

"You're forgetting someone, what about puppy is she not invited?"

"What are you going to call her?"

"How about Jezebel, nice and dramatic don't you think?"

Dave looked at the innocent little puppy and disagreed so they discussed a few options but as they couldn't agree they decided to ask Mary later.

Jonathan put the puppy down and she immediately squatted and peed on the carpet. He picked her up and took her to the kitchen. He got out a bowl from under the sink and a cloth and disinfectant and went back to the longue to clean up the mess, with the puppy at his heels.

Dave carried the box that came with the dog into the kitchen and Jonathan followed with his new born. The box contained a sleeping basket, bowls and puppy food, together with an instruction booklet on how and when to feed infant shepherds.

Jonathan put the puppy into the basket as she immediately fell asleep. He sat at the table and read the booklet. Dave sat opposite him and started the crossword when his mobile rang.

Dave greeted the caller and, as much as he tried not to, Jonathan listened. It was obvious that the caller was Dave's sister and although he could only hear one side of the conversation he caught the gist.

It seemed that Carol was supposed to be coming to London to finalise the sale of the Casino by signing the last of the documents. There was some sort of problem and she wanted Dave to bring the papers to New York instead. Dave refused but then left the room and went upstairs.

Jonathan sat for a while imagining how the conversation would conclude. He picked up the pen Dave had been using and turned over the booklet happy to find the back page was blank. He scribbled a list and waited ten minutes then put the booklet in his back pocket and went up to the bedroom.

Dave was lying on the bed looking up at the ceiling and his breathing was like a series of sighs.

"Hey what's wrong?"

"It looks like I have to go to New York" he said through deep breaths.

Jonathan got onto the bed and sat astride him. He leant forward and started to rub Dave's shoulders in an attempt to get him to relax and it seemed to work a little. Then he withdrew the booklet from his back pocket and handed it to the prone man. "Jonathan, why are you giving me this she's your dog so you have to learn to look after her, not me?"

"You fucking grump, turn it over."

Dave read the list and looked puzzled. It was a list of places in Manhattan.

"What's this, I'm not going on a sightseeing trip? I'll be in and out in a day." He threw the booklet onto the bed.

"That's my Christmas present to you."

"Jonathan you're talking in riddles, you know there is no way that I'd do any of these things."

"You are dense sometimes. I said it's my Christmas present so I have to be there to take you to these places. I'm coming with you and you're paying. First class please." He knew that would make the conversation easier as Dave would insist on paying anyway.

"You want to come with me? What about the dog and your studies?"

"I don't want to come with you, I am coming with you. There's no way you're going alone, no way. My last lecture is on Tuesday before the Christmas break and mum will look after the puppy. We can have a holiday and you can show me New York. It'll be our first holiday together where we share a bed. It'll be just us, it'll be great."

Dave grinned, "Even I want to go now, you manipulating bastard. Now you can get off my legs, the left ones gone to sleep."

As Jonathan was about to get off Dave punched him.

"What's that for?"

"I should have known you'd make it right, you sly git."

Jonathan returned the punch and they ended up wrestling until Dave went limp and just held him. They were about to get amorous when Dave suddenly sat up.

"Stop, we can't, look at the time, I've got to start cooking dinner"

"Dave it's only one o'clock and it is kindda still my birthday so come here."

By two thirty they had showered and gone down to the kitchen. The puppy was awake and ran over to greet them.

"Oh my god she's crapped everywhere. Dave it's disgusting."

"It's your dog so I'll let you do the honours. Don't worry too much we have a visitor tomorrow who will help us. He's a dog trainer and he's supposed to be excellent."

"Can't he come now and clean up this lot?"

"There's always a little trouble in paradise so enjoy the good bits and clean up that fucking shit."

"Yes Granddad."

Dave clipped him around the head and started preparing dinner when his mobile rand again.

"Hi Rachael how did you get my number?

"Oh Dolly right."

He listened for a while then laughed. "That's so funny and I don't mind one bit.

"Yes he's here. Jonathan, it's Rachael, she wants to speak to you."

Jonathan took the phone and Rachael sounded very apologetic. The newspapers were full of pictures of the two of them and there was one of them leaving the party and it described Dave as a body guard. Jonathan also thought that very funny and he reassured her that it was all fine.

"I'm too happy to let anything upset me today. Dave bought me a puppy for my birthday and she's beautiful. We don't know what to call her though any ideas?"

Rachael wasn't at all helpful but she was relieved at the men's reactions. They passed a few pleasantries and hung up.

The phone rang again and this time it was Dolly with much the same story, then Mary rang and said she would bring the Sunday rags with her.

She arrived a little early and showed the men the photographs. She left the People until last.

It was the picture of them leaving the party and sure enough it described Dave as a bodyguard. What was more alarming was a picture of Jonathan and Rachael dancing, smiling and gazing into one another's eyes. The caption read 'The look of love' and it said underneath that Rachael had been overheard telling her mystery man that she loved him. It went on to say that they had discovered the identity of the handsome Latin lover. His name is Juan and he's a Spanish flamenco dancer and of course there was also a picture of Jonathan dancing flamenco.

Mary saved the best till last. "Look there's one of us leaving and guess what I'm in it. I'm so excited I've never been in the newspaper before and look here I am. It describes Dave as the bodyguard, does that bother you Dave?"

"Not at all, in fact, I like to think I am some times."

Dave watched Jonathan for his reaction expecting him to be upset. To his relief, Jonathan thought the whole thing ludicrous and funny and asked Dave why he wasn't outside the house doing his bodyguard duty.

He looked pensive and after a few moments he said, "I should go to the press and tell them who I am and the whole thing will go away once they realise there's no story to it."

Dave agreed but Mary objected. "This is the most fun I've had in years plus the fact that it gives Dolly a lot of free publicity for herself and the foundation. Rachael told me that she's had loads of offers since that ball you went to and I dare say she'll get a lot more now. It's the life blood for those sorts of people. Just leave it as long as it amuses all of us. That does include you Jonathan, it's not that it's a daily occurrence after all, is it?'

"Mum, you're a real case and I never thought of you as an attention seeker and your right it's not like it happens every day and I actually like some of those people. If knowing them puts us in the public eye, so be it."

Over dinner they discussed the puppy's name and Mary also wasn't impressed with Jezebel and suggested Bathsheba if they wanted a biblical name. She explained that she had been Solomon's mother and that a biblical name would be apt as the sweet puppy belonged to David and Jonathan. They agreed and they would call her Sheba for short. Mary held Sheba on her lap all through dinner and readily agreed to look after her whilst the men went to New York.

She went home at nine thirty and Dave and Jonathan went to bed shortly after. They took the dog basket up to their bedroom and put Sheba in it to sleep for the night. No sooner were they in bed than Sheba started to whimper. They left her for a while but Dave's conscience got the better of him so he got out of bed and brought her back with him. She lay between their pillows and licked their faces in turn. Dave sighed and said they could say goodbye to their sex life and promptly fell asleep.

The dog trainer came the next morning and gave them a lot of advice amongst which was not to let her sleep in their bedroom. She had to have a comfortable place but alone at night, so the kitchen was to be that place. Jonathan asked if it was ok to take her for a walk but was advised against it until she had finished her course of injections. Jonathan was a little disappointed as that wouldn't be for a couple of months. The mantra was to be, routine and reward for good behaviour.

Mary called round at lunch time on the pretext of wanting to ask about Christmas but could easily have done that on the phone. She found herself slightly thwarted in her real mission as Mrs Hayes seemed not to want to put Sheba down.

Mary had to revert to the Christmas enquiries. She said they were all invited to Karen's for Christmas and they would go on Christmas Eve and stay until the day after Boxing Day.

Dave looked alarmed and said sheepishly, "I'm sorry Mary but I'm booked for Christmas Day."

Jonathan looked puzzled he knew Dave wouldn't desert him on Christmas day so he asked what he meant.

"Well the members of the foundation cook Christmas lunch and serve it in the soup kitchen to the homeless. It's the one hands-on thing I do and it's just once a year. I'm sorry I didn't mention it before but things have been happening and it slipped my mind."

"Dave why shouldn't it, no need to apologise. Mum that's two of us that won't be coming, I'll go with Dave. Maybe we can come on Boxing Day."

"That's a good idea, I'll tell Karen she has to have two Christmas days and we'll all go on Boxing Day. She'll understand."

"Jonathan, you and your mum go to Karen's and I can come the next day, I really don't mind."

Mary chuckled, "And leave you to have all the fun, not likely?"

"Well I'm not going without you Dave but what do you mean about fun mum?"

"We'll all go and help at the soup kitchen and in the evening Dolly has invited us round for supper. I think that would be so nice and Christmassy."

"Mum you knew all the time and you've even made plans for all of us, you're a wicked woman to put Dave through that."

"I didn't know if he'd changed his plans because of you so I'd have gone along with whatever he wanted. I thought I was being considerate."

"And so you were Mary. Thank you, so that's Christmas settled."

"Don't you two have to be somewhere today?"

"Jonathan has no lectures today so he's dog sitting, if you and Mrs Hayes give him a look in, and I'm off to the Casino in about an hour."

Mary was looking pleased with herself and said she thought she had made a real friend with Dolly as it seemed like they'd known each other for a long time.

"I've not had a real friend since my early twenties and it feels so nice. It's such an unlikely match but I think Dolly's the same. She said it's hard to make friends in her business. She's coming round on Wednesday and we're going to spend the day gassing."

"Mary I've known Dolly for a while and I know her well enough to know that she wouldn't bother with anyone she didn't like. Look at me. She only ever bothered with me when she needed something and made it clear that I wasn't her favourite person. I know she likes you but enough of that we have things to do."

Dave called his office and asked them to book their air tickets to New York for Sunday coming back the following Saturday and to sort out their hotel reservation.

Jonathan went on line and quickly received his authorisation to enter the US under the visa waiver program. Dave already had a visa which he got before his earlier aborted trip. So they were all set to travel.

Dave's office also emailed his sister Carol a copy of the document that needed signing so she could get them checked out by her lawyer, then there would be no arguments when he met her. He had earlier offered to courier them to her, in the hopes she would sign them and send them back the same way. She had declined and said she wanted him there as she had another matter she needed to discuss. Before moving to New York, Carol had been close to Dave but that soon turned sour when she found a new life. She now seemed to get great pleasure out of being the bitch she had become.

Dave left for work and Jonathan went and commandeered the dining room table to do some studying. Mary and Mrs Hayes were left to fuss over Sheba.

CHAPTER FORTY TWO

Dolly arrived just after twelve. They had coffee and chatted for a while. Mary took on a serious demeanour when she was about to ask if her new friend would let her unburden herself of a secret.

"I know it can be unfair to ask someone to keep a confidence but even though I hardly know you, I trust you. Do you mind?"

Dolly looked at her new friend and said of course she didn't mind and that she wasn't the scatterbrain the most people thought. Then she laughed a wicked laugh and said she loved secrets and was very good at keeping them.

"If I told my dear husband half the things I did before I met him his hair would fall out, what's left of it. Come on unburden yourself my dear Mary."

Mary related her secret to a silent Dolly. It took her about twenty minutes and there were points in the story when Dolly gasped or her eyes opened wide in wonder.

When Mary had finished they sat in silence for a while and then a tear fell from Dolly's eye. This brought Mary's emotions to the surface and she burst into tears and Dolly followed suit.

After about a minute the crying turned to laughing and then back to a controlled conversation.

"Dolly I really don't know if I'm doing the right thing."

"I think you're doing exactly the right thing and given the circumstances you really don't have a choice. You are truly wonderful. It's a bit cold outside but the sun is shining, let's go for a walk and I can digest all that you've told me. I passed an organic food place on Portobello road that looked ok, let's go and get some lunch."

They walked arm in arm down Portobello and found the cafe and sat at a table in the corner. They ordered and Dolly began to offer some observations.

"I met your son for the first time a little less than three weeks ago and you exactly two weeks today. I have never met more interesting and influential people in my life. Your lives are so complex and interesting although you might not see it that way. From the little I know of you and Jonathan, I could write a book."

Mary looked perplexed.

"My dear Mary your son looks like and angel and he has absolutely, transformed someone's life, as angels do of course. Did you know that until the foundation party I thought Dave was just a miserable, coarse, boring, rich bugger? I could go on. I really wasn't looking forward to having to look at his dreary face all night. That Dave didn't turn up. A different, funny, laughing and entertaining one did, who looked ten years younger. I'd always thought of him as being forty plus. I was amazed. At first I thought he was on drugs but it was your son who did that and there's no doubt about it.

"Then there's you, you've been so kind and I know it's nothing to do with celebrity. You really care. You recognised I have a problem and you went out of your way to find a specialist and coming with me so you could understand what I needed. You're helping me come to terms with the fact that I have to live with Parkinson's for the rest of my life. You did it all so discreetly.

"If that wasn't enough you now tell me the most beautiful love story I've ever heard and it's not a play, a film or a book, its true life.

"On top of that you're a witch," she said to lighten the mood.

"You have enriched my life in a matter of weeks, thank you dearest Mary. Do you know I feel that somehow I've known you a long time. We are officially friends so you will have to tell me all your secrets."

They both laughed and the gloom lifted.

"Dolly I know by telling you, nothing has changed but I do feel better in the knowledge that you would do the same in my position. Thank you so much for listening."

"There is one thing I'd like to ask you but tell me to mind my own business if I'm intruding. How do you feel about Jonathan being with Dave?"

Mary pondered the question for a minute.

"I could see it coming and I did tell Dave. He refused to talk to Jonathan after that and it broke his heart and my poor boy's and my interfering eventually drove them together. How do I feel? Well I don't think Jonathan would ever have another girlfriend. He really loved Gabriella and I think there's only room in his head for one major experience of a kind. It's 2013 and it seems fine for same sex couples to live together. If Jonathan hadn't found Dave, and that's the way it happened, I think he would never have known love again.

"You know until you just asked I hadn't really worked it out, I just try to ignore it. I like Dave a lot and he's done wonders for Jonathan and they really do love one another and that's obvious. I'm good with it in fact I'm happy for them and happy for me."

Dolly nodded, "You're a modern woman amongst other things. I think they're great together but think of the disappointment of all those poor girls who'd like to be with either of them."

They had only picked at their food as they were distracted coupled with the fact that the food hadn't interested them. At Dolly's suggestion they left the cafe and took a slow walk to Notting Hill Gate. The sun was still shining and the air fresh and it felt invigorating. Mary felt as if she had shed a load and imagined she was almost floating up the Lane. Dolly lead the way to a bakery that sold great coffee and huge slices of chocolate cake.

"We deserve this indulgence don't you think, after all we didn't eat much lunch."

"Dolly you're incorrigible but I must admit this is delicious. I think you've been recognised, people are staring."

"Ignore it, it's not as though we're doing anything naughty is it?"

"Oh I don't know. I can see the headlines now 'Dolly Worthington eats chocolate cake'."

"Then let's cause a major scandal and have another piece."

"Dolly there is something else I need to tell you. Dave made me promise not to tell anyone but somehow it doesn't seem right, you of all people should know. I didn't lie to you but I purposely mislead you. The money from my Joe's estate did come from there but Dave gave me an equal amount as a gift as he put it. So it really came from him and it's made me feel a bit of a fraud."

"Somehow Mary that doesn't surprise me and I won't let on. Thank you for telling me and the last thing you are is a fraud."

Dolly spoke excitedly about her rehearsals for the upcoming play and said it was all going swimmingly. She said her character was a bit of a manipulating bitch but she remembered seeing a recording of Peggy Mount play it as a real old battle axe and she was going to do the same. She was loving being over the top and she explained that you could do that on stage but it never works on film or T.V.

They drank more coffee and chatted about life in general when out of the blue Dolly announced, "I'm coming to visit. I love Malaga and the sun will revive me. We finish in time for Easter so I'll come then. Please say that's ok."

Mary beamed a grateful yes. She said there was plenty of room and Dolly could stay as long as she wished. The beach was within easy walking distance and the local night life was a little more elegant than the Costas.

"There is only one condition Dolly, you have to come alone."

"Of course, I understand that and I can leave my lot behind with a clear conscience. It will be great just to get away and now I'm part of your story, I want to experience it. You're a very brave and noble woman Mary Martinez.

"Well Dolly Worthington that makes two of us. You know somehow the name Dolly sounds fine when I think of you as an actor but sitting here with you it doesn't seem to suit you. I hope you don't take offence but it's not a very elegant name and you are a true Lady."

"It's not my real name. My birth name is Grace but that was a problem when I first started acting.'

"That suits you so much better, why was it a problem?"

"My family name is Kelly."

They both laughed and carried on talking for another hour.

CHAPTER FORTY THREE

Jonathan had just the one lecture on the Tuesday after the party and wondered if he would get any comments about the press photographs. Some fellow students had been suspicious after the ball but there were some that knew he danced flamenco so that photo was a dead give-away.

He resolved to do something about it. He asked Dave if he would drive him to Uni and pick him up later. Dave readily agreed without question. Dave went to pick up the car and when he got back he was amazed to see Jonathan in his suit looking clean shaven and absolutely beautiful.

"Are you sure about this?"

"Dave I think they would have worked it out by now, I just want to be honest with my fellow students."

Dave bit his bottom lip and tried not to laugh.

They got stuck in a jam and Jonathan only just made it to his lecture. Everyone was already seated when he walked in and the lecturer watched Jonathan take his seat. With a smile on his face he said, "Who are you young man?" There was a buzz in the room and Jonathan stood up.

"I'm Jonathan Martinez sir, sometimes known as the mystery man. The reason I look half-way decent today is that I know that some of you have worked it out and I want to be honest with you. This isn't me, the real me is the scruff and the reason I choose to look like that is because I don't handle attention very well. I'm not seeking any publicity and I've attended just two events and obviously met the people who do. Hence my picture being plastered everywhere. I only went to those events because my partner asked me to and I like to please him. I'll be back to my old self in the New Year. I was going to tell the press but some people think its fun to keep them guessing. It's been particularly helpful to one young lady. So now you're in on the secret it's up to you. I really don't mind either way. Sorry for taking up your lecture time sir."

There was a brief silence then everybody clapped. The lecturer then said, "Well are we going to keep the secret and let Jonathan live in peace."

There was a chorus of yeses and they, like honest lawyers, kept the confidence.

Mary decided to move into the upstairs flat whilst the boys were in New York. They had a small garden in which Sheba could roam around and hopefully do her business. She arrived on Sunday in time to see them off. She couldn't help herself calling them boys, motherly instinct she supposed.

The car arrived at seven to take them to Heathrow. Their flight was at ten fifteen and would get into JFK at one twenty five New York time. Jonathan had surprised Dave the previous weekend by asking him to go shopping with him. He only had one suit and no decent casual or warm clothes and he thought it was time he started to dress appropriately when required. Dave didn't object and he took him first to Regent Street. They found a nice suit in Jaeger, another in Burberry and casual clothes by various designers in the plethora of shops along the road. They ended up in Austin Reed and bought a very sober, navy blue overcoat. Now he was fully kitted out.

They checked in at the first class counter, and made their way to the entrance for departing passengers where they cleared security and then went and sat in the airline lounge. They boarded the flight at nine forty five and Jonathan was about to start his first, first class journey. He was excited but kept that to himself. During the flight he played a few video games and watched a movie. Dave slept the whole way and Jonathan requested the cabin crew not to disturb him.

Jonathan nudged Dave into consciousness as they were about to land. "Put your seat up Rip, we're about to land."

"We're here already? God I've gone from being an insomniac to someone with sleeping sickness."

Immigration seemed to take forever and when they arrived in the baggage hall their bags were already on the carousel. There was a car waiting to take them to The Pierre. Jonathan gazed out the window of the limo and watched as Manhattan approached. He was a little disappointed as it didn't seemed as dramatic a skyline as you see in the movies but Dave explained that it was great at night and that they weren't seeing it from the best angle.

They checked into the hotel at four thirty and their room was spacious, beautifully decorated and came with a view of Central Park.

Dave called his sister and arranged the meeting for the next morning.

"That's odd she's moved and the address is nowhere near as good as the old one, not even close. She used to live not far from here just off Fifth Avenue but now she's on the upper West Side. Maybe it's fashionable now, who knows.

"Let's go exploring. Where's your list? Ok we'll do the Empire State Building and you can see the city in all its glory. It'll be properly dark by the time we get there and that's when Manhattan comes into its own. We'll use the subway so that'll be another thing you can tick off your list."

Jonathan found a subway map in the desk draw and some information leaflets. He thought the subway system looked vast and hard to read but Dave said it was really easy once you got the hang of it.

They found where they were going with no difficulty and took the elevator up to the viewing deck. Jonathan thought the city lights were brilliant, without meaning that to be a pun. They wandered over to Lexington Avenue and admired the Chrysler Building and then onto Bloomingdales. Mary had told him to do that, as Rachael in the Friends sitcom worked there for Ralph Lauren. They bought Mary Ralph Lauren perfume, some other bits and pieces and had them all gift wrapped in Bloomingdale's gift wrap paper.

It had started to feel cold so they headed back in the direction of their hotel. Dave was starving and spotted a steak restaurant and in they went. They were told they had to wait about twenty minutes and were directed to the bar. The bar seemed to be stocked with just about every liquor Jonathan had ever heard of and even more he hadn't. He tried to play it cool and ordered a martini. The barman asked him if he wanted it dry and with a twist or an olive. He tried not to look ignorant so said yes he'd have it dry and with an olive. Dave was trying not to look amused and ordered a beer for himself.

"I didn't know you liked martinis."

"I've never tried one but I've seen them drinking them in old movies and it always looks so cool."

When their drinks arrived they toasted themselves and took a sip. Jonathan pulled a face and Dave laughed.

"So much for being cool, this is horrible. How can anyone drink this?"

Dave was still laughing, "It's an acquired taste. What you just ordered is almost pure gin with a touch of vermouth for flavour. Let's swap."

Jonathan did so happily.

They sat down for dinner and ordered steaks and it wasn't until they arrived that Jonathan realised he wasn't hungry.

"I ate non-stop on the plane and I'm still full. This does look good though and it's normal size."

"You sound disappointed."

"Well I thought that all meals were huge in America."

"A misconception especially when it comes to New York. People are very health conscious here but I'm not feeling that way today so I'll eat your steak and you can nibble the veg."

They took their time and washed the food down with a nice bottle of wine. When it was time to leave Dave suggested they walk back to the hotel. Jonathan pointed out that he was still on UK time and it was three o'clock in the morning for him, but Dave was obviously fine having spent seven hours asleep on the plane. Dave waved down a cab.

They got into bed and Jonathan switched on the TV and although he was tired he couldn't resist channel surfing and was amazed at some of the things that were shown. Talk about the land of the free, wow.

After about an hour he became very sleepy and switched it off. He hadn't notice Dave fall asleep and he shook his head and smiled. He switched the light off and fell into a deep peaceful sleep.

Jonathan woke first as usual. It was seven o'clock so he slipped out of bed quietly so as not to wake the sleeping giant. He stuck his head under the closed curtains and looked out at Central Park. It seemed that like London this was the time all the crazy people came out in the form of joggers, fast walkers, cyclists and the whole gambit. He watched for about ten minutes and then showered. At seven thirty he woke Dave and suggested that he might get up or they wouldn't have time for breakfast. Dave stuck his head under his pillow and told him to order room service.

Jonathan pulled back the bed covers and ordered him to get up as he hadn't come to New York to sit in a hotel room, as nice as that one might be.

Dave groaned and headed for the bathroom. Jonathan put on the bottom half of one of his new suits and one of his new shirts and checked himself out in the mirror. His hair had grown since he had it cut for the ball but it still looked pretty good. He was clean shaven and not his usual scruffy self and he was feeling bold and confident but still hoped nobody would look at him.

Dave quickly dried himself and dressed and they went down to the hotel restaurant for breakfast. Jonathan was in awe of the choices on the menu but ended up having a boiled egg and toast. Dave had just about everything he could throw down in an hour. Jonathan loved the splendour of it all and the brilliant service. He ate his breakfast and watched the other guests until he noticed some were looking back.

"Dave you do know that I've only ever stayed in hotels twice before and both times with you. This place is amazing, are all four star hotels the same?"

"I haven't stayed in that many but I'm sure they all have their own charm."

At nine they returned to their room and got ready to leave. Dave had booked himself a hotel car for nine thirty as he was to be at his sister's by ten.

Dave looked at Jonathan who was now wearing the top half of a new suit to match the bottom half. "Wow you look really good, have you got a date or something?"

"Well I suppose I have."

"Do you want me to drop you off somewhere? I suppose it's some museum or other?"

"Something like that, it's on the other side of the park. Is that ok?"

Dave wanted to probe further and it was killing him not to know but he knew Jonathan was playing with him so he pretended not to be interested. Dave grabbed his briefcase and they went to find the car.

Once inside the car, he asked Jonathan in the most nonchalant manner he could muster where he wanted to be dropped.

"Dave, if you think I'm going to leave you alone in this city, think again? I'm coming with you. You said her lawyer will be there so you're taking yours."

Dave had an uncomfortable feeling but knew it was hopeless to argue.

They arrived at the address which was an apartment building which made Dave curious as they used to live in a Brownstone. It was a nice enough building but a long way off the elegance of their old house.

Dave hadn't been given an apartment number hence he hadn't realised it wasn't a house so he asked the concierge who called up to the apartment. He then gave them the number and told them to go up to the twenty-first floor. They rang the doorbell and Carol opened the door almost immediately. She gave Dave an air kiss and asked in a very unpleasant manner whom his companion might be. Dave introduced Jonathan as his friend who helps him with legal matters. She looked dubious but admitted them both.

Her lawyer was sitting at the dining room table and they joined him. The lawyer asked a few questions and Jonathan, who had read the contract thoroughly without telling Dave why, was able to answer to his satisfaction. Jonathan explained to Dave that as the contract was drawn up under British law there were some minor differences. The lawyer looked impressed by the young man's knowledge and continued talking to him whilst Dave and Carol looked on. It was agreed that all was in order and Carol signed.

Whilst Jonathan was engaged in conversation with the lawyer Carol had been speaking on and off to Dave. She spoke to him as if he was something the cat had dragged in. Jonathan had heard every word and he didn't like what he heard and was starting to feel very defensive on Dave's behalf but knew he had to stay calm.

The lawyer said he was leaving and asked Jonathan to accompany him to the door. When out of earshot he said, "Thanks kid for going along with that. If I had nothing to say, that bitch wouldn't have paid me. Enjoy New York."

Dave put the documents into his briefcase and stood as to leave but Carol ordered him to sit down."

"You," she said looking down her nose at Jonathan, "can go.'

Dave shook his head and said Jonathan would leave when he did.

"I have something to discuss with you and its private, so get rid of him."

"No."

She went red in the face and said, "This is my home and I can choose who I want here."

Dave got up to leave but Jonathan remained seated. He gave Carol the longest stare and then said, "You really are a very rude unpleasant person. Is that why your husband left you?"

"He didn't leave me; the divorce was by mutual consent."

Dave sat down.

"Did you tell him?" she spat.

"How could I? I didn't know until ten seconds ago."

"Then how does he know?"

Dave looked at Jonathan, smiled and shook his head.

"Carol he's just magic ok?'

"Fuck off you stupid idiot. Are you really that gullible? He's been checking up on me."

"Carol when you moved to New York you became a monster, especially to me. Now if you have something to ask me please ask now because I want to get out of here."

"Get rid of him first."

"No."

She took a deep breath and said, "I'm thinking of moving back to London so I'll be staying in the upstairs apartment, from the first of March until I decide what to do. The children are with Tom, so I'm pretty much free to do what I like. Tom junior is at university and Francoise will be going in about eighteen months. They can visit me during the holidays if I decide to settle in London. By the way when do I get my money?"

Dave was about to open his mouth when Jonathan said, "I'm sorry you can't use the flat."

"What's that got to do with you? I asked you to leave, now go."

Dave knew something was about to happen. Carol had more than met her match but hadn't realised it yet. He knew that Jonathan wouldn't be mean and wondered where this conversation would go. He sat back and decided to enjoy it.

"No I'm not leaving without Dave and you won't be staying at the flat. Dave owns the whole house now you've signed the contract it's his to do with what he wants. He's already promised it to someone else, so tough find your own place to live."

"Who the fuck is this?"

"My trusted adviser," Dave said with a broad grin.

Carol burst into tears and rushed out of the room. She returned a few minutes later, composed but she slumped into her chair.

Jonathan read the body language and said, "We're going to have coffee at a place close by which we passed on the way. You're more than welcome to join us. Maybe we could start this conversation again. I know Dave would like to help you so please come but can you leave the mean bitch here."

Carol looked at him in horror. She stood up, left the room and came back wearing her coat.

"Come on then, let's go." She said it as if battle was about to commence.

Dave stood and rubbed Jonathan hair, "How do you do it and more to the point why do you do it?"

Jonathan leaned towards him and whispered, "I do it for you and only you."

Carol said "It's rude to whisper but I suppose I should approve as I'm the rudest person on Earth."

They walked a couple of blocks to the cafe and sat at a table by the window. Jonathan changed the tone and the subject of conversation by asking Carol about life in New York. She was still a bit frosty but was definitely warming and talking like a reasonable person.

Jonathan finished his coffee and asked Carol if she had left Mr Hyde back in her apartment. This time she did smile and nodded.

"In that case I will leave you siblings alone to discuss your past, present and future. Dave I'm going for a wander. Take as much time as you need but call me when you're done and I'll let you know where I am. I'll probably be stuck in museums all afternoon so please, absolutely no rush."

Dave nodded and watched him go. Carol watched too. "Who is that person?"

Dave called two hours later. Jonathan was in Central Park and said he'd get a taxi and come and pick him up. Dave laughed down the phone and said he was quite capable of catching a cab, so Jonathan said to meet him at the Natural History Museum. When Dave arrived they went inside and checked out the exhibits.

They emerged at three o'clock and made their way across the park, over Strawberry Fields, to find the Metropolitan Museum of Art.

As they walked Dave told Jonathan all about his conversation with his sister. She had apologised for being so horrible and said he was right, she is a bitch.

"We had a really nice conversation. She asked how you knew that she had split from Tom. I told her that I didn't know and she should ask you yourself."

"So you invited her to dinner, you bloody great softie."

Dave grinned. "We went back to her apartment and made a reservation for seven thirty tonight at Sardi's, luckily they just had a cancellation, so Sardi's it is. Can we check out the art tomorrow and go back to the hotel instead?"

"No, you're going to have to play second fiddle to New York whilst we still have things to do on our list, as tempting as that is."

Dave put his arm around Jonathan's shoulder as they walked as he desperately needed some physical comfort. They spent more time than they had planned, being enthralled by art neither of them had seen before, and had to rush back to the hotel and quickly shower and change.

They arrived at the restaurant to find Carol already there. The place was bustling and everyone seemed happy or excited which meant the noise level was very high. They ordered drinks and whilst looking at the menus carol nudged Dave and said, "Well what did he say?"

"I didn't ask him, you ask him."

"I am here you know."

Carol pulled a face and said "I'm really sorry about my behaviour and Dave you're my only sibling and we're orphans. Since I moved to New York I've been a terrible sister and a terrible everything else. I probably wasn't that good before, in the sister stakes, but I quickly turned into a monster when I got here.

"Jonathan how did you know about my divorce, Dave said you're an all seeing Gypsy, but really how?"

Jonathan study their expectant gazes and waited for a minute before he answered.

"It was easy really. Dave had said you had moved from a swanky house in the best part of town to something not nearly as good. There was no sign of anyone else living with you, yours' was the only coats hanging in the hall. There were pictures of your children but no husband and you have a mark where your wedding ring used to be."

"You sound like Sherlock Holmes."

"Mum taught me to be observant and to make connections around what I heard and saw. That's it, simple really. Now do you mind if I ask you a question?"

"No go ahead."

"Why did you come to the cafe?"

"I thought that I'd get myself together and give you hell when we got there but something happened. As we were walking I noticed Dave for the first time and realised that he had changed back to the Dave I knew before I left England. He was no longer giving off the thug aura and he seemed really happy. I wanted to know what had happened. When we got to the cafe I was still thinking of getting my claws into you but you look so angelic and I was too afraid of your blatant honesty to get into a row I had no chance of winning."

Jonathan smiled and she hung her head for a few seconds.

"When you left, Dave told me what happened to him in prison. What a cow I am. I didn't even visit my own brother. I was ashamed for myself, not good in social circles to have a criminal in the family. He told me that he loves you and it's not hard to see why and I'm very happy for him. I spent the whole afternoon thinking about what I've become and you gave me a reality shock. You see nobody ever tells you, they just seem to put up with it. Nobody has ever called me a bitch before but I bet they were all thinking it."

"What makes you so unhappy?" Jonathan asked.

She thought for a while. "I married money and status, not for love and day after day I regretted it, it just started eating away at me until I invented the new me for protection, the hard-nosed bitch. My husband put up with me until the children grew up but even he'd had enough. The kids prefer him too me and who can blame them. I have no real friends and those that do call me are as bad as I am. Dave was kind to me this afternoon and I don't deserve it but I'll take that kindness I really need it."

"So did you discuss coming to England. We do have more than one bedroom you know so you can stay with us."

Carol burst into tears and dashed to the ladies room. She returned five minutes later looking like she had reapplied her make-up.

"I'm sorry for that but I've been bursting into tears for no reason ever since my conversation with Dave. I don't deserve kindness from anyone, especially either of you.

"Dave says that you are a fearless, honest, protective person when it comes to him. I've never had anyone in my life that would stand up for me, I envy Dave. You're also very beautiful, if that's the right word to use for a man. You must spend your life fighting off admirers."

"No I don't. I avoid people as best I can and I'm only half way companionable when Dave's around. I'm a total introvert but Dave gives me confidence and everything's good when I'm with him. I don't need anyone else and if he wasn't around I'd go back into my shell and stay there."

"It must be love and it's nice to see Dave happy. You do that for him and now I'm going to cry again."

The men both laughed and Carol took a deep breath and joined in.

Dave told Carol she was right about the attention Jonathan gets when he scrubs up. He related the mystery man saga and Carol was intrigued.

"You don't always look like this then?"

Dave took out his phone and showed her some pictures of Jonathan in his natural state and she confessed that she still found him amazingly good looking.

"I don't know if you've noticed but every woman in here has noticed you and some are even taking detours around our table on the way to the ladies."

"He wouldn't have noticed and now he'll probably start feeling uncomfortable and we'll have to go," said Dave shaking his head.

"I'm fine and we won't have to go. So Carol have you decided when you're coming to London?"

"I do miss it so much and it would be an opportunity to start over but I have no friends there anymore."

"You have us," said Dave.

"Oh don't please or you'll start me off again. I need to get my head together and I don't want to feel like I'm running away. It's about time I stopped wallowing in my own self-pity and took stock of my life. Tom's a good man and I have unfinished business there and I don't mean that I want to go back. I just want to show him that I can be civil. I need to step up to the plate as they say here. When I feel the time is right I will come back to London."

They enjoyed their dinner and Jonathan listened to the stories of their growing up and the villain they called dad. They drank a lot of wine and laughed a lot. They then proceeded to a bar where they drank more and talked until two o'clock in the morning. They caught a cab together as Dave insisted that they take Carol home first as she was a little worse for wear.

When they got back to their hotel room Dave picked Jonathan up and threw him on the bed and laid on top of him.

"You're a bit heavy big Dave and you're squashing my dinner."

"I don't care, you can't escape me now.'

"Why would I want to do that?"

"I don't know. I keep pinching myself to make sure it's real."

"Me too and you're drunk so get off you big oaf."

"Only if you promise we can stay in bed until midday."

"What and miss breakfast?"

"Fuck breakfast I'd rather spend time in bed with you, we haven't had sex in days."

"Ok but if I wake up I'll nip down to breakfast without waking you and get back into bed afterwards ok."

Dave agreed and rolled off. He got undressed and just threw his clothes over a chair, brushed his teeth and got into bed. Jonathan meantime was meticulously hanging his clothes and finding a laundry bag for his shirt and underwear. He also brushed his teeth and got into bed only to find Dave fast asleep once again. He laughed to himself and snuggled up to the gentle giant.

Somewhere during their drunkenness the previous night, Jonathan had invited Carol to join them on their sightseeing excursion and luckily she had the foresight to call them to make sure it was still on. It was eleven o'clock when the phone rang and they were both still asleep. Dave answered in a groggy voice and arranged for Carol to come to their hotel for lunch at one. Jonathan put his head under the pillow and asked what the time was.

"It's eleven."

"We could have met earlier and had lunch out." Jonathan mumbled.

"We have some unfinished business to take care of so come here."

Carol arrived on time and they lunched as planned. They planned the rest of their day in a logical way so that they could end up taking a round trip on the Staten Island ferry as it got dark so they could see the lights of Manhattan on the way back.

Carol confessed to never having done that or having been up the Statue of Liberty. In fact she had seen very little of the city beyond mid-town to the upper-east side. She seemed genuinely excited at the prospect of wandering around the city she had called home for over twenty years.

They did all they planned and ended up in Greenwich Village for dinner. They were all exhausted by ten so made their way back. Jonathan asked Carol to join them the next day but she declined but said she really wanted to see them again before they went home. They agreed on Friday and parted company.

They had two days to themselves and didn't try to cram too much in. They wandered the city streets in the day time and bought theatre tickets for both Wednesday and Thursday and booked restaurants on the recommendation of the hotel concierge. They were both really enjoying themselves and would have liked to extend their stay but for the fact that it was Christmas.

On Friday they met Carol and spent the day together. It was a beautiful day although a little chilly so they went to Central Park and strolled leisurely through its winding paths. Carol said she had called Tom and had a decent conversation with him for once. She hadn't apologised, or anything like that, but she also didn't make any of her usual cutting remarks. The whole conversation was quite civilised.

She laughed and said, "He asked me if I was well, meaning I supposed I hadn't been my normal bitchy self. I've been thinking Dave about you having to sell the business that you've worked so hard to make so valuable and if you want you can tear up the contract. I don't need the money and well, it's your life."

"That's a great offer but it's a bit too late for that. I want to sell, I really want to do something different and get a life with normal working hours. I think my earlier reservations were due to some misguided loyalty to dad, after all he started it. I have a new life now and I want to be able to enjoy it."

"What will you do?"

"I've got another year before I have to decide that, then I'll get my head round it."

"I told Tom that you were in town and he said he'd like to meet up for a drink if you have time but don't feel obliged."

"That's fine we could do that."

"Ok so where do you want to meet. He'll probably suggest his club."

At this point Jonathan intervened. "There's still one place on our list that we haven't done. It's Mc Sorley's and it's on E. Seventh St."

"I'm not sure that's Tom's thing but why don't you ask him yourself."

"Jonathan wants to go to Mc Sorley's so that's where we'll go; after all we are the tourists in town."

Carol gave Dave the number and although he sounded a bit dubious, Tom agreed.

They left the park and stopped at a cafe and had sandwiches and coffee. At five thirty Carol said she should go and let them make their way down town.

"Jonathan, what do you think of that?" Asked Dave.

"Not much as it happens. Carol you're coming with us."

Carol objected but Dave insisted and said they wouldn't go if she didn't. She reluctantly agreed so they hailed a cab.

The place was crowded and noisy and felt like going back in time. As they entered some people were vacating a table so Dave and Carol quickly sat down and Jonathan went to the bar. He ordered three beers and got six in smallish glasses.

"Carol I hope you don't mind but I got you beer. You should at least try it, it's famous."

She said she was fine with that and admitted to not having drunk beer since she left England. She was pleasantly surprised.

They were all thirsty and downed the beer quickly. Jonathan stood to get more when he saw a well dressed man approaching their table. Dave stood up and greeted him. Tom was older than he'd imagined, close to sixty he'd guess but well preserved. Dave introduced Jonathan. "And this is my sister Carol but you know that."

Tom was shocked but almost managed to hide his surprise. He commented on how Dave had changed from a lanky teenager to an Arnold type. Jonathan got beer for everyone and when he returned it seemed the atmosphere was a little frosty so he weighed in with some light conversation.

"Have you been here before Tom?"

"No never, not my sort of place."

"Really, presidents including Abraham Lincoln have been here, it's an institution."

"Been reading up on it young man?"

"Sure, I did some research on Manhattan before we came and this place really has a lot of great history."

The conversation carried on in that vein and then Tom started talking to Dave, more or less ignoring Carol. Dave tried to bring her into the conversation by asking her if was still enjoying the beer. She nodded and Tom commented on it. "I've never seen you drink beer before, thought it was beneath you."

"I used to think so too because that's what my teacher taught me." The words were sharp but said in a gentle manner and with a smile.

Tom seemed to ignore it and returned to his conversation with Dave.

"You know I've always felt bad about not visiting you in prison."

"That was my fault, I told you not to get involved. How bad was that?" confessed Carol.

Tom looked at her puzzled. "What, you actually admit to something? I'm sorry we shouldn't get into an argument, we have company."

"I'm not going to argue, say what you like it can't be worse than what Jonathan has already said to me. He said I was real bitch amongst other things." She patted Jonathan on the shoulder.

"Carol something's happened to you. You seem almost happy. Did you run out of lemons to suck?"

Carol laughed, "Something like that."

They drank more beer and slowly Tom and Carol started talking, mainly about the children. They both seemed to have relaxed, thanks to good old McSorley's ale. Jonathan seized upon the moment.

"Carol's thinking about coming to live in London. That'll be great."

Tom looked surprised but then said, "This city never really suited you did it?"

"I think it was more a case that I didn't suit this city."

"Are you really going, what about the children?"

"They're hardly children but I'll talk to them first. I don't suppose they'll mind either way. I haven't exactly been the model mother now have I?"

"Carol what's happened to you?"

Before anyone could answer that Jonathan said, "She's been reminiscing with Dave and I think she's remembered who she was. Be careful though she's been a bit weepy."

"Carol cry? The only time I've seen you cry is when you're angry."

"Enough Tom please, I know I been a cow and I can't change that but can we have a pleasant conversation without raking over the past."

Tom nodded and they had a relatively pleasant evening.

Tom left around nine o'clock and the three of them caught a cab to the upper east-side and found a casual bar/dining place.

They had a bottle of wine and some steak and Jonathan edged his way out of the conversation so Dave and Carol could talk about stuff he didn't know about.

Carol became aware of this. "I'm sorry Jonathan we seem to be leaving you out."

"Nothing to be sorry about, I'm enjoying learning about Dave's life and I really mean that."

"I noticed what you did by the way, to get me talking to Tom."

Dave grinned, "He does those sorts of things to me all the time. An odd word and I'm gladly doing things that I didn't know I wanted to. It invariably turns out for the best but it fucking annoys me sometimes because I should be able to work things out myself. That's what he did tonight with you but let me tell you he wouldn't do it for everyone only his loved ones."

Carol smiled, "Does that mean I'm a loved one."

Jonathan took her hand and gently said "I think we're family." At which point she burst into tears and laughter.

They finished their dinner and said their farewells, which brought on more tears from Carol. They left for London the next day. They arrived home at eleven thirty and the house was in darkness. Mary had obviously retired for the night and there was no sign of Sheba.

They made tea and toast and then went to bed. Dave got into bed wearing his boxers and he had put on a tee-shirt. Jonathan fell about laughing.

"What's funny?"

"You won't get naked with mum upstairs right?"

"Too true."

"I know what you mean. It's a bit off-putting but we might have to get used to that one day.'

"We'll see."

CHAPTER FORTY FOUR

Dave woke up at eight o'clock and Jonathan, for once, was still sleeping. He got up and put on his dressing gown and went down to the kitchen. Mary was sitting at the table drinking tea with Sheba at her feet. The puppy was delighted to see Dave and she bounced around his feet. Dave bent and picked her up and she licked his face frantically.

"Good morning Mary, everything been ok?"

"Good morning Dave and if everything means Sheba, then absolutely, she's a darling little dog. The trainer came on Thursday to see how we were coping and he gave me some useful tips. She's getting the hang of doing her business outside because she gets a nice treat every time she does it. She's a clever baby aren't you? She's still making a few mistakes but she'll get there. There is one problem though."

Mary pointed to the chair leg which was showing signs of Sheba having feasted on it. "If you let her into the rest of the house without watching her, she'll chew everything. Now let me pour you some coffee. Would you like some breakfast?"

"Just coffee please I need to get my skates on I have a meeting with some of my staff at ten. Thanks Mary for looking after her."

"It's that boy upstairs who should thank me. Is he still asleep?"

"Unusually yes, did Mrs Hayes take care of you?"

"Yes she's a lovely woman. She insisted on cooking my meals and when I objected she said that's what you pay her for. She's a good cook and I felt like I was on holiday. I have something to show you, I hope you don't mind but it was a joint effort by me and Mrs Hayes."

Dave wondered what was coming, as Mary told him to follow her to the lounge. He did as she said but was asked to wait a second at the door.

"It's ok you can come in now."

Dave entered the room and saw it had been filled with Christmas decorations and a big, real Christmas tree covered in lights and baubles with gift wrapped presents underneath. Dave stood silent and Mary felt a sudden panic.

Jonathan came down the stairs and saw the lounge door open so he put his head round and wasn't sure what he was looking at. Mary was standing with her hand to her mouth and Dave was looking up at the ceiling with tears streaming down his face and a puppy in his arms.

Mary said, "I think I've done something wrong."

"No mum, you haven't."

Dave turned towards her and mumbled through his tears, "Six weeks ago I wanted to die."

Mary burst into tears and said "You poor, poor boy."

Jonathan took Sheba and put her on the floor and he embraced Dave at which point Dave let it all out and started sobbing. These were the tears he had never shed through the worst of times and he cried until he couldn't cry anymore. Jonathan stood with his arms around him offering no words of comfort.

Jonathan kissed Dave gently on the cheek and said, "When you're ready."

They stood like a frozen scene, nobody moving. Dave eventually raised his head and smiled through his tears. "I'm sorry Mary." He said, trying to control his self, "It looks wonderful."

"So tell her why you're crying Dave."

It took him a while to get the words out, "I've lived in this house for over ten years and I've never put up decorations. Before that I lived with Dad and we always went away somewhere for Christmas and he said it stupid to bother. I vaguely remember when mum was alive we had a Christmas tree but I was very young."

"I'm sorry Dave I didn't mean it to upset you."

"It's not that. My life has changed so much this year. I've gone from being a lonely, bitter head case to a happy, happy man with a family and a Christmas tree."

Christmas went as planned. They went to the soup kitchen and helped cook and serve Christmas lunch to the homeless people who wandered in. They went home to change and went to Dolly's for supper. Dolly had bought them all presents. The men hadn't actually given that a thought but Mary had and she had presents for Dolly and Dicky which saved their embarrassment.

They left at ten on Boxing Day for Karen's taking Sheba with them. Dave had not met Karen and her family before and was feeling a bit nervous but was soon put at ease. As requested Karen had prepared a Christmas lunch and everyone helped out. Dave wondered what the sleeping arrangements would be and was surprised and relieved to find he was sharing a room and a bed with Jonathan. Sheba was a big hit and behaved reasonably well. Nobody seemed to mind when she messed in the house or chewed the legs of the kitchen chairs.

Karen's husband, Nials, and her children were all there and of course Lou the matriarch, it was all very easy. Lou was in great form and asked what might have been embarrassing questions in different company. Dave found her very amusing and she seemed taken with him and much to everybody's amusement started flirting. As usual she drank too much wine and became quite outrageous but no one minded. That was Lou.

Nials was interested in Dave's business and said he'd read about the sale of his company. He asked how he managed to grow the business so successfully.

Jonathan had been listening and he offered with pride, "Dave is extremely skilled around business matters and has been given awards for it. He sorted out our finances which were a puzzle to mum and me. He likes investments too. He has a big portfolio of shares and studies companies for fun. It's all way beyond me but it's like a hobby to him."

Karen was also listening and she said, "Nials has been having problems trying to grow our business, maybe you could give him some advice."

Dave looked at Nials waiting for him to ask and he did. "That would be great if you could. I wouldn't want to take up too much of your time but it would be good to have a fresh eye look at it."

Dave said he would love to help and agreed to stay a few extra days to go through their finances and strategies. Mary decided to stay on too so they ended staying through to New Year. Dave was very pleased that he was given the opportunity to give back something to this family by doing what he was good at.

He soon found the problem although the solution was quite complex if you didn't have the skilled people who could implement the solution. He helped Tom write a business plan and produce a budget to support it. They needed a capital injection of about half a million pounds to fund the purchase of new equipment and Dave had a solution. He turned to Jonathan and asked, "What do you think?"

Jonathan looked puzzled but Dave didn't offer any clarification. He knew that he must be able to help with the solution otherwise Dave wouldn't have asked. Then the penny dropped.

"Nials I could help you there. I have money in the bank doing very little, so why don't I invest some in your business? Half a million right, I can manage that."

Nials was taken aback that Jonathan should have so much money and Jonathan wasn't really sure he did but he knew that's what Dave wanted him to say.

Dave smacked the table and said, "Great that's settled then, you can keep it in the family."

Nials was impressed and very grateful.

When Dave and Jonathan were alone they discussed the investment.

"I don't know if I've got that much money. You know what I'm like with money. I know I've got a lot but what if I don't have enough?"

"I did a quick calculation. Twenty years rent, plus your trust fund, which you've never touched, plus interest, coupled with the fact that you don't spend much means that you have at least four hundred thousand and maybe more."

"But that's not half a million."

"We'll consider this your first foray into capitalism. If you see a good investment then you borrow the shortfall."

"The bank wouldn't loan me money, I don't work yet."

"But your private banker would." Dave said it with a smile on his face. "I didn't want to offer because I know Nials would have refused. He'd probably think that's why he asked me to help in the first place. Anyway it's a sound business and with a little help from your bank balance it will only get better. It's a sound investment."

"Dave when we get home you'll need to go through my finances and if I have to borrow from you I'll want a proper loan document. I don't want to take your money, I'll pay you back."

Dave sighed. "Sure, whatever."

Within a year they started to see the results and Jonathan and Dave found themselves being invited to Karen's on numerous occasions. Dave loved to watch Tom's new success and was happy to give advice whenever asked. Jonathan had borrowed a hundred and fifty thousand from Dave and they agreed that it would be paid back by Jonathan handing over his dividends from the investment to Dave until it was all paid. Dave thought that it was all fucking silly but Jonathan wanted his financial independence, so that was the way it had to work.

The New Year was soon upon them and Dave went back to work. He had a year to train up his replacement and he took that job very seriously, after all his father was the business founder. He tried to keep his hours from ten to seven but still occasionally worked late into the night.

Jonathan got stuck into his studies and sailed through his exams and he got a first. He started his Bar Professional Training Course in September. He opted to do it as a two year course as Dave would be leaving his job in December and he wanted to spend more time with him.

Mary had returned to Spain at the end of January and had shipped a lot of her personal possessions which made Jonathan suspect it was a permanent move. She remained very secretive about the whole thing but he knew it was pointless asking. The rest of the things she wanted to keep were moved to the upstairs apartment. The Portobello flat had been let and Jonathan was now receiving rent from two properties.

Sheba grew very large and was kind enough to leave her hair wherever she went. One or both of them walked her every day and she became, with help from the trainer, a very obedient and rewarding companion.

Dave suggested they go on holiday in July. Mrs Hayes has offered to take Sheba so they agreed the dates with her. Jonathan suggested they visit Mary in Malaga for a few days and then rent a car and explore lesser known parts of Spain. Dave thought it sounded like a great idea so Jonathan called Mary.

To Jonathan's surprise and disappointment, Mary was not agreeable to the idea and said she was far too busy to entertain them. She made various excuses and Jonathan got the message. Dave could see he wasn't happy and tried to cheer him up by saying she was a nurse and took her responsibilities very seriously. Jonathan became philosophical about it and accepted the fact that it was inconvenient. He and Dave discussed it trying to work out why she didn't want them there and came to the conclusion that the person she was nursing must have needed a lot of attention. Jonathan was half-way happy with that explanation but not fully.

"Jonathan I've got a good idea, why don't we just stay home. I'd be happy with that."

"That's something I'd really like but if your staff got wind that we were here they'd constantly be calling you for advice, so no. We're going on holiday so you can eat and sleep as much as you like without interruption. Let's go somewhere nice but not too far."

"Have you been to the Riviera?"

"No, but that sounds good as long as we don't have to go to the casino in Mont Carlo."

"Done, we'll stay in a great hotel somewhere like Nice and just chill out. No work calls and no studying for two whole weeks."

Dave found a very expensive hotel in Nice and they did as planned. They soaked up the sun, went on long walks and ate the best food Jonathan had ever experienced.

Dave had been asked to extend his contract for one more month so it was the end of January when he finally said goodbye to his old company. As much as he wanted to leave, the parting was tinged with a sense of loss. Jonathan had asked him if he'd started getting his head around what he would do now he was unemployed and he'd told him that he was not going to be rushed into anything. He would take a year off whilst exploring his options and at the same time rationalise his finances.

Jonathan had said he shouldn't leave it too long as he was pretty ancient, the reply to which was a raised eyebrow.

"You're used to working hard, won't you get bored?"

"No, I don't think so. I only did the last year because it was a deal breaker for the sale, not because I particularly wanted to. Mind you the rewards were great too."

He paused and said," The new company has offered me a job at twice what they were paying me, in Las Vegas."

"So what did you say? I mean that's a real opportunity isn't it?"

"I didn't even think about it. I just said no."

"It wasn't because of me was it?"

"No, it was because of me."

"So I didn't enter into your thought process at all?"

"No."

"You bastard, I might have wanted to go and live in America and you didn't even give that a thought."

Dave laughed. "It's not to do with anything other than the fact that I just don't want to do it anymore, pure and simple. I want to spend more time at home with you, so get used to it. You're stuck with me mate."

Jonathan was happy with the response and it was never discussed again. He left Dave to cogitate on his future enterprise.

Mary hadn't come home for Christmas saying she couldn't leave her patient for any length of time. She did come home for a few days in May but seemed distracted and didn't offer much information about what was going on. She'd bought a house the previous year and had moved her patient into it as she was needed twenty four hours a day. She was paid extremely well, much more than she needed and she often had help. That was all she would tell them.

She asked if they would move Joe's old chest out of her room as she'd never liked it and anyway it really belonged to Jonathan. Dave moved all the documents to a filing cabinet in the downstairs office and the chest to their bedroom. The chest fascinated him. It was obviously very old, yet very well preserved. They'd established that it was of Arabic origin and was probably Moorish as it came into the family in Spain. Other than that it was just Joe's magic box.

Dave sent a picture of it to a fine arts auctioneer but he was not able to help but did say it looked like a fine piece and Dave should explore its origins as it might be valuable. He had lots of free time which he was enjoying enormously so he decided to do some research and try to discover the age and origin of the chest. He was about to embark on a mission, a mission of discovery.

Jonathan was studying in the kitchen and Dave put his head round the door and told him he was going out for a while.

"Do you want to come?"

"No, I'm alright."

"You didn't ask me where I was going."

"You would have told me if you wanted me to know."

"Well I suggest you get off your backside and get ready to go out because I think you might want to come."

"Where to?"

"The British Library."

"Well I wouldn't miss that now would I?" He put on his shoes and grabbed a jacket and off they went. Sheba looked a little disappointed that she wasn't going out so went and found Mrs Hayes for company.

They looked through the computer files at the reception and found what might be interesting. They checked in and gave their list of books to the receptionist and went to the relevant reading room. They had chosen a number of books on Islamic art and furniture. They also selected books on the Moorish places of interest in Spain.

They didn't find anything helpful so they started looking for the names of experts in the field. There were a number of people but Jonathan found the name of the curator of Islamic art at the British Museum, one Dr Ismael. They left the library and caught the Northern line train from Euston to Tottenham Court Rd and walked from there to the British Museum. Jonathan didn't think the chest could really be of interest to anyone but didn't say anything to dampen Dave's enthusiasm.

They found an information desk and asked if Dr Ismael was still at the Museum and were told he was and the person behind the desk asked the nature of their business. Dave explained as best he could and a call was made and Dr Ismael located. They were asked if they had a photograph of the item and Dave said he did. This was relayed to the person at the other end of the phone. They were asked to take a seat and someone would be with them soon. A youngish, bookish looking lady came to greet them and led them to the coffee shop. They found a free table and the young lady took their coffee orders and went to the counter to purchase their preferred brews. As she returned so Dr Ismael appeared. He seemed to be as ancient as some of the relics.

"So young gentlemen shall we get down to business?"

Dave pulled out his iPad and displayed a number of photographs that he had taken of the chest, both the outside and inside. The curator was obviously interested and asked how they came upon it.

Jonathan explained that it had been in his family for generations and his father had inherited it, as he had now.

"Probably Moorish then, can you bring it here for me to take a proper look?"

Jonathan was surprised that the British museum could possibly be interested in his dad's old chest but kept that to his self. Dave said they could bring it the following Monday and that was agreed.

Dr Ismael asked a number of questions but Jonathan was unable to answer most, it was just an old chest. Dave called him a Philistine and told the curator that the photographs didn't do the piece justice at all. He personally thought it to be a work of art. The old man seemed very interested and said he was looking forward to viewing the chest at which point he stood and said his goodbyes.

It was a glorious day and London looked amazing. The architecture here was different to the City, being a mixture of what seems many different periods, the rest of the City having stark contrast between ancient and beautiful to modern and stunning and not much in between. They walked south to the river and crossed Blackfriars Bridge and strolled along the South Bank. They stopped at a pub and had lunch on a terrace and soaked in the warm sunshine. They were supping their beer in silence when Jonathan asked Dave why they couldn't deliver the chest until Monday as it was only Wednesday.

Dave looked down his nose at Jonathan and said, "Well maybe I might have something important to do over the next couple of days."

Jonathan didn't rise to the bait but just took a sip of beer.

"Well aren't you going to ask me?"

"You're going to tell me anyway so get on with it."

"I got a phone call from the BBC and they want to talk to me about an opportunity to do some radio. They said they liked what they heard when I did a guest appearance on one their chat shows about homeless people, do you remember?"

"Yes of course. Dolly was supposed to do it but sent you instead. I was glued to the radio listening to your dulcet tones."

"Fuck off, you piss taker. Anyway, I have a meeting tomorrow at ten thirty. I will see what they want and take it from there. There's something else."

Jonathan waited without comment because he had a good idea what was coming next.

"I'm going back to LSE in September to take a two year course in macroeconomics after which you'll have to call me Dr Dave."

Jonathan had seen a letter from LSE that had arrived that very morning and guessed something of this nature was in the wind. He didn't say so as he didn't want to spoil Dave's moment. Instead he said, "Wow you're going to do a PhD?"

"Yep, I didn't want to tell you until I was accepted. A letter came this morning and I've been accepted."

"That's brilliant, but why are you bothering to go to the BBC if you're committed elsewhere?"

"Jonathan you're beginning to sound like a nagging spouse. Don't you think I'm capable of thinking it through by myself? I can do both if that's what I choose."

"Sorry god, interrogation over. Why are you so touchy?"

"I'll finish my course about the same time as you finish your pupillage so we can have a joint celebration as of course we will both be successful. I'm sorry I seem touchy but I feel a bit off, maybe it's the prospect of two new things, or maybe not, I don't know. I'm sorry I didn't tell you what I was planning."

"That's ok you don't have to tell me everything, I know you will eventually.'

That didn't make Dave feel any better.

Dave suddenly looked and felt troubled and he wasn't sure why.

The next day Dave returned from his BBC interview at four thirty. He found Jonathan in the bedroom lying on the bed reading.

"Why are you in here?"

"Staying out of Mrs Hayes way she's got the vacuum cleaner going."

Dave slumped onto the bed and lay on his back looking up at the ceiling light.

"Is that exhaustion from your day at the BBC?"

"Maybe, I am tired, I didn't sleep well last night probably giving it too much thought."

Jonathan rolled over and put his arm around Dave and told him to have a nap. Dave closed his eyes and drifted off into a troubled sleep only to be rudely awaked by Sheba jumping onto the bed and slobbering all over his face.

"Off Sheba, where's Jonathan and what's the time?"

Jonathan poked his head around the bathroom door and asked Dave if he'd found a way with communicating in dog language and in case he hadn't got a satisfactory answer, the time was six.

Dave got off the bed and took a shower. Dried and dressed they went down to see what Mrs Hayes had left them for dinner. Jonathan looked at the beef stew in the microwave and declared that he was taking Dave out for dinner.

They strolled down to Holland Park Avenue to a tapas restaurant. They ordered beers whilst they were making their selection. They ordered a wide range from the menu and a bottle of wine.

Dave sat back in his chair and took a large gulp of beer.

"Well aren't you going to ask me what happened today?"

"No you might fall asleep again."

"I promise I won't. I just had a lot on my mind and as I said I hadn't slept well last night."

He had met the guy that had called him and he'd explained that they were looking for someone to front a weekly, half hour radio program about current economic affairs. He had been told that they thought he was perfect for the job given his background in business and his education. They knew he sounded good on the radio as they had heard him being interviewed about the homeless foundation.

Dave had explained about his PhD and was told that there was a team of researchers attached to the program so it wouldn't take up much time during the week but someone else would explain that if he was interested. He said he would like to know more so a call was made and within minutes a woman appeared. She introduced herself as Fiona, the program producer.

She explained in more detail the program's focus and asked if Dave had any ideas he could put forward. He gave her a number of topics he thought were of general interest and some that particularly interested him. She said she liked what she heard and invited him to a recording studio for a sound test. He was asked to read a script and then to talk for five minutes on London as an economic force. Fiona was very impressed by Dave's free flowing talk and his obvious knowledge on the subject. She had offered him the job there and then.

The program had been scheduled to run initially for three months and would be extended if it was successful. The planning for the first program would be a long affair as it would mean a lot of brain storming around content and logistics. Dave said he had plenty of time at the moment so was free for as long as he was needed over the next couple of months.

Jonathan sat listening with great interest and also a sense of pride.

"So when you start at LSE you'll have time for both your studies and a radio show, right?"

Dave laughed, "It's not a show. It'll be a thought provoking program that will be of interest to everyone. It's not going to be an intellectual exercise per se but we'll cover subjects that touch everyone and we'll do it in a way that doesn't talk down to people."

"Sounds like you're there already. How much time will you need to spend on this?"

"The subjects are pre-planned and there's a research team that will send me a copy of their results at the end of every day Tuesday to Friday. I'll add my comments and we'll bounce ideas off by email so that's probably no more than an hour a day. On Saturday we'll brainstorm the final output and record the program on Sunday."

"Won't that interfere with your study time? Stupid question I forget how brilliant you are and I'm nagging. So have you committed? Is this something you really want to do?"

"It seems so and yes the more I think about it the more I like the idea. It might even be useful for my PhD research, who knows? We have a month to do some mock up shows and we do the first real program the following month."

Jonathan raised his glass in congratulations and they drank a toast to Dave's success.

"To our new radio star of intellect, how much do they pay you?"

Dave almost choked on his beer and when he gained his composure from laughing he said, "I forgot to ask."

Jonathan suddenly looked a little less enthusiastic but it was nothing to do with money. Dave knew exactly what he was thinking for once and gave a big grin. "I finish at one thirty on Saturdays so we have time for football."

"Now who's a mind reader? Well that's great but if you can't make it for football that's ok too."

"Oh, no it's not."

"And why's that?"

"I bought us four season tickets."

"Four?"

"Two for Rangers and two for Chelsea, Rangers take priority ok?"

Jonathan declared his love for the big man and Dave returned his in a rather loud voice much to the interest of the diners in close proximity and much to Jonathan's amusement.

"Now I'm going to blow my own trumpet for once. They said I sounded young and vibrant on air, how about that?"

"Just as well it's not TV then. You will tell them not to disturb you at nap time old man."

It was the wrong thing to say. Dave took a deep breath.

"I've been thinking about that a lot lately. I'm going to be thirty five this year and you'll still only be twenty three. When I'm forty you'll still be in your twenties and that's a big difference."

"Is that what's been bothering you?"

Dave nodded but knew it was more than that but thought the rest was better not said.

"Dave when I first met you, you looked at least forty and it didn't make a difference then and the age thing will never matter to me. Oh maybe when you're ninety and I'm a spritely seventy eight I might think about it. I know I wind you up about it but you're a fucking idiot do you know that?"

"It really doesn't bother you?"

"Never has, never will so if you so much as mention it again I'll buy you a wheelchair. Really you never have to worry about it. I'm not going anywhere."

"Thank you, I think I needed to hear that. Now here comes our food. Christ I think we ordered enough to feed an army."

"You ordered enough food not we, anyway you need it to keep up with your exercise routine and maintain that mountain of a body, go for it pig."

Jonathan paid the bill and Dave sighed.

When they got home Jonathan made tea and took it into the lounge where Dave was sprawled on the sofa with Sheba lying next to him with her head on his chest.

"This is a nice cosy domestic scene, no room for me though." He sat in an armchair. Dave you still don't look right, glum even, what's up?"

Dave sighed. "You're young and you don't do any of the things people of your age do. That's because of me."

"Oh back to that one are we?"

"It's not just that, I'd like to do things for you but you never need me to."

"I think Dave Wilson is feeling a little insecure."

"Maybe that's what it is. I look at you or think about you and I have to pinch myself to make sure it's real. Why are you with me?"

"I don't know what's brought this on; too early for mid-life crisis. Let's take this one thing at a time. I don't do things other guys of my age do because those things have never interested me but you know that. I do more since I met you than I've ever done in my life. I didn't go to pubs or restaurants and definitely not functions. We go to football, talk and have even been known to watch TV. You're everything I didn't know I wanted and if you weren't around I'd just go back into my shell and stay there forever."

"That's nice to hear. I don't know what's wrong with me."

"I think I do."

Jonathan left the room and came back holding an envelope which he gave to Dave.

"I know you've been unsettled lately but I didn't want to say anything until I was ready but that was a bit stupid because it's only prolonged your misery. Well open it."

Dave obeyed. "It's a will, your will and you've left everything to me. What about Mary?"

"What about her? If anything happened to me you'd take care of her, I know that.'

"Of course."

"Right so when did you change your will?"

"How do you know these things? I changed it about a year ago."

"This isn't about age is it? When you speak about money or home you always say ours and yet I still talk about my flats my bank account and my turn to pay. That's not what spouses do is it? We are married remember?'

"November 18th 2013 in your mum's kitchen, by your mum."

"Right so do you want to get married properly?"

"No as far as I'm concerned we're married."

"But it doesn't feel like it does it? So here's the deal. I'm going to transfer all my money to you, all my millions and you're going to take care of all financial matters. So now I don't owe you anything for the Nials' investment. It also means you have to deal with the letting agents for OUR Portobello properties and we'll change the ownership to joint names. We'll have a joint account and I'll have a debit card so that I can spend our millions at will.

"I'll be starting my pupillage in the not too distant future and I'll have to dress accordingly and as you're the one with great sartorial knowledge you will help me. You will be responsible for me leaving the house looking half-way decent. Agreed so far?"

"Agreed."

"There is one other thing." Jonathan put his hand in his trouser pocket and held his clenched fist out to Dave.

"Hold out your hand then."

Jonathan dropped the contents of his hand into Dave's. Dave's jaw dropped. He'd just been given two gold bands.

"Well put yours on and give me mine. I think these things will settle your insecurities for the time being and I'm sorry for being so dumb. I should have realised some time ago. I'm just so happy that I forget we don't always have the same needs. I've usually got my head stuck in a book or in the clouds and well I suppose I must seem a little insensitive."

Dave didn't know what to say. Jonathan was right as usual and he'd been acting like a silly schoolgirl.

"Jonathan I'm the one that should be sorry. I'm really stupid sometimes but only where you're concerned."

"Well we both know that. If ever you feel insecure it's probably because I don't always pay enough attention to you. I just know you'll always be there and you are. Please if I get too stuck in my books and forget stuff, tell me or thump me but don't suffer it, ok?"

Dave felt like the cloud had lifted. How could he not know that he meant so much to this young man? He had to believe in himself and in this situation it wasn't always easy but he'd get his head around it.

"So if I'm going to do all this stuff for you, what are you going to do for me?" he asked smiling.

"Ah, you think this is all one sided do you? Well I'll tell you what I'm doing I'm learning how to cook. Mrs Hayes has been giving me lessons surreptitiously and I'm getting the hang of it. I wanted it to be a surprise. This might seem like a good thing but I've been reading about diet, nutrition and weight. You've not been exercising as much as you used to but you're still eating as much and that's not good for you. You said a while ago that you were going to lose weight but if anything you've gained."

"Are you saying I'm fat?"

"No surprisingly you're not, at least not yet. I wouldn't care if you were other than for the fact it would be unhealthy. You weigh a lot and it's not good for your heart in the long run. Your dad died of a heart attack and I'm not letting you go the same way."

"So what does that mean, do I have to go on a diet?"

"Not exactly, you just have to change your eating habits to match your exercise regime and it's beginning to worry me how much red meat you eat. So we're going for a full medical check-up and we'll start from there."

"Are you nagging me?"

"Yep and you like it don't you."

Dave nodded and grinned from ear to ear.

"There is one other thing; can we have air conditioning in the bedroom? It's been so hot lately I find it hard to sleep."

Dave agreed and the following week it was installed just as the weather changed for the worse. They only used it once in the following two months.

CHAPTER FORTY FIVE

On Monday they took the chest to the British Museum. They showed their passports at the service entrance and were told to wait. Two men in overalls appeared and loaded the chest onto a trolley. Dave had bubble wrapped it to avoid any damage. They followed the two men through the corridors of the great institution which looked decidedly shabby compared to what Joe Public sees. They were taken to Dr Ismael's workplace and together they unwrapped the chest.

Dr Ismael scrutinised it both inside and outside and declared that it was an interesting piece. He asked if he could keep it for a few weeks or maybe longer as there was research to do and people to consult. They agreed and left their cell phone numbers saying there was no hurry.

In the weeks following, Dave spent time at the BBC learning the ropes. They did their practice runs which went well and Dave was able to make significant contributions around content. The team was cohesive and Dave was well pleased with their enthusiasm.

The first program was broadcast in mid-June. It was recorded on Sunday, edited that day, and was aired according to plan the following day at seven in the evening. It was repeated on Wednesday and Friday lunch time.

Jonathan listened to the Monday evening program and insisted Dave listen with him even if it did make him cringe at the sound of his own voice.

They were both busy and had forgotten about the chest. It was the middle of July when Dave received a call from Dr Ismael asking if they could meet him at the museum the next day.

They arrived at the appointed time and Dr Ismael greeted them looking very serious. He told them that he had completed his research and all the experts agreed that the chest was Moorish in origin and dated back to the fourteenth century. It had probably been looted after the fall of Grenada from one of the rich Moor's palaces. There was no evidence to indicate that it came from The Alhambra but that was a possibility. It wasn't listed anywhere as stolen property so it seemed that Jonathan was the rightful owner. The Dr waxed lyrical about that period in history explaining how the Moslem world produced the best craftsmen of that time. He spoke of scientific discoveries and art with much pride before returning to the subject of the chest.

Addressing his comments to Dave he said, "You were right young man, this is truly a beautiful piece of craftsmanship and is representative of the best of its kind in that era. As you said the photographs didn't do it justice. Have you had it valued?"

The response was negative.

"Well young gentleman, it's probably worth a small fortune to the right collector but that's of no import to me. To me it's invaluable and shouldn't be confined to someone's bedroom that would be such a waste. This beautiful piece belongs here in this museum where the world can appreciate it. I assume that as you don't know its value that it is not insured."

Again the answer was in the negative.

Jonathan stopped the Dr's flow with, "What are you suggesting?"

"I would like to place it in the Islamic exhibition and give it a permanent place here. You should donate it, it belongs to the world."

Dave asked if the museum would be willing to buy it but Jonathan interceded.

"I've been here many times and I know you have many pieces here that are on loan from different organisations and that's noted on the blurb that goes with it."

"Yes young man that is true."

"I will loan you the chest for five years and there will be a dedication to my father on the description to say 'On loan from the estate of the late Jose Martinez'."

"That can be done and after five years?"

"We'll cross that bridge when we come to it sir but in the meantime it's yours to display in your collection."

Dr Ismael shook his hand and grinned. "Thank you so much, I really thought you would say no but I misjudged you. You're a very generous young man."

The old man furrowed his brow trying to remember something and then raised his hand, "Aha, I remember there's something else. I fiddled with the tiles inside the lid and found that they could be extracted which solved a puzzle. The Arabic writing didn't make sense but it was easy to see why. Two of the tiles had been transposed so I reversed them and now it's clear. The picture is that of a beautiful garden and it now says, simply in Arabic, Paradise. When I removed the tiles I noticed something which I removed."

He went to his desk and picked up an envelope. "I found this tucked inside so I return it to the rightful owner which must be you Jonathan."

He handed over the envelope and Jonathan asked what it was. The Dr said he had no idea as he hadn't opened it. Jonathan put the envelope into his pocket and they said their farewells.

On the journey home Dave said, "Well, aren't you going to open it?"

Jonathan looked pensive and replied, "I don't know why Dave but I've got a bad feeling about this. Let's wait until we get home."

They parked the car and walked to their house. Jonathan slumped onto the sofa and sighed and Dave sat next to him watching him finger the envelope. After a few minutes he took a deep breath and opened it. He withdrew a sheet of paper and a key. He unfolded the paper and read it looking puzzled and then handed it Dave to see what he could make of it. Dave read it and shrugged.

"I think it's obvious what it is but why was it hidden?"

"Dave it might be obvious to you but it's not to me. Can you explain please?"

"It's the name and address of a branch of a Swiss bank in Zurich and the number must be the bank account. The key looks very much like a safe deposit key. Your dad really was a mystery man."

"How do we find out, do we have to go to Zurich?"

Dave picked up Jonathan's iPhone from the coffee table and keyed in the name of the bank which took him to a website. "I've got it but there's no phone number. There's an email address for enquiries though so let's do that."

He typed in his enquiry and pressed send.

Jonathan was restless all afternoon and kept asking if there had been a reply.

"Jonathan whatever it is, I'm sure it's ok."

"I just have an anxious feeling in my stomach. Something's going to happen because of this. I'm sorry but I really can't help it."

"No but I can. Come on we're going to the pub."

"You're just trying to distract me."

"No I'm not I'm going to get you drunk this early in the day so it will take your mind off it. It's called taking care of you and I'm allowed to do that remember."

"Sure, thanks. I think that might actually help."

They went to the pub but it was crowded. There was what seemed like an office party so they had one beer and went back home and took a couple of bottles of wine into the communal garden.

"Let's play a game. We know your dad was a bit of a mystery so let's make up stories about what all this could mean."

Jonathan liked that idea and it helped release the knots in his stomach, that and the wine. They came up with some outrageous suggestions and a number of really silly ones. Without knowing it Dave got some of it right but the truth was to be far from any of their guesses.

Jonathan received an email from the bank the next morning which asked them to call a UK number to make an appointment. Jonathan called and was told that the number was for the London City branch of the Swiss bank. He was asked if he could go along that afternoon and bring his passport to which he agreed.

Dave went to his filing cabinet and retrieved Joe's birth certificate, death certificate and the copy of his will, just in case they needed it to prove Jonathan was Joe's beneficiary.

They arrived at the bank at three and were shown to a small meeting room. Within minutes a woman appeared, introduced herself and took a seat at the table. She was holding a print out and she took a quick look at it and asked Jonathan if he had brought his passport. Jonathan handed it over together with the other documents which he said she might want to look at. The woman looked at the passport and then at Jonathan with surprise.

"Excuse me but when you called you said your name was Jonathan."

"That's what people call me but my real name is Juan."

"Oh I should have asked because that changes everything. I assumed you were the son of either Juan or Jose but that was obviously a wrong assumption. I'm sorry for my error."

Jonathan was puzzled as to why that would make a difference but said nothing.

"You said you also have a key, did you bring it with you?"

Jonathan extracted the envelope from his pocket and handed it to her.

"Do you mind waiting a few minutes I need to check something."

Jonathan said that was fine and she left the room. She returned ten minutes later with another printout. Addressing Dave she said, "Would you mind waiting outside, this is confidential?"

Dave stood to leave but Jonathan beckoned him to sit.

"There's nothing private between us. In fact he's my money manager." He said to the bank official.

"Ok, if you're sure."

"I'm sure. Is it bad news or something I might not want to hear?" Jonathan enquired.

"Not at all, the reason I had to leave was I had to retrieve the account details as I'm sure you want to know how much you have."

"How much I have?"

"Yes. The account number you gave me is in your name. The account was created from an existing account by a name change in September 1993. The original account was in your father's name, Jose Martinez. The balance on the account today is four hundred and thirty-two thousand Swiss Francs, that's about three hundred thousand pounds sterling at today's exchange rate. The key is for a safe deposit box in one of our Zurich branches but it's still registered under your father's name. As you are the sole beneficiary of your father's non-specified assets then whatever is in the safe deposit box is yours. Before you can access it we will need to verify the documents you gave me. I'll pass them on to our legal department and I'll contact you when that's done. It might take a week or two. The deposit account is yours to access whenever you wish. Would you like the account to be transferred here in Sterling?"

"I'm not sure; I'll think about it and let you know. Thanks for everything and I look forward to hearing from you." She gave him her business card, smiled and they said their farewells.

They took the underground home and didn't speak the whole way. They got off at Notting Hill Gate and went for a very late lunch.

They ordered their food and Dave tried to suppress a laugh.

"Ok what's funny?'

"Well it seems that your dad was full of surprises. Did you check under all the mattresses to see if he had hidden anything else?"

Jonathan laughed, "As it happens mum did just that after he died. There's something bothering me though. Dad worked for the Foreign Office and one of their guys named Gideon something came to see mum a few times and as it happens just before she left for Spain permanently. He said he was a colleague of dad's. He was at the funeral too so mum said. On each occasion he asked mum if she had found anything that might belong to the foreign office and specified a key. Well that's why mum searched the flat after dad died but didn't find anything but now we have a key. Maybe it's that key he wanted."

"Maybe but we'll hold onto it until we know what it means."

"Mum said this Gideon fellow is a real slime bag and dad had mentioned him to her once it a way that made it obvious that he didn't like him."

"Well then my Jonathan, fuck Gideon and let's have an adventure."

"Why would dad have a bank account and a safe deposit box in Zurich? Maybe I should call mum."

"I shouldn't, the last time you spoke to her you said she seemed worried no point in upsetting her more. She'll be here for a week in October, tell her then when we know more. You know you haven't even mentioned the money."

"You're right about mum and what shall we do with all this money, it just seems to fall out of the sky whenever dad is mentioned?"

"That's my department remember. Let me worry about that."

"Yes you big banker. I did say banker didn't I?

Dave's radio program was a success and he managed his time well. He wanted to get into a rhythm that would ensure he'd have enough time for his studies when he started. He was happy that he'd done that and would still have some free time. He loved the research aspect and his team were great at digging out facts. He'd write the script on Friday afternoon and send it to Fiona and they'd review it on Saturday mornings and that took only about an hour which was great. They recorded between nine and ten on Sunday which meant Dave was in time for mass at the Oratory. Jonathan would meet him there and then lunch somewhere. They even occasionally accepted invitations to lunch with the Worthingtons.

Dave had been asked to speak to the TV guys about doing the day time news but he said he wasn't interested. He told Fiona and also asked if the program was going to get an extension as the original three months were up.

Fiona bit her bottom lip and said that the TV guys had priority and maybe he should rethink his refusal.

"And if I don't what then?"

"We'd have to see."

"See what Fiona, either you want me to do this or not. Those guys have no claim on me."

"Dave you do a great job, that's why they want you."

"Well let me save everyone any trouble here. I've contracted for three more programs after which I'm out the door. This is my life and not anyone else's. Good morning." He left and went to mass hoping it would cure him of his murderous feelings.

After mass they did their usual thing, having coffee on Knightsbridge.

"Dave you came into church looking like thunder and you still look a bit angry." Dave told him what had happened.

"Fiona called the house just as I was leaving. She said you weren't picking up your hand phone and she really needed to talk to you. Are you going to call her?"

"When I've cooled off a bit."

"Wow you could have been a TV star."

"Fuck off piss taker. You'd hate me to be famous, too intrusive."

"I hope that's not what stopped you."

"Of course not I, like you, have no ambitions in that area of life. I'm going to be Dr. Dave and that's my secondary focus in life."

Jonathan flashed his disarming smile and said, "And I'm your primary focus."

They walked over to the park and sat on a bench. Dave pressed the missed call button and Fiona picked up immediately. Jonathan could only hear one side of the conversation which was a series of monosyllabic responses. Dave ended the call and looked pleased with his self.

"Went well then?"

"She said that she had spoken to the head of programming and explained my situation and he apologised to her and said he'd deal with the guys that were trying to put pressure on us both. She also said that we have a six month extension on the program and, if I could forgive those tossers, she will have a contract for me to sign next week."

Jonathan passed his driving test the next day and on the following day, Tuesday, the Swiss bank called and asked them to go along for a chat and to collect the documents they had left. They did as requested and met the same woman. Jonathan asked her what the next steps were and she laughed.

"I'm sorry Jonathan but I'm going to sound like a TV program, you can open the box." Now they all got the joke.

Dave told her that they would leave the money where it is for the time being and she made a note.

They went into a coffee shop on Poultry and whilst Jonathan was ordering Dave booked two tickets to Zurich for that evening. He then booked a hotel within walking distance of the bank which was on Bahnhoff Strasse.

They arrived at the hotel at eight that evening. They dumped their bags and went for a walk along the lake and found a nice looking cafe for dinner. Dave insisted that as this was Jonathan's first time in Switzerland he had to try rosti and he ordered for both of them. The meal was simple but good and after they continued their stroll along the lake to Bahnhoff Strasse. They found the bank they were looking for and headed back to the hotel.

Jonathan commented on how clean and orderly everything seemed but he couldn't see much as it was dark. Dave said he was in for a treat the next day as Zurich is a very picturesque city compared to places like London.

The next morning they took a slow walk to the bank and Dave was proven right, it really did look nice. The sun was shining and the lake glistened and Jonathan was surprised they could see mountains in the distance. It all seemed far from the hustle and bustle of London which calmed his nerves which had been jangling since he woke up.

They entered the bank and stated their purpose. Dave was asked to wait and no amount of protest from Jonathan made any difference. Account holders only were admitted to the safe deposit area. Jonathan went through a security screening and was asked to leave his mobile phone with the security officer. He was taken into a large room and was told to ring the bell when he had finished. He found the locker without any trouble and unlocked it and removed the box which he placed on a table provided. He lifted the lid and held his breath. His dad had proven himself full of surprises so what was he about to find?

Inside he found a large envelope and two velvet, drawstring bags. He looked inside the bags first, then closed them and returned them to the box. He opened the envelope which contained numerous sheets of paper. He sat down and started reading them. After about ten minutes he rang the bell and the security officer opened the door. Jonathan asked him if there was a photocopying machine he could use and was told there was. He put the box containing the bags back into its slot and locked it. He photocopied the papers and returned the originals to whence he found them.

He left the bank with Dave in tow and told him he'd show him what he had found once they got back to the hotel. Dave rather thought they should stop for coffee and a bite and talk about it then.

"No way Dave, we're going straight back to the hotel."

When they were safely ensconced in their room Jonathan gave Dave the copies he'd stuffed in his Jacket pockets.

"I didn't know what to expect but certainly nothing like this. I think I'm dreaming, read."

Dave sat on the bed and read the documents and whistled with surprise. "Are these the originals?"

"No I used their photocopier and put the originals back. That's not all I found, there were two small bags full of diamonds or I suppose they were diamonds."

"Wow, you were right to put everything back. This is serious stuff, what do we do now?"

"I hope that was a rhetorical question because I was hoping you'd know."

"Let's put these in the safe and go for a walk, the fresh air might help us think. We don't leave until tomorrow so there's nothing we can actually do whilst we're here."

Jonathan agreed and added. "There wouldn't just happen to be a nice restaurant on our route by any chance would there?"

"You know me too well and anyway you know I think better on a full stomach."

They walked back to the main part of town and tried to make sense of it

"Do you think my dad was a thief."

"No I don't. You knew him, do you?"

"I'd like to think not but what was he then?"

"Reading that stuff it seemed he not only worked for the foreign office but also the secret services. That's possible because I read somewhere that they both have the same reporting line. He mentions MI6 and two names."

"Yes I read that and it sounds like he didn't trust either of them."

"I agree so we can't approach them. He mentions that Gideon fellow that your mum said was a slime bag and it seems she was right. Well here's the restaurant so let's eat and think. We shouldn't discuss this though in case we're overheard."

"Now I feel like a fucking spy. It's all a bit much to take in. Order for me whilst I find the gents, I want the same as I had last night, that was good."

They ate lunch and avoided talking about the find with great difficulty so they spoke about football to take their mind off it.

They walked back along the lake when Dave suddenly stopped. "A full stomach really helps. We can talk to Dicky Worthington, he works at the foreign office. We'll ask him what to do."

"Yes that might work, you're brilliant, food really helps," he laughed, feeling a little easier. They took a boat ride and walked some more. Dave said he felt like they were people from a Len Deighton book. It all felt surreal and somehow exciting.

They returned to London the next morning and Dave called Dolly as soon as they got in the taxi from the airport. He asked if they could call on Dicky that evening and she said they must come to dinner. Dave explained that they needed to talk to Dicky in private and she seemed unphased by the idea as if it was a normal occurrence. She said they would have a lovely dinner and she would leave them alone to talk to Dicky over coffee.

They arrived at seven as instructed and ate dinner and drank fine wine with Dolly for light entertainment. Dolly said her goodnights when coffee arrived.

Dicky put a cigar in his mouth but never lit it. "Dolly tells me you boys need some advice and she said whatever it was sounded serious."

Dave told Jonathan to relate the story. When he got to the references to MI6 Dicky put his hand up and told him to stop there.

"Jonathan I don't need or want to know any more details. Do you have the documents with you?"

Jonathan withdrew the folded envelope from his Jacket pocket and handed it over.

Dicky looked at it and said "Good it's sealed," and took a ball point pen out of his pocket. "Sign across where it's sealed two or three times and write today's date and the time." Jonathan did as he was told and handed it back.

"I cannot get involved with anything to do the Secret Services but leave this with me and I'll get it to someone who might be able to help. I need the names of the persons mentioned to make sure they are avoided of course but no more, understand?" he said in his usual mild manner.

Jonathan nodded and told him the names which Dicky committed to memory. Many thanks were offered and they went home.

They lay in bed looking up at the ceiling both lost in their thoughts. Jonathan got up and switched on the air conditioner, not because it was hot but he thought it would be nice to snuggle under the duvet and feel safe.

After about fifteen minutes Dave asked if he was asleep.

He grumpily answered no.

"Thinking about your dad's stuff?"

"No, that fucking air conditioner is making a funny noise and it's driving me made."

Dave almost fell out of bed laughing and got up and switched it off and opened the windows. He got back into bed still laughing.

It was the middle of September and Dave was starting at LSE the next week. On Monday he was asked to join a conference call with Fiona and the team and she announced that they had managed to get the Chancellor of the Exchequer for the coming Sunday. He agreed to come as long as it was televised as well as radio. Dave wasn't sure if he was ready to handle such a big fish on his own and television so he asked if he could invite Professor Duncan, the head of economics at LSE. Fiona thought it would be a good idea and asked if Dave was comfortable doing TV. He said he wasn't but he knew they couldn't miss such an opportunity. The program wasn't going out live so they could edit out any gaffs, so he was ok.

Dave called Professor Duncan himself as he had known and respected him since his student days. The professor agreed and offered Dave some advice on what to focus on and Dave took that advice on board.

This was important so Dave insisted on a conference via Skype every evening. The team were coming up with some interesting stuff based on the advice given by Professor Duncan. The program was to be split in two halves. The first fifteen minutes were to be prearranged questions which left Dave only fifteen minutes for the real interview so he had to be succinct.

Dicky had invited them both for lunch on that Monday but Dave was unable to go, so Jonathan went alone. When he arrived he was shown to the library where Dicky and another man were seated. They rose to greet him and introductions were made after which Dicky beat a hasty retreat. The other gentleman had introduced himself as Sir Jeremy Whitley and now explained that he was number two in MI6.

"Jonathan, Dicky passed the envelope you gave him to me and the contents, I must say, are of a rather sensitive nature. I understand that your friend has seen these documents and it's unfortunate that he couldn't be here today. I'll tell you up front that we've done a thorough check on you both and, apart from a wrongful imprisonment of David Wilson; you both came up squeaky clean. Even so because of the subject matter, I would ask you both to sign the official secrets act."

Jonathan cleared his throat. "I'm a private citizen and I came by this information fortuitously and I'm at liberty to use it any way I see fit. It's private property, my private property and evidence of wrong doing by your people. In saying that I do want those responsible for my father's death brought to justice and if you commit to bringing that about I will sign. Dave Wilson will not however until I have a satisfactory conclusion."

"By signing, you do realise that you will not be able to discuss this matter with him beyond what he already knows."

"Yes I do and he'll be ok with that."

"Dicky said you were smart and it seems you understand what you're in possession of and what the consequences of publication could be. We need you as much as you need us."

"Well does that mean that you will do everything within your power to help?"

"It does, so are you prepared to sign?"

The document was produced and Jonathan signed in good faith.

The first course of action was to happen the very next day.

"I want you to help me test out a new gadget. We've tested it but haven't used it in a live situation, so you'll be our guinea pig so to say."

Jonathan started feeling like a James Bond type, which rather amused him. "Sure, my honour."

"You don't wear glasses I see, contact lenses?"

"No sir, nothing."

"Splendid," he said fishing out a glasses case from his attaché case. "Try these on, the lenses are plain glass."

Jonathan opened the case and put the glasses on and was given an explanation as to their purpose. He was impressed by the technology which seemed like a variation on those available from Apple.

"They're the sort of thing your father would have worked on if he was still with us, poor chap. In the morning you will have to go through security so you must take them off at that point and put them in their case. You mustn't forget to do that."

They did a test and Jonathan was even more amazed by the demonstration.

They discussed the plan of action and Jonathan offered a suggestion which Sir Jeremy thought splendid. After they finished they went to find Dickie and had lunch with him and Dolly without uttering a word of what was said.

When he got home Dave was busy at his laptop. He looked up and asked how it went.

"You're going to hate me."

"Why's that?"

"I mustn't talk to you about it other than what you already know. I signed the Official Secrets Act."

"What, like never?"

"They want you to sign too but I told them no. You see you're my guarantee that they will really help. I said you'd sign only when we have a satisfactory conclusion. Do you mind?"

"Of course I'd like to know what's going on but that was a smart move. It's probably just as well at the moment because it would be a major distraction," he lied. "As you know I've got the Chancellor of the Exchequer on Sunday and its being televised. I'm scared shitless."

CHAPTER FORTY SIX

The next morning Jonathan arrived at the secret service headquarters at ten o'clock and did as instructed. He passed security without a hitch. He was asked to deposit his phone which seemed standard and was given a seat and asked to wait.

Sir Jeremy was informed of his arrival and picked up his office phone and keyed in an internal extension.

"Charlotte my dear, I have a young man down in reception who wants to see me. I'm a little tied up, so I'm sending him to you, don't mind eh? He's the son of Joe Martinez who used to do odd things for us, Foreign Office security, remember?

"Yes you do have to see him and please be civil."

Jonathan was escorted to the office of Charlotte Tully. He handed the security slip he'd been given to Marjory, Ms Tully's P.A. She checked the details and when satisfied it was all in order she escorted him into her bosses' office.

Charlotte looked up from her desk and saw a rather scruffy young man with glasses and an unshaven face and enquired, "What can I do for you Juan Martinez." She said it with what was meant to be a smile but looked more like a smirk.

"Juan is the name on my passport but I'm known as Jonathan I have something that should interest you." He was told to take only the two sheets that related to the unauthorised thefts. He explained how they had come to be in his possession and handed the oldest one over first. It was a building plan which showed precise details of a large house and its security system. He asked her to turn it over and read the notes on the other side. She read without reaction then looked up at Jonathan and said, "So?"

"It appears from those notes that my father was instructed to do what he often did for your department but he was asked to do it alone. As you can see when he returned to Switzerland he examined what he'd taken and after some enquiries suspected that he'd committed a robbery that had nothing to do with the good of our nation. That was what he thought at that time."

He handed over the second sheet and said it was much the same only this time he was certain. Charlotte sat silent but appeared unmoved, so Jonathan continued.

"He sounds worried when he says that since you took over he had no recourse to anyone, other than Gideon Charles and he felt he couldn't trust him. He also says that before you took over he had a secure line to someone in authority should he need it but you took that away. He tried to see you several times but you refused."

She sat silent for a while before giving a considered response. "Your father did try to speak to me once but I only talk to people who report directly to me. Does that explain it?"

"Not really, what my father did, he did for your department and that's your responsibility isn't it?"

Still cool and calm, "I don't need you to tell me what my responsibilities are, thank you. You're way out of your depth you know."

"He says that you were the only person that had access to plans and had the authority to allocate jobs so you must have known."

"So what do you expect me to do?"

"My father was subjected to unwarranted danger by you and I believe that's what got him killed."

"I know nothing of this so it's nothing to do with me."

"Gideon Charles reports to you and it's your responsibility to ensure that your staff, act according to instructions so he must have been acting on your behalf." Jonathan was extremely calm which rattled her a little. "If you look at the top of the plans you can see my dad wrote the addresses, surly you could check if these were legitimate?"

"Now you're telling me how do my job."

"It seems you need to be told. You should be in prison for what you've done. At a minimum it's dereliction of duty which led to the death of my father but you're obviously also directly implicated, so it's murder and more."

"A nice little speech, I notice these are photocopies, where are the originals? You're breaking the law by holding on to property that belongs to the state, the Security Services to exact."

"They're in a safe place and I have every right under law to have them and do what I see fit with them."

"No you are not, I could have you arrested."

"No you can't and what you're saying is misrepresentation for personal gain in other words to cover your own arse. Now that is an offense under English law."

Jonathan was in perfect control of his emotions and the situation. Charlotte looked like she was losing it.

"You seem to think you know a lot about the law, well whatever that is, it doesn't apply here."

"Madam it does. I'm in training to be a barrister and I'm good, really good. I'll be called to the bar in a year or so. What you're saying is false. Your actions were illegal and they led to the death of my father and you are going to pay dearly."

A victorious grin came over Charlotte's face and she called Marjory who appeared almost instantaneously.

"Draft a letter to the bar council explaining that this young man is a security threat to our nation and under no circumstances should he be allowed to ever be called to the bar. Do the letter now please."

Jonathan smiled at the woman opposite who was now looking self satisfied. Jonathan said, "You have no conscience do you? What are you going to do about Gideon Charles?"

"Nothing, I have no evidence to suggest he's done anything wrong."

Marjory entered the office and handed the letter she had typed to Charlotte who scanned it.

"Your father was a traitor and if he was alive today he'd be put in prison for treason," she spat. Now she had the bit between her teeth and was enjoying it.

Jonathan gave her a huge smile and said, "Now that's slander aren't you going to sign the letter that ruins my life?"

She glared at him signed it and instructed Marjory to have it hand delivered immediately.

Jonathan was now looking most amused. "Now that's a really serious offence, abuse of power leading to the destruction of a young man's life and vocation, tut tut Tully." He laughed.

"Marjory get this fucking thing out of my office."

"Certainly, Jonathan Sir Jeremy will see you now and he wants you to go along Charlotte. Oh and he said bring your handbag."

Charlotte was suddenly feeling very nervous. "What's going on, tell Sir Jeremy that I'm too busy."

"Charlotte he told me it was an order not a request and there are two security men here to escort you both."

They were taken up two floors and shown into Sir Jeremy's office. Sir Jeremy stood up and greeted Jonathan with a huge grin and a thumbs up. "Hello young man, nice glasses keep them on, splendid job, absolutely splendid."

Now Charlotte felt very nervous. "What's going on Sir Jeremy?"

"Oh nothing, I think they suit him don't you. Right Jonathan my dear boy, I trust Charlotte was helpful?"

"Not really sir."

"Oh come now she's always helpful. Tell me."

"Well firstly she dismissed my evidence of wrong doing. Then she told me that she had no responsibility for my father's safety."

"Really, is there more?"

"Yes, she knew who my father was and that he needed to talk to her but she refused. Then she threatened to have me arrested for being in possession of something that is rightfully mine."

"Now, now this doesn't sound a bit like Charlotte. Charlotte is this true?"

"No none of it, he's just trying to twist words for his own benefit. I think he's got a bee in his bonnet and he's trying to stir up trouble."

"Anything more substantial Jonathan?"

"Well yes there is, excuse me for a second."

He returned with Marjory. "Marjory can you give the letter to Sir Jeremy please? Thank you."

"You can see clearly sir that she's advising the bar council that I'm a security risk. She also slandered my father by saying he was a traitor."

Charlotte was beginning to feel desperate. "None of this is true I only had the letter typed to rattle him."

"Marjory my dear what do you have to say?"

"Well Sir Jeremy, I was told to have the letter hand delivered immediately and normally it would have been well on its way so she did intend to send it. The bit about Joe being a traitor was absolutely true and despicable under the circumstances. Joe was such a nice man and if anything he was a hero."

Charlotte was horrified. "Marjory what is this?"

"Truth Charlotte, truth."

"I deny it all"

Sir Jeremy looked as pleased as punch when he said, "Jonathan please take off your glasses and put them on the coffee table over there. This is so exciting."

Jonathan obliged. Sir Jeremy pushed a button on a device that was sitting on his desk and suddenly a hologram appeared of Charlotte. The whole conversation was there and they watched with fascination. It looked almost real. Charlotte was apoplectic.

"Clam down now Charlotte, Marjory can you ask Stanley to come in now please?"

Stanley appeared. "Stanley old chap it seems that your glasses worked. They didn't send the data directly so it must have picked up our radio detection system so that worked. It got through our security system so that worked but we now need to upgrade our security system because we don't want the opposition getting through now do we? By the way this very clever young man is Jonathan Martinez, Joe's son."

Stanley shook Jonathan's hand and told him he had worked closely with his father. "He was a great guy bordering on genius." He looked at Charlotte and said to Jonathan, "I don't know why you're in the same room as that woman she was horrible to your dad. She's a real cow. Sorry sir it just slipped out."

"That's fine Stanley she's been giving out plenty of insults of her own today. Well Charlotte it seems the evidence is irrefutable. What do you have to say for yourself now?"

"We're MI6, nobody can touch me and you won't do anything because it will damage the department."

Sir Jeremy nodded his head, "Charlotte was it two years ago that our chief was grilled by MPs live on TV? He promised transparency so shall we oblige? Jonathan you legal whizz, how many criminal charges are there here."

"Three sir and I told her each time."

"If you could only choose one which would it be and why?'

"Abuse of power, the new act concerning public servants would mean she'll get ten to fifteen years."

"Charlotte, would you be happy to settle for that?"

"No I wouldn't and I'd blow the whistle on everything."

"My dear you don't know everything and there are ways of keeping you quiet which you know. Our dear friend Jonathan knows we don't like having our name dragged through the mud so he came up with an ingenious idea. Is it time Jonathan?"

"Five more minutes sir but I don't have my phone."

"Marjory my dear please call security and have them bring Jonathan's phone here immediately."

The phone arrived and at the allotted time Jonathan made a call. He greeted the party at the other end in Italian and then handed the phone to Charlotte. "It's for you and it's very important."

Charlotte took the phone and asked who it was. She turned as white as a sheet and just listened. She gave the phone back to Jonathan and started shaking and said "You bastard, you fucking bastard."

Jonathan nodded and said, "Just desserts don't you think?"

Charlotte went silent.

Sir Jeremy had tracked down the contact details for the mobster that Joe had been asked to rob. Jonathan had called him the night before and explained what had happened all those years ago and without compunction gave him Charlotte's name and address. The gist of today's phone call was that friends were keeping her husband company and that he'd agreed to sell their house and pay over the balance of their bank accounts in repayment of the stolen one million dollars. The value of all that amounted to three million pounds which the mobster had said was capital and accrued interest. It was also the price for letting them live.

Charlotte spoke, "Sir Jeremy did you know about this?"

"Not the details my dear, just the general outline but I think justice has only partially been served. There's still the issue of Joe's death."

Jonathan interrupted, "Sir I think she will have to live in fear all her life and be broke at the same time. She might have been party to my father's death but I don't think she did it. If she tells me what happened now I'll let it go, well at least for her."

"Well Charlotte?"

"I didn't order anyone to die and I don't know what happened. It was to do with the diamonds I suppose and a meeting with Gideon but he wouldn't admit any involvement. He said Joe was mugged and it was convenient for me to believe that. Talk to him, he'll be back on Saturday."

"I don't know why sir but I believe her."

"Ok, Charlotte you have committed crimes here and you deserve punishment. Of course you no longer work here and you will be held in protective custody until your husband notifies me that your business with mobsters is settled. When you are released you will leave this country and never return. Your parents live in New Zealand so that's where you will go. Take her away." She was escorted out.

"Fine days work Jonathan, shame you have no ambitions to work for Her Majesty but that would be pushing it a bit if I tried to persuade you. You'll make a fine barrister, cool under pressure and right to the heart with your questions and comments. Good Job, now we have to deal with the other one."

Jonathan stayed for two hours whilst they formulated plans to deal with Gideon Charles. Sir Jeremy made it very clear that it could mean danger for

Jonathan but that was brushed aside and Jonathan committed to the plan. He had to know the truth and he would do anything to get justice for his father, so it was settled. They would aim for Sunday morning as Dave wouldn't be around.

Jonathan went home pleased with what had happened so far and he felt a sense of excitement about Sunday's plan. Dave was glued to his laptop and looked up and said, "How did it go? I won't ask you any details just tell me good or bad."

"Good thanks, in fact very good. It doesn't seem right not being able to discuss it with you, I'm bursting."

"I'm glad it went well and I must admit I do feel like I've been sidelined. We both know it's for the best so let's live with it."

"Ok I thought this BBC thing wasn't going to take up much of your time."

"It hasn't so far but with the Chancellor and TV to consider, it's got to be one hundred percent."

Jonathan put his arms around Dave's neck and rested his chin on his head. "You'll do a great job. Does TV take longer than radio?"

He felt awful being devious but it had to be done.

"I'll have to be there at eight and we don't expect to finish until two or three." Jonathan was relieved as that gave them a bigger window of opportunity than he expected.

On Saturday Jonathan got the call he was expecting. Charlotte had done her part, under close supervision, having phoned Gideon to give him the good news that Jonathan had found the diamonds. She had told him that Jonathan had called her office trying to locate him and she gave him the mobile number he needed.

The call was short and to the point. Jonathan had the diamonds and Gideon could collect them at eleven thirty on Sunday morning at his house. He gave the address and put the phone down with his heart pounding in his chest.

On Sunday morning Dave left at seven and Jonathan made a call. The police arrived within fifteen minutes and placed three listening devices around the lounge where Jonathan was to guide Gideon. When it was all done they retired to the upstairs flat and tested the equipment and then just waited. Sheba was restless, she didn't like all these men being around her master and she growled a few times much to the policemen's discomfort and Jonathan's amusement.

At ten thirty it was all set and the detective inspector who was leading the team came down to confirm that and to check that Jonathan was OK.

Gideon arrived at eleven thirty on the dot. Jonathan opened the front door with Sheba at his heels. She took one look at Gideon and bared her teeth so she was shut in the kitchen to make Gideon feel more at ease. Jonathan led the way to the lounge and closed the door.

"So you're Jonathan, you look like your father only a bit taller and scruffier. Your dad prided himself on his appearance, always looked good did Joe. I knew him for many years, you know. We worked closely together on a number of projects. He died shortly after our last one, most unfortunate. Charlotte told me that you've found what he retrieved on his last mission."

"I believe I have but I need you to tell me what it is you're expecting. Whatever it is, it's in the safe upstairs so I need to be sure that what I have belongs to the Foreign Office and it's not dad's personal property."

Gideon looked a little unsure. "I'm not sure I should tell you this but as it was such a long time ago, I suppose its ok. It was a consignment of diamonds that had been earmarked to fund a terrorist group. Is that what you found?"

"What I found was this." Jonathan produced a sheet of paper, "its dad's notes from that job. He says that he didn't think this was really an authorised MI6 job. He says that you mislead him. You see when I retrieved the diamonds I also found a bunch of documents which I have safely tucked away. This is one of them and it suggests that the owner of the diamonds was a legitimate trader. I've checked and he was and still is. So what was the real purpose of that mission, to make Gideon Charles rich?"

"You shouldn't stick your nose into government business; it's none of your concern."

"Oh but it is my concern, you see the diamonds are mine as my dad left everything to me in his will."

"You're too clever by half kid. Where are they?"

"First I want you to answer a question. My mum told me that whilst dad was away, obviously on this mission, she was bundled into a van and taken for a short ride and then dropped off, without any explanation. The kidnappers put a bag over her head so she didn't see anyone and nobody spoke. She said she told dad when he got back. He went into the bedroom and made a phone call and then went out. He hadn't even unpacked. That call was to you wasn't it"

Gideon knew this wasn't going to turn out the way he hoped so he'd have to deal with it the only way he could.

"Yes it was me he called."

"And it was you that arranged for my mum's little ride."

"Sure, you're dad was making all the wrong noises and it was a way of ensuring I'd get what I wanted. Real family man your dad, I knew his weak spot."

"It was you he went to meet that night."

"Of course."

"But you couldn't have taken my dad on your own. I could beat shit out you, you're a scrawny weasel."

"Hard case, like your dad, eh but you see I had a little help from my friends. He wasn't meant to die but one kick too many if you know what I mean?"

Jonathan took a deep breath to help control his rising anger. Now was not the time to tear this piece of shit apart.

"So you made it look like a mugging."

"Clever boy."

"Why are you telling me all this, you know I'll use it? I don't get it."

"Son, I know where your mother lives on Portobello Road. I've been there for a visit before and had a cup of tea. Now if I have any trouble from you, your dear mum will find herself six feet under and not dead."

"Christ, leave my mother out of this."

"Sure just give me what's mine."

Jonathan feigned nervousness and fear but the only emotion coursing through his body was of extreme anger. He had to continue as planned.

"Look my mum's suffered enough and I reckon you owe her. I'll give you half the diamonds and when you've sold them I'll give you give a hundred thousand pounds, then I'll give you the rest."

"No deal son, I already have a partner."

"Is that the woman dad mentions in his notes, Charlotte Tully?"

"You're too clever for your own good, sure it's Charlotte. She gets the lion's share, so there's nothing left for your poor old mum," he said sarcastically.

"I suppose it was all her idea, you don't seem that smart."

"No, the diamonds were my idea. The first job was hers. It was her that told me to put the frighteners on your old man. It was her that told me you wanted to talk to me about something. That's how I got your number."

"This is all too easy, why are you confessing all this? If you're not going to give me a share I'll go to the police, that's if I don't kick the shit out of you now."

"Ok, go to the police, you're not so fucking bright after all. We're MI6; the police won't go near us."

Jonathan took a step towards him and as he did Gideon drew a gun from under his jacket.

"I brought this just in case, now where are the fucking diamonds?"

They both heard footsteps coming down the stairs. Jonathan thought it must be the police.

"Who the fuck is that kid?"

Jonathan had to think quickly.

"Must be the housekeeper, she's the only one with a key."

They stood still, just a little way from the door, listening. Whoever it was had gone into the kitchen. Jonathan knew it was too early to be Dave but why would the police go into the kitchen?

The footsteps were now heading for the lounge. Then it all happened. The door swung open and Sheba bounded in and made a lunge for Gideon. Dave saw the gun and landed an almighty punch on the side of Gideon's head. The gun went off and Dave fell to the floor and blood appeared on his forehead. Gideon had been floored and Sheba was chewing at his arm. Jonathan picked up the gun and aimed it at Gideon. The police rushed in and the inspector shouted, "Don't do it son, he's not worth it"

Jonathan squeezed the trigger.

CHAPTER FORTY SEVEN

The team was all ready in the recording studio and the Chancellor was brought in. The formalities over, he took his allotted seat as did Professor Gordon. Dave asked the preset questions. The Chancellor was enjoying blowing his own trumpet and they overran his allotted time by five minutes which left only ten minutes for the questions the team had prepared. Dave had been told that this part was not going to be edited so he had to ensure he got through it all as quickly as possible.

"Sir you outlined your plans, which included three major projects that will benefit the North, which is admirable and long overdue."

"I agree" nodded the Chancellor.

"One of those projects is to build a new airport between Preston and Blackpool. What will happen to Manchester and all the smaller airports in the area, will they have to close down?"

"Of course, they won't be needed. The project has been well received in the area which is borne out by the enthusiastic results when we polled the locals."

"I have a copy of the poll's findings here. It was only conducted in the area which is in close proximity to the site of the new airport. We conducted a poll using the same questions in Manchester and Liverpool. We did a cross section of residents and existing airport workers and the overall results showed that ninety percent were against it."

"Well you polled the wrong people."

Dave didn't respond to that. He continued, "How many new jobs will be created?"

"We estimate that it will be somewhere in the region of four thousand."

"That includes all the concessionaires I understand and the number of jobs that will be lost will be more than that."

"I'm sure you've got your numbers wrong."

"My numbers come from a government working document, so I assume they are accurate.

"You're also planning to embark on a major house building project in the North, the like of which the region has never seen before. There has been a lot of concern expressed about this as the numbers far exceed any shortage and that's even if you take into consideration the re-housing of those in existing poor quality homes. So who will live in the homes that appear to be well in excess of current demand?"

"People of course," he laughed.

"Your family own one of the biggest construction companies in the country. Will they be part of the bidding process?"

"Every qualified company will be part of that process and I hope you're not insinuating foul play."

"It wasn't even in my mind but, now you mention it, don't you think that might be a view held by some especially as it's not a priority housing area?"

"If so then they'll be holding an erroneous view. Can we move on?"

"The North has been seeing a pick-up in jobs over recent years but the unemployed rate is still well above the national average and that coupled with the fact that there isn't a pressing housing shortage begs the question why do this? Wouldn't the money be better spent on job creation in the region?"

"We're a conservative government and we believe in Capitalist ideals, so we rightly leave job creation to the private sector."

"Professor, can you comment please?"

"David I agree with you. What the North needs is a good stimulus package to encourage investment. There are so many new industries popping up around the world that we could encourage them more to locate to UK and specifically to the North. Unemployment numbers would drop, the social ills that are created by long term unemployment would dissipate and the reliance on benefits reduced. I'm from the North and we're proud people, we want to work. Investment has been long coming and as there now seems to be lots of money in the coffers to spend on white elephants, why not divert it to where it would make a real difference?"

Dave turned to the Chancellor for a response that was not forthcoming. "Chancellor, you have pledged to reduce the deficit, reduce borrowing without any new or increased taxation. You've also said that there will be no reduction in spending on defence, NHS or education. The only place that increased spending and major savings can come from is social services, so is that where you intend to make the savings?"

"We'll tweak here and there, we'll find it."

"Sir we are talking multi- billions of pounds. You don't get that sort of money by tweaking."

"Young man, you're a radio presenter. I don't expect you could possibly understand the machinations of the treasury."

At this point Professor Duncan interjected. "Sir, David got a first in economics, and sailed through his masters both at LSE. He's one of the brightest students I've ever had the privilege to teach. You might like to rethink that statement."

The Chancellor look at the producer for support but none was forthcoming, she just indicated to continue.

"So back to my question the only places you've not pledged to maintain spending is pensions and benefits. I understand that you're planning major reforms in these areas."

Dave had not intended to make the interview controversial but this pompous prick was starting to make his blood boil and he dropped his notes and went off script.

"Well sir will you answer please?"

"We never do anything without testing the nations pulse on issues and when it comes to cutting benefits we have huge backing from the people. We conducted a poll and got a 70% positive approval rate for cutting benefits."

"I also have the results and methodology for that poll. It was conducted in London only and then in areas where predominately well off people reside. We didn't have much time to conduct our own poll but we managed a sample size of one thousand. We did it in the borough of Brent and the target audience was British citizens who were in full time employment. Our result was very different from yours. 80% disapprove of reducing benefits."

"Stats, you purposely chose a borough with a vested interest."

"As did you sir, and you're right the people we polled do have a vested interest because their jobs are always in danger of disappearing through the actions of bankers and government. I'd like to make it clear what you are proposing. It's planned to raise the retirement age to seventy and to reduce benefits by 30% in most areas and up to 70% in the rest."

"Well yes but that still needs some work."

"Professor, your views please."

"If you do that then you will push anywhere up to two million people below the poverty line, especially the long term unemployed."

"Chancellor?"

"That's the problem isn't it? These people should find jobs or their families should support them. Benefits only encourage idleness."

"That is your view, is it also the view of the Prime Minister?"

"Of course, he backs me to the hilt."

"Sir, do you know you have a nickname in Westminster?"

"No I didn't know that."

"They call you Pol Pot."

There was an audible gasp from the production team. This information was not supposed to be aired.

"That's insulting, that man was evil. I'm not evil, I serve my country."

"They call you Pol Pot because you conduct a manipulated poll to justify whatever it is you want to do, whilst you're driving our country to pot."

"This is outrageous."

Now Dave really lost it. He didn't care if he was never allowed anywhere near the BBC again.

"What's outrageous sir is you. Look at the camera. The people who will be watching you are citizens of this country and they are not stupid. They don't believe that spending money on white elephants is a good thing. They don't believe that forcibly creating poverty is a good thing. They don't believe that penalising people who have worked hard all their lives only to have their pension hopes dashed is a good thing.

"It took the people of this country a millennium to break free from the ruling classes and get a decent share of the wealth they create. Now you come along with your old school tie, aristocratic friends and want to reverse all that and you've made it clear that the PM is amongst that group. That's what's outrageous. You think your fellow countrymen are idiots. The only idiot I can see is you."

Dave stood up and said, "This interview is over."

The Chancellor had gone red in the face and he spat, "This program will never be aired. The Director General will not allow it. He's a personal friend of mine. As for you, I'll see you never work in the media again and that goes for all of you who've conspired to create this pantomime."

Someone beckoned the Chancellor from the wings and as he got up to leave the whole crew, whistled and jeered. Professor Duncan stood up and applauded and the whole studio joined in.

Dave said something into Professor Duncan's ear and then held up his hand for quiet. "I'm leaving now and I'll probably never be allowed to return. Thank you all for your support. You might want to open some windows there's a bad smell in here. It must be all the shit that guy talks."

He left the studio to more applause.

It was still only eleven. He slowly walked to Marble Arch station and caught the train to Holland Park. He was feeling angry and a bit disappointed in himself for letting the team down. He knew there would be consequences and not only for him. There were four teenagers on the train and they started bothering an elderly woman. Dave got up and without saying a word grabbed two of them and put them off the train at the next station. Their friends seeing the size of the problem followed. Dave sat down and the lady thanked him. He just nodded.

He got home just before twelve and went into the kitchen where he was surprised to see Sheba shut away. He thought Jonathan must be out but Sheba pushed past him and he followed her to the lounge still feeling that he'd like to punch someone's lights out.

CHAPTER FORTY EIGHT

A policeman removed the gun from Jonathan's hand. Jonathan looked down at Dave and saw blood dripping down his face. He knelt next to him and saw that his eyes were open. He cradled his head and said, "You've been shot."

"No I haven't. I tripped over Sheba and hit my head on the coffee table. What a fucking horrible day."

Jonathan felt a wave of relief. He looked over to where two policemen were standing over Gideon. "Did I kill him?"

The Inspector answered, "No, you didn't even shoot him but you did manage to shoot a hole in your ceiling. The shot fired by this guy went straight through your garden window. Just as well nobody was in the garden."

Gideon came to and was escorted out of the house to a waiting police car.

One of the uniforms said that they should take Dave to the hospital but Jonathan said it wasn't necessary. "Go upstairs to the first room on the right and you'll find a first aid kit in the bathroom in the cabinet above the sink."

Jonathan cleaned Dave's wound and saw it was just a small cut with the beginnings of a bump appearing. He cleaned it off and put a large plaster over it. Sheba helped by licking the other side of his face by way of comfort.

The policeman who had found the first aid kit said, "I don't like to tell you this but the bullet you shot through the ceiling went straight through your air conditioning unit. Dave and Jonathan both burst out laughing.

The policemen all look at them in bewilderment. When he stopped laughing Dave said, "One of those stories when you had to have been there to appreciate it."

They all went into the kitchen and Jonathan made tea for all, which included the two uniforms and the detective inspector. They sat at the kitchen table and the detective said, "You two have a lot of balls, I must say."

Jonathan ignored the remark and asked Dave why he had reached home so early and was the interview a success. Dave grimace and was about to say something when the house phone rang. Jonathan nodded to a uniform who answered it. "It's for Dave a lady called Fiona."

"Tell her I'm not home."

The uniform relayed the message and stayed on the line for a while before hanging up. "She heard you. She said that she's been trying your mobile for the last fifteen minutes. She said it's very important but you can see for yourself if you watch the BBC news which is just about to start. Shall I switch on the tele?" Dave nodded expecting the worse.

They only had to wait two minutes before the news began. "This is Lucy Hoskins and here are the headlines. Sensation in the BBC studios, War in Angola, President Putin makes an announcement and plague in China. Our main story is about events that happened right here in the BBC studios. The social media is on fire with snippets of an interview that took place today with the Chancellor of the Exchequer and our very own David Wilson. We'll show you the piece that's caught the public's imagination but you can see the whole program at one thirty, directly after this news bulletin and only here on the BBC."

Suddenly there on the screen was Dave sitting between the Chancellor and Professor Gordon. Dave closed his eyes.

It started with Professor Duncan saying that if the government went ahead with their plans they would push two million people into poverty and ended with Dave mentioning the Chancellor's nickname.

"Our reporters have been trying to contact both the Chancellor and the Prime Minister for comment but both are unavailable. It appears from the press secretary that Downing St hasn't yet viewed the program and has asked for a copy of the full recording. Watch after the news it really is sensational."

Dave got up and switched the television off. The room was quiet until one of the uniforms, Stelios, said "You really do have balls to talk to him like that, good for you."

"You haven't seen anything yet, the rest is much worse, if they dare to show it."

The other uniform, Rick, asked Detective Inspector Merchant if they had to wait or should they go back to the station.

"We have to stay here until Sir Jeremy Whitely arrives and he'll give us our instructions then. Meantime Stelios call the station and ask them to send someone round to fix that window. We won't disturb you two any further we'll wait outside."

Jonathan said they couldn't do that because he was sure they didn't want to miss Dave's performance.

"Do we have to watch it?" said a mournful looking Dave.

"I wouldn't miss it for the world and we're all going to watch it with the star of the show."

The phone rang again. Jonathan answered. They were all listening to his end of the conversation.

"No he can't come to the phone, I'm Jonathan his partner, you can tell me and I'll pass on the message."

Pause.

"Yes we did see it and yes we are going to watch the full program."

Longer pause.

"Yes I'll pass on the message but there will be no interview today, maybe tomorrow and you can stick your contract up your arse. I'm his legal advisor and if you don't back off I'll give an interview to Sky myself and then you're screwed."

There was a short pause.

"I'm glad we're on the same page. Dave isn't around tomorrow until about four so call back then. Thanks and bye."

They all looked at him. "She said it's the biggest coup the BBC has had in years. One of the cameramen was so incensed he leaked part of the interview to social media. The Director General himself ordered the program to be aired. She also said they wanted to interview you today but I think you got the gist of that one. I can't wait to watch the whole thing. She said you might have brought the government down. What did you do Dave Wilson; no don't tell us we'll watch it ourselves."

Dave looked like he wanted to be elsewhere. "I'm not watching it. I suppose it's just as well there are policemen here because there will be an arrest warrant issued for me very soon."

Jonathan insisted that Dave stayed so he made sandwiches and coffee for everyone once the formal part of the interview was over. At one point the four viewers cheered, then they booed and at the end they all stood up and clapped. To Dave's horror, the cameras had continued rolling until he left the studio catching all his comments.

Dave made more coffee and tried to dodge the comments. Jonathan took his arm and put it up in the air. "Champion Dave by a knock out."

The detective's phone rang and he answered saying he would take a look and to hold on. He went upstairs and looked out the bedroom window, which overlooked the street. He told the caller that he'd call him back and returned to the kitchen.

"This is awkward, there's a whole bunch of press out front wanting to speak to Dave and MI6 security said that Sir Jeremy will be arriving in fifteen minutes."

Dave thought for a moment and then made a suggestion. "Inspector, as you're not in uniform you are the only one that can do this. There's a back entrance through our small garden to the communal garden that leads onto Lansdowne Rise. The problem is we don't have a key to the street entrance, the houses opposite do though. If you go into the garden and climb over the fence you could knock at one of the houses opposite and borrow a key. I'm sure a policeman will not be refused and we can't ask Sir Jeremy to climb the fence can we."

"Well I suppose there's no alternative." Dave let him out the back and gave him the key for his return.

Dave came back and sat down at the table with the others feeling extremely miserable.

Stelios the uniform said, "Cheer up; you're a bloody hero twice in one day. It's been one hell of a day for you hasn't it?"

Dave grunted and Jonathan got up and stood behind him and rubbed his shoulders. "Relax everything's fine. Just focus on starting back at LSE tomorrow. As Stelios said you're a hero, enjoy the moment."

It was Rick's turn. "You're both bloody heroes. Look I hope you don't mind me asking but are you two, like a couple."

Stelios looked horrified and said it was none of his business and as police they were not supposed to ask. Anyway it really isn't important.

Jonathan smiled. "That's ok, yes we are a couple."

Rick looked at them both, "You'd never believe it. You're not what people expect to be gay, if you know what I mean."

Stelios looked exasperated, "You walk pass people every day that have same sex partners and you just don't know. You're stereotyping, so just quit will you?"

It was Dave's turn. "We're just regular people. We do the same things other guys do, like going to football, the pub and that stuff. The only difference is we don't have to part company at the end of the day."

Stelios said "Satisfied Rick now no more ok? If they had been opposite sexes you wouldn't have asked if they were hetro would you? What's the fascination?"

"Ok but there is something that I will ask. Jonathan I keep thinking that I've seen you before. My wife buys all those celeb mags and there's was a lot about some mystery man dating Rachael Young a way back and she cut out a picture that said 'The look of love'. She stuck it on the fridge and it's still there. She said I never look at her that way. That was you wasn't it?"

"Guilty as charged but if you breathe a word of it I'll get Sir Jeremy to have you jailed under the official secrets act."

"Good one. I won't tell a sole but can I tell my wife that I met you both? She'd be thrilled to bits. She'd have seen the news today so she'll be right into you Dave. She likes big men."

Dave stood and asked Rick to give Stelios his phone. He and Jonathan went and sat either side of him and Stelios took a picture. They did the same for Stelios.

Rick was very excited, "I'll get a bonus when I get home, if you know what I mean."

The backdoor opened and in came Sir Jeremy with Inspector Merchant in tow. Sir Jeremy congratulated the inspector on his ingenuity, bringing him in through the garden. Before he could confess that it wasn't his idea, Dave told Sir Jeremy that these policemen were a smart bunch and had been very helpful. The inspector nodded in appreciation.

"Jonathan is there somewhere private we can go?"

They went into the small office and Dave was also invited.

"Did Jonathan tell you anything, David Wilson the government destroyer?"

"No he didn't and I don't think I like that moniker. I suppose you're going to lock me up in the tower."

"Not at all, you were spot on. If it brings down this useless government, you will have done the nation a great favour. I can assure you that you have done nothing untoward and there will be no repercussions. It's been a most eventful day for you both. I listened to the tapes and you were splendid Jonathan. Before we go on though I need Dave to sign you know what."

Dave signed.

"Now you two can discuss everything at your leisure. I haven't got long I'm afraid so I'll be brief. First the good news, Gideon Charles is dead."

Dave went as white as a sheet, "Oh Christ did I kill him?"

"No, no. If anything we did. He was taken from here straight to headquarters and interrogated. When he learned that his ex-boss had squealed on him, he keeled over and died. We checked his medical records and he'd had a heart problem for many years. I don't think we explained but he was no longer with the department, he was pensioned off a number of years ago because of his condition. Well, that's a big problem out of the way. Happy with that Jonathan, justice done?"

"I suppose it is what's next?"

"We will make it seem like it never happened and that way your father remains a good and faithful past member of Her Majesty's service."

"Thank you Sir."

"No thank you young man. The inspector filled me in on the events that took place here and he said you were a pair of super heroes along with a very protective dog. I'm not sure I'd go that far but if either or both of you ever want a job with HMSS just give me a call. Truly thank you for all you've done.

"Now onto logistics, Jonathan I need you to go back to Zurich and retrieve the original documents and the diamonds. Someone from the embassy will go to the bank with you and unburden you of your load. The booty will be placed into the diplomatic bag and sent to me. I need to read everything to ensure we haven't missed anything and then the documents will be destroyed. As for the diamonds, well we checked and the owner claimed on his insurance and its best we don't rock the boat there. That means the diamonds are yours Jonathan. When they were stolen the insurance company paid out fifteen million pounds and my people tell me that they are probably worth as much as double that now."

"Sir those diamonds got my father killed. I don't want any part of them."

"Then what do you suggest we do with them?"

"Where did they come from?"

"They were mined in Botswana."

"Well then I think that's where they should go. I read that there are many orphans there because of the Aides epidemic. Find an orphans' charity and give them the diamonds."

"You really are a remarkable young man. We'll sell the diamonds at auction and we will find the most reputable orphans' charities and spread the money around. Who will the donor be?"

It was Dave's turn. "The donor will be the Anglo/Spanish children's society."

"Does that exist?"

"It certainly will even if only for a few days."

"Right Jonathan when can you go to Zurich?"

"I can't go tomorrow as I'm taking Dave to LSE for his first day back at school, so Tuesday. Just book me on a morning flight coming back in the afternoon as early as possible. What I need to do won't take more than a couple of hours."

"That will be done, just as we are. I will keep my ear to the ground so that I can follow your progress, both of you. As for you Dave Wilson, I don't know if you realise what you have done but I assure you it's a favour to this great nation. So David what are you going to be doing at LSE?"

Dave explained and Sir Jeremy nodded in approval. "So will you be Chancellor one day?"

"You are joking of course."

"Then what will you do?"

Jonathan answered for him. "He's going to lecture at LSE and write papers on economic reform."

Dave looked at him and said, "You do this all the time, how could you know?" Addressing Sir Jeremy, "He's a mind reader, we've never discussed it and yet he knows." He put out his hands as if to strangle Jonathan.

"Jonathan, that's a very useful attribute that will serve you well when you join us."

"Never and anyway, I can only do it with him."

Sir Jeremy left the way he'd come. A minute after the phone rang again and Stelios was asked to answer it.

"It's that woman from the BBC again. She said to turn the news on again in two minutes. She also asked me to tell you that your program is going to be featured, on every BBC news program until the story dies. Quick put the television on. Oh and she said that she was very sorry but didn't say about what."

The headlines were that the PM had called an emergency news conference to announce that he had accepted the resignation of his Chancellor. He distanced himself from the accusation by saying that he was not in any way of the same opinions as those expressed in the BBC interview. The political analysts that followed doubted that the government would survive. The media were all calling David Wilson the new David Frost and all wanted an interview. Then they showed a shot of all the press gathered outside of their house.

"Oh fuck look at that lot, how am I going to get out of here tomorrow morning?"

Inspector Merchant answered that, "I'll send a car to pick you up at eight and we'll use the same escape route we use for Sir Jeremy. We can do that in the morning but I suggest if you want to return to a quiet life you give that interview that everyone is looking for as soon as possible."

"Thanks, you're right of course, the more I try to avoid them the longer this will go on. I'll make a call soon."

The police departed through the front door which sent the media men into frenzy. Dave called Fiona and said he would stop by the studio the following afternoon and film the interview she wanted. Fiona apologised again but explained that exclusives were the life blood of the news media.

He gave the interview and made it clear that the encounter with the Chancellor was the first and last TV news program he would host. Asked if he would continue his radio show he told them to direct that question to Fiona. She said she had a new contract for a year sitting on her desk waiting for Dave to sign.

CHAPTER FORTY NINE

The following Saturday they were both at home reading. Dave got up to make coffee but they were almost out of milk so he said he'd take a walk to Tesco's and get some. Jonathan reminded him that they hadn't returned the garden key to its owner so Dave offered to do that first.

He found the house he was looking for and rang the doorbell. It was a large house, very similar to theirs, occupied by just one family, which was evident by the one doorbell. The door was opened by a young woman who was probably in her early twenties. She had thick shoulder length naturally blond hair, large blue eyes and was pretty rather than attractive. Dave explained why he was calling on her and was about to introduce himself when she smiled and interrupted him.

"You're David Wilson the whole country knows who you are."

Dave Grimaced.

"You're Jonathan Martinez's friend I've seen you together several times."

"How do you know Jonathan? What's your name?"

"I'm sorry that was rude of me, I'm Emma and I went to School with him. It was just sixth form and we did some of the same subjects, French and Philosophy."

"Did you know Gabriella?"

"Yes of course, Romeo and Juliet." She gave him a look that was almost apologetic and yet rueful at the same time.

"Emma, are you busy right now because I'd like to talk to you?"

"Not really, why don't you come in?"

"No I really don't want to put you to any trouble, maybe we could go to a coffee shop on the Avenue?"

Emma got her jacket and they found a table at the patisserie.

"What was Jonathan like at school?"

"I didn't know him that well, in fact nobody really did. There were two boys in our year that had known him since they were five and they said

Jonathan had never been one to mix. He was too intent on his studies. He never attended parties or functions. He was almost reclusive, yet he wasn't at all shy, if you know what I mean."

"What was Gabriella like?"

"Oh dear, Gabriella, she was an enigma but unlike Jonathan. She always seemed happy and would talk to anyone and everyone, except when Jonathan was around. She's tall, very beautiful, long black wavy hair, olive skin and big brown eyes that we're vaguely oriental. Her father is half Chinese and I suppose that's what made her look exotic. She looked like a model and moved with the grace of one. She and Jonathan could easily have been brother and sister, the resemblance was that strong. Of course Jonathan is beautiful, if one can call a man beautiful. I saw his photograph in newspapers and magazines a while back and it easy to see why the press was interested in him."

"What was she like as a person, her character, was she nice?"

"Initially all the girls wanted to hate her because of Jonathan. We had only been at school for a few days and she had interrogated all the boys that knew him to find out what he was like. Jonathan didn't stand a chance. The first lesson they had together was the beginning of a love story, she just went for him and got him.

"I'm making her sound manipulative but she wasn't, she just knew what she wanted and went for it. She was such a nice person that we all ended up liking her. She really loved Jonathan and I mean really. He wasn't anywhere as near as demonstrative as her but you could tell he loved her too. Her sudden disappearance must have upset him but we never found out because after prom night, he never came back to school and of course he wasn't friends with anyone but I can imagine he was devastated."

Dave got the picture and he hadn't learnt much new but he was pleased to hear that she was nice.

"I've just got to pop into Tesco's will you come with me and I'll walk back with you and we can stop by our house to say hello to Jonathan?"

"Jonathan would probably not remember me and that would be embarrassing."

"I doubt that, no in fact I know he will remember you."

"Have you known him long?"

"A few years but I don't remember what life was like before so it feels like forever."

"When I see you together you seem not to notice anything other than one another. I almost bumped into you once but neither of you even glanced at me. Are you a couple?"

"Yes we are, so are you coming?"

Emma was feeling a little nervous when they arrived. They went straight down to the kitchen where Jonathan was reading.

"You've been a long time getting a pint of milk." He said without looking up.

"I've brought someone to see you."

Jonathan raised his head and then stood.

"Bloody hell it's Emma."

Dave smiled and Emma blushed.

"I told Dave that you wouldn't remember me."

"You once clarified a problem that I was pondering. Love thy neighbour as thyself."

"Wow you remember that?"

"I remember most things, like the spotty fourth year that lived near you and hung around the school gate so he could walk home with you. He was besotted with you. Your French was brilliant and you ran the four hundred metres and you were the best at it. Does that do for starters?"

"You're a sly one. Spying on people and feigning disinterest."

"I can clarify that one. It's not that he's not interested in people it's just he's more interested in learning. He can sometimes be extremely observant as I often find to my chagrin."

They chatted for a while and drank tea. To Dave's amazement, Jonathan suggested Emma join them for dinner and she accepted. They ate and talked and all in all had a very pleasant time.

Dave walked Emma back to her house and returned to find Jonathan filling the dishwasher.

"Well that was a surprise. Actually it was more than that, for you that was amazing. I've never known you talk to someone that much except me."

"It was nice to talk about school and stuff and she's very nice. She's smart too. She said that she works in IT and it sounds like she has a really neat job. I enjoyed myself."

"So did I we'll have to invite her round again."

"Steady on, let's not go overboard."

As it happens they did see more of Emma and over time they all became firm friends, another surprise for Dave.

CHAPTER FIFTY

Life soon got back to normal and they found themselves, most evenings, sitting at the dining room table studying. It pleased them both enormously. Occasionally they'd go to the pub or out to dinner and football was still high on their agenda. Jonathan perfected his cooking and Dave lost fifteen kilos. Mary's visits got less frequent and shorter in duration and they still hadn't received an invitation to visit her. Unbeknown to both, Dolly's trips to Malaga were becoming more frequent.

They sometimes accepted invitations for dinner with the Worthington clan and even socialised occasionally with Dave's radio crew. Dave had become a BBC fixture and was well respected in the media. When Dave spoke people listened.

Dave was given his PhD about six months before Jonathan finished his pupillage. Dave was appointed to a lecturer's position at LSE with a strong endorsement from Professor Gordon. Jonathan was called to the bar the following year at the age of twenty six.

Dave was sitting in the lounge one evening doing the times crossword. Jonathan was going to be late as he had been given his first brief and had a lot of work to do. Dave put his head back and gazed at the ceiling remembering what life had been like just a few short years ago. He shuddered at the thought and it reminded him how lucky he had been to have met Jonathan purely by chance. That's what it was, chance. That evening's football team meeting should never have happened but it did. The subsequent events of a few weeks could easily have put an end to any form of acquaintance but it didn't.

Just then the phone rang and shook him out of his reverie. It was Mary.

"Hi Dave, I just tried to call both your hand phones. Jonathan's is off and yours just rings and rings."

"Jonathan's not home yet. He's working on his first case so he's switched his phone off so as not be disturbed and sorry I left mine upstairs. How are you, is everything alright?"

"I'm fine I was just wondering if you and Jonathan could come over for a few days and pay me your first visit."

"That sounds great. There's a bank holiday at the end of the month so we could come Friday until Monday if that works for you."

"That's perfect, short and sweet after all you might not like it here."

"Nonsense of course we'll like it. It'll be great to see you in your secret environment."

"We'll see about that. Will you check with Jonathan to make sure he's alright with it?"

"I will but I know he will be."

"You sound very sure."

"I am certain."

They chatted for a while and then said their goodbyes.

Jonathan got home at nine and dropped his things in the bedroom and went to find Dave. He was very excited about his day and related all his research and preparations for what was to be his first day in court solo, next Monday.

"Your mum called and asked us to go visit her."

"What, bloody hell she's ok isn't she?"

"She's fine. I told her that we'd go the last weekend of the month as it's a bank holiday. I booked the flights for four thirty in the afternoon, coming back on the following Monday evening."

"Great, Christ something must have happened."

"She sounded fine and said everything was wonderful."

Jonathan was doubtful.

"Everything's ok, don't worry. Did you see that the house next door is up for sale? Maybe we should think about buying it."

"Yes I did and why would we want another house?" Jonathan replied suppressing a smile.

"Investment maybe, do you know I haven't seen the owners for ages?"

"You're not very well informed Mr Dave, they moved to Malaysia and there're not coming back. Carol said her son was moving to London and that she would be looking for a place so we could convert it like this one and she could live in one of the flats."

"I suppose she could but would she? How do you know about the neighbours?"

"I called Carol this morning and forgot the time difference so I woke her up at five in the morning. She said she'd love to live next door. I also called the estate agent and he told me about the neighbours. The house has been sold already."

"Bloody hell that was quick. Oh well that's that."

"What's what?"

"Well we can't buy it then."

"We already did. I offered two hundred thousand below the asking price for a cash sale. The agent called Malaysia and they accepted as long as it can all be done by the end of the month. So get liquidating some investments."

"You did that without asking me? Shouldn't you have at least discussed it?"

"The outcome would have been the same and don't try and pretend you're angry with me because I know you're not."

Dave had a stern face. "I called the agent this morning to find out how much they wanted and it seemed like a good price and you got a discount. Fucking hell you should be in business."

"Does that mean I did well?"

"You're incredible and yes you did well. This is great when can we look at it?"

"Tomorrow, I'll get home earlier and we can look together."

"I'll need to call the solicitor."

"Done."

Dave laughed, "Are you trying to muscle in on my territory?"

"Not at all, we're just swapping roles for a day, so where's my dinner, I'm starving."

CHAPTER FIFTY ONE

They arrived at Malaga airport at six thirty and were in a taxi by seven. They gave the address to the driver and it took just twenty minutes to reach their destination.

Mary had heard the car pull up and she come out to greet them. She took them through the house to the garden at the rear. She sat with them at the patio table and then went to make tea. The house was larger than they both imagined and there was a tranquil air about the garden. It was still light and warm. Mary returned with a tray and poured tea.

"This is what I bought with the money you sent over. It's so nice here but I do miss London."

"Then why can't you come home?"

"I can now and I will soon but I'll keep this place because it's so full of memories, good and bad."

"Mum you've been living a life about which we have absolutely no knowledge. Where's the person you were nursing?"

Dave was thinking exactly the same thing.

"Not so fast Jonathan I'll explain in due course."

Mary changed the subject and asked the men what had been happening back home. They had been talking for about ten minutes when they heard a car pull up in the front drive. Mary excused herself and said she'd be just a moment.

Mary stopped at the patio door and said, "There's someone here that you must meet."

They were both expecting to see her secret boyfriend. Mary turned and beckoned someone to come out. It was a small girl.

"Introduce yourself my darling."

Dave didn't need an introduction. He knew exactly who this beautiful child was.

"I'm Josephina but Mary calls me Jo. I know who you are. You're Jonathan and you're Dave or David."

Dave stood up and said, "Well Jo. Why don't you show me around so Mary and Jonathan can chat?"

"Ok." She took his hand and led him to the end of the garden and opened the gate. They turned right along a narrow path. Jo held his hand tightly and said, "You have very big hands in fact you're bigger than I thought you'd be."

"You're right, I am big. Where are you taking me?"

"There's a big stone a little bit further on and it's my favourite place to sit. You can see the sea from there."

They walked for about five minutes and reached their destination. They sat on the rock and gazed out across the Mediterranean Sea, which looked as calm as a mill pond.

"You can see lots of boats some days but there are not many today."

"It's a nice view."

"I like it better when the sea's rough all the boats bob up and down."

"Yes I can imagine that would be fun to watch. How old are you Jo?"

"I'm seven and I'll be eight in November. Mary said we're coming to live with you and Jonathan in London."

Dave did a quick calculation and suddenly lots of things made sense.

"And so you are. Will you like that?"

"Very much I think. Gabriella said I have to go to boarding school so that I don't bother you and Jonathan too much."

"Well I went to boarding school and it was alright but you won't do that. You'll live at home and go to day school. Maybe the same one as your" he stopped and corrected himself, "As Jonathan did."

"That would be nice but Gabriella said I should."

"Did she make you promise?"

"Not about that, no."

"Then Jo you're not going to boarding school."

The little girl gave him an unmistakable smile.

"Where is Gabriella?"

"She died last year. I'm not sad though. I did love her very much. She was always sick ever since I could remember. She said I would have two lives, one until the day she died and another for as long as Jonathan lived. I'm not sure I understood that but you're here now."

Dave understood.

"I suppose Mary has been looking after you both all this time."

"Yes Mary has always been here. I love Mary." With that she started singing a song in Spanish.

"That was a nice song."

"Do you speak Spanish?"

"A little but I didn't understand all that you sang. Maybe you'll teach me when we get to London."

"My Grandfather taught it to me. It's about a boy who thinks nobody loves him and then he meets a princess and they fall in love and live happily ever after. He said it's about him and my grandmother. I think that's nice but they're very old."

"I thought your grandmother was dead."

"Not that one silly."

Dave wanted to laugh. So much to take in, he wondered how Jonathan would react. They sat looking out at the sea and the strangest thoughts entered Dave's head. Which room will Jo have? Should we change our wills? We should be smart and set up a trust like Joe did. What does she eat? What does she like to do? The questions were racing around in his head.

"I wonder why we weren't invited before."

"Oh that's easy Gabriella said we had to wait until Jonathan had finished everything. Mary wanted to ask you last year but granddad said Gabriella wouldn't like that because we made a promise."

"What's your grandfather like?"

"Granddad is very nice and very kind. You will like him very much and he will like you very much."

Now Dave did laugh. "I know we're going to have a lot of fun Jo and I think it's time to get back."

They took a few steps along the path and Jo stopped.

"What's up, why did you stop?"

"You can see the whole world from up there and all I can see is bushes."

"We'll that's easily remedied."

He picked her up and put her on his shoulders.

"I can see everything now."

"Josephina, I think we all can."

THE END

Printed in Great Britain
by Amazon